Andrew Klavan was born in New York City in 1954 and educated at the University of California. Before becoming a full-time writer he worked as a newspaper reporter and radio news-writer and editor. He is the author of five novels under the pseudonym Keith Peterson, and has gained enormous acclaim as a thriller writer under his own name. He now lives in London with his wife and two children.

Agnes Mallory

ANDREW KLAVAN

An *Abacus* Book

First published in Great Britain in 1996
by Little, Brown and Company
This edition published in 1997 by Abacus

A CIP catalogue record for this book
is available from the British Library.

ISBN 0 349 10683 5

Typeset by Palimpsest Book Production Limited
Printed and bound in Great Britain by Clays Ltd, St Ives plc

Abacus
A Division of
Little, Brown and Company (UK)
Brettenham House
Lancaster Place
London WC2E 7EN

I am very grateful to everyone who helped me with this novel: Michael Freund and Christy Rupp for their detailed descriptions of the world and work of sculpture; Robert Hartman and Glenn Borin for their insights into New York City law and politics; Sarah Amelar for her labor as my research assistant; Ellen Klavan, as always, for her patience and editorial suggestions.

This book is for Tom and Jean Flanagan.

There was a wooded hill across the street from the cottage where I lived. That's where I saw her first. Or glimpsed her, really, because she ducked back quickly behind the ruined stone root cellar in the middle of the slope. I'd just caught a movement at the corner of my eye that I took to be the movement of her hair and there was a sense of color that might have been her face or her clothing. These stood out against the gray of the winter hardwood trees and the white bark of the birches.

I gave a brief, derisive snort into my coffee mug as she dodged out of sight again. I'd had a penchant for romance too once.

For a few minutes more, I stood there at the window, polishing off the last of my coffee. There was no further sign of her. I turned away then, and carried the empty mug downstairs to the kitchen.

It was about three miles into town, an hour's walk. I wore my old city overcoat and the leather gloves lined with fur. No one had worn hats when I was part of humanity, so I didn't have one. After the first mile, my nose was running and my ears burned with the cold.

My daydreams these days seemed to have become more benevolent than in the past. Or they were going through a more benevolent phase, at least, because these things do change back and forth as time goes by. Now, anyway, it seemed I used my magical power over the universe for nothing but small mitzvahs. The curing of sick children, unbidden Christmas gelt to widows in their shacks. I stayed away from sex fantasies in the mornings, because the hardons made it difficult to walk briskly. So it was all more or less benign and ridiculous stuff.

Now and then, I returned to reality — guiltily, because the woods really were beautiful at the edges of the road. Fathomless interlacings of branches and vines. A visible stillness going back and back with just the sough of the faint wind in there, and the unseen river, the water running under a sheen of clear ice. I would resolve to pay attention to it and then slip back into my fantasies, walking along. I'd stopped trying to recreate my now-famous walks home from Agnes's house (famous, that is, in the untold legend of my life). I'd given up on that sort of soul-tingling awareness. Today, though, I noticed I did wake up to things a little more often than usual. It was the cold, I guess. And the suspicion that the girl was out there somewhere. Following along, watching me. Full of childish mystery. The idiot.

At the post office in town, feisty old Mr Codger gave me my envelopes. Shuffling to the counter in his overalls. Going through all his patented ticks and grumblings. I could never remember his real name because I didn't care whether he lived or died. I put the envelopes in a canvas bag I'd kept folded up in my overcoat pocket. I strapped the bag over my shoulder and stepped outside and saw her again.

The town — a wealthy Westchester commuter town — had been maintained as a sort of theme park by the ancient locals with the help of the later escapees from New York. Colonial New England was the general idea. The Buy-Rite hardware and the Rexalls pharmacy and the real estate place, a Century 21, had all been whipped smartly into line. Their white clapboards, green shutters and rooftop fillips matched them up nicely with the brick library and the wooden town hall which were actually over two hundred years old. Even the stretch of two-lane where the speed limit dropped to thirty was still, wistfully, called Main Street.

The post office was colonial too, a no-nonsense clapboard box as feisty-by-ginger as old Mr Codger himself. And in front of it, in the middle of the junction between Main and Highway 44, was a triangular island of grass they called the Green, a remnant of the pre-Revolution original where the sheep had grazed. Across from the Green, on the far side of the junction, there was Ye Olde Burying Ground. An iron railing with a grassy slope behind it. A few black maples on the slope, sweeping low to the earth. And gravestones — maybe two dozen gravestones — washed near mute by rain and time, but slanting quaintly in the light and shadow as the sun rose opposite and the wind moved the branches of the trees.

That's where she was standing, in there. Unbelievable what they think of when they're young. She was standing alone among the graves, watching me steadily. The shadow of one of the maples angled across her. Her hand rested on a modest stele. Her long tan hair was stirred by the morning breeze. Like the cover of some gothic novel: Fiona, Girl of The Suburbs. *Amazing.* With her jeans and her red down vest and her fuzzy black earmuffs. I shook my head. I guess if she'd worn the usual flowing white nightgown, her ass would've turned to an icicle.

I shouldered my sack, disgusted, and headed off for home.

I knew her. I'd never seen her before, I couldn't name her, but I did know her somehow. It bugged the shit out of me. It's mysteries like that, mystery in general, that I'd had my fill of. Mystery and Romance. Standing among the graves! I mean, for Christ's sweet sake. I put the town behind me, and walked back the way I'd come, along the sidewalk of Route 44.

The highway was whooshing with commuters' wives. BMWs and Mercedes speeding to the Shop-Rite down the road. The hoary white mansions on the edge of town catching the snootfuls of exhaust up the spreading hickories on their lawns, up the flutes of their pretentious columns. I stalked by them, thinking: what could it be? What was the Dark Secret behind the Girl in the Graveyard? And how I hated to give her the satisfaction of wondering. It was probably nothing, after all. Someone must just have said something — in the old days, when people still said things to me. Or I must've seen a photograph. Back then, when I was still part of the general scheme of things. Something — something must have suggested her or even somehow foretold her to me because she sure as hell looked familiar, considering I'd never set eyes on her before. Well, I gave it three more minutes, walking under the hickories with the bag on my shoulder. Then, resolutely, I put it out of my mind. I was sure to remember eventually, I figured. It'd come to me and it'd be some dumb thing or other. Everything has an explanation — not just a reasonable one, but a physical one — that's the thought that keeps you steady. Steady in that thought, I approached the corner of the forest road.

Here, the hidden river broke out of the trees and out of the ice. It grew wider, maybe ten, fifteen yards across. It squeezed itself up under a wooden bridge, getting jazzed, and then broke forth with the accumulated energy; toppled through lacy ice fringes and sparkling ice crags in a broad and scenic falls. I came marching along past it, all steadied. Puffing frost balls out ahead of me, starting to sniffle *again. Paging through the Fantasy Juke Box, trying to select a good one for the forest walk home. And just at the corner, with the falls shushing, what should I come up with instead, through the courtesy of free association, but the ever-popular Memory of Agnes On The Riverbank? The memory of her body, that is, lying at the spot where it had washed ashore, just across from the campgrounds, down beyond the high steel bridge. No respecter of the Human Miracle this Death — that's what I remember thinking as I stood there, drenched, hobbled, calf-deep in mud. She was all deflated by it, though she'd been alive not an hour before. Her skin was still brown with the sun and soft-looking and life-like, but it had collapsed on itself somehow. Her breasts and her belly seemed to sag inward. Her ribs jutted out. And with her mouth hanging open and the glassy look in her open eyes . . . well, it was a big letdown, I don't mind saying, after what she'd been to me. There was a broken branch lying across her hips. And there was a strip of yellow plastic from an exploded raft or inner tube tangled in her arm and in her black hair. And that's what she seemed to me: a thing, just another thing. Truly, it was a disappointment. After the allure of her all those years; the romance and even her agonies, even mine. That she should turn out to be this, really, under it all. A thing. A mannequin. Animated for a while. Choosing sugar in its coffee and philosophizing about art and talking about love — and then switched off, deflated, tossed out with the branch and the yellow plastic. All that drama and suffering: it had just been a puppet show, it turned out, a puppet show done with corpses. Very disappointing indeed, having believed in it for a while.*

Well, such are the joys of free association: this hoary anguish, this helpless rage. But association with what? *That was the question that was really nagging at me. I mean, I passed that corner every day just about. But I usually reserved Agnes At The River for my reveries in the dead of night.*

The cottage I lived in was a rental. A 1700s shinglesides; a real one, not like the Buy-Rite or the Rexall's. I got it cheap from a steel-haired Daughter of the American Revolution when the real estate market collapsed. It stood at the edge of the forest road, looking across at the hill and the root cellar. Two stories, not counting the basement where the kitchen was. It was white and splintery outside with a black front door and black shutters on the windows. Inside, it was stout floorboards painted rust red and thick brown beams beneath the low ceiling. I sat, most of the day, in my workroom on the top story. Bent at my desk under the pressing eaves. Crachitt-fingered with the cold that poked in through the knotholes. Surrounded, in my solitude, by untold dozens of steel-haired DARs in their more stately mansions in the surrounding woods. Pissing a little Jew into the colonial beer.

I'm sure I could've had a newer place, certainly a warmer place, something more convenient to the town. Marianne would've chipped in. She's a charitable creature, goofy as she is, strapped for cash as she is herself sometimes. But I figured she had the grief, she and the kids, she might as well keep her money, what money there was. And anyway, I liked it here. With its breakneck-narrow stairways and their rope bannisters. With its fireplace in the dead center of the main room downstairs. Agnes and her tragical bloodlines back to Goshen notwithstanding, I'm still an American myself, yessiree bob. The habit of my misspent youth, and ignorance of anything else, no doubt. I liked it here, clinging to a ledge of the mythic country, me and the mansion daughters settled in their wood.

Of course, in concession to this century – and it's late in the day, almost Century 21 – I did live by charity all the same. The envelopes from the post office, the papers splayed over the desktop now: they were all from friends. Those good folks I laughingly call my friends. Lucky lawyers, I mean, who were left out of the indictments, who were sick with relief and gratitude when I decided to keep my mouth shut. Well, call it charity, call it blackmail. At least I wasn't out on the street with sad eyes and a paper cup like everyone else.

Instead, I worked through the day, God love me. Word processor, telephone, pen in hand. Bankruptcies were big right then. Some deed transfers. Some trusts. Paralegal stuff, but then I was a disbarred kind of a guy.

Anyway, there was nothing to it. Nothing to engage the soul or ignite the passions. With me now, that was the main thing.

Black, chesty, gravid clouds swung in over the grey maples in the afternoon. I had to chuckle to think of her out there. When I went down to the kitchen for coffee at about three o'clock, I thought I heard her clanging around in the old barn out back. I imagined her stepping on a rake, bopping her head with the handle. Tripping over hubcaps. I laughed out loud, though it might just have been a squirrel.

By five, not only was it night, but the wind rose and even the wind was black. The trees rattled and groaned in the updraft and shivered when it died away. And I shivered at my desk, the branches chattering at my workroom window, the cold eating between sill and sash. Valiantly, my freezing digits zapped paragraphs from a testamentary trust. Five-thirty came, then quarter to. Then another noise started: pat, pitter, pat. And I thought: Oh, you're joking. But no, a half-frozen, kamikaze rain had begun to hurl itself against the lightless glass. Well, youth is youth and romance is romance but enough, by inference, is also enough. I couldn't just let her freeze to death, the little twit. I copied my work onto disks and shut the computer down; stacked my papers in careful piles — still determined not to hurry on her account, not to fall victim to the extortions of her stupidity. Then, finally, with heavy paternal sigh, I padded down the narrow hall, ducking the eaves. Lowered myself by rope and raw courage down the quick twist of stairs. Took two irritable strides under the beams and, seizing its brass knob, yanked open the door.

The cold marched over me like a parade and the icy rain stung me. The wind went wild in the tortuous dead trees on the opposite hill. There was turbulent swaying of branches; howling, eeriness; the whole horror-show effect.

'For Christ's sake,' I shouted, 'you wanna catch pneumonia?'

All nature did not exactly pause at the sound of my voice. The rain seemed to grow stronger, in fact. It beat a savage tattoo on my forehead and cheeks. And the air continued freezing. But, for a second or two, the winds did settle a bit. They quit their howling and seemed to skulk away into the forest depths. The trees on the opposite slope fell hangdog over the ruined root cellar. I spat a cube of hail into the night and squinted at the darkness. A moment passed.

'Goddamnit,' I muttered.

Then, slowly, out she came. Out of the woods. Side-footing down the hill. Crossing the street — checking both ways for traffic first, the good girl. Stepping into the cone of light from the open door. A sullen mess she was. Her down vest plastered to her. Her fuzzy muffs drooping with rain. Hail sparkling in her hair and melting on her cheeks like tears.

Man, she was young. Sixteen, seventeen, eighteen — definitely no older than that. So what did she have to come here for? What could any of it matter to her? What could I matter? I was out of it now. I was not pertinent to the question at hand – to any question at any hand. When I wasn't scratching out my living with meaningless bullshit, I was reading – old books, old novels, old histories, histories of art. Anything concrete enough, specific enough, to conjure up the past, the dead, the sense of the dead, Agnes's sense of the unnumbered, the unforgiving dead. That was my life now. That'd been my life all these years since Agnes had died, that and rolling from one side of bed to the other, tearing at my hair in torments of remorse. And it had made me distinctly unpleasant to know, let me tell you. Narrow-eyed, scowl-faced, old in my mere forties, acidly indifferent to whatever waif-like concerns she was traipsing in here to plague me with.

So why should she turn off the warm way of the world to come worry at me who did not want her?

And how could I tell her this story if she wasn't even wise enough to despair?

— 1 —

Agnes would've started it with Auschwitz. Or the American Revolution maybe. Or Jacob's Pillow — I don't mean in the Berkshires either, I mean Jacob's fucking pillow. Agnes never saw a tear fall but she blamed it on the *fiat lux*. But, by my lights, it was some time after the creation of the world when I first saw her. An autumn in the Sixties. An autumn dusk.

I was playing fungo, first, on Hampshire Road. The dark was thickening. When I whopped the tennis ball into the air, it would nearly vanish in the purple line of sky between the trees. My friends, Freddy and Dave — the two who had not been called in yet for dinner — would wait for it down the street, frozen, mitts tensed at their thighs. Then, out of the twilight, the dirty old thing would fall. Bounce right between them more often than not. And there would be much lunging, pivoting and hurling as we had seen it done in ballgames on TV.

We played in the street in front of a house, a specific house, which was directly in line with the sewer we used for home plate. It was a small ranch-style house, the broad boards painted gray. It had a picture window out in front — that was the main point, that was the whole idea. When it got dark enough like this, and the lights were off inside, the wide picture pane took on an ebony sheen on which soft reflections rippled: the branches of the apple tree on the narrow lawn, the sweep of the batter when he came around, and so on. When this time came, when you couldn't see, in other words, through the glass, Andrea Fiedler, so I believed, would stand inside the house and watch me. I didn't dare to glance over much, not much, but I thought I'd spotted her outline hovering in the dark interior once or twice. Always, to be safe, I assumed she was stationed there, looking on. It brought out the masterful in me. The home-run swing, the hot corner snag when the ball was tossed back; every movement very dramatic. The window was a grand canvas – and baseball was a fine setting – for my heroism, my rectitude.

I was nine years old then. I was blond and lithe and fine-featured with noble blue eyes. I was a leader on the street or in the playground, looked to by the others for rulings and judgements. At games like these, bat in hand, I would stride the field, pointing to errors, settling disputes. Smaller kids would appeal to me as if by nature when they were shouldered out of a play. And when bullies – like Ira Wertzer and his pals – biked in to start trouble, they saw that I was on the scene and pedaled past. I was a man of peace, of course, but quick with my fists when I had to be. Better yet, I had perfected a menacing glint in my blue eyes from watching old movies like *Davy Crockett* and *Shane* on TV. All this, a measure of all this, was being drunk in, I figured, by the window's ebony depths, by Andrea's shadowy form behind the glass.

Now, as night gathered finally, I had set myself up for one last Homeric blow. My bat was in my right hand, the barrel on my shoulder. My left hand was slung low with the ball cupped in it. I had to squint to see my friends out there. I heard them laughing about the dark. The smell of wet leaves and the cold were in my nostrils and I could feel Andrea watching me, I could imagine her eyes.

'Car!' Dave called from the outfield.

'Hey, Harry!' said Freddy. 'Isn't that your Dad?'

I looked over my shoulder. I saw the widely spaced headlights of my father's Cadillac. He had the dome light flicked on inside so I could make him out behind the wheel. He beckoned to me. The headlights went off, then on again, then off, then on.

'Now I just want to tell you one thing,' my father said as we drove along. He was speaking in his Serious Voice. 'Your grandfather is very ill.'

'I know, I know.'

'Well, I just want to tell you.'

'Well, I know,' I said.

I slumped in my seat blowing long breaths from puffed cheeks. Tapping out a rhythm on my folded baseball mitt. We were zipping quickly along the road to the train station, a wider road than most where the huge Caddy could flex. Outside, in the dark, in the fall wind, the waggling fingers of the trees had a nicely spooky effect. The yellow lights of houses at suppertime seemed very cozy as we passed them by.

'Well, he might look different, that's all,' my father said. 'I don't want you to be shocked or to say anything that might hurt his feelings.'

'I won't, okay? I won't,' I said.

He made me very uncomfortable, my father. Just his presence. His aura of obscure misery. The sloped shoulders, the podgy middle, the thin, patrician face beginning to grow saggy and foreign and Jewish. Even the way his skin smelled, even the hair on the back of his hands as he gripped the wheel. And whatever it was about his life that made him this way, I was always aware that I could never make it up to him.

Tonight, he was making me even more jittery than usual: the way he was making a state occasion of this. Coming to get me this way, speaking now in portents. I didn't know my grandfather all that well anyway. I'd only seen him once since he'd moved to town, several months ago. Before that, once or twice each year, he had come out from Brooklyn. Patted me on the head. Brought me silver dollars. I had a stack of them on my shelf next to my president milk bottle tops and my Martian invasion cards.

Gazing out the window at the eerie trees and the homey suburban windows shining in the night, I thought about him now. Grandpa. I thought about him looking 'different', being 'very ill'. It made me nervous, yes, but I was excited too. I had to keep my face turned away from my father to hide my smile of anticipation. I had never seen real sickness before. It might be neat, it might be gruesome. I could already imagine myself casually tossing off gory details to my friends.

The anticipation swelled as we arrived at the end of the

road, at the railway station. It was fueled by the sight of
Grandpa's building. Ours was a well-to-do Long Island
town of stalwart houses and imperious lawns. There weren't
many apartment houses around, hardly any. But there was
a block-long collection of them here across the street from
the station. The Colony Arms, they were called, or the
Estates or the Towers or something like that. Clean, old
brick buildings with courtyards and gardens – but foreign
and even forbidding to young Harry, who hadn't been in
such a place since I was three. There were great thuddings
in my chest as we got out of the car, as we walked side
by side through the lobby, rode silently up in the elevator,
as we went down the hallway together toward Grandpa's
apartment. A ghost house journey, it seemed to me, down
this thin corridor, toward that closed door. Amber lanterns
burning dull on the wall. Custard wallpaper with port paisley
flock; burgundy carpet that muffled your footsteps – uncanny
colors at once posh and sepulchral. And smells; there were
smells – or I imagined smells: slack skin and old men's potions,
cobwebs, dust, orange photographs, porcelain shepherd boys
from another country, the old country.

Now – creak – the ghost house door was opening – my
father had a key. And he was there, Grandpa, in his big chair,
in the circle of light from a standing lamp, with the TV glow
flickering on the carpet beneath him but not quite reaching
his slippered feet. My father had not exaggerated. It was a
creepy thrill to see him all right. He looked like a marionette
collapsed in the plush chair; a homemade marionette, just
matchsticks held together with twine. And the skull sort
of jogged up when he saw us, and the arms bounced and
danced just like a puppet's pulled by strings.

'Harry . . . Harry . . . Oh!' He was so happy to see me.
'Come give your old Grandpa a kiss.'

I ran right to him. I was a Good Guy, I knew how to
be brave. I leaned into his lap as the stick arms flopped
around me. I kissed him a good one on his rough, moldering
cheek.

'Harry . . .' he said.

I smiled up into his rheumy eyes. 'How are you, Grandpa?'

'How am I?' He beamed down at me. He gave a phlegmy laugh. 'Listen to him. How am I? What a good boy. How should your old Grandpa be? He's great. He's never better. You're a loving boy. You know that? Huh? So – what? You do well in school, Harry?'

'Uh . . . yeah. Pretty good, I guess.'

'Sure. Heh, heh. A smart boy this Harry. Eh, Michael?'

My father had moved to the television and turned it off. He didn't answer. I don't think he'd heard. He was gazing at my grandfather across the dim room with a kind of vague, angry wonder. What was he thinking? He was thinking: *An astronomer!* That would be my guess. Because he remembered the old man as he used to be. Stolid and imposing; dark, brown, hairy arms pressing out of his plaid short sleeves; a head hewn out of stone, jagged and Moses-browed, the deep eyes glistering with wisdom and necessity. Sneering at him. *An astronomer! Mr Big Shot, Mr Intellect. Who becomes an astronomer and makes a living? A lawyer. A lawyer can always study the stars. What does an astronomer know about the law?*

'Very smart boy,' Grandpa repeated. He pressed my head so close to his bathrobe that I saw the green fabric blur. He clamped his flaccid lips shut over a cough. He coughed harder and had to grab a handkerchief off the nearby stand with his free hand to wipe the spittle from his mouth. 'Heh heh,' he said, patting my shoulder. He noticed my jacket now. 'Baseball. Uh? You play baseball, right?'

'Yeah. Uh huh.' My smile was getting a tad painful about now, but I couldn't smell him anymore and that was something.

'A regular Babe Ruth, right?' he said. 'A Lou – what's his name? – Garnig? Gellig? He died, I don't know. You hit a lot of home runs, Harry?'

'I'm okay.'

'What? Hanh?'

'I'M OKAY!'

'He's okay. Sure you are. Heh heh. A good boy. A good boy.'

He nodded for a while, his skull leaden, the string jerking it up and down. My father stood slumped by the TV set. Contemplating us, his hands in his pockets. Thinking: *My life! Oh-ho, my life!* Or words to that effect. Remembering a woman now. By way of submerging himself in this oceanic emotion of loss, remembering a woman he had loved, the only woman ever. He had driven her home one day from the Boardwalk in Atlantic City. He was twenty-two, just back from manning a desk through the War. He had talked to her about the stars, about how much he loved the stars. He had told her about his mother's finger pointing out the pictures of them in *A Boy's Book Of The Constellations*. The flesh tones of the naked Gemini, the scarlet skirt of Andromeda, the silver flash of Perseus' sword – all gleaming in a Brooklyn of brownstones, in the heavy velvet atmosphere of their rooms above his father's pawn shop.

Grandpa noticed him now, standing there. 'How are you, Michael?' he whispered to him over my head.

My father blinked. 'Hm? Oh. Good. I'm good, Dad. I'm really . . .'

'What? What?'

'I'm really good!' he shouted. 'It looks like . . .'

'What?'

'Looks like I may have a chance to run for the Planning Board.'

'Eh? The Planning Board?'

'Yeah, I may be running for it!' my father cried out.

'The Planning Board . . .' Grandpa went on nodding, his head slowly dropping lower, lower. 'The Planning Board. Work. Eh. You can't always think about work all the time, Michael. Remember that, Harrela.' He regarded me heavily, his chin nearly grazing the grizzled wedge of flesh above his robe. 'Children. Children are the important thing. Remember that. Heh heh heh.' He laughed breathlessly, giving me a little shake. He coughed deep in his chest. 'What a good boy,' he said.

We drove home a different way. Down Middle Neck Road, the town's main drag, bright with streetlamps and traffic. The card shops, drug stores, clothing stores were all mostly closed already. But the deli door was still swinging out and in, and the two movie theaters with their marquis confronting each other across the street were selling tickets for their last shows of *Mary Poppins* and James Bond. We went more slowly now than we had coming. There were stoplights and narrow stretches and lines of parked cars. And other Cadillacs too, coming at us, squeezing us over. All Cadillacs. Jews still didn't buy Mercedes back then.

'You all right?' my father asked me. Glancing over, working his sad jaw.

'Sure,' I said. 'What's for dinner?'

'Steak, I think. Did it frighten you – seeing Grandpa?'

'Nah.'

I fiddled absently with the new silver dollar in my fingers. I looked out the window as the big car cornered onto Piccadilly Road.

Dad meant to go on being fatherly, to draw out my feelings on death, reassure me on the subject of illness and so forth, but his mind drifted. There were few streetlights here and the shadows enfolded him, and thickened between us, and in the dark – the sad mouth working – he began to consider himself and became absorbed. He was thirty-eight, he thought. Thirty-eight years old and he had lied to impress his father. That crap about running for the Planning Board. Bill Farber, one of his partners at the law firm, had mentioned the possibility to him. But that was it, that was all. He wasn't running for anything. He'd lied to win some praise, he'd demeaned himself. And his father – *Work! You can't always think about work!* Dismissing him. Just the same as always. The same massive, beetle-cragged, ham-handed, bouldery, sarcastic tyrant. Trying to look benign in his cancer costume, behind his cancer mask. Holding me in his lap like that. *Children are the important thing.* As if he had ever taken *him* on his lap and kvelled so. *Astronomy! What a smart boy! What a good boy! A regular Albert what's-his, with the frizzy hair, Einstone . . .*

We drove up the hill toward the next corner. In that last moment before he fell in love for the second time in his life, my father's hands were wrapped so tightly around the Caddy's steering wheel, his teeth were clenched together so hard that it was as if a bolt had shot through him, a thunderbolt of rage. And when the rage let him go, it let him go and go, down into the tarriest depths of his loss and his longing.

What am I doing? he thought. Aching, aching. *Am I crazy? Why am I torturing myself with all this old business?* He really didn't know the answer; it was too big, it was right in front of him. *Thinking of that drive home from the boardwalk.* He had never gone out with the girl again. She had never answered his calls. He had even humiliated himself, gone to her house to find her . . . *Why am I bringing all this up again now?*

As for me, I was still staring out the window just then. Twiddling my silver dollar. Sometimes, at home, watching television, say, I would daydream that I had magic powers. The show would be boring and I would think: I'll change the channel without moving from this spot, I'll change it with my mind – *twink*. At night, awake in bed, I would go farther, mentally moving any object I pleased, controlling events around me with alternating wisdom and mischief until the entire elementary school became my private Punch and Judy Show. Ira Wertzer would be vanquished, Andrea Fiedler would be in my thrall, Miss Truxell, my fifth grade teacher, would be kowtowing before my superior powers . . .

And now, in the car, gazing out the window, I was dreaming that I would come to Grandpa. I would sneak from my house one night through a downstairs window, I would walk the miles to the Colony Arms. I was working out every step of it, building it logically to the dramatic climax. I would stand before Grandpa's big chair. With my brow heroically contorted, I would raise my hands. I would zap Grandpa with an extra-super mental blast. At the very touch of it, he would well from his big chair like an inflated bop toy. *Harry! Harry! I'm healed! I'm well! Oh! What a good boy!* The entire fifth grade would rise up and call me blessed. Andrea would have her hands clasped, her lips parted. Miss Truxell would be on her very knees . . .

But wait, the car had stopped. We'd come to the corner, to a stop sign. We'd stopped and now we were just sitting there, the engine idling. I turned to my father.

'What's up, Dad?'

He was looking my way, his face in shadow. The down-ward lines of his features, the melancholy glint of his eyes, were focused on my window, through my window. I turned back to follow his gaze.

There was nothing particular out there that I could see. A white house on a little lawn. A line of trees rising behind it, branches swaying in the wind. The downstairs windows were cosily lit. And through one window, the one to my left, you could see a ways into a small den or parlor. You could see a woman in there, reading a book to her daughter. They were sitting on a sofa together. The mother looked very domestic and appealing with her hair tied back and her lips moving and her eyes serenely on the page. The daughter, a brown-haired girl about my age, sat beside her with her hands folded passively in her lap. She was staring off into space very solemnly.

'Sorry,' my father murmured. 'I – I just wanted to see something about that property.'

He stepped on the gas and we drove on up the road as I tried to pick up the thread of my fantasy.

And that was the first time I saw Evelyn Sole – and her daughter; Agnes.

How do you know? That would be her first question. This damp little visitor of mine, my mystery guest. If I even began to tell her, if I even tried to make a start – how do you know? she would ask me. What your father was thinking about. Or what your mother was afraid of, or what happened to Agnes that last night behind the closed door, or any of the pieces of it that had nothing to do with you? Because she was a kid – my lady of the root cellar – she was seventeen, eighteen. Life was still such a riddle to her. How do you know what other people were feeling or thinking about? Did your father break down in tears in his old age and confess all? Did your dying mother draw you to her bedside with papery hands, croaking, 'I have to tell you, my . . . son . . . everything . . .'? And no, as a matter of fact, they didn't. My father till he died last year never let fly a peep outside the standard paternal self-justifications. And Mom's doing quite well in the complex, thank you, and can even carry on a rational conversation if you avoid talking about government conspiracies or the mafia's role in the Kennedy assassination or the nature of love.

Well, then, you're just making it up, she would say. You're just turning people into characters in your head. It's all just about you really, that's all. Isn't that the kind of thing kids are always saying? When they aren't drooling drug-sluggish monosyllables and listening to loud, bad music and blowing their brainless politics out their ass. How do you know? If the chair still exists when you turn away? If the universe is a grain of sand on a policeman's hat? If a great poem is great? If the truth is true? Because they're kids. Because they think all kinds of things are possible. Instead of only a few things. Maybe even only the one thing.

Oh, and all right, because, of course, I *don't* know. Some of it, much of it, all of it. I never knew. My parents sure never told me. They never told me anything, not if it smacked of human emotion, of suffering and pain. My mother's two miscarriages, which left me an only child? Never heard of them. My father's disappointments in local politics? I simply wasn't informed. I had a dog when I was seven. Clancy. He got sick; they didn't tell me. They had to put him down; I never knew. I just came home one day and – whammo – he was gone. Like walking into a wall.

But then; ah then, the things I understood, the gamut of things. Lying awake at night, wandering alone by day in the backyard where the terrier and I had roamed together. Imagining the trips to the vet while I was out, the whispered parental conferences behind my back, the drive in the station wagon down the last mile . . . I saw it all – all of it – then.

And likewise, that winter – all that time between the night we drove past the Sole house and the evening I saw Agnes again – I built my merry igloos in the snow, I had my snowball fights, I engineered great tunnels beneath the wind-hammered drifts – and Dad watched Grandpa die and never said a word about it. He stood by the old man's bedside. He squelched his horror at the lung-retching agonies. He wrung his heart dry through the glazed, uncommunicative end. And never told me. No one ever told me. My parents boxed that old man up and buried him and didn't mention a thing, didn't break it to me till months and months afterward. All that winter went by in ignorance – and then suddenly – whammo – without understanding why – I met Agnes, and the rest of it happened.

And that's how I know.

That day – the day I met Agnes – was an April day. A Friday, with spring just coming. The weather, I remember, was incredibly fine, the air wonderfully sweet – it was the kind of weather a sloppy drunk remembers when he maunders about the past. The sky was blue, the breezes were cool and wistful. I ate breakfast in our back room, surrounded by high sliding windows slid wide, and the air wafted in through the screens, smelling of the grass, the backyard, our cherry tree.

My father had already gone to work. My mother sat at the foot of the table across from me, working on the *Times* crossword puzzle and her greater familial mysteries as well. I was prattling at her through gobfuls of Special K. Gabbling all the more urgently as I could see she was distracted. Telling her stories, mostly, of my courage and integrity. Of my stand for justice against the fire-breathing Miss Truxell, my raw bravery against the bully Ira Wertzer and his gang. They were, all these yarns, about half-true, and I knew she only about half-believed them. But it was imperative somehow that they be told, that she hear them. I needed her to know what a good, what an honest guy I was. So I talked fast, embellishing with a broad stroke, as breakfast was only a matter of minutes with me, and childhood only a matter of years.

My mother's pen hovered and hesitated over a twelve-letter word for 'monopolized resort,' and she wondered to herself, *How much has he told her? How much does she know?* Thinking about Aunt May, that is. Her younger sister, my Aunt May. She had had a phone call, a series of phone calls over the last few days. Aunt May's marriage was collapsing. This much I had overheard though it was mostly a matter of indifference to me. Aunt May had fled the man Mom called Mr Slick Hollywood Producer. With his half-buttoned flowered shirts and the *chai* medallion gleaming on his hairy chest – everyone had to know how *Jewish* he was, Mom said because she felt it was not quite the thing, being Jewish, though Jewish she was.

Anyway, May was down in Florida now, sobbing out her troubles to their aged father. And my mother had invited her to come north and spend the summer with us. This, as I'd gleaned from certain grumblings in the walls, did not make my father happy. Dad and Aunt May had never gotten along, I knew that. It couldn't be pleasant: the two of them sharing a house all summer. My mother knew it too, but she had had to invite May anyway. She had not been able to help herself somehow.

My mother was never pretty, not even as a girl, which

was important, because her sister was, Aunt May was always beautiful. Mom got all the Litvak features, the babushka stuff, the beezer, the hound dog eyes, the cheeks like lead. Aunt May was the Austrian rose, with black hair you wanted to lift to your face in handfuls, skin like blushing ivory, and mysterious, beryl, love-song eyes. She had bigger tits than Mom too. And a waist you could touch your fingers around. Poor Mom, in youth, had been reduced to imitating her younger sister, mimicking her frailty, her whispery fascination with even the boys who bored her senseless: a desperate attempt to lure some of May's suitors, even one of her suitors, into saving her from her parents' gloomy house in the Jersey marshes.

It was mortifying for her, I guess. But then as now, Mom consoled herself with her intelligence, her deductions. I think they really were still deductions at that point; they didn't become paranoid fantasies until later on. She deduced motivations, she uncovered buried histories. Why her father's gaiety had faded. Why her mother used to sit by the radio cursing the newsmen in some unknown tongue. Why was her family so poor for so long? Why had they moved from place to place all through her childhood, falling and ricocheting from the Bronx to Lower Manhattan to the Jersey outlands like a pachinko ball? These questions, which were never discussed in her home, Mom had answered, or thought she had answered, figuring out her own life-story from half-heard clues and conversations. Silently, all her childhood long, she shared her father's tribulations; knew them without revealing that she knew; understood his tragedy without telling him she understood. She had always prided herself on this and on the fact that May had never had an inkling of any of it. It was the achievement of my mother's youth, I think. And now, as I cleaned the bottom of the breakfast bowl, as I recounted my historic Rescue of the Little Kid From Ira's Clutches, she thought to herself, *What is he telling her down there? How much is he letting her know?*

It bothered Mom: her father and May alone together in Florida. It gnawed at her that they were down there, talking about who knew what. And that was why, over my father's groans of protest, she had invited May to spend the summer with us. Though, of course, Mom wouldn't have admitted to herself that that was the reason. Her own motives, in this as in everything, were an absolute enigma to her.

So she sat at the end of the table with her pen poised and her sad saggy aspect and her quick but inward-turning eyes and the birdsong and spring aromas all around us. And she looked up, suddenly, startled, when I pushed back from the table and said, 'I gotta get to school.'

She blinked and came into the moment. 'Be careful,' she said, her eyes lingering on my strong limbs, my blond good looks, the beauty she loved. 'Be careful.'

The rest of the day, until Agnes, was pretty much my usual thing: all-powerful in the morning, a sniveling turd by afternoon. In the morning, that is, I walked to school, hiking jauntily up Bunker Hill with books beneath my arm and daydreams of sovereignty beneath my semi-crew. News of the telepathic mind-burst I'd used to heal Grandpa had spread and I'd been made king of the world now, nine years old though I was. I was a greatly intentioned king. Enlightened rule for the entire planet was just around the corner. First, though, I was working out the details of an apocalyptic purge. Mobsters, Russians, rapists, Arabs, the guys who'd killed Kennedy — it was a bad day to be any of that gang. As I walked along beneath the budding canopies of trees, I imagined myself, slouched on a throne, wearing a short-sleeved polo shirt I particularly liked with blue horizontal stripes. In trooped the population of the earth to stand before me. With a slight tilt of my scepter I sent them left or right. Good guys into the dawn of a magical new era, mobsters et al into a black room where a red ray made them dance in agony for a while and then dissolved them. Frankly, it all seemed to be going like clockwork . . . and then the next thing I knew, I was sitting in my combination chair and desk, inwardly cowering as Miss Truxell prowled up and down the classroom aisle. It had somehow become two-thirty — the morning was suddenly dreamed away. We were doing Reports — Reports! for the pity of sweet heaven. We were supposed to have one prepared today on one of our Founding Fathers. Mine was supposed to be on Jefferson and I knew exactly nothing about him except that he had a ponytail and spent a lot of time gazing off into the horizon. I slouched and ducked and trembled as Miss Truxell went up the aisle right past me and down the next aisle right past me on my other side. Monstrous with her razor smile, her blackboard stick, her frizzy hair receding from a high forehead that was mottled and stained. Scanning the rows of neatly trimmed heads for someone to call on next. There seemed no hope the schoolday could end before she saw through my attempts to become invisible and singled me out to die the death of the ignorant and ignominious.

And yet, minute by minute, three o'clock came. Susan smugly proclaimed the life of Hancock, Freddy mumbled his way through Franklin – and the bell rang and I was free. By three-thirty, I was out on the baseball field, shouting manly encouragement to the baserunners, settling disputes. Striding around with my arm outstretched toward the trouble spots, trying to keep things fair for one and all.

I figure it was about six-thirty, and just beginning to get dark, when I finally set out for home.

There was no homework that Friday so I wasn't carrying any books – God knows what I was planning to do about Thomas Jefferson. I walked with my hands in the sidepockets of my windbreaker. Daydreaming mostly, then sometimes taking notice of things. The air was a little cooler now, but it still had that hankering spring smell in it. There were robins pecking around some of the lawns and sparrows perching here and there on the telephone wires.

I went up Bunker Hill a block, then cut across Warwick past Jay Friedman's house just for a change of scene. The sidestreet was shaded over by budding oaks and maples so the light was already reddish here and dusky. But even on Piccadilly Road up ahead, the day was growing pale. Still, it was brighter when I reached the corner and stepped out from under the trees. I cut across the lawn of the nearest house, and was just coming down onto the sidewalk, when I heard a car door thunk shut behind me. I glanced back casually down Piccadilly and then away – and then looked back again, surprised. There was my father.

He had just stepped out of the brown Cadillac. It was parked at the curb about a block away. I stood still and watched while he came around the front of it. He hadn't seen me, and I thought if I was careful and crept up quickly I might be able to shout boo and spook him. As soon as he had his back to me, I started forward, smiling in anticipation, crouching low.

Then Dad did a sort of odd thing. As I was creeping up on him, he walked straight over the sidewalk onto a lawn and headed between two houses. Piccadilly wasn't lined with trees like Bunker Hill was. There were more lawns, more open spaces. The houses on the south side, though, where he was, across from me, had trees in back, a thick stand of tall hickories, maples and dull-green pines. Behind these, and down a short slope, was a stream. Not much of a stream, a run-off of some kind that flowed from a culvert at the top of the hill to I don't know where. You couldn't see it from the road, but I'd been to it a couple of times for rock battles with my friends – standing on either side of the water, tossing rocks in to splash each other – so I knew it was there. It seemed to me that my father was headed for the trees behind the houses, and for the stream.

That stopped me a minute. Why would he be going in there? I straightened and watched. My father went out of sight behind the houses. Interested then, I crossed the street, trotting after him.

When I got to the opposite sidewalk, I saw him again. He was threading his way into the screen of hardwoods. Bending the leafless branches down with his hands. Heading in toward the stream bank. He looked weird to me in that sylvan setting, wearing his navy suit and his thin tie. And as he started down the slope to the bank, he became an obscure, dark figure, moving behind brown trunks and conifers.

I started after him again, panting now, though mostly for show. I plunged into the trees with great shuffling and crackling. Battled my way to the crest of the slope and then side-heeled my way down it to the stony strand. It was darker there. The opposite side of the stream was steeper and pretty high. The trees on its rim were taller and there were more pines and hemlocks that blocked the westering sun. In this twilight, I found my father again. He had planted himself in the black mud of the bank. He was looking away from me, his hands in his pants pockets. Beside him, the stream trickled around rocks and over pebbles making its small noise.

I loped up to him, panting for all I was worth.

'Dad!'

It spooked him, that's for sure. His whole upper body whipped around to me, his hands flying out of his pockets, out to the side.

'Harry? *Harry?*'

'Hi. I saw you from the road,' I said, between heavy gasps for air.

'You scared the heck out of me.' He smiled wanly. His eyes really looked wide and frightened. He reached out and squeezed my shoulder. 'Jeepers. What are you doing here?'

'I was going home this way. How come you're down here by the stream?'

'I . . . I'm meeting someone.' A branch snapped downstream. He whipped around at this too. Then came back to me, nervously. 'A client,' he said. 'I'm meeting a client. We have to talk about a parcel of land back here. Why don't you go on home, and I'll be back in time for dinner.'

More branches crunched. I tilted over to look around my father. I saw two figures coming toward us along the bank. A woman and a girl, moving in shadows. They came on slowly, and passed into a patch of latticed sunlight. The woman, I saw then, was tall with tawny hair worn long. She walked with stately care, a sweater over her shoulders, a long skirt swaying. I could hear her talking pleasantly to the little girl. The girl was thin and had dark hair in a braid down her back. She was carrying a basket over her arm. She answered her mother in a low voice. I didn't remember seeing either of them before.

'Go ahead,' my father said again. 'I'll be back for dinner.'

The woman indicated a place by the stream and the little girl carried her basket to it and knelt down cautiously. The woman left her there and continued along more quickly by herself. By this time, it did seem a good idea to get out of there before I had to talk to her. But it was too late. The woman greeted us before I could make up my mind.

'Hello, Michael. And hello,' she added to me.

She seemed nice enough. With round cheeks and brown freckles and not much makeup. Nervous hands; fretful eyes. A Mom, and pretty. She made me shy. I managed to mutter something to her.

'This is Harry,' my father said. 'Harry, this is Mrs Sole.' The two grownups exchanged a look. I believe my father shrugged at her and sighed. 'I was just saying he should go home while we do our boring business. Go ahead, Harry.'

'Agnes has some people she made from cookie dough,' said Mrs Sole. She made a reticent gesture with her hand. 'She's playing in the stream with them, why don't you go have a look. We won't be long.'

'Nah, thanks, I'll just go home,' I said.

'Oh, she's not playing house or anything,' said Mrs Sole kindly. 'In fact, I think she's drowning them.'

My father laughed in a peculiar way, a phony, dinner party laugh. 'Well, you won't want to miss that,' he said.

I wagged my head. It did sound kind of interesting. 'Okay.' I moved away from them.

'He's at *shule*,' Mrs Sole said softly behind me – a remark which meant nothing to me then and didn't recur to me until I was seventeen, when it made me sit bolt upright in bed and rollick my head in my two hands.

Now, though, I just continued down the bank to the girl.

She had moved downstream from her original position and was kneeling by the water again farther on. I approached her in the semi-dark. The low voices of the grownups fell away behind me. Bashful, I walked with elaborate caution over the soft earth of the bank and stared down at the stream as I went. As I came closer to the girl, I saw something white in the water. I stopped to squint down at it. It was one of her figures. She'd put it in the water to float along, I guess. It had snagged on a twig and the current was nudging it and slipping around it on either side. I pulled an appreciative face: it was pretty good, pretty real-looking, almost like something you could get in a store. A girl figure, hand painted with a red skirt and yellow hair and pink skin. As I watched, it worked free of the twig and went turning and bouncing downstream.

'Here comes your figure,' I said. I followed it from the bank until I was standing over her. 'It's going by.'

For another second, the girl didn't even look up. She just went on, arranging her three other figures in the sparse waterside grass. Then, slowly, she did look. A long, slow look up at me. Very queer. She had a small brownish face, grim, constricted; a face like a monkey working out a chess problem. Kneeling there in her little green jumper with her little bare knees in the dirt, she made her eyes go all wide and magical.

'That one's my sister,' she said.

She said it in a half-whisper, intoned it, with low echoing notes. A witchy business there in the shadows. Without thinking, I took a nervous peek back over my shoulder, checking to make sure my Dad and Mrs Sole were there. They were – still talking in the gloaming under the trees. Standing very close, Dad gesticulating in the small space between them. Now and then the sound of their voices rose wordlessly over the gurgle of the stream.

I turned back to the girl. I shrugged. 'Yeah. My friend Freddy has a sister. He wants to drown her too. He says he wants to set her on fire while she's asleep.'

But the girl took no more notice of me. She'd returned her attention to the figures in the grass. Arranging them, pacing them through some mysterious, girly hoo-ha. I stood over her, hands in my pockets, observing distantly. The figures were two men and a woman, just as life-like as the one she'd drowned. One of them even looked like a soldier, which was admirable enough. I wasn't too sure about this cookie-dough angle – it smelled of sissiness – but I couldn't help thinking: You could make whole armies of these things. Any kind of soldiers you wanted. Romans, say, with swords and shields. Or the guys from the Alamo. You could work out whole massacres not sold in any store. You'd be the only one who had them.

I relented, squatted next to her. 'So, like, you made these?'

She nodded. Grimly. Working her witchy work.

'Out of cookie dough, huh?'

Another solemn nod. 'You glaze them. And bake them in the oven,' she said. And with another sorcerous glance my way: 'That's what turns them real.'

'Uh huh.' I saw what she meant. They did have a quality about them. Shiny, pliant-looking; made you want to touch them. 'I'm no good at art. If I made them, they would all just be . . .' Doody with arms, I wanted to say, but I was a gentleman. 'Lumps with arms,' I said.

At that, she surprised me by letting out your standard issue giggle – and then immediately kneaded her grin back into the wrinkled mask.

I plucked up courage, reached for the soldier. 'Can I see one?' She didn't stop me. I picked it up. Examined it appreciatively. No gun, mind you, but a very promising barbarity about the mouth and eyes. 'Man, you could sell these,' I said. 'You just gonna let that one float away?' Actually, the girl figure was caught now in the roots under the bank a short way down. 'It looked good.'

'It was good,' she said softly. 'I told you. It was my sister. Lena.'

'Yeah. Yeah. Well, I'm an only child.'

Slowly, she turned her spectral gaze downstream. 'So am I.'

Right. That called for another reassuring glance upriver at the big folks. Uncomfortably enough, the light seemed to have faded some around them since my last look. They were dappled shapes now, gesturing at each other against the grainy vista of naked trees and burbling water. Their faces, in-leaning, were laced with branch shadows, and Mrs Sole had one of Dad's hands clapped in both of hers – as if she were trying to slow him down so she could get a word in.

'I thought you said you had a sister,' I said to the girl again. I handed back the soldier. She took it from me with tiny girl fingers that brushed against mine. She lay it in the basket. Picked the others from the earth and bedded them down too.

'I do,' she said.

'Well, what is she, like, imaginary?'

'No. She's not imaginary.' More eyes, half-whispers,

sorcery. 'She's a ghost!' And back she went to the figures in her basket with much mysterious maneuvering, voodoo passes of her hand. 'She died before I was even born. She's a ghost now.'

Well, I reckoned it was getting late: just about time for me to run screaming for my life. With a casual grunt, I stood out of my squat. Stretched. 'Yeah, well, you know, ghosts aren't real. Or anything,' I told her. 'There aren't really any ghosts.'

I do believe she'd been saving this last glance of hers. It was something out of a horror movie. She turned it up at me from where she knelt. Blasted me with a couple of campfire eyes, a grand smile of insane knowing. 'That doesn't mean you don't see them,' she told me. 'You *have* to see them. Ghosts. They're like the sky. The sky isn't real. There *is* no sky. It's just particles that make us see the blue in the light.'

'Yeah. So?' I said. 'I knew that.'

'But you have to see it. It's not like other things, other things that aren't there. Like dragons or . . . or monsters or something. You can't just say it's not there and stop seeing it. You *have* to see it. So it *is* there. Like ghosts.'

'Well, yeah, but . . . I mean, you could go up through the sky with a rocket, so it isn't there really,' I said desperately.

'Yes,' she answered, 'yes.' And she finally got that face off me, turning back, motherly, to her basket of creatures. 'Yes. That's what makes it so strange.'

Whatever else I was going to say, I swallowed it, glug. Things were spooky enough already. It made me feel dizzy, in fact, this sky notion. Made me feel light on my soles, adrift. A sky's the sort of thing you want nice and solid. Climb up your ziggurat of an evening, give her a rap. Yessir, screwed on tight. For a second there, I lost that sense of it. I had a sense instead of being in a shoebox tableau with the lid suddenly pulled off and everything floating free. Trees, earth, grownups floating. Stream floating up in gouts and droplets. Everything around me spreading thin like smoke, parting like the fabric of smoke and atomizing in twilit space. A bizarre glitch in the general proceedings.

I tried to steady myself with a wet-dog shake. Tried to anchor myself again on Dad and Mrs Sole. She was appealing to him now, eyes upturned into a stray gleam of sunlight. He was running one hand through his thinning hair, the other on his hip, pushing his jacket back to show his paunch.

'Is that your Dad?' Without warning, the girl was standing next to me. Holding her basket placidly in front of her jumper. And oddly, it was a look at her that righted things for me. The sight of her worried brown nugget of a face brought me down with a clunk.

'Yeah,' I said. 'Yeah. Is that your Mom? Mrs Sole?'

She nodded. 'She's your Dad's client. He's nice, your Dad.'

There was a delay before I heard this. I was still busy looking at her. Feeling earth, trees, water, feet sucked back into place. I looked at her so long I had to say something finally. 'My name's Harry, by the way,' I said.

And flash, there was her smile, ordinary, like her giggle, like any girl's.

'Hi,' she said. 'I'm Agnes.'

My father saw the two of us coming toward him and spoke up quickly, 'Okay, Harry? Ready to go?' Cut Mrs Sole off in mid-sentence. She whipped around quickly with a bright smile for us.

'All done?' she asked her daughter.

'Yes,' Agnes said.

Mrs Sole waggled her fingers at me. 'Well, then, bye, Harry. Nice to meet you.' And at Dad, 'Thanks, Michael, we'll talk about it again.'

'Right-ho,' said Dad.

And he and I stood side by side a moment, as mother and daughter walked away from us along the shadowy bank.

'Agnes is a nice girl, isn't she?' my father asked, as we climbed out of the trees and started across the grass to the street. The light had gone here now too. It was dusk.

'I guess so,' I said. 'The figures she makes are pretty good.'

'Her mother, you know, is a client of mine. We're discussing some business. A piece of property back there . . .'

'Yeah, you told me already.'

'Oh. Did I? Right.'

He was quiet after that. I was glad. I wanted quiet. There was something going on, in me, as I walked beside him. I wanted to check it out. I felt peculiarly alert; I guess that's what it was. Historians may disagree whether this was technically the first of my legendary Walks Home From Agnes's, celebrated in song and/or story from generation to generation. I mean, I only walked over the lawn to my father's car that day. But the formative principle was there, no question. That weird, cool feeling of transparency, the light wandering through me; of permeability, me waxing subatomic and the whole scene buzzing in and out of the interstices. Which just comes down, really, to an odd, inhabitive awareness of the assembling crickets and their calls and to the worsted texture of the graying day, to blade of grass on sneaker tip, and to the one-dimensional look that houses get just at that hour, as if they were cardboard cutouts raised against the sky. And the sky, just at that hour . . . What a bizarro girl, I thought suddenly, and I suddenly goose-pimpled under my jacket sleeves — because the sky at nightfall, I discovered then, actually *does* lose its solidity. It becomes granular and vertiginous and deep.

I was glad, I don't mind saying, to find that it was a momentary thing. When I wrapped my hand around the cold metal handle of the Caddy door and raised my eyes one last time suspiciously, I could see that the order of the sky's distance and substantiality had been re-established, thank you very much, by the gradual appearance overhead of Vega in Lyra, the night's first star.

— 3 —

For each of three Fridays thereafter you could find me, just
before dusk, Shwinning down Piccadilly, clean out of my
way. Not confessing it, but looking for her. Just passing by,
you understand, but secretly calculating the proper hour for
voodoo ghost-sister drownings – on the chance it might be
a regular sort of thing with her, you see. I would lay my bike
down on a lawn and wander in there, in among the trees
behind the houses. Peek in at the stream, do a quick study up
and down of the sun-pocked strand. Just popped in to guzzle
some serenity, I'd tell myself, searching the snarled branches
for her and the shade under the budding leaves. Just here for
an aftertaste of the transcendental blast, nothing to do with
monkey-face. Oh, but I was undeniably intrigued. Well, I had
no overview of it, no perspective on that alchemic pinch of
zen she'd dropped in my nine-year-old pudding. Nine years
old; Jesus – I hadn't even grasped the truths that would later
crumble around me. I hadn't seen her deflated corpse at the
roiling river's edge, or sleep-walked into corruption day by
dreamy day like anyone. I didn't know I *was* like anyone,
like everyone. I had the strangest feeling that all this, this life
business, was happening specifically to *me*.

Anyhow, she never showed. I biked home each Friday,
secretly disappointed, secretly relieved. And the only new
wrinkle in the Harry universe I can remember was the
occasional laying aside of a daydream or so during the walk
to school those weeks; a stern, forced, philosophical converse
or two with the heavens as I tried to recover that weird, vivid
sensation that had hit me that twilight after our first talk. Then
I'd drop it, start to dream again – dreaming about this purge of

mine. Wondering: wouldn't it be more interesting if when the population came before King Harry to be judged, they were naked? The women especially. If they had to parade up to me like the girls in Freddy's father's magazines. Naked and pink and trembling . . .

Just a thought, you understand. And on I'd bounce up Bunker Hill.

The next week I gave up the search and – wouldn't you know it – bumped right into her. I was pedaling home from a ballgame down Plymouth Road, where she shouldn't have been. But there, in fact, she was, walking along on the sidewalk up ahead of me. Marching behind her chin like any stuck-up schoolgirl, her braids going tick-tock behind her neck. It gave me quite a start to realize that it was she.

Coolly, nevertheless, I continued to bike up the street. I rattled past her – then faked a double-take and put on the brakes.

'Hey, aren't you that girl who makes figures?' I asked as she reached me. I pretended to search my memory. 'Agnes, right?'

'Oh yes,' she chirped primly. 'I remember you. You're Harry, Mr Bernard's son. I have to get home by sundown,' she added, to explain why she kept on walking.

I pedaled along beside her slowly, wrestling the handlebars as my front wheel wobbled. 'Are you, like, religious or something?'

'No. Well, we light the candles. But then only my father goes to temple. He says I can decide for myself when I grow up.'

I nodded – and conversation lagged. This wasn't the sort of talk I wanted to hear from her, and I couldn't think of anything to add to it. I considered telling her how I'd overheard my mother say religion was all hooey, but that didn't seem very polite . . .

'Uh . . .' I said.

Agnes began to sing. '"Oh, Mary Mac, Mac, Mac, with silver buttons, buttons, buttons, all down her back, back, back . . ."' She eyed me sidelong. 'That's a jump-rope song. I was jumping rope with Jessica. She's my friend. I was over her house today. That's why I'm coming back in this direction. "She jumped so high, high, high, she touched the sky, sky, sky, she didn't come back, back, back, till the fourth of . . ." You don't go to JFK, do you?'

'Uh . . . No . . . Bunker Hill.'

'Oh. Jessica and I go to JFK. I like it there. I'm in third grade.'

A car coursed by and my front wheel switchbacked. Agnes pulled ahead of me as I righted myself. This gave me a moment to consider. What was going on here? I felt like I'd taken a cold douse in the kisser. I mean, here I was, talking to a girl about a jump-rope song, for crying out loud. Talking about her friend Jessica. With a girl younger than me. And with her braids clocking. And with her prissy nose in the air. *He came for witchcraft, he left with cooties* – I could see the headlines now. What a let-down this was turning out to be.

I pulled up alongside her again just as we reached the corner of Piccadilly. I wanted some answers here. Where was the eerie girl I'd met by the stream? How come she was so different now?

'Uh . . .' I said.

'Well,' said Agnes. 'I have to go. Bye.'

'Bye,' I managed to get out.

She turned off, marched away. I pedaled up to speed and got the heck out of there.

So that was the end of my plaintive pining streamside. No more hankering after Agnes either. It definitely was a let-down, but not the worst surely. I couldn't even recall exactly what it had been, down there by the water; what she'd been like exactly that day that had put the spook into me so. By now, my soulful converse with grass blades on sneaker tips etcetera had more or less rotted away to the purely philosophical. Illusion, reality, the reality of illusion – who can say when you're nine years old? And after that, who gives a damn?

So the next Friday, I was back out on Hampshire Road playing baseball as the sun went down. Up at the sewer, with Dave lobbing them in this time, Freddy and Rick sharing the narrow outfield which went only from curb to curb. I had invisible men on first and third, two outs and two fouls on me — and we allowed foul-outs in this game to keep it moving so I could go down with any swing. And it was that time of day again, the light failing. And the big front window of Andrea Fiedler's house had gone ebony again and was shimmering with the reflection of gnarly apple branches, sparsely blossomed. My Louisville Slugger, circling over my shoulder, was pictured on the glass as well, and so was the tennis ball coming in. And her shape, her silhouette, Andrea's, was also there, I imagined, melding with the other blackness as she hovered spectral in her living room, watching me perform.

Dave's pitch reached me. I swung. Gave it a thok, a real shot. Usually I pulled those over the housetops, a long strike, but this one stayed true. Soon, it was bouncing way the hell down by the corner of Hartford and Sloane. Rick, who was fast, was tearing after it, but he had no chance of catching up. He could only watch where the ball landed and report back.

'Home run,' he shouted.

I made only the most restrained gesture of triumph, yanking the air in front of me into my fist. Then I pivoted from the plate to walk off the energy. And I saw that the light had come on in the Fiedlers' window.

Mrs Fiedler was in there, setting the dinner table. Then, as I watched, a toilet flushed faintly in the distance and Andrea skipped in too and started to help with the cutlery. She came in, I saw, from the back of the house somewhere. She hadn't been stationed at the window, in other words. She hadn't been watching me.

I returned to the sewer for a few practice swings, while Rick and Freddy relayed the ball back to the mound.

The next day, Saturday, was a warm, pleasant day in May, but I awoke somehow in the tar pits of meditation. I didn't know why I was in such a funk. I even watched the cartoons scowling. In pajamas till ten, my hair uncombed. Nothing satisfactory. Finally, somewhere between 'How come we never have any *good* cereal?' and 'This is a stupid house, there's nothing to do here,' my mother got sick of me. 'It's a lovely day,' she said. 'Why don't you go outside and play?' And I was banished to the suburban streets.

Like a lonesome cowpoke, I wandered aimlessly. What was life? What good was anything? Why did I have to be stuck in Miss Truxell's class? It had ruined my existence. Nothing was ever any fun anymore. And where was my dog – why had my parents killed my poor dog two years ago without telling me? Oh, Clancy, Clancy, if only you were here. Eyes on the macadam, sneakers kicking stones, I shuffled east to Plymouth and then Piccadilly Road. I was going to think this world out, I decided. I was going to know what I believed and stand for it and never complain and watch everything with an air of dangerous quiet and make terse, profound statements through tight lips. And hey, what if the women were not quite naked but were in their underwear and leaned forward and said, 'Please, please, King Harry, you can do anything you want to me?' The sun was at my back, the lawns were dewy, birds sang, and the air was like sponge cake, soft, warm and sweet.

A screen door banged. I raised my eyes and up ahead was Agnes.

This time, she was not only flouncing smugly from one lawn to the next, but was decked out in green beret and brown smock – a Girl Scout uniform. Now she was selling Girl Scout cookies, for Cripes' sake. She headed up the path to the next door, primly toting her sample boxes, clipboard and order form. Disgusting. I shook my head, determined to mope right past her.

So, of course, there was no one home at her next stop and I came abreast of her just as she laid off the chimes and came prancing down the front walk toward me.

'Hi,' she said.

I stopped. Lifted my world-weary visage, as if surprised to see her there. She was standing flat-footed on the sidewalk, facing me straight on in that unnerving way girls have. I tipped her the lorn, lonesome wave of the ambling saddle tramp.

'Taking a walk?'

'Yeah,' I sighed, grimly remembering how I'd killed a man in a gunfight in Abilene.

'I'm selling Girl Scout cookies. I've done twenty boxes so far just this morning, although my mother took five. Jessica and I are going to share our sales so neither of us has more than the other. And that way we'll both have more than Michelle. She's our friend too but she's kind of annoying.'

I nodded with a sad, kind of faraway look in my eye.

'Well . . . I have to go home for lunch now,' she said. 'You could come if you wanted to. We're having wagon wheel noodles and Girl Scout cookies for dessert.'

Normally, I'd have refused out of simple shyness – and, too, it was just about time for me to be movin' on to another town. On the other hand: wagon wheels and Girl Scout cookies – those vanilla creme sandwiches especially . . . And it'd teach my mother something if I just didn't turn up for her lunch.

I shrugged. 'Okay.'

And we walked off together to the top of the hill.

And so, The Queer Lunch. There's no doubt it was the beginning of something. And it sure was queer, too, right from the start, right from the minute I walked in the door. There was the smell of the place, first of all. Not your usual kid's house smell, open to the air, the screen door banging, laundry going, lunch on. It was that other smell, stagnant and ripe, plush with the must of another country. Not that I actually thought of Grandpa or the Nouveau Riche Hotel Of Parental Death or anything. But the defeated-looking stuffed chairs in the living room, and the rattle of Hummel shepherd boys on the mantelpiece and of hand-sculpted glass on the coffee table as I tromped through after Agnes – these did feel familiar to me, even as they felt unalterably foreign.

The kitchen was better. Brightly lit with a window on the trees out back. Yellow wallpaper and shiny floor tiles. And the starchy smell of noodles steaming. And there was the Mom, Mrs Sole, hair up and apron on, comfortably at her stove, a recognizable and reassuring presence.

'Hi, Mom, I'm home,' Agnes said.

She turned from the noodle pot, wooden spoon in hand. Smiling. 'Oh, hel . . .'

Did I register the way her eyes went flat, the way her

cheeks, pinkened by the noodle steam, drained suddenly to chalk? Her smile was back in place in a pulse beat.

'And Harry! How – how nice to see you.'

'He was taking a walk,' Agnes said. She dropped her cookie-selling stuff on the kitchen counter. 'Can he have lunch with us?'

'Lunch?' whispered Mrs Sole. We regarded each other, she and I, she with her wooden spoon upraised.

'I'm hungry,' said Agnes. 'Can we eat now?'

'Yes. Yes,' said Mrs Sole. She glanced desperately back at her noodle pot. 'I guess we have enough, I . . .' She looked at me again. I looked up at her blankly. I wondered if she was feeling sick or something. 'Of course,' she said finally. 'You're more than welcome to stay, Harry. We'd love to have you.'

'He's our friend Mr Bernard's son,' said Agnes.

'Yes. Yes, I know,' said Mrs Sole, and cleared her throat.

'Are we eating now? Should I call Daddy?'

Mrs Sole turned slowly back to the stove. She put her spoon back in the pot – weakly, it seemed. She stirred with slumped shoulders. 'Yes,' she said softly. 'Call Daddy. He's on the back porch.'

'Come on,' Agnes said to me. She scampered out the kitchen door. 'Daddy! Daddy!' we heard her call.

I'd lingered there and stood behind Mrs Sole, squinting up at her back. 'Excuse me, Mrs Sole,' I said. 'I ought to call my mother.' Her head came up; I heard her make a noise – a laugh, I think. A sort of wild, frightened laugh. 'To tell her I won't be home for lunch,' I said.

'Of course, Harry.' She turned, just barely, pointed with her wooden spoon at a phone screwed into the side of a cupboard. 'The phone's right over there.'

So over I bounced. Lifted down the receiver. Dialed Mom. 'Hi, it's me,' I said. 'I'm staying at a friend's house for lunch. Okay. Okay. Bye.' I fit the phone back in its cradle and turned around.

Agnes's Mom was staring at me. Bent over her pot, gripping her spoon, holding it into the steam without stirring. Staring at me over her shoulder like a terrified animal. She licked her ashen lips – she seemed about to

smile, about to speak. But then her stare, as if at a shrill
alarm, shot elsewhere. Nervously, I followed the line of it
to the kitchen door.

Agnes had returned. She stood in the doorway. She was
hanging happily onto her father's sleeve, bouncing up and
down by his trouser waist, as he surveyed the kitchen, me,
his wife, through inconsolable eyes.

'Lunch time!' Agnes sang.

Dr Sole. Dr Chaim Sole. The first thing that struck me about
him, naturally, was how old he was. You couldn't help but
notice it. The way he walked, shuffling slowly in pants a size
too large. The grizzled wattle at his neck, his limp yellow-gray
hair, his damp, uncertain lips, his rheumy eyes. Even I, blithe
and stupid, thought he must be Agnes's grandfather really. But
Agnes said, 'Daddy, this is Harry. Harry, this is my Daddy.'
And in they came.

He's what I remember best about The Queer Lunch,
what made it truly queer, deeply queer, though he said
hardly anything to me. Just brushed by above me with a
distracted smile when we were introduced, and patted my
hair with his dry palm − like any old man. We ate in a
sunny alcove off the kitchen, with screen doors letting onto
the slate patio, the small yard, the treeline and the spring
weather. There were modern paintings on the white wall,
I remember. Drips and smears of pastel that you couldn't
focus on, and that were oddly disturbing. The Doctor sat
at the head of the glass table. He ate salad and bread and
spoke to his wife, when he asked for anything, in a thick
voice with some sort of accent. He spoke with formal, courtly
sweetness to her: it was nerve-wracking, and made me sit up
straight and say, 'Thank you' a lot and keep my mouth shut
otherwise whenever I could. Agnes, though − she chattered
away. Seated across from me, her eyes brown and bright, her
head up like a twittering bird's.

'Jessica says she's not sure she's even going to invite
Michelle to her birthday party because she's so annoying,
but she says she probably will because Michelle is still her
best friend although I'm her best best friend. Michelle thinks
she's so great because she can do cartwheels, but Jessica says

she'll teach me to do cartwheels too, she taught Michelle and
she says it's not so hard . . .'

'The bread please, my dear,' said the doctor.

Mrs Sole handed me the basket and I passed it on to him,
then stole a glance back at her. She was sitting like a ramrod,
watching him. Her breath held, her cheeks still pink as if with
kitchen steam, her eyes fairly glittering with hectic terror.
Only when Agnes's prattling paused, did she seem to come
awake, round on her daughter desperately with:

'Have you told Harry we visited a farm, Agnes? Why don't
you tell him about the farm?'

'Oh. Yes. That was fun. Well, we went to a farm . . .'

And off Agnes went again. And up again sat Mrs Sole,
swallowing with relief, resuming her anxious watch along
the table. And I, with my nose buried in my bowl of wagon
wheels, oppressed by Mrs Sole's strange nerves and Dr Sole's
bizarre old age, and with the foreign aura of formality and
a gothic closeness that pressed in on top of me like gloom,
only just dared, clamping my mouth on my buttery spoon,
to hazard a look also at Agnes's father. And, well, he, during
all this, was staring at the bread. That's all he was doing.
Staring at a hunk of bread he'd lifted from the basket. What
an expression he gave it too, as he held it there like Yorick's
skull, absently mashing his salad with flaccid, lettuce-flecked
lips. A hunk of hand-sliced rye, it was. He turned it a little,
this way and that, as if studying the facets in the light; the
shape, the crust, the seeds, I don't know. Tragic, intimate,
ardent, amused, enraged: if you held in your hand your own
malignancy and found it had the face of the woman you love
– that was the gaze he was putting on that wedge of rye. While
Agnes blathered about funny-smelling sheep, and Mrs Sole
sat rigid, flushed and saucer-eyed; and I, finally, laced into
those noodles again, scraping the bottom of the bowl with
my spoon, and politely declining seconds.

'Why don't you two take your cookies outside?' said Mrs Sole
when she had doled them out to us two apiece. 'Agnes, why
don't you take Harry down to the stream and play there?'

It was a relief to tumble with Agnes out the patio doors
back into that pillowy spring day, and lunch was forgotten at

once. Agnes, still in her Girl Scout uniform, her scraped knees bare, skipped along ahead of me, over the slate, then over the grass, then up to the edge of the trees where we could hear the stream riffling below us. I came up beside her and we stood munching our vanilla cremes intently until our hands were free. Then, when our mouths were stuffed, we dusted the crumbs off our fingers. Agnes gulped her cookies down.

'Now!' she said.

And there, at last, it was again. A genuine thrill to see it, too; a goosey scare even. Her crimped face was of a sudden all witchery, with arched brows and torchlight eyes. Her voice was that mysterious whisper. The weird voodoo girl I remembered from last April had returned.

She pressed in toward me until I nearly leaned away. 'Now,' she hissed, 'I'm going to take you to . . . the *star rock*! Follow me!'

Arms out like wings, she ran into the trees. She'd left her Girl Scout beret inside, and her braids, which had been pinned up before, bounced around free behind her. I felt a little stupid, I reckon, but I sure enough jogged after her all the same. Losing her for moments in the maze of trees. Sliding down the slope to the muddy streambank. Leaping the water on a bridge of stones. Then scaling the opposite slope over rocks and roots, litter, beer cans and pine needles until finally, panting, we pushed together through another stand of conifers and oaks, and came out into an empty lot.

Not much romance here at first sight. A dusty half-acre. Gravel, scrub and broken glass. The far side was bordered by a chain-link fence and down to the right you could see the brick medical offices on Middle Neck Road. You could even see the rear of the parking lot and hear the traffic down there. But the sky was big above us, pale and blue and laced with clouds. And there was a great gray boulder rising from the dirt on the edge of the treeline, and Agnes was full of its mysteries.

'Come on,' she said.

She climbed it, scraping the scabs from her knees afresh. She knew the rock all right, because she went straight up the smooth surface like a beetle while I had to run my fingers over the stone like a blind man to find the obscure points of purchase. Soon, though, I stood panting over her where she sat with her oozing knees drawn up and her arms wrapped around them and her chin in close. I surveyed the view and drank in the power of it: houses through the far fence, cars pulling in and out of the medical parking lot – the town going about its business, in other words, while I watched without being seen.

'This is the star rock,' Agnes breathed with her creepy stare at nothing. 'This is where I come to put my spells on the stars.'

I snorted. 'Oh yeah?' But she lifted her scrunched face to me and somewhere inside my dim boy's brain I registered the neediness beneath the necromancy. So I played along gruffly. 'Well, what kind of spells?'

And she put her chin on her knees again. I sat down next to her, drawn despite my qualms to her worried little profile.

'The stars aren't really close, you know,' she said. 'They aren't really next to each other the way they look, they're far apart in space. Some of them aren't really even *there* anymore.'

'What do you mean?' I blurted out – I forgot to pretend that I knew that already.

'They're dead,' she whispered. 'But the darkness hasn't reached us yet from so far away so we still see the light.' And here she fell into an eerie kind of sing-song. 'And so I climb up to the star rock sometimes – and I cast my spell – and all the stars come together in people's eyes – in constellations – Orion . . .' she nodded toward the west, then a little eastward, 'and Gemini, the twins, and the big dipper and the lion. And everyone has to see them even though they're not really there – no one can look without seeing the shapes of the constellations in all the stars even though they're really dead and far apart in space.'

She paused and licked her lips. My nervous check on the broad and domey sky confirmed the daylight there and the wispy clouds across the blue. But I could sense them, I confess, night and the stars, lurking right behind that scrim: like a gaze behind a veil, like a village in mist. What a spooky little girl she was.

'Like the sky, you mean,' I said, mostly to hear my own

voice. 'Like they have to see the sky even though it's not there?'

She shook her head slowly. 'No. No. Because this is my spell, that I put on them. And sometimes, when I feel like it, I can climb up to the star rock and wave my hands . . .' And she did, sitting up, lifting them crossed before her face and drawing them apart in a slow arc. '. . . and take it off, and all the constellations disappear and there's just one star after another, a million zillion stars, far and close and dead and not dead and every one alone, even in the Pleiades, even in the Milky Way, and no pictures in them anywhere, only stars, star after star after star after star, millions and zillions.'

Yes, well, of course, there's not a whole lot you can say to something like that, so I kept my mouth shut. And she'd fallen silent too, peering up into the veil above us. I couldn't help watching her, studying her. Her crimped features, her permanent expression of wariness and concern. She must've felt me doing it, I did it a long time, but she didn't stir, she let me.

Then, without thinking at all, I piped up, 'Hey, Agnes, how come your Mom was so nervous at lunchtime?'

'I don't know. She wasn't nervous,' she said. She turned her head, lay her cheek on her knees and peered back at me dolefully.

'Well, maybe not nervous,' I said. 'She just seemed . . . I dunno. But I mean, how come your Dad stared at the bread like that? He was looking at the bread, I dunno, really funny.'

'No, he wasn't.' Her voice was small now, a monotone, as if she were answering mechanically.

So, what the heck, I shut up again, scratching my head. I was getting tired of this game. I felt cooped up as if I'd been indoors too long. I had an almost homesick yearning for Hampshire Road, Freddy and Dave, a game of ball.

'Sometimes I don't want to talk about my parents,' said Agnes, in that same small voice. She nested on her knees another silent second or so while I shifted uncomfortably. Then, all at once, her head popped up. Her eyebrows lifted, she gave me the big lamps, the whisper: 'I know! From now on, let's only meet here! Okay? Or down by the stream.

And we won't see my parents, and we won't see anybody. Okay? We won't tell anyone. We'll only meet here and it'll be secret. Okay?'

I returned her stare without answering. This, more than anything, spooked me good, made me sour inside – nearly nauseous – with fear. What sort of compact was I into here – and so suddenly – and with a girl besides – and with this girl, this queer, queer creature?

Yet there was no time to think and I was mesmerized and even the instinct to make excuses had only a weak glimmering power beneath the other forces that drew me in with her.

There we stared back and forth on that rock together silently. And then I heard myself saying: 'Okay. Okay.'

— 4 —

Freddy and I were digging in my backyard — chink, chink, chink — trowels in the stony earth. This was months after the Queer Lunch and the star rock. Summer was just coming. School was out for good tomorrow.

'No more Miss Truxell,' said Freddy, spearing the loose soil.

We faced each other across the hole, on our knees.

'Wouldn't it be awful,' I said, 'if she taught sixth grade too?'

'Or what if you just had to have Miss Truxell forever?'

'Oh God!'

The hole was almost two feet deep now, and wide, maybe a foot and a half across. We had set it just at the back gate, which led out onto Chadwick Road, around the corner from our front door. Next to the hole, we had the front page of the *Times* lying in the grass. *LBJ PLEDGES SUPPORT FOR SOUTH VIETNAM*, it said. *CALLS FOR GREAT SOCIETY*. We piled our spadesful of turned earth between our dirty knees.

'Boy, I am really dying to get to camp,' Freddy said. 'I found out yesterday my team is called the *Tigers*. I'm gonna play second. We're gonna win the league, I swear.'

He was going away for the full two months, to a baseball camp. They played a whole season, with two leagues, and then a World Series too. I had to admit it sounded pretty cool.

'That's deep enough,' I said.

We lay our trowels aside. We lifted the newspaper, carefully, both of us, each holding two corners between thumb and finger. We lay the paper down gently over the hole, like making a bed. It covered the hole and then some.

'Okay,' I said.

We started placing pebbles on the paper's corners to hold it in place.

I was only going away to camp for two weeks, at the beginning of August. It was my first time at sleepaway. I was glad it was such a long way off.

Gently now, gently, we began to spread the turned earth over the surface of the newspaper. Sprinkling it on with our hands at first then using the trowels to spread it thin and even. Fragments of words, photographs, fists, bearded mouths on angry faces appeared through the dirt for a while, then they were covered over. The entire newspaper began to disappear. Our hole began to look like just another section of the yard.

'Oh man!' said Freddy. 'This is great! If Ira comes by here, we'll just shout something at him, like, "Hey, Ira, your mother wears boots to bed." Then when he comes running after us – boom! – man, he's gonna fall right into the trap, he'll, like, break his leg and we'll make him lie out here until he starves to death. I mean, you could really do this in a war or something, you know. Like when the Japs came at you, you could just, like, run away . . .'

There was still a whole month, I told myself. I shaped the dirt, not listening to Freddy. All of July, I thought, before my camp began. I didn't think: all of July – with her. I didn't think about her at all, or about our solemn hoodoos by the stream the night before. Or about all the nights we had been together through that spring. What I did think about – while Freddy, bless him, put paid to Pearl Harbor with a few well-positioned ditches – was afterwards, the walk home from her house alone, the bizarre welling in the long summer dusk of the dreamless quiet inside me, the flamboyant, nearly garish limning of the details without – the barking of a distant dog, the smell of mown grass, house lights through maple leaves – and that dizzying sensation that came and went of the world's objects loosed from their moorings, floating, my attention lodged within them, toward infinite night and outer space. It was always like that after I'd been with her.

'Wouldn't that be great?' said Freddy breathlessly.

Really spooky, I thought. A spooky, spooky little girl.

The bell rang on the last half-day of school and I with the other kids gushed cheering out the doors into the summer noon. We boys shouted to each other in loud, high voices, bursting with exquisite witticisms about Miss Truxell as we strode down the path to the road and freedom. Hilarious puns about trucks and old maids flew back and forth among us. We even stood on the corner an extra few minutes to further abuse that poor, ugly, lorn and probably miserable creature before we finally parted to go home for lunch, secretly sad about the whole thing.

I, with a fine summer melancholy on, went by way of Piccadilly — out of my way completely, that is. Not that I expected to find Agnes by the stream this early in the day. I just figured I'd sit there by myself a while and toss pebbles in the water and take stock of things. I came down to the bank from the culvert, the secret shortcut I always used when I did meet her. Really all it was was cutting through the woods near the ghost house at the top of the hill. Skirting past the wooden shack's darkened windows always gave an extra spurt of terror to the proceedings, and then I could jump Batman-like off the rim of the big culvert and stroll with casual heroism along the bank to our usual spot.

So I did — and I was surprised to see that Agnes was there after all. She was kneeling by the water, bright and small with the sun right above her, the trees full green and bright overhead and the stream glittering. I was glad to see her, glad for the company, and quickened my pace. But Agnes only looked up briefly when she heard me coming. She was fiddling with something on a rock and there was a puckered scowl on her round monkey mug.

'Hey, Agnes,' I said, giving it a try anyway. 'Hooray, huh? School's over.'

'So?' she said. 'I hate summers!' I could see now that she was mashing up some Play-Doh, savagely kneading the jolly reds, blues and yellows into a single ball, streaked, mucky, brown. 'Jessica and Michelle are going to camp together, all summer. I'm going to fly there at night and haunt them! I'm going to scare Michelle so much she'll turn white and die.'

'Whoa.' I tugged my ear, stifled a yearning for lunch and my mother and home. These moods of hers could be suffocating, but they were part of the spirit of the place. 'Can't you go too?' I asked.

She mashed the clay against the stone. 'My *father* won't let me. He says I'm too *young*. He says he'll be too *worried* about me. My mother says I can't upset Daddy; no one can ever upset Daddy. She says I should make *other* friends.' Oh, the thunderous little frown she lifted to me. 'I'll bet *you're* going to camp too.'

'Well . . . not until all the way in August.' But I didn't want to think about that. I sat down next to her at the stream's edge and began plucking up my pebbles. 'Aren't you going to go to day camp or anything?'

'I hate day camp! I'm not going to go. I'm going to lie in a coffin all summer, all alone, under the ground. Then I'm going to come out at night and fly to Jessica's camp and stand by Michelle's window and sing a horrifying song.'

'Well, yeah, I guess you could do that,' I said. I looped a stone into the rushing middle depths with a satisfying *plink*. 'Or you could just go to day camp and make some new friends like your mother says. It might be easier.'

'I don't want to meet new friends.' It was really determined talk now through hardened jaws. She worked at her clay steadily. 'I want to meet old people. I'm going to meet people so old that they're in the past. They'll be ghosts, like me. I'm going to go with my sister into her garden.'

I aimed for a fiery ball of reflected sunlight in a shallow eddy on the far side. Bullseye — shattered it into sparkles. 'What do you mean? What garden?'

She was so long in answering, I looked over. The streaked Play-Doh was beginning to take shape into a figure now. Not limbs and head stuck onto a trunk either; a thing entire just sort of oozing out between her fingers. I'd never seen her actually do it before and it caught my attention. It gave me a thrill.

'I had a dream one time,' she said, 'where Lena came.'

'Your ghost sister. Yeah?' I rolled my pebbles in my palm.
I watched her work the clay.

'She came and met me in a ghost place – a big, kind of –
I don't know – a big, kind of brown place where everything
was broken. There were all these broken, old things lying
around in the mud and some of them had arms and heads
reaching out of the mud like monsters trying to crawl out,
you know? And there were all these . . .' She straightened
a second to describe them in the sunlit air with her hand.
'. . . scary trees, like, all around, that looked like monsters
with giant fingers and scary faces staring down at us. And
the sky was scary too with, like, clouds. And it was all cold.'
She returned to her figure, the little girl figure she had formed,
Lena's figure. 'And Lena came there – wearing a white dress –
she came there and met me and she said, "This isn't where I
really live. This is just where I have to come so I can meet
you. Where I live it's like a big garden with beautiful flowers
all over everywhere like a carpet, and all the mothers are with
their children and all the fathers are playing with them and
everyone's laughing." And she said I could come there with
her.' She looked up, caught me gaping at her hands. 'She said
I could come with her to the garden where she lived.' She
took her figure from the rock and sat back in the dirt with
it, bracing it against her scraped knee, shaping the details. 'I
wanted to go, too. I was going to. Only I didn't know if she
was telling the truth or not. Once you went to the garden,
see, you couldn't come back and what if it was all like this
place, I mean the scary place we were in, you know, with
the trees and things and I could never get back – never.'

She stopped and I figured she was finished with her story
and I couldn't help saying something about this incredible
figure she'd made and I blurted out, 'God, Agnes! God, that
is so neat! How do you do that?'

She hiked one shoulder, made a grimace of disdain. 'I just
make what I see,' she said.

'Yeah, but, I mean, could you, like, make . . . like a
monster or something, like a Frankenstein, something really
cool like that?'

She rolled up off her backside back onto her knees, back
to the edge of the burbling stream. She held Lena's figure

close to her in one hand. Braced with the other hand on
the bank, she gazed down into a quiet pool sheltered from
the current by stones.

'Oh, come on, Agnes,' I said behind her, 'don't drown it.
Make a Frankenstein or something, make something cool.'
She hesitated. 'Come on, Agnes.'

After another moment, she sat back. She was still gazing
away sort of dreamily – or maybe sort of insanely, I don't
know – into the shadow-pocked slope on the far side. But
she wagged her head. 'I could make a Frankenstein.'

'Yeah!' I dusted the last pebbles off my palms and went
over to her on my knees. 'Only not a Frankenstein.' I already
had the Aurora Frankenstein monster model on the shelf in
my room. 'Something else cool,' I said. 'Like a skeleton or
something.'

Dreamily, Agnes folded Lena in two between her palms.
She mashed the figure back into the muddy ball whence it
had come. 'You can't do a good skeleton with Play-Doh,'
she said, gazing off. 'Because of the ribs. Play-Doh's too soft
to make good ribs. I could do a skull though.'

'Yeah! Great! Okay! Make a skull!'

Slowly, reflectively, Agnes seemed to come back to herself.
She heaved a deep sigh and set about the task. I knelt beside
her on the sunlit bank, by the dribbling stream, under the trees
heavy with leaves on the ridge above us. I watched her as she
worked. I was mesmerized by those delicate little fingers in
the clay.

And she made a skull, all right, a great one. She let me keep it
too. It would be worth – what? – about two million dollars by
now. Unfortunately, that autumn – just around the same time
I was flipping my baseball card collection into piles of burning
leaves – I accidentally knocked the skull from my shelf and it
was dented by the fall. Somehow, when I picked it up, when
I saw how lopped it was, I became fascinated. My thumb, as
if of its own volition, slowly burrowed into the skull's side,
making it crumble, the clay having dried. Then, in a trance, I
crushed the thing, and rolled the hardened bits into a clump.
After that, I played with it for a few minutes distractedly, and
finally threw it into the trash.

But not that afternoon. I carried it home carefully that afternoon. I held it balanced on my palm. Going over and over its ghostly eyes with my own, admiring the detail of its evil grin. No one had one like it, no one – on Long Island, in the whole world – it was a oner. God, if she weren't a girl, and such a spooky girl, and so mysterious and so hard to approach for things, she could have made a million cool things – we could've set up a stand outside my house, like a lemonade stand – we'd have made enough money to buy a car or something . . . But that was just a thought. I was content enough. Absorbed in contemplation of the thing and with wisps of Agnes's creepy dream drifting across my imagination and with that incandescent, floaty Walk-Home-From-Agnes's feeling permeating the periphery of verdant foliage and scrabbling squirrels and summer sky. Raising my eyes as I came home to Old Colony Lane was like being interrupted from a TV show or a good book. There was my house suddenly barging in on my meditations. A big, homey colonial – white clapboards, green shutters – it seemed strangely unfamiliar to me for half a second. And, as I came around the hedges, there was something else – something really unfamiliar that brought me out of my revery the rest of the way. Another car was in the driveway. A family-style Ford of some kind, a Thunderbird I think, shiny and blue but stodgy in a way – and anyhow a foreigner, an intruder in the house, which made me grimace when I saw it.

I remembered who it was, though. My mother had mentioned it to me a week or so before: my Aunt May had finally come for her visit. She was going to be staying with us for quite some time.

— 5 —

'I cannot, cannot tell you how happy I am – how happy I am now that this is over. This is the thing I dreaded above all else, above everything, being alone like this, and now that it's finally here I feel so – so free! I just can't tell you.'

Even I knew she was beautiful, even then. And glamor came off her in waves like perfume. The magazine-cover makeup that preserved her flushed-ivory complexion, the low front of her navy summer dress and her ensorcelling cleavage through a fringe of lace, her bare arms and the movement of her arms and the dramatic phrases she used and the smell of her, even a little too much fragrance in an aggressively feminine cloud around her: it all made her seem spotlit to me. The grand sideboard behind her, ranged with display plates and pewterware, became a sort of dim backdrop. My mother and father, at either end of the dining-room table, seemed to fade into the shadowy wings. And I, sitting across from her in the elegant and windowless alcove we used for company, could only finger my crystal of Seven-up and occasionally chew the lump of pot roast lying on my lower jaw like lead, and try and fail and try again not to stare at her.

'Well, I never should have gone back to him. Oh God, it was the mistake of a lifetime. But, I mean, picture the scene: with me all alone and no money and nowhere to go, poor thing. You *can't* imagine it, Claire: you're so lucky, with Michael and Harry and a house and a life like this. Well, I wanted some of those things too, that's not so terrible. And, you know, he'd set his picture up at Fox, and there was money again, and he said everything would be different. I was absolutely, completely, totally convinced that he wanted to have the baby.'

'You know, I don't think we really have to go through all this right now,' my mother said. She wore an expression of stony disapproval – and a shapeless green muu–muu meant to hide her fat.

May pulled up at the rebuke. 'Oh . . . I'm just saying, Claire . . . you don't know how lucky you are, that's all. Here with your family . . .'

My mother's baggy face contorted once, and she pushed her last string bean through its butter with her fork. We all looked down, in fact, and our plates were strewn with only bones and wisps of mashed potatoes and streaks and puddles of butter. The carving board was down to a few gristly strips and there were just crumbs on the napkin in the bread basket. May's plate alone was nearly untouched, but then she'd taken so little to begin with. And though she lifted her fork now, she only sat poised with it. Her head bowed, her black hair pouring forward.

'You just don't know, Claire,' she said in a high, squeaking voice. All at once, the disaster of her tears was upon us. We repressed Bernards – who knows? – we might've died of the embarrassment. But luckily, May lifted her head quickly, and knuckled the damp cautiously from her underlids. 'I don't know why I should be crying. I'm so, so happy now – now that it's over. But I mean you don't know . . . every day he would come home, night after night, creeping into bed at eight–thirty, nine o'clock, hardly saying a word to me.' She gave a juicy snuffle.

'Are you done?' my mother said to me. 'Why don't you go upstairs and I'll call you when dessert is ready.'

I would've gone, I wasn't all that riveted by this grownup stuff. It was the sight of her more than anything that held me. But May, turning to Dad now, just carried on, hoarsely: 'I finally confronted him, Michael. That's how it finally happened. He was leaving for work, he was going down the stairs. We had this beautiful curving staircase going down to this marble foyer with an absolutely magnificent chandelier hanging above it. And Ben was going down the stairs, and I was still in my nightgown. And I thought: "No. Just: No."

And I got out of bed – and this was with the worst, the most awful morning sickness anyone anywhere can imagine, just crippling, utterly crippling nausea – and I just didn't care, I just ran – I ran – to the top of the stairs. I said, "Ben, you have to tell me what is going on. You have to tell me right now." And, Claire . . .' Because Mom and I were watching her again. 'Claire, I just wish I could describe, I wish I could paint for you the lofty, sanctimonious expression on his face. If I could paint some sort of . . . patron of Renaissance art being shown flying up into heaven, that was Ben, that was the look on his face. He says, "May . . ." That was his lofty voice: "May, I've joined Alcoholics Anonymous. I've found a higher power to help me deal with all my problems from now on." I mean, he was that self-satisfied. And so I said, "Well, what is that supposed to mean? You're just going to go to bed every night and leave every morning from now on? You have your higher power, so you don't need me anymore? Is that it?" And I can't, I can't convey the holier-than-thou expression on his face. "Oh, May," he says, "Oh, May, stand with me now, this is the crisis point of my life." And I just said, well, you know, "What about my crisis? Ben. I'm the one who's pregnant. Everyone says, oh that's so wonderful and everything – and then everything you do is a big, important crisis?" And he was just going to walk away from me! He was just going to turn his back and walk away. That was his answer to everything. And I just couldn't take it anymore. I just *couldn't*. I said to him, "You're not walking away from me this time. You're not. Absolutely."'

'May. I mean it. That's enough,' my mother said. 'For God's sake. Go on, Harry, go upstairs.'

'Oh God! Of course, of course,' said May, lifting her fork again. 'I don't have any children so I forget. I'm so, so sorry, Claire.'

'Go on, Harry,' my mother said. Her face was the color of concrete, with the cracks in it too. There was no getting out of this.

'But what happened?' I said. I was wrapped up in it now. 'What did Aunt May do?'

'Michael,' she said, 'would you tell your son to go upstairs?'

'Go on, Harry,' my father said heavily. 'Do what your mother says.'

'But what did Aunt May do?' I insisted.

'Harry, do you want there to be dessert?' said my mother.

'She lost the baby,' my father went on in the same heavy tone. 'She was going to have the baby but she lost it, it died. Now, go ahead, go upstairs or no dessert.'

I looked back at them once as I retreated toward the stairs and still – hell, more than before if anything – she was luminous. Aunt May. Eyes glistening with tears, cleavage heaving in the dull glow from the brasswork toplight. My parents flanked her in low relief, drab of aspect, drab of expression. My mother giving Dad her Damn-It-Michael look, my father shrugging at her for answer.

As I started upstairs, I was already wondering what I could find to watch on the TV in my parents' bedroom, but I did hear my father say softly behind me, 'Well, these things happen, Claire. You can't protect him from everything. It's only life.'

She moved into the guest room, down the hall from me, right across from Mom and Dad. I didn't like it much; she was a stranger among us. That room – and the bathroom too – she made them alien territory. Scented atmosphere, stockings and frilly brassieres in plain sight, blouses bright as gardens – thrilling, you know, but foreign, invasive. She would come out of the bathroom some mornings in a cloud of steam with her hair in a towel and her leg flashing from her bathrobe and the white V beneath her throat showing. She would sit at breakfast and say, 'Oh, it's so peaceful here,' and stretch with her hands intertwisted high above her head. She would talk about Hollywood, which bored me, but the whispery flute of her voice was so light it made everything else around her seem heavy and harsh. My parents' very jowls sagged as they listened to her. They seemed to sit around her like those Bronze Age monoliths, those squat boulders plumped upright.

I heard the hiss of her shower in the morning sometimes and lay in my bed an extra few minutes, dreaming of dominion, stretching, arching, playing my dick like a trombone –

not masturbating yet, just tugging at it. And once, when May asked me to run upstairs to her room to fetch a book, I left the lights off and just stood there; just breathed the alien air, the perfume. Then I crept to her closet; I reached inside; I rubbed a slip of hers between my finger and thumb. It was so sheer it seemed to catch on the ridges of my fingerprints. My little heart played rock 'n' roll.

With no camp till August, I had a free July. Breakfast in front of the TV. Reruns by daylight – *My Little Margie, Topper,* all the mindless greats. The humid torpor of it, the rancid PJs, the mental drone; ah, whither are such summers fled! Most of my friends were gone during the day in one kind of camp or another, and I was prince of all their territories, running free from backyard to backyard, full of fantasy, alive with summertime and basically, yeah, bored out of my head. Luckily, stumbling through a hedge one morning, scratched nearly blind, I managed to discover an enclave of younger kids, some seven- and eight-year-olds, playing pirates in a lawn sprinkler. They were wary of me at first, but when I showed peaceable, they were sort of honored to let me tromp and splash around with them a while. I went back there most days to be with them. We played soldiers together and I taught them everything I knew – which was that Pickett charged with his hat on his sword, Civil War guys had to have their legs cut off without being unconscious, and Japs shot you in the back just when you thought you'd cleared the island of them. Slowly, indignant at the injustice of the world and the oppression of the weak everywhere, I organized these young scallywags into a band of right-seeking outlaws known forevermore as Harry's Raiders. Our hideout was a teepee of old lumber in one of their backyards. Our exploits were trumpeted far and wide. We once stole an entire box of toybox cookies right out of Mrs Zimmerman's kitchen while she was on the phone in the next room. Then, descending like the wind on the Allenwood Park playground, we distributed these, and mothers be damned, to a group of five-year-olds playing there in the sandboxes. One of these tots actually hugged me for it. 'That's all right, son,' I said, squinting into the middle distance, 'just thank . . . Harry's Raiders.'

Whereupon I vanished, followed by my merry band, into the woods, and legend.

In the afternoons, after four o'clock, when I knew she'd be home from camp, I'd usually wander up to Piccadilly Road and climb down to the stream to see Agnes. Sometimes, I would get there first and wait for her, skimming stones, floating sticks. Other times, as I sauntered down the bank from the culvert, I would hear her there already through the low overhang of summer leaves, chattering girlishly to her figures or, better yet, gutturalizing hellish incantations echoed by the softer gutturals of the water.

Sometimes I didn't see her at all, or couldn't come, or came too late, like the night I arrived as dark fell, and climbed up the bank and struggled through dense maple and hickory boughs, and came to the very edge of the treeline, my hand resting against shagbark, and saw her through her house's glass doors in back, spied on her there. Not that I witnessed anything too shocking. They were lighting the Sabbath candles, the three Soles. The dining room amber around them, the candelabra set on a corner table. Agnes with a shawl over her hair, furrow-browed with concentration, looking like an old peasant woman as she stretched the match out unsteadily to draw a tear-shaped flame from each wick in turn. Her mother hovered over her, likewise shawled, and apple-cheeked and attentive, the firelight in her eyes. And the old doctor, on the far side, chewed his wrinkled lips and looked about the room impatiently.

I watched a while, then, lonesome, melted back into the territory of shadows whence I'd come.

'In March – that's when my birthday is – Gemini is right there, right in the middle there.'

We were on her star rock at the edge of the vacant lot at the very beginning of a night soon after. She was pointing straight above us to where she'd just sketched Bootes, which I couldn't really make out, and the star Arcturus, which was neat because it was orange.

'Gemini is the twins,' she said, bringing her arm down, wrapping it round her knees, resting her chin on her scabs.

'One twin was regular, and one couldn't ever be killed because his father was one of the gods. Then, one day, the regular one, Castor, was hit by a spear and he died. So Pollux, the god one, he asked his father — I can't remember his name — if Castor could live in his body one day and Pollux would be dead, and then the next day, Pollux would live in the body and Castor would be dead. And the father said yes. So that's how they lived forever after that.'

She paused. I nodded appreciatively, though of course she was gazing off mystically God knows where. Still, it was a pretty cool story and, boy though I was, I wasn't too proud to admit that I'd never heard it before — or seen Bootes before or Arcturus. I wasn't too proud about any of that with her anymore these days. In fact, I could almost admit to myself how much I liked to have her tell me such things. I was almost conscious of feeling close to her when she did, and when we sat like this together, with the warm, quiet darkness of the lot lapping at our rock and then stretching away as far as Middle Neck Road where streetlights beamed and headlights hissed softly past. That evening, I guess, that was probably the best of us. That was our peak before Aunt May said what she did.

'One night, we were in our village,' Agnes said then, 'and policemen came.' She had dropped her voice to her ghostly whisper, and I perked up, my spine going icy.

'What?'

She swung her huge, spiraling glare on me. 'They took all the children out of the houses and made them march down to the river. And if the mothers and fathers tried to stop them, they hit them, or they shot them with their guns.'

I snorted. 'Come on. What do you mean? That can't even happen. Policemen don't shoot good people.'

'This was in another country where the police were bad,' Agnes intoned. 'And they made the children line up at the edge of the river, and then they pushed them in — even the babies. And all the children drowned in the water, even the ones who could swim, because the policemen wouldn't let them come out. We just had to do the dog paddle in the river until we got so tired we drowned too. It was night and so dark. I kept crying for my father, but he couldn't come because the police wouldn't let him. He wanted to, he wanted to a lot, but they wouldn't let him. And the river was so cold. And it was black, it was blacker even than the blackest night you could imagine.'

She paused to swallow. She swallowed hard, swallowed her own terror it sounded like.

'Well, I'd have killed them first,' I said.

She shook her head. 'You couldn't, because they had guns. They were the police.'

'You can't be the police, Agnes, if you shoot good people. I'd have gotten my own gun, anyway, and shot them back.' I thought about this a second, and felt very sure of it. 'You know what I would do if I lived in a country like that? I would get a band of outlaws, and we would hide in the woods and then if stuff like that happened we would come out suddenly and rescue people.'

For a moment, her round, worried face just hung there dimly in the night, still inner lit and full of witchery. Then, all at once, she burst out: 'I wish I were like you, Harry! I wish I could be a hero like you!'

I was surprised at that, completely. And pleased: well, I swelled like a bullfrog, I was that pleased. But even as I shrugged modestly, full of myself, a bulb went on in that dim bean of mine, and a frightening thought took half the wind right out of me. 'Well, wait a minute,' I said. 'Like, what is this? Is this something real? Is this, like, what happened to your sister or something, to Lena?'

And in the same anguished little voice Agnes cried, 'Sometimes I *am* my sister, Harry.' She swallowed again. She went on breathlessly: 'My father is so sad. My mother says he's so sad and misses her so much. So sometimes – sometimes I let her live in my body – so she can be alive too, like Castor and Pollux. And then I have to go and live in a coffin in a grave until she's ready to come back. And then I can live again.'

I looked at her, and she at me. I think I can safely say that was just about the spookiest thing anyone had ever said to me. One faction of the inner Harry was lobbying hard for flight, but another . . . no. As scared as she made me, as big as she made the dark around me seem – well then, we were that much more together on our star rock island, weren't we? In fact, I do believe I wanted to be even closer to her then. I wanted to throw my arms around her, to hold her tight. To do *something*, anyway, I didn't know what. I didn't know much about sex − for all the bare-assed slaves who paraded through my imagination, I still had only a technical sort of inject-the-baby notion of it − so the impulse flooded through me as an inarticulate ache to be nearer, nearer than near, to her frail, creepy being and I wanted . . . what goodness for myself of her, what protection for herself in me I really couldn't have begun to say. And I really couldn't have begun to know whether I was bursting like this in solitude or whether she felt it too or − or what. We just gaped there at each other with a wild surmise.

And then I said quickly, 'Wulp, guess I better be getting home.' And pushed to my feet, dusting off my bottom.

We were out later than usual that night − yes, it was the best of us, no question. I walked her back up to her house even though she said I didn't need to. I saw her inside manfully and then − not for a moment about to go back into those scary woods the way I felt − ducked my head and sneaked past the side of her house and over her front lawn to Piccadilly Road.

I began walking home, hands in the pockets of my shorts, whistling tunelessly for fear of the night around me. The looming tree silhouettes, the spidery alleyways of hedges and grass between the houses: each seemed spring-loaded with potential horror. The ghost house − the abandoned shack lurking in overgrowth at the top of the hill − peered out at me with broken windows. I jogged past that, I confess. But then, as I came round the corner onto Wooley's Lane, as I started down into the gracefully descending prospect of homes and oaks and willows, that sensation welled in me, as it did so often when I'd left Agnes in one of her weirder moods, that sensation of terror and intimacy somehow working to produce a dizzying clarity of vision. The inner monologue quieted and I became aware − swimmingly aware − of the silken warmth and blackness of the night, the ragged borderlines of leaves against the sky, the depth of the stars beyond them, the whole reality shebang. And, startled, I became aware too that someone was walking on the road before me.

In the normal way of things, that might have made me nervous. It was a grownup — a man — about twenty yards ahead. I might have been cautious of him and held back. Instead, in that queer post-Agnes state in which I halfway seemed to become whatever I beheld, I fell in with him — mentally, I mean. Strolling along behind his slumped, brooding figure, observing all, in with the spirit of all, I entered into his rhythm as well, his progress, the very fact of his being there together with me on the sloping road in the vasty night. Sometimes there was simply a peaceful unison with him, knowing we meditated over the same pavement or heard the same electric frizz of cicada from a pacysandra patch nearby. And at other moments, I do declare, there were rushes of dissolution, almost passionate release, in which my goofy nine-year-old self seemed to extend to him, to envelop him, to balloon through him to global dimensions — and I loved him, to use the right word for it, I loved that man on the street ahead of me, downright fearlessly.

And so I tagged after him, loafing through these emotions, all the way to Plymouth Road, and around the corner to the short connector lane called Andover and thence finally to the bottom of Old Colony Lane and to my own house where I hung back only long enough to let him go through the door before me, and then followed him in, wondering what was for dinner.

6

One night, as I was watching TV with my mother and Aunt May, my father came storming in through the back door. He was limping. He was holding what looked like a tattered rag, shaking it in the air like a DA with an indictment. Particles and clods of dry earth were shaken from it and pattered onto the floor.

'Did you do this?' he said fiercely. He was looking at me, rattling that thing. 'Was this your bright idea?'

Until then, I had been reclining apathetically on the sofa, resting my elbow on the armrest, resting my cheek on my hand, staring at the set. Aunt May was next to me, smelling too good and chattering too much through the program, and my mother was in the cushioned chair with her crossword, too far away. It was beginning to occur to me that my trip to camp was not as far off as it used to be, hardly more than a week or so away. The dread of it was weighing heavy on me and I wanted to be near my mother, and alone with her for comfort, without the visitor's interference.

Then my father thundered in.

'Damn it!'

Whoa! I thought, quailing: My father had cursed.

He hobbled to the breakfast table, leaned on the back of a chair for support. My mother was already up and waddling toward him. I stood up too, and May cast her beauty in his direction.

My father pushed the indictment at me with his free hand. 'I could've broken my leg!'

'What is it, Dad?' I said, stalling for time. I knew what it was all right. Even from where I stood, I could now read the faded scrap of headline through the encrusted dirt: *LBJ . . . VIETNAM . . . GREAT SOCIETY*.

Dad turned to Mom. 'It's a piece of the newspaper. Your . . . *son* laid it over a hole and covered it up with dirt. Someone could've come by and broken his leg and sued us for a fortune.'

'I was just playing around with Freddy!' I cried out. 'We were making a trap!' I had forgotten all about it. It was weeks ago.

'Well, it was a damned stupid thing to do!' my father said.

My mother was working him into the chair, calming him, saying, 'All right, all right, let me see your foot. Can you move it?' She took the paper from him and put it on the table. I thought I detected the tremor of a smile at the corner of her lips. I felt awful, scared and awful, but it looked like it was going to be all right. I was almost beginning to breathe again.

And then, from the sofa next to me, May had this to say: 'Michael, what is it you do on all these secret night-time rambles you're always on anyway? It's no wonder you fall into things, creeping around the backyard in the pitch dark like that.'

It was an instinct I think she had – I've known people since who've had it too, people whose early lives proved unreliable somehow and collapsed around them. They develop this sort of compulsion to test the structure of things by jarring the stones that support it. May, I guess, was like that; she must've felt most at home with the catastrophes that followed, whatever the cost to herself. Her timing, anyway, was just impeccable. My father looked raw murder at her – raw murder, like nothing I'd ever seen in him before.

'Go to your room, Harry,' he said in a soft, strangled voice. He never took his eyes off May.

'Go on,' my mother said to me, but no one had to tell me twice.

'Sorry, Dad,' I said miserably. And, hangdog, I got the hell out of there.

There had never been anything in my house like the screaming there was then. My parents didn't scream as a rule — it was, in fact, exactly what they didn't do — and so I knew nothing about that kind of unbridled, free-galloping rage. It must've been building up in all of them for some time. But me, I'd had no idea. And to hear it now coming up through the floor of my room, well, it seemed as if hell had yawned belowstairs without warning. I seriously wondered if there would be anything left of home and family and everyday life when it was over. I lay on my bed, wobble-lipped, wet-eyed. My Yankee pennant was blurry through my tears. The models on my bookshelves — Frankenstein's monster, a knight in armor, Kennedy's war craft PT 109, even Agnes's grinning Play-Doh skull — seemed to hover over me in helpless pity like cherubim viewing the Crucifixion. I prayed for courage to my framed photograph of Mickey Mantle.

'*But you don't know what it's like to be alone!*' These words, Aunt May's unholy wail, reached me clearly. And my father's carnivorous rumble after that. And then the low warble of my mother — who never cried — pleading with her sister in tears.

Then May again: '*Where am I supposed to go? What am I supposed to do? You have everything, Claire! I don't have anything!*' The words seemed to be ripped brutally out of Aunt May's throat. '*Keep your money! I don't want your dirty money!*' And her sobs — it sounded to me as if they would tear her apart. '*Oh God! Oh God!*'

I tensed on the bed almost to the point of trembling and stifled a sob or two myself as I heard her footsteps rushing to the stairs, rushing up the stairs, closer and closer to me. I half expected her to burst in through the door next, shrieking, 'See what you've done, with your stupid trick!' I didn't mean it, I thought, clenching my fists, bracing myself.

But she veered off, of course. The guest room door slammed shut. I heard her sobbing and coughing in there, calling on God. I thought that it was just chaos, chaos everywhere, chaos and the end of the world.

Then, the next morning, everything was fine. Dad and Aunt

May were at the breakfast table with me. Mom was in and out of the kitchen, bringing us cereal and bowls. Dad's foot was fine, much better, he told me when I worked up the courage to ask. He sat abstracted over his *Times* while Mom, a little stone-jowled maybe, still came and went, keeping her thoughts to herself. May? She couldn't have been sprightlier, all clear weather after the storm. Trailing scent with balletic sweeps of her downy arm. Catching the morning sun from the big window behind me. Her voice, as always, trilled its jolly little tune.

'I thought I'd drive down to Washington to do some sightseeing,' she called over her shoulder into the kitchen. 'I might even go to Florida by way of Atlanta – I hear it's beautiful down there.'

'Just be careful in the South these days,' my mother said darkly, re-entering. She dealt the bowls out to us. 'Put an American flag on your aerial or something. You don't know what those people are up to.'

'So you'll finally be rid of your old Aunt May,' Aunt May said to me now. 'Will you miss me, Harry? Just a little bit?' I made a face and hunched my shoulders. She laughed delightedly, and reached across the table to tousle my hair. 'Just grateful to have your bathroom back, I'll bet. Oh, Claire, you don't know how I envy you – really.' She smiled at my Dad; he had looked up at the sound of that laughter of hers, half bray as ever, half heavenly psalm. 'To think,' she said, 'your husband might have been mine if I'd only been smart enough to jump at a good thing. You have to admit you were at least a little in love with me before Claire stole you away, Michael.'

'Do you want Rice Krispies or Raisin Bran?' my mother asked me.

'Uh . . . Rice Krispies,' I said.

'Everyone was in love with you, May,' said Dad. He opened the paper wide so that he was hidden behind it. 'You were a great beauty,' came his voice. 'You still are.'

'Oh, the gallant gentleman,' said May. 'Harry, you wouldn't believe it, but your father used to be so romantic. He drove me home once from the beach in Atlantic City. Oh! He was Prince Charming.'

I poured milk on my Rice Krispies and tilted my ear to the bowl to hear the snap, crackle and pop.

'All right, May,' said Mom. She lowered herself formidably into her seat at the end of the table.

'Well, he *was!*' squealed May, notwithstanding. 'All the way home, he talked about the stars, that's it. He could absolutely turn a girl's heart to sauce, Harry. I remember it as if it just happened. Do you remember, Michael? That drive we took? You have to remember. What all *did* you say?'

'Uy,' my father groaned. He turned the page and shut the paper, folding it over expertly.

I was spooning sugar into my cereal now, one teaspoon after another, the spoon clinking against the sugar bowl. I liked to pile the sugar up, then watch it sink slowly into the milk of its own weight. When the cereal was finished, I liked to eat the milky spoonfuls of sugar on the bottom.

'Well, he was the total, total cavalier, Harry,' May said, and I think she glanced my way as I studied how the sugar darkened just before it was submerged, as I thought to myself, *We're taking on water, Captain! The ship is going down!* 'Talking all about the sky and the stars, that's it,' May went on. 'Oh, and how the sky was like love because you couldn't make it go away even if you knew it was an illusion. God, we were young. And that the – what do you call them – the constellations were that way too, only sometimes, if you concentrated, you could make them go away and you would just see the beautiful, beautiful stars themselves. You see, I do remember, Michael, even though I didn't understand it all. You see how you stole my heart? And you told me all those stories about the constellations too. I remember. About the two brothers – right? – and how sad it was because one of them died, poor thing, and they had to live together in one body after that. And what else?'

My sugar sank – and, before I even realized why or what had been said or how it poisoned everything, my little Harry heart slowly started going down with it, glub, glub, glub, Captain . . .

'Oh well,' said Aunt May, sighing like an ingenue, 'I guess you can never bring back the past.'

* * *

My first reaction to an emotional blow was always indifference. Kind of a mental anesthetic, like when a dying man has visions of a passage into divine radiance rather than, say, a clown face shrieking, '*So long! You're ceasing to exist!*' Whenever cause for anguish struck me, I'd be as if immersed into a solution of indifference and then drawn out only slowly, maybe over days, into what you might call a general atmosphere of pain. By the time the last of the indifference evaporated, I would usually have lost the connection between my misery and the original source of it: I would just feel bad somehow − bad for no reason or for some other reason, the wrong reason. Camp, it was this time. From that breakfast onward, I began to grow depressed because I didn't want to go away to camp.

Aunt May left us, but the house did not seem our own again, not to me. To me, it just seemed empty and odd, with the floral smell of her lingering, like the music of her voice, like the soggy nylons on my bathroom towel rack that no one removed for days. For days, I wandered through the rooms, all fraught with woe, shuffling after my mother, repeating, 'I don't wanna go to camp,' over and over again. My mornings in front of the TV grew longer. I could zombie-glide right through the game shows sometimes, *The Price Is Right* and *Concentration*, both of which I hated. 'Harry, would you turn off that TV and go outside,' my mother would say. And I would roll onto my back and stare up at her with hollow eyes. And whine at her: 'I don't wanna go to camp.' Before she could bully me into my clothes it was nearly lunchtime, and when she hurled me outdoors, I would linger in the backyard like my own ghost, haunting her with an I-don't-wanna-go-to-camp stare through the kitchen casements. Harry's Raiders were soon disbanded on account of this depression. How long could they sit in the womblike dark of the lumber pile with their fearless leader sunk in dejected reverie?

And as for Agnes − I did not see her. In all that time, that whole last week. I didn't understand that she was at the heart of this, I just didn't feel like going over there anymore, that's all. Sometimes, some afternoons, I would wander aimlessly up toward Piccadilly Road, but I was

never abuzz with the old expectations. I was steeped instead
in fantasy: King Harry at the Judgement Day, his dread
sceptre tilting left or right, the naked women wailing in
their terror, and flailed across the tush, many of them, to
insure obedience or simply for good measure not to mention
that it was such breathless fun. And then, somewhere along
the road, at the top of Wooley's Lane usually, before the
curve, before the ghost house, I would stop. I would look
around me and find myself cotton-headed with dreams and
out-of-sorts. I did not want to see her; even the thought
of it depressed me even more. I wanted to go home, to
spend these precious moments of the fleeting July with that
dear, dear mother from whom I would too soon be cruelly
sundered.

So, shrugging, sighing, miserable – God, miserable – I
would turn again and head back down the hill, angrily
kicking stones, angrily dreaming, wasting what could have
been our last days together, Agnes's and mine, and laying –
or so I tell myself on those nights I want to rip my own head
off in paroxysms of regret – the groundwork of our lifelong
ruination.

Signs of the Dreaded Day accumulated: Mom sewing name
tags into shorts and T-shirts, clothing strewn on bedspreads,
suitcases brought up from the basement and a camp trunk,
with stout metal hinges and latches everywhere, brought
home from the city by my Dad. My parents were taking
advantage of my absence to spend a week in Europe so the
packing was general and, to my tragical mind, it looked as if
my entire existence were being struck like a set.

Finally, as it must to all men, Sunday came, the eve of my
departure. The various packing paraphernalia had converged
in the guest room. Thoughtful, nimble, my tubby Mom
stepped among the neat piles of clothing on the carpet there,
returning inevitably to the suitcases set open upon the bed
and the trunk on the floor, all of which became, inevitably,
nearer and nearer to being full. The condemned man sat in
the midst of this. On the edge of the bed with head hung
down, with hands clasped between his knees and shoulders
bowed under at least a ton of fear, homesickness, helplessness,

dread. And something else, some nameless suspense. Outside, through the glass door that led onto the garage roof, the sun could be seen setting, a dragon-toothed splotch of light poised on the peak of the Rothmans' roof next door.

'Why do you have to go to Europe?' I groaned.

'We'll be back before you get home,' said my mother wearily. She pressed a finger to her lip as she swiveled indecisively between a poncho and a pile of underpants.

'I don't wanna go to camp,' I said.

The underpants, Mom decided, and leaned down to lift the stack between her two hands.

'I don't wanna . . .'

'Oh, Harry, it's only two weeks. You'll have a wonderful time. Just be careful, that's all. Don't go crazy.' She divided the stack in two and bent to set it neatly into the trunk's corners. 'Don't start any trouble. Don't let them make you do anything dangerous.'

My whole slumped body rose and fell with a moaning breath. I lifted my head slowly against the weight of apathy and doom. Now the sun was sinking past the Rothmans' roof and turning yellow and throwing shadows of the burly trees across the pitched slate. Time, that's what the suspense was, the running out of time. And nothing I could do. I was pilloried with despair. I looked around the room. The mounds of clothing were fewer and fewer. The suitcases were nearly full. The ordinary contours of the room were returning. I wished it was more familiar, a room we used more, a room I knew, I wanted to embed myself in those known things. But the guest room always seemed strange. Not colonial like the rest of the house, more modern, like my room, with white walls, and orange carpeting and indigo bedspreads. There was a dresser in the far corner from me, a piece I almost never noticed. Not the sort of exact thing my mother usually liked, but just functional, knobby, stained tan. I saw now that there was even a picture on it that I had never seen before. Something May had left behind maybe. A black-and-white photograph veiled with yellow age. A young man in funny old clothes, wearing a high collar, stiffly holding a derby under his chest with one bent arm. He was standing off to one side, proudly displaying the legal offices behind him. I wanted to ask who he was, but was too lethargic to say the words.

I glanced out the glass door again. The sun went down behind the roof. 'Why did Aunt May leave?' I asked suddenly, without thinking.

Mom, already holding a pair of pants, averted her face as if searching for something else. 'Well,' she said with some gravity, smoothing the pants absently over her arm, 'she had to go back to her own life.'

'Why is she so strange though?' Blurted again, almost with anguish, with some new emotion anyway glimmering under the big dark dolmen of all the others.

Of course, Mom was interested in this, whatever truths about her sister a child might stumble onto. She set a smile on her lumpy, sagging features, and asked me, 'Why strange?'

'I dunno. She just . . . she always has to be in everybody's business and part of everything. I dunno.'

My mother snorted softly. Finished folding the pants and avoided my eyes as she set them in a suitcase. 'Oh, these things,' she said. 'They're just sillinesses. People carry them around with them. They ought to just get rid of them. But they don't –' She gave the packed pants a definitive pat. '– and that's why there's so much silliness in the world.'

Thus my mother's wisdom; make of it what you can. I only half heard it myself anyway. My attention was on the window and the first hulking violet of this final night. I did not want to pull myself away from my mother's side, not even to think of it. There was so much still to say to her: I don't wanna go to camp, for instance. But there was this other urgency percolating now. I stood up. With a beleaguered, nasal drawl, I said: 'I'm gonna go out for a while.'

And my mother, surprised: 'It's almost seven o'clock, where are you going?'

'Out. I'll be back.'

Behind me, as I went out the door, she called: 'Not for too long, Harry. I want you in bed by eight, we have to get up very early tomorrow.'

I took my bike. These Shakespearean tragedy links – I have nightmares about them. I'd never taken my bike before because there was nowhere to hide it and Agnes and I had this vow of secrecy between us. But tonight I took it, afraid, after all this time, that she wouldn't wait for me by the stream. I stood on the pedals up Wooley's Lane, anxious to be on, eager to get back. I didn't even park it by the ghost house at the top but raced it dramatically, with flurrying feet, down the steep of Piccadilly almost to her front walk. Recklessly, I set the kickstand on the sidewalk just a little before her driveway. And even so, I didn't realize what a dither I was in for a rendezvous until I looked up to see the peaked white aluminum cubes of the Sole place sinking into insubstantial shadow against the still summer background of trees and sky. The house was dark. Although an air conditioner was muttering in an upstairs window, the lights were all out – it seemed no one was home – and I could've torn my hair in aggravation. This made things more dramatic still. I ran without caution past her windows, across her back lawn to the stand of trees. Panting heroically, I worked my way among the thick leaves of oak and hickory, the spindles of pine, over the acorns bulging up beneath my Keds, through the spider webs clinging to my lashes and lips. I crashed through to the top of the slope above the stream. It was already thick dusk there, the leafy tree crowns on the far side huddling against the sunset. And, posed rather handsomely in the last movement of my dynamic breakthrough, I peered along the banks through the uncertain light.

And there was Agnes, kneeling quietly at the edge of the water.

I hated her. I only realized it when I set eyes on her. I was furious at her, so mad it was as if the whole reason I had had to come – the matrix of the suspense and the urgency that had got me there – was that I needed to tell her what a stinko she was. I was metamorphosed on the spot. I wasn't going to give her the satisfaction of seeing how I'd hurried to find her. I stopped panting. I stuffed my hands into my pockets. I skittered casually down to the bank, and strolled along it toward her as if I'd just happened by.

A twig snapped under me and Agnes looked up. Looked up, and lit up when she saw it was me.

'Hi, Harry!' She got to her feet, smiling, dusting off her shorts and her scabby knees. 'I thought you went to camp or something.'

I shrugged. Grunted a hello. Gave her the side of me, and swung my foot, kicking a clod of dirt into the water. It hadn't rained in weeks and the stream was low, an avid trickle humping it over the bottom rocks. 'I'm going tomorrow,' I said.

'Oh,' she said. And then: 'I guess you were busy and had to get ready and everything.' She jutted eagerly at my grumpy profile. 'I almost didn't come out tonight. Only there's a full moon and it's supposed to come up just at dark.' I sniffed at that; I gave her nothing. She tried again: 'See, the moon comes up at different times, a little later, every day, every different size of moon comes up at its own . . .'

'I know how you know all this stuff, Agnes. My father tells you.'

The heave of rage, the way my mouth twisted, the way I spat out the words: I'd been so busy putting on the show of anger, I was surprised at how real it turned out to be. I didn't have the foggiest idea what this was, this acid in me. What did I care about what my stupid Aunt May said?

But Agnes, Agnes the Witch, she got it right away. She was meek. She was conciliatory. She made an offering. 'Some of it my mother tells me.'

'Oh yeah, right! Because my father tells her.'

'Well . . .' She licked her lips. 'Maybe he'll tell you too soon. He probably tells you lots of other things.'

I glanced at her to see if she was making fun, but she was all face, desperate for forgiveness. 'Sure he does,' I said nastily. 'He tells me lots of things. He tells me things all the time.' I kicked out again − a white stone plinked into the trickle. 'Anyway, I just didn't want to come here cause I don't want to play on your stupid rock anymore, that's all. It's all stupid.'

With which, unnoticed, gray, grainy twilight with no friendly intent closed in around us poor two. Agnes frowned as if she would cry. Maybe she did cry, but by then, she was kneeling again so I couldn't see, standing some twigs in the soft earth where the stream had receded, laying others in the small current as part of her secret ritual — it's what she had been up to when I broke in.

'My Daddy never says anything,' she said. The priestess now, incanting it to the elements, but small too, a little voice, pitiable. 'He never says anything. He can't. He can't talk.'

'Oh, he can talk,' I said. 'I heard him.'

'No, I know, but he can't tell me about anything. I couldn't ask. My mother says so. It would make him too sad. He's not like your father.' And, lifting to me all at once her graven suffering, she broke forth right earnestly: 'I'm sorry, Harry!'

Well, the Har was moved. A guy's not stone, after all, even in his rages. Even hurt — and hurting stupid too, because I didn't know, not even now quite, what the hell this was all about — I began, in increments for pride's sake, to relent.

'Well, what's he so sad about? Your father.'

Back at her twigs, swallowing hard, she laid it out for me. 'He was there — in that place I told you about? — where they killed all the children. He had to watch them being killed. They killed his wife — his wife before my mother. And my half-sister, Lena. That was his daughter. They killed her too.'

Around us, unnoticed, the volume of the place was slowly rising, the night syncopations of frogs and cicadas coming up from the grass, hatches of gnats and mosquitoes buzzing under the trees, birdsong floating from the topmost branches, from the high leaves. I shifted my shoulders suspiciously. 'What did they kill them for? Where was this?'

'In Poland, where he's from. They wanted to kill all the Jewish people.'

'What, you mean, like, the Nazis?' I'd heard about that, of course. Nazis killing Jews. A very bad thing. Fortunately, my father had gone over there personally to help put an end to it. 'The Nazis killed them?'

Agnes nodded, kneeling there. And — though it was getting harder and harder to make her out, to distinguish her outline from the thickening obscurity — I could tell that her hands were unsure in their movements now, going from twig to twig, place to place, hovering frantically, never quite coming to rest.

'Yes,' she said. 'They had a place they had to go to. My mother told me.'

'Was she there too?'

'No. But she knows about it. She told me some of it. She said everybody had to go to this place, all the Jews did, to see Hitler – he was the King Nazi. And everybody had to go up to him. First they had to give everything they had to the other Nazis, all their money and everything, even their clothes. So they were all naked so they couldn't do anything, and they had to stand in line and walk up to where Hitler was, and he would point with his, what do you call it, that stick king's have . . .'

I stared down at her through the darkness. 'A scepter,' I said softly.

'Yes. He would point with it, with his scepter, like, to the left or to the right. And the people he pointed to the right had to go in a big room to be killed. And the people he pointed to the left had to be his slaves and do, like . . . I don't know, like, hard work, in the snow and everything, like breaking rocks with a hammer or something. I just know it was very hard.' She shook her head, her braids stirring. 'I don't want my Daddy to have to talk about it. I don't want him to have to be sad about it anymore.'

Night fell then, mercifully dropping its velvet veil over my slack-jawed stupidity, my willed density, the stone synaptic wall I'd thrown up between connection and connection. Even hidden though, even with all that self-deception – woof! The guilt, the ignorant guilt. The poignant whining within to be justified to her. 'I'm only going to sleepaway for two weeks,' I said for no reason I could think of. 'I'll be back for the whole rest of August. Okay? We can go back to the rock or whatever then. I didn't really mean it was stupid or anything, okay, Agnes?'

As if mollified on the instant, Agnes hopped up. 'Then you'll be back in time for the Perseid showers,' she said. She stood so close to me that her features loomed – loomed pleadingly. 'They're late at night, but maybe we could get to stay up for them. Or maybe – maybe I could watch from my window and you could watch from yours and we'd be seeing them at the same time.'

'Uh – okay. Sure.' I sounded a lot more eager than I felt, a lot less nauseous than I felt too. And I forced myself to ask – I didn't want to, knowing the source, but I made the effort: 'So, like, what are they? The – what showers?'

'Perseid. 'Cause they're in the constellation Perseus. They're meteor showers. Showers, like, of falling stars. You want to go up on the rock? I could show you where they'll be. We could watch the moon come up, okay?'

For the first time, finally, I remembered that I had to be home – and now that I did remember, I couldn't tell her. How could I? And leave it like this between us, everything messed up, alchemy reversed, her mystic enthusiasm forced, or sounding forced to me at least, and the night leaden – black and loud and summery, but leaden, dead; etched in close by the usual forest lineaments, the alleyway of fresh stars between the high leaves above us, but flat-seeming and leaden; the invisible water's gurgling, the oompah frogs, the rest of the chattering insect masses – all supposed to be charged and twinkly with our conspiratorial demonry and just small, I don't know, messy, plopped too close to the road and the lights of houses, and with me plopped in it, leaden too in the belly, wanting to be home, sick and heavy and sour at the prospect of hearing this shower stuff, my own father's meteor stuff, from her – what could I do? I was desperate to restore our ruined thing.

'Okay!' I forced myself to say. 'Great!'

And we leapt the stream energetically and clawed up the far bank side by side, making our expressions seem bright and excited.

In the big sky above the lot, the stars were out, the first layer of bright constellations, Cygnus, the dipper, Cassiopea.

'Perseus will come up later, there,' she said when we had climbed the rock. She pointed hard above the treetops just behind us. We didn't sit, we were standing together on the boulder, our shoulders touching, our faces lifted, hungering, toward the sky. She strained for that tone of mystery, and began to tell me the Perseus story and it was a good story too but Jesus, it was agony, agony to listen to it. Everything she said now seemed underlaid, thick with hauntings, palimpsests and pentimenti. Her forced whispers, her outsized gestures were warped by all the storytelling I'd been gypped of, the forfeited ranges of paternal chumhood. I mean, I might have known this stuff and told *her!* She'd stolen it from me, maybe innocently, but still. I tried hard to do the rapt audience bit. I nutcracked the logic of the arcane Greek offenses and the unnecessary hero trials, and I conjured a seaweedy ocean god like the ghost of a sunken man, and I even chimed in with a gout of blood for the beheading scene, always a major plus. But my mind drifted too, and at the same time that Perseus was doing that neat trick of reflecting Medusa on his shield so he could decapitate her without being turned to stone, I was half-imagining homey scenes that might have been, in my home, in her home, in some television home — who knows? — with a sort of red mist of unacknowledged rage hissing up over everything. What a shame, what a shame. Because there it all was too, or would be, she said, come the middle of August, right up in the sky by way of the constellations. There was Cepheus the King and Queen Cassiopea — all right, she looked like a lawn chair but there she was; and Perseus was rising; and just now, the brighter stars in Andromeda and in Pegasus, the winged stallion — a real stallion with wings just like the Amoco gasoline sign! — were burning their way through the purple dark. And at midnight, when deep August came, so she told me (so my father must have told her), the kraken would breach the eastern horizon to devour the chained princess and Perseus would hie it to the rescue brandishing the basilisk ugliness of Medusa's head (still gouting) to turn the monster to stone. And stars would fall, dozens of shooting stars like fireworks to celebrate the event — I mean, what would it take to get us in the mood?

Whatever it was, this wasn't enough, not tonight. I tensed every time her shoulder brushed me. I felt morose. I wanted it to work too badly; too much damned presence of mind ruined the best effects. And then, anyway, the moon rose, the full moon she'd told me about. Back in the trees but bright enough to whitewash the dimmer stars away just as they struggled to show themselves. And it bared us to each other too, fruit-of-knowledge-like, more's the pity, so that Agnes finally gave it up, falling silent during the embellishments, and we looked at each other hopelessly in the silver light. I almost said: I have to go home now; and I did have to – to get to bed, to get ready for camp. But I fought the impulse. How could I say it? How could I go? After our whole spring together, after all July? Was there nothing we could do?

'Hey!' I said too loudly. 'You wanna pretend it? Like I'll be the Perseus guy and – this could be the rock and you could be chained here? Okay?'

She hesitated – it was a little rowdy, a little boyish – but then she agreed, and we began to play it out in the empty lot.

Lord, Lord, Lord. I will not tell her this. My little visitor from the root cellar, from the sleet-streaked night. I will not tell her, I will not tell anyone. When I think what they would say – what Agnes's biographers would say, and the art critics, and the feminist angerheads. When I imagine the dental vaginas, and the castrated witch-mothers they'd come up with. The post-Holocaust Jews relating to the western myth inheritance, they'd say, or an early experiment with the transubstantial artistry that turned monsters that night to statues, to stone. When I picture, I mean, the vomit of words they would drench those children with, those two poor defenceless waifs – the little girl dead now, the boy vaporized to an unsalvagable walking fart of corruption – oh man, I would rather drink blood than tell them, than breathe a word of this to anyone. Leave them alone, you bastards! I shake my fist at you! I goblin dance like Rumpelstiltskin till you run away. (Because you're all cowards else you'd get out and work for a living, get some exercise.) I'll die a wooden Indian, a blank tomb, an ur-stone. I'll live a mirror: you can all trace your own fucking faces in me till you drop. I alone remember – I alone am survived to not tell thee – how the big purple-white sky was littered, behind our self-consciousness and the moonglow, with creatures, damsels and champions which we, small and far below in the broad, dusty lot, so desperately reflected and replayed. And how the stones crunched beneath my sneaker soles. And of Agnes's hilarious 'Help, Perseus, help!' And the way I almost forgot myself a moment as I thought to intertwine my fingers in the snakes of the gorgon's hair. Soul-heavy though I was, I remember, I forced out a TV-adventure riff – 'Ba-dum

ba–daaa!' – as I galloped on my Amoco gasoline steed with
the squiggling Medusa–head upraised. And I meteored down
as best I could, so sick at heart, to petrify the breasting beast.
And Agnes cowered very convincingly against her star rock
and twisted in her chains and made a fuss, though I think
she was praying all the while – I could just about hear her in
my own mind – for the impossible resurrection of our late,
lamented zing. And the air was warm and clear and smelled of
dust. I was there, you assholes. It was my life, I was there.

And that, at any rate, was what we were up to when I
heard my mother calling me from the road.

We stopped, breathless. My mother's voice reached us again.
'Harry?'

I lowered the hand with the gorgon's head in it, my fist
still clenched. 'That's my Mom,' I said. 'I gotta go.'

Agnes stepped away from the rock. Halfway across the lot,
I could see her clearly in the moonlight. 'Bye, Harry,' she
said. 'Have a good time at camp.'

'Okay. I'll meet you by the stream when I get back.'

'Bye,' she said. She stretched her hand out to me, waving.

'Harry!' my mother called, sounding more worried than
annoyed.

I waved to Agnes. 'Bye, Agnes,' I said. I felt her looking
after me as I jogged past her and ducked into the trees.

My mother called one more time as I carefully made my way
over the stream in the dark. 'Harry!' Then, as I was climbing
the opposite slope, I heard her start to call again – and stop.
When I broke out of the trees, I could see her at a distance.
She was standing on the sidewalk beside my bike. She had
spotted it, my bike, as she drove around in search of me.

She was standing in the light: the light of the full moon,
which had risen here above the treetops, and the headlights
of her Country Squire station wagon which she'd left running
at the curb. And there was light too in the upstairs window
of Agnes's house – the window that had been dark before:
it shone brightly now. I could see my mother with her face
upraised, staring at it. My poor, dumpy, onion-shaped Mom.
I could see her frozen there, trying to frame her reaction to

what she'd just witnessed – bemusement, indifference, fury.
I called out to her as I ran across the Soles' lawn, but she
didn't turn. She kept staring up at that window. It was
empty now – I checked it, vaguely curious, as I ran. The
guilty parties had recovered, I guess, from their first panicky
reflex when the sound of Mom's voice reached them over
the air conditioning. They had ducked down again although,
of course, too late. But Mom kept staring, staring. Poor old
Mom. Always working out the family secrets, always getting
to the bottom of things. It was what she had instead of beauty.
It must have taken all her motherly fortitude just to turn,
when she finally did; just to smile at me ruefully, to shake
her head mother-like, to croak in a distant, unsteady voice:
'Oh, so there you are. I was worried about you. Well, put
your bike in the back, and I'll drive you home.'

Camp, it turned out, was fine. I had a good time for the most
part. I got a certificate for winning a badminton tournament
and my softball team lost only once the whole time I was
there. I used to join in the general uproar of complaint
about the freezing waters of Lake Placid, but I had a wry
fondness for it secretly, especially in the morning, with the
mist coming off the surface and the surface like steel and the
sky an uncanny blue above the green-blue foothills of the
Adirondacks which ringed it round. I was homesick only
three times – badly, I mean: The first night, when I lay
on my bottom bunk in tears, clutching a Civil War soldier
I'd brought with me, and biting my lip so as not to call
out for my mother. Then another night when some jerk
told a story after lights out about how a guy had drowned
in the lake a hundred years ago and how now, every so
often, bubbles rose to the surface and popped with a soft
cry of 'Help! Help!' Then, on a night toward the end of the
second week, Uncle Chuck or Bobby or Neil – one of the
college-age counselors – led us out to a campsite in an open
field beyond the surrounding woods. We had a fire and sang
songs and roasted marshmallows till nearly midnight. Then
we lay on our backs in our sleeping bags and oohed and
aahed into the deep black sky where meteors streaked back
and forth across the Milky Way in unimaginable numbers,

dying in July Fourth explosions in the bowl of the Dipper
or the Great Square, leaving trails of white fire burning all
the way back to Perseus, whence they had come.

As my mother predicted, it was all over before I knew it.
And as I boarded the motor boat to go, I felt very brave and
vowed to come back for the whole summer next year which,
for one reason and another, I never did.

It was kind of depressing to be home, in fact. Only a few of
my friends had returned so far. There wasn't that much to
do. I missed my camp buddies. School loomed.

My first day back, I scouted out Dave and we biked over
to Allenwood Park and played catch. That was all right.
But as the afternoon came on, I began to feel somewhat
heavy-hearted. I knew I had to give Dave the slip and head
over to Piccadilly. I'd said I would, after all, those many days
ago. And, as I put it to myself, I did sort of want to go, but
I sort of didn't too.

Around four, with a suave excuse − 'I gotta go, Dave, I
got stuff to do,' − I parted from him. He headed off to his
Bunker Hill home, and I to Old Colony where I parked my
bike in the garage and started out again on foot.

I was nervous as I crossed under the ghost house and into
the trees. I was excited at the thought of seeing Agnes, but I
wanted things to be different between us too. Camp, I felt,
had changed and matured me. I wanted to act with more
authority around her so she wouldn't always ensorcel me so.
I didn't want everything to be just the same as it was.

I jumped the culvert and strolled the bank and reached
our spot, but she wasn't there yet. I waited for her, splashing
stones, but the light ebbed and she didn't come. Finally, as
I sometimes did, I climbed up the bank and wove through
the trees to the edge of her backyard. I came to the brink
of the treeline and poked out into the Soles' lawn. It looked
different somehow. I couldn't figure what it was − then I
could. The patio furniture was gone. So was the sprinkler
the Doctor generally left lying around. In the house, the lights
were out, but it wasn't night yet and the more I looked, the
more I sensed a certain emptiness indoors as well in the dining
area which I could just make out through the glass doors.

Moving closer cautiously, it began to seem to me that the dining room table was gone, that *all* the furniture was gone. I edged closer. I leaned forward, peering through the glass. Yes, it was gone, all right. And, moving around to the side of the house and trying a window there, I could see the furniture in the living room was all stacked up. There were boxes in there and upside-down tables and rolled carpets. I kept moving slowly around to the front.

There was a *For Sale* sign planted in the grass. The garage was empty. The Soles' name had been taken off the mail box — I could see the outline of the letter-stickers on the black metal.

I stood on the front lawn with my hands in my pockets — the first of the several times I would confront that empty place.

Hmph, I thought indifferently after a moment, *I guess they moved away.*

Then I shrugged and ambled back up Piccadilly, daydreaming.

*She was in now. The root cellar girl. I had shut the door. She stood
dripping on the wooden floorboards. Peeling off her sodden earmuffs.
Prying her down vest away from a blue workshirt, which matched
her jeans, both of them dark in patches with rain.*

*'Let me get you a towel. How come you're spying on me?' I
said.*

*I climbed back up the narrow stairs, hauling myself up by the
rope bannister, panting.*

'I wasn't spying on you,' she called after me.

'Yeah, yeah, yeah,' I whispered.

*Head bent beneath the eaves, I ducked down the hall to the
bathroom. I still couldn't remember who she was, or who she
reminded me of. Or why Agnes — why Agnes came back to
me now. Only I did know too; it felt obvious. I was blocking
it, that's all.*

*The towel was hanging on the inside of the bathroom door. I sniffed
it for mildew. Very nice, lovely. I headed back down the hall with it.
Well — the Agnes part was easy enough. What else could it be, after
all? Aside from Marianne and the kids sometimes, who else came
around here, and who else snuck around outside, who else besieged
me like this? Agnes's biographers. And the occasional glitz-eyed twit
from the feature mags. Maybe some hunched newspaper hawkshaw
looking for an anniversary follow-up. Even the TV people came once:
I was actually on screen slamming the door in their faces.*

I worked my way downstairs and tossed the girl the towel.

*'I wasn't spying on you,' she said again. She began to dry her hair.
Her long hair. Brown, it turned out, when wet. She was fresh-faced
I saw now, freckle-faced, and pretty. And, Christ, young. Young,
young, young. She had draped her vest on one of my chairs, one
of the colonial Windsors from the junkshop. She'd balanced her*

earmuffs on top of the vest. Both dripped water onto the floorboards, pit, pit, pit.

Outside, the wind was up again. The freezing rain lashed the house. The gale hurled great stones of ice against the windows. Like a poltergeist.

'I'm a journalist,' she said. She sneezed loudly. Wiped her nose on my towel. Shivered painfully.

'Oh, bullshit,' I said. 'No, you're not. I'll get you a brandy or something. Hold on.'

I headed for the other breakneck staircase, the one down to the kitchen.

'What does that mean: I'm not,' she said. 'Yes. I am. I'm a . . . I'm, like, a reporter for a newspaper.'

'Bullshit. You're not old enough.'

'I'm twenty-three!'

'Bullshit.' I headed down the stairs, bracing myself on the white planks of the narrow walls. 'Come to think of it, you're not even old enough to drink,' I called back to her. 'I'll make you coffee.'

She came to the door above me, just her soggy sneakers visible. 'Christ, I am so. I want a brandy. I want scotch, in fact.'

'My ass,' I muttered. Yeah, but who the hell was she? Agnes's ghost, maybe, judging by the flood of feeling. Only not this sparkly-eyed little goy, not the ghost of my witchy Jew-girl, no sir.

The kitchen was in what used to be the cellar so the ceiling was low. I could just feel it brush what used to be my hair as I moved to the sink. I hunched over a little as I filled a pot with water.

'I want scotch,' she warned me, when she heard the faucet go.

I tossed the pot on the old gas stove, turned up the flame. 'You take milk and sugar? I don't have any milk.'

The wind howled. The rain pattered against the downstairs door. It was a dark and stormy night.

'Look,' she said wearily from the stairs. I was leaning against the stove, studying her stupid sneakers. My arms crossed, my soul leaden with sorrow. 'I just didn't want to approach you too fast. I know you don't like journalists. I saw you on TV: slamming the door? That's why I was watching . . .'

'Oh, admit it: you were being mysterious and romantic.'

'Jesus!' One of her little sneaks gave a little stomp. 'You sound just like my father.'

Fortunately, this arrow went directly through my heart and came *out the other side so there was no need to have it surgically removed, which can be expensive. The pain, however, was not to be denied. It wasn't just that I had happened, at that moment, to be reflecting on her youth, my middle age, my regret — which is pervasive actually, but was taking the form right then of regretting — that I would never hold a woman that young in my arms again and that her firm tits would probably have rippled lusciously as she came beneath me screaming, which I had a very clear mental image of, not having been laid in about six weeks. But it was also that, well, I could've been her father. I had a sudden, deep, aching sense of that when she said it. Of that, and the other so many things, the billions of things, infinite things, that could have happened, that hadn't. That never would.*

Apropos of which, I flashed back here to the Sole house — or the Lieberman house, because an old German couple bought it after the Sole family was gone. That small, modest work of aluminum and wood: it called to me, of course, as the years went by. Often and often I had returned to it. In the suburban dusk. When I was eleven, twelve, when something had made me cry. A sentimental tyke, sitting on my Schwinn by the curb, I would tell my troubles to the ghosts in there, even sometimes — I blush to tell it — calling to them, whispering their names.

When I grew older, I mostly avoided the place. I even took the longer route to high school to stay out of its range. But then too there were occasions when I came back, folly-worn, seeking a draught of adolescent melancholy and nostalgia. The house never failed me. I would stand outside with my hands hooked rebelliously in my jeans, my shoulders up around my ears — that was the way kids stood then, to look alienated, to look sullen. I've been hurt, man. I would tell the house; I've been through the mill. Fifteen, sixteen years old, with death's-head patches on my denim jacket, my hair down long around my ears. Listening for the sound of the brook out back, and fairly melting to a delicious goo of tristesse. Once, a younger kid, about nine years old, coasted up behind me on his bike, his wheels clicketing. Like the phantom of my former self (a romantic conceit that wasn't lost on me).

'You know,' he told me, 'that house — it's haunted.'

So perfect, such a setup line. I felt as if I were in a movie. I tightened my lips, hardboiled, and gazed off wistfully into the middle distance.

'Yeah, kid,' I said. 'I know it is.'

When I was eighteen — my last year in town — a younger couple bought the place from the Liebermans, though they didn't move in right away. Soon after the For Sale sign went down, pickup trucks arrived in the driveway, workmen started hammering inside. They were always inside. You hardly ever saw them, just heard them, wham, wham, wham reverberating in the stillness of May. For weeks, the exterior looked the same as ever, just a little murkier, a little hollower at the windows, as the house was gutted. One summer dawn, during this period, I parked by the lawn in my father's Volvo. I'd fallen asleep at Kate's, at my girlfriend's. Had to creep out her back door before the neighbors saw and informed on me to her mother, a kite of some ferocity. This wouldn't last into college, Kate and me, and I was beginning to realize that, so I went to the Sole house. Stepped from the Volvo, shouldering my usual sack of blues.

I walked to the door across the dewy grass. It wasn't locked — it didn't even have a latch — it just swung open. In I stepped and saw the waste-scape they had made of the place. Every wall that wasn't holding up the roof had been demolished. There was lumber lying here and there, electric wires dangling. From the doorway, I could plainly see a window that used to be in a back room down a hall. I could see right to it, and through it to the mists of dawn and the slender trees that overhung our brook, Agnes's and mine. That was the only time in my life, standing there, that sounds, smells, presences ever came back to me that clearly. The clink of lunchware, the steam of boiling noodles, the louring of the ancient survivor with his rheumy eyes. Woeful stuff. Unbearable. Ah, what might have been! I did the whole maudlin routine. I even spotted movement at the corner of my eye and turned to see if anyone was really there. Nope. No one. Not a Sole.

In the end, when I was heading off to college, I went to say goodbye to the house, but it was no good. A disappointing experience. The exterior was finished and the whole place looked completely different. Bigger, huskier, healthier. Siding gone from white to jolly yellow. Red shutters; I swear it. The garage had been walled in, a story added over it, a new garage tacked on. A great rolliking burgher's manse had been constructed where the old joint used to be. Bozo the house. What a gyp. I felt as if the pants had been yanked right off my melancholy, the polka dot boxers revealed underneath. All those memories, regrets, yearnings scattering like foreign coins on the *sidewalk. Worthless in this country, corresponding to nothing except maybe themselves. Ho ho, m'boy! the house seemed to say through its chuckly door, Where are these things I hear so much about, these million things that might have been? I don't see 'em — you? Show 'em to me. Go on, I dare ya.*

The Sole house — the Finkelsteins' now. What could I do? I pulled up my melancholy, gathered my shekels, and shuffled off into the next chapter of life.

With which instructive detour completed, I returned my attention to the water in the pot, which was boiling.

'Oh God!' she said, rolling her eyes, when I brought her the coffee. I'd poured a scotch for myself too, just to annoy her. She accepted the mug from me all the same. Cradled it in both hands, in a gesture both womanly and childlike. She was sitting on the living room loveseat now in front of the old fireplace. Dampening the loveseat's green velour. She blew on the coffee, shivering.

'I'll build a fire,' I said. I put my drink on the mantel out of her reach and knelt down under it, unwrapping a fire starter. I could feel her watching me, hear her slurping coffee as I stationed the briquette on the grate.

'I don't hate reporters, by the way,' I said. 'They disappear, you know, if you just stop reading the newspapers, or watching TV. They stop mattering to you.' I picked up a log from the carrier and faltered at the feel of the rough bark in my hand. Now why was that? I put the log down quickly beside the briquette. I went on nervously. 'You're always arguing with them in your head otherwise.' I lifted another log — got another nervous thrill. What the hell was this? 'Or not with them exactly. With the world's opinion. Reporters are just . . . cogs in the machinery of the world's opinion. Grinding everything into World Opinion Paste.' I dropped the log in the grate as if it were already burning. 'Used to be the church, grinding up everything. Now it's the world's opinion.' I put my hands on my knees, breathing too heavily. Glanced around at her where she huddled over her mug. 'I mean, look at you. You're probably in college, right? Some professor teaching you the going thing — late-post-modern-feminist-correctism — grinding up everything into the going thing. You probably haven't had an original idea since you were three years old.'

She plucked her rosy lips from the mug's rim. Gave me a blast of placid superiority: Hell, she had a father; she was used to the *ravings of bitter old men. 'Thanks a lot,' she said killingly. And wrapped the rosebud round the rim again.*

I turned back to the fireplace, braced myself to grab a third log. 'Well, pardon me if I don't want to feed my life into the machine. I don't need it to be ground up into your philosophy or commentary or . . .' Ah, but now I did it: I wrapped my fingers round the log, felt the shaggy wedge where the axe had split it. And three was the charm all right. It came to me — not who she was — but why I recognized her, where I'd seen her face before. Oh boy. No wonder the Book of Agnes, the Boy's Book of Agnes, had to be opened again. Shit.

'I'm not in college, you know,' she broke out in a so-there voice.

I lay the last log across the other two, over the briquette. Sagged, ass on heels. Shit, shit, shit. 'No . . .' I had to clear my throat. 'No?'

'No.' Smarty-pants, she might've added. But she slurped her coffee. 'Okay, you're right, I'm not a journalist. Okay? And I'm not twenty-three.' I shook my head at the pyre in the grate. 'I'm seventeen — but that doesn't mean I'm an idiot. And I do have original thoughts, I don't just, like, believe whatever anyone tells me.'

'Good for you,' I murmured, stunned by the suddenness of my understanding.

'That's why I didn't want to go to college in the first place.' She snorted. 'But try explaining that to my father.'

I nodded. Reached, with mortal sigh, for the box of matches by the carrier. Her father. Right. Of course. And her facades. And her arrogance. Her barely hidden turmoil. The pure self-absorption, too, of a girl who'd bother to hover about in graveyards and root cellars. She'd come to me with all of it, hadn't she?

I stole another look at her sitting there. Physicists tell us that what seem to us solid forms are really only hot spots in the continuous field of energy and composed mostly of empty space. I think this is particularly true of adolescents.

I came back round to the pyre, plucked out a wooden match. Set the blue head against the flint on the side of the box. Oh boy. Oh, Agnes. You witch, you witch from beyond the grave, you. Whoever she is, this creature of yours (and I was already beginning to guess), she's brought me her ever-fascinating young

*self, hasn't she? Her arrogance, her turmoil, her father, the whole
shmear. Her all-absorbing self to save. She wants me to help her —
how would she put it? — get her head straight, get her shit together,
get her show on the road? I'd bet that's it. I'd bet anything. She
wants you, Agnes. She wants me to give her you.*

'So,' *I said* — *hoarsely* — *after a long pause.* 'You're some kind
of artist then.'

That took the child aback — *to her, there still seemed so many
other possibilities.* 'Well . . . yeah,' *she said, surprised.* 'At least,
I mean — I want to be.'

*I struck the match. I torched the briquette. The flames danced
quickly up into the dry wood.*

*Soon, the fire was snickering merrily, and the girl was posing on the
sofa with downcast eyes. Arranging her face into various expressions of
milky sensitivity with which she hoped, I guess, to meet this last, long
silence of mine. I was standing by the window, looking at the window,
drink in hand. Secretly studying her reflection there, searching it for
vestiges of that other face I remembered — and for vestiges of Agnes
too, for any resemblance at all. Then, after another moment, my eyes
shifted and I saw myself, my own reflection. If it had been a movie,
I thought, there'd have been my transparent image upon the pane
and, through that, the water trickling down the glass like tears, the
tumult of the storm in the silhouetted trees — visually representing
my turbulent inner state, see, with maybe a symbolic commentary
on the veil of perception. And well, that's how it was, that's just
what I did see. Which galled me. Because it was her movie. Because,
I mean, it must've been something like this when she imagined it,
in the movie that went through her mind when she was deciding to
defy her poor old Dad and come: First, I'll lurk in the trees, then
I'll hang out in the graveyard, then, by the fire, I'll be beguiling
— mysterious yet somehow innocent and poignant — and the gruff
but lovable old exile, touched, will wrestle with his inner anguish
and finally purge his autobiography into my inspired eyes, freeing
his tortured soul and mine at once and giving me the power to go
forth, tra-la.*

*I swallowed my gorge. Gruff but lovable. Dear God, had it really
come to that?*

In college, in Byronic mood, I used to follow girls down the street sometimes — nothing threatening; at a distance, I mean — if they had black hair and small heads and a certain sinuosity: that was the way I imagined Agnes had grown up, you see. It was funny, because that wasn't what I wanted at all — in women, that is — in the long run. I took what I could get, of course, but fey blondes were what I set my hat for. Fey blondes with crystal blue eyes. Large-ish round breasts were also a favorite or small, shy, refined ones that perked up when you touched them. I taught a few such girls what it was to be adored, anyway. My little letting-outs of breath when they'd strip down, the more off-handedly the better. My raptures at the sight of their vaginas and buttocks — the fact that they had vaginas and buttocks — how wonderful! — I could go on and on about it. What must they have thought, the poor creatures, sitting on the things all day, casually crossing their legs this way and that over them, to have some dreamer go all religious about it? They must have wanted like crazy to believe me — who wouldn't? — especially at that age, feeling all misshapen and messy and secretly deficient — to be told, no, no, it's the greatest, it's the Coliseum. Well, I was tied to the cock-rocket like any young man and the transcendence went out of me with the gism and the girls would be hurt and disappointed, having gotten their hopes up. But fey blondes and their pudenda — call it a third-generation American trying to dive dick-first into the melting honey-pot, but I was there, and the physical facts took precedence — these still, always, drew me on.

And yet — and yet, I'd follow a sinuous black-haired girl down the street now and then, someone like Agnes, my version of Agnes, though the rest of it, of our time together, had more or less receded from me. I'd forgotten the details, the actual incidents. I never thought about them anymore. And it was only much later that I began to think she might have had any real, any lasting effect on me, or have left a part of herself in what I hankered after. To give an example: I think I've always been a fairly conservative sort of person, in spite of my youthful liberalism. Work and money, living in houses, dressing in ties, I've always liked all that stuff. Even at NYU, in the early seventies, leftism fading but still a habit, a glow: even then, when I was sitting tailor-style in the dorms, wearing jeans and shaggy hair, smoking hashish, calling the president a fascist and so on, I always admired his suits — Nixon's. Even then, the Jewish tradition of extravagant condemnations of the corrupt and the hard-lined, while convenient for the time, sat uncomfortably on me.

*Later on, I made a philosophy out of this. I would point out that
the embattled bourgeoisie, for all its complacencies, was really the last
bastion of practical tolerance; that the left and the right were always
imposing their wills on others, and finally forging their perfect worlds
with censorship and guillotines and gulags and concentration camps.
Only the middle ground knows how to live and let live, I'd say.
But that was just a philosophy. The real point was that always, in
my heart of hearts, I was a bourgeois, always. I always suspected
that even the very best rock songs were simplistic, poorly written
tripe, and that eventually, in every system everywhere, the sedate,
the industrious, the pleasant were meant to inherit the earth. All
right. So — that said — I studied Zen. This is what I mean about
Agnes. I was deep down a practical, thoroughly un-mystical kind
of a guy. Except when it came to yellow-haired pussy, satori was
nowhere on my deepest agenda. Yet twice a week, all through college
and law school too, I would close my books and tramp down to the
Washington Square subway; ride the train all the way to and from
Amsterdam Avenue; walk to the rundown brownstone off Columbus
Avenue, and climb the narrow stairs to the shabby, plant-infested
third floor one-bedroom apartment where Janet Hastings held her
Transcendence Seminars. Pretzeling my legs with deep, cynical and
witty groans into the half-lotus position I would sit narrow-eyed in a
circle with six others, a candle burning among us on Janet's thinning
living room carpet. I would try to carry out her solemn instructions to
'Follow your energy,' or 'Visualize your breath.' This, even though
such language struck me as incredibly vague and silly. And the
discussions afterward — gad, they made me downright squeamish.
Janet was into the New Testament in a big way and always quoted
Jesus as if he were some great guy she knew personally, a dutch uncle
whose advice was so clear, so in keeping with eastern principles of
inner vision that all this Catholic and Protestant nonsense that had
been going on these past twenty centuries would just make him slap
his knee with holy hilarity. The joy of clarity and revelation would
well up in her throat when she talked and into the others' throats
too and even into my throat sometimes, which just made my hair
stand on end. I distrusted it entirely. But — but the meditation itself
— helped along sometimes by Janet's mystifying Zen tales of broken
buckets and tasty strawberries — that kept me coming back for more.
And I think — think now though it would never have occurred to
me at the time — that it was Agnes I was after, my lost Sole, that*

Walk Home From Her House feeling. It didn't come naturally to me without her and I missed it. I wanted it back.

I would even go so far as to say that this had something to do with my marrying Marianne. Marianne with her fairy tendrils of corn-colored hair, and her upstate dairy farm childhood, and the gray leotards she meditated in which served to inflame my suspicions that she sure enough possessed the articles of my one true faith. She was one of Janet's students too. In fact, she worshipped Janet. She would tell me, breathily, *'Janet is so deep. She understands so much.'* The goof. This made me jealous, on the one hand, but it also suggested a talent in her for selfless devotion, something I wanted in a wife, and which I saw confirmed in her vulnerable, domitable not to mention crystal blue eyes. She was – not to oversimplify, but to make the point – everything I was looking for, yet with just that added filip of kookiness that was the legacy of my lost little girl companion.

Turned out there was no resemblance. Not only between Marianne and Agnes but between the soggy ghost on my sofa here and the dead sculptress of beloved memory. She, the girl on the sofa, was more my type, the Marianne type. Light hair, apple cheeks, bright, pellucid, innocent eyes. And it saddened me to realize this, oddly enough. As if America were rinsing the mad Jewish witch out of its bloodlines and leaving this pale spectre of itself to go searching across the graveyards of the earth blah blah blah . . . Dear Christ, listen to the bullshit. The big thoughts, the stupid generalizations. She was doing it to me. Sucking me bodily into the cinema of her soul.

I tore myself away from the window and, in doing so, rounded on her dramatically, which must've been just what she wanted. God, how to break the fetters.

'All right then,' I said, *'what do you want? We've done the root cellar, we've done the graveyard. The journalist lie, the age lie.'* She tried to look smart-assed but her cheeks colored. *'What do you want?'* I said again.

And surprise, surprise – call me a feather and blow me away – she leveled her baby greens at me and said – said gravely as if expecting a chord to strike:

'I want to know about Agnes Mallory.'

7

Her letters started twenty years later, in the era of Buckaroo
Umberman. Buckaroo was a Manhattan real estate attorney.
Also a part-time tax commissioner. Also the president of the
MacBride Democratic Club, with offices in the heart of the
Deuce. He was also, I've come to suspect, my id, foul as
he was. I think that had to be it, else how could he have
corrupted me so easily? Of course in those days, when I
was young and so half mad, everyone was something to
me. Ralph Myers was my father, Marianne my mother,
Umberman my id, and so on. Some hooker who called
herself Juliet I think was my vacuous, beautiful, sold-out
soul. Everything fit in somewhere. That's what craziness
is: imposing the template of your psyche on an indifferent
world. Of course, that's also what sanity is, which is what
causes so much of the terror and confusion about the two
states. But crazy or sane is not the point: it was youth. I was
young, and as far as I was concerned, everyone had a role to
play in the extravaganza of my existence. That's what they
were there for.

So the lights come up on me again when I'm twenty-nine.
Briefcase in hand, I'm storming with virile and righteous
anger past the reception desk at Myers & Weiss. The
secretaries loved me when I was like that. They'd go
slack, their pupils dilating. Six feet tall and very thin,
blond still, with boyish features, I usually tried for an
expression of old-fashioned, square-jawed rectitude tempered
by man-of-the-world cynicism which of course failed to quite
conceal my indomitable fighting spirit. It was good stuff. Even
Weiss, the junior partner, wanted a piece of it. When I passed

his open door, he called out to me. 'Hey! Harry! Hold on!' When I stopped, all impatient and dynamic, he came around his big desk to me, partner though he was.

In my arrogance then, I could find no easy way to relate to Weiss. I liked him, but looked down on him too. Even literally, down on his amiable pug features, his bald head with the frizzy black fringe. At forty or so, he had gone where he was going more or less, whereas I radiated a Big Future. He liked, therefore, to play adviser to me, get his licks in, secure his mentor role in my biography. The pleasanter I was about it, the more he sensed I was merely tolerating him and the more desperate and pushy he got. It was not a comfortable relationship.

'What's up?' he said, laying a friendly hand on my shoulder.

'Plunkitt Towers,' I said grimly. 'The fix is in.' I'd been reciting this phrase to myself all the way in from the Bronx and thought it sounded great.

'This is the Article Five case.'

'Yeah.' It was one of my favorites. Its outrageousness made it a tale worth telling, especially as I was on the side of the angels. Having left Legal Services a couple of years back, it was just the sort of thing I had to root around for more. Briefly, Plunkitt Towers was part of a Fifties slum-clearance project: subsidized low-income housing on the West Side. Originally, it was packed with deserving, mostly Jewish, mostly socialist types. According to the law, as these people prospered or died or moved away, the new low-income groups, namely blacks, Hispanics, Orientals and so on, were supposed to move in. But that's not the way it happened. When the Lincoln Center theater complex went up, the value of the neighborhood went up with it. Suddenly, the Plunkitt Towers residents found themselves living in a very low-rent goldmine. In the meantime, some of those same residents had become fairly powerful themselves, with connections to the city government and political clubs. So, while the city Housing, Preservation and Development Agency turned a blind eye, the residents stacked the building's waiting list with friends, relatives and heirs, and the new low-income people had to go fish for somewhere else to live. Okay – now, in Washington, president Reagan and the Republicans had arrived. Real Estate Summertime: the borrowing's easy and the market runs high. On top of which, the City's contract on Plunkitt was about to expire, which meant that, with a two-thirds majority vote from the co-opers, the building could go private, ensuring large profits all around and leaving legitimate low-income folks out in the cold. Just another New York scam: fine speeches and good intentions twisted to line the pockets of the powerful. But wait! What's this on the horizon? Is it? Yes. Sir Harry of Bernard, riding in *pro bono* to stop the vote on the grounds that a lot of the voting residents shouldn't have been in the building to begin with. A cry of 'Huzzah!' Followed by a loud: 'Shit!'

'They gave the case to Judge Montanti,' I told Weiss. 'The opposition walks in with Murray Seidenfeld, who just sits there, right? Just giving the judge the eye. So Montanti suddenly decides I have to serve the entire board – most of whom are out of town – and he lifts the TRO on the vote, which is next week.'

'*What?*'

'I gotta talk to Myers.'

I marched on, eager to get away from him before he loaded me up with bad suggestions and weak contacts I'd have to waste time on in order to soothe his ego. For his part, he hurried ahead and managed to be the one who burst into Myers' office first.

'They set the kid up on Plunkitt Towers,' he announced, pointing a thumb at me. 'Listen to this shit.' We all loved to talk like that.

I went through it again for Myers and he listened quietly, slumped in his swivel chair, his pants riding high on his round paunch. There was a moist smile on his face – a face like crumpled putty in which the eyes glittered mildly, full of Jewishness, Jewish wit and wisdom. When I was done, he shook his head.

'You can't win this one, Harry, they want it too badly. Murray Seidenfeld owns the whole surrounding block. He doesn't want all those low-income people moving into Plunkitt; it would kill his property values. And if Seidenfeld is involved, so is Hank Cohen. And with Montanti on the bench, the best you can do is make 'em keep whatever low-income units are left.'

'Yeah, but once they go private, the ballgame is over,' I said.

Nodding absently, Myers considered. I watched him and so did Weiss. Our respect for Myers was powerful, all our feelings for Myers were very strong. At moments like this, in fact, I admired him so much that it was important to me to remind myself why I was essentially better than he was. He was old, for one thing. He was satisfied with his lot. He was Jewish in the old-fashioned way and was satisfied with that too, with his rabbinical softness, his sighing acceptance; he said 'oy' a lot, and used Yiddish expressions – '*Fidugula*. You know what's a *fidugula*? You don't know a *fidugula*? What kind of a Jewish *bocher* doesn't know what's a *fidugula*?' I was proud not to understand what the hell he was talking about. Still, there was no denying what I felt for him. Now, for instance, watching him, I experienced real tremors of excitement and anticipation. What would he say? What was the word from on high?

He thought a long time, nodding like that. Framed against his modest window with its modest view of the Municipal Building. He was senior partner; he could have had Weiss's panorama of downtown, the Brooklyn Bridge, the twin towers.

'Maybe we could blackmail HPD,' Weiss chimed in, 'wake 'em up with some scandal stories in the *Times* . . .' He was just throwing this out in the hopes he'd get lucky and get to be my expert this time. But his voice trailed off as Myers made a moue and shook the suggestion away.

'I think,' Myers said finally, 'a case like this: you might just be able to go to Umberman.'

'Umberman. Who's Umberman?' I asked.

'"Who's Umberman!"' snorted Weiss, enjoying his superiority while he could.

But Myers – this is what Myers answered, shifting in his chair, sinking into what I believed to be a shamanistic trance – and this is why, at the hard core of feeling, we all worshipped the man:

'Well, until two years ago, you know, Manhattan and

the Bronx were a single judicial district, and Freeman in the Bronx only controlled a third of the nominating panel's delegates. Everytime he tried to sell a judgeship, the Manhattan reformers got in his way, which embarrassed the mayor no end, since he'd have been only too happy, his deal with Freeman being what it was, to let his nominations ride. Now two years before that, Freeman had already tried to split the districts up, but the reformers got to Governor Carey first and shot him down. So this time, Freeman – and Cohen too, for that matter – approached Umberman, who's now president of the MacBride Club but at the time had some Carey plum and was very in with the Governor. To make a long story short, Umberman sold the district split to Albany, Freeman got his own judicial district to play around with and, in return for the favor, he gave Umberman one Bronx judgeship for himself. Which, in the fullness of time, was presented to our boy Montanti. All of which means that, even though he's a Bronx judge, Montanti belongs to Umberman.'

I mean, I loved this stuff, *loved* it. I loved the whole city when it was explained to me this way. Political New York. We all loved it, the whole youthful firm of us, and Myers was its master, he had it down pat. The layers, the details, the intricacies of corruption. No one did it like he did. You didn't even have to understand what he was saying to appreciate the way he said it, the dropping of names, the sardonical phrasings – 'our boy Montanti,' 'the fullness of time' – the gimlet in-ness, the gimlet eye. When Myers starting talking, it was like looking at one of those cross-section models of the earth in which you can see the strata and the roots, the interchange of minerals, the slug-life, all the underworkings of the innocent's green-blue surface world of trees, houses, avenues and lies. We lived to breathe that knowing of his, that unshockable grasp of chicanery with its bedrock of unstated moralism. We too would be incorruptible but know the ways of the corruptible and walk among them, as he did, without sanctimony but weary-faced and wise.

So now I perched on the edge of his desk and gestured with my hand, just as I would have if we'd been wearing snap-brim hats and smoking cigarettes like the tough guys in old films. 'Why should Umberman do a dance with me?' I said.

Myers answered with a classic Semitic gesture: closing the eyes, tilting the head, spreading the hands a little. 'I'll call. We'll talk. He'll dance.'

As we were walking away from our audience with Myers, Weiss, completely overshadowed, had to get in his word. Hands in his pockets, he hoisted his shoulders. He corkscrewed his lips knowingly and shook his head. 'Buckaroo Umberman,' he said musingly.

In my condescending compassion for him, I took the bait. 'Buckaroo? Why Buckaroo?'

And Weiss, pausing at his office door, dropping his voice, tapping the fingertips of his open hand against my shirt front, a little too eager, a little too giddy, a little too little informed, did his version of the great Myers' routine. 'The babes love their Umberman, see. Don't ask me why, okay? It's a mystery of female sexuality. Anyway. When he was up in Albany, he was *schtupping* all of them. Constantly. Every aide, every secretary, every court clerk he can stick his dick in, he *schtups*.' Glancing toward the secretarial caroles, he moved in on me. I could smell the egg sandwich on his hot breath. 'So he starts to play this game with his staff, all right? He gets a girl into his office and gets her to bend over. So he can *schtup* her from behind, see?' He was almost whispering now out of one corner of his mouth. 'Then, just as he's going good, right? – *schtupping* her – suddenly, four or five of the guys in the outer office burst into the room. You know, they shout, like, "Hooray!" Well, of course, the babe is horrified. She tries to get away.' Weiss's face reddened as his whisper rose to a high-pitched squeak of laughter. 'Only Umberman won't let go, right? So she's screaming and throwing herself around like a bucking bronco and Umberman holds on for dear life, and the guys are shouting, "Ride 'em. Ride 'em, Buckaroo." I swear to God. They used to take bets, they used to time him to see how long he could stay on. That's why they call him Buckaroo.'

Weiss's high-pitched giggling went on for some time. He shook his head, his round face scarlet. He had to knuckle-dry his eyes. I did my best not to hurt his feelings, of course, glancing heavenward, murmuring breathlessly, 'You're kidding. Are you kidding me?' and so on. But this was no good. It was not a Myeresque story at all. It was even faintly pitiful that he would tell it. For one thing, it probably wasn't true, or was an exaggeration, which Myers would have pointed out. And for another thing, it was cruel. Humiliating some girl like that. That was awful. That wasn't like selling a judgeship or miscounting a vote or signing a dead guy to a nominating petition. Those you could admire in a way: the endless ingenuity of greed — that was part of the idea, part of our easy, cynical knowledge of human nature. But this: this stank. It was brutal. You didn't stand there and giggle about it. Cruelty — rape, murder, child abuse — you could joke about these things under Myerism if no women were around, but only to mask your outrage, to relieve your heart. 'Oh, a wonderful guy our Mr Umberman,' you might say. Or 'Hell, in Albany, that's how they treat all the voters.'

And then, too, the story was demeaning to womankind. We Myerists didn't do that. We believed in women, as coworkers, mothers, wives. We treated them with court-liness and bemusement. And if there was something a little patronizing about that, well, it was because we knew, in spite of their trumpetings of strength, that a certain gentleness was required for the maintenance of their humanity which was not required with us. Some of them might insist, in the abstract populism of the age, that there was no difference between their sex and ours, and the courtly Myerist would go along. Hell, the world would be a lot easier and a lot fairer if that were true. But facts were facts — that was the foundation of our creed. Women, whether they liked it or not, were strange and mysterious and wonderful beyond their own control or understanding. You did not abuse that or truck lightly with those who did.

And finally, the story gave me a hardon. A big one. Not right then, while he was telling it to me, thank God, but later, when I had time to consider it and form a picture in my mind. In the cab going up to see Umberman a few days later, for instance, I had to keep my raincoat over my lap: my

dick could have cut glass. I looked out on the Park Avenue
pedestrians as they headed into the strong September wind,
under a gray sky, under imperious walls of white brick and
red brick. I fixed a solid image in my mind of the imagined
Umberman's satyr-like thrusting, the girl's bare ass bouncing
and bucking as she struggled to get away from him. I imagined
her high-pitched cries. I suppose I half believed it had actually
happened now, if only for my own excitement's sake. Then,
a jack hammer riddled the pavement and I came around. I
saw a colossal crane hoisting a girder on a side street. Hard
hats and scaffolding. A grinding steam shovel. Pulling out
of the daydream, looking up ahead, I saw Grand Central
drawing close, the big clock and Mercury with outstretched
arms. I knew I had to ditch the erection before we pulled up
at the MacBride Club, and I cast around for neutral thoughts.
My pregnant wife . . . no. My last handball game at the NYU
club. All the construction everywhere, all the money and
property changing hands as the government led us on a
borrowing and spending spree. That did it, and nervousness
helped too: my fear at the big meeting, my general anxiety
these days.

My dick safely receded. Still, moments like this were
very difficult for me. I had a feeling sometimes, when I
was pried from my imagination like this, as if a barrel ring
had been removed from my Self, as if the barrel staves of
my personality had fallen away and I was left naked, with no
personality at all. Anxious, acidic, depressed, really, for no
reason I could think of, I had to remind myself what a happy
guy I actually was. An up-and-coming legal star fresh from a
good-guy apprenticeship at Legal Services. Loving husband
of a beautiful, gentle and service-minded wife. Father-to-be
of our first baby. Everything, as people kept telling me, was
going great.

But the Inner Man, oh, the Inner Man. With my wife,
for example. Just that morning, I had snapped at her, and
pretty savagely too — about towels no less. She had used the
last towel in the bathroom and hadn't replaced it. I had to
come out into the hallway sopping wet to get another. I'd
snarled at her all through breakfast and while I'd managed,
by an effort of will, to keep from turning really cruel, the

Inner Man – oh, the Inner Man was in an uproar about it. To Him, it was a problem with universal implications, these missing towels. It showed her lack of consideration. It demonstrated women's refusal to accept responsibility for their actions. It was indicative of a falling off of courtesy and respect for others throughout the entire society. God knows what else. The Inner Man had been spouting silent jeremiads like this all morning. He was practically on fire with them. Whereas I personally felt like shit for being mean to her, Marianne, the sweet, whispery soul.

And it was like this a lot. I was not at peace with Him, this Inner Man. He was angry at my wife more than half the time, even when I would have been perfectly placid. He was flamingly enraged when I might have been merely annoyed. He sniped at her enterprises, was scornful of her condition. He was a total stinker. And it wasn't just with her either. It was everything; His whole outlook, His attitude. I was concerned with big topics. With the liberalization of the Law versus the responsibility of the State, with the intrinsic relationship between corruption and democracy, blacks and whites, women and men, rich and poor. With the decency of my own career, with doing Good, with being Good. The Inner Man, meanwhile, was preoccupied with topics such as shit. Literally shit. He could go on and on about it. Oh, that was a good one, He'd say, just the consistency I like; stick with that cereal in the morning. Or: I feel a bit of pressure, maybe we should do it now, save us trouble later on. Or: What do you think, if we fart here, will the stench have cleared away before anyone comes into the room? On and on and on like that. In sexual matters, too, He was awful: infantile, domineering, secretly terrified. Made giddy and giggly by words like titty, tush, bounce, buck, thrust. Nourishing his sultanic fantasies. Avid for news stories about rape. Nauseous at the mention of castration or impotence. And politically: He was secretly glad – glad, I tell you – that Ronald Reagan was in the White House and the right in power; we'd make more money that way. And He'd thought many of my poor black clients had been lazy idiots. He burst out at them sometimes, right across the desk: *Nigger! Ignorant Nigger!* Christ, what if I accidentally spoke aloud?

Call it a version of the old mind-body problem — well, I guess it was — but that made it not one whit less painful and disorienting for me personally at twenty-nine. All that rage, all that fear, all that shit. And the suspicion — no, the conviction — never articulated, hardly framed — that He was I, this Inner Man, that I was a mere construct, a falsehood, no one.

I was ready for Umberman to come into my life. I make no excuses. My very confusion conjured him from beneath the sidewalks of New York.

The most memorable moment of our first meeting was just before the aide opened his door. The aide — or whatever he was — was a sinister, sharp-faced young man in heavy, black-framed glasses that showed, I thought, an almost vengeful disregard for fashion. He led me through the wide outer office of gunmetal desks and strewn paper and campaign bumper stickers stuck to the wall. He took me to a door at the back, let me approach it first. Then, while I stood there, he reached around me. He twisted the knob, pushed the door open. What was I to think? Was this it? Would he shout, 'Hooray!' Would they be there, right there before me, the struggling girl, the thrusting Buckaroo? Would I be confronted with the entire spectacle? Worse, would it render me helplessly lubricious? Would I stand flabbergasted, breathless and erect while some poor woman's dignity was violently stripped from her and her round, rosy, convulsing buttocks bared for all to see?

This — this fearful anticipation — was the only comic anecdote I came away with afterward, although I had to modify my own reactions in the telling. I had to delete, that is, my panting excitement. Comic anecdotes, see, were an important element in my defense against the sovereignty of the Inner Man. When told with wit and apparent modesty, they established the decency of my Real Self in the admiring minds of others. You just had to lie about what you were really thinking, that's all.

Anyway, nothing actually happened, of course. The door was flung in and there was Umberman. An enormously fat man with thinning black hair and heavy features: jowls, lips, nose, eye-pouches all heavy and drawn toward the earth. I couldn't imagine women exactly swooning at his feet. He didn't get up from behind his desk when I came in but leaned back in his creaking chair, spreading his arms to welcome me in a gravelly voice.

'Harry Bernard! We meet at last!'

I laughed, coming forward to shake his hand. I felt superior to him already. He reeked of the way of things, and I was clean. 'I wasn't aware we'd been missing each other.'

'Ah now.' He wagged his finger at me. 'A name gets around. A man has a reputation. A man has a future. Nothing is secret in this city, Harry.'

He gestured me to the metal chair across from him. I was much too concerned with my own image, with projecting confidence and the moral necessity of my cause, to take much notice of the surroundings. There was a good view of the Terminal and Mercury through the window behind him, and I got a sense of some pretty fancy prints on the wall, seascapes and sailing ships he might have picked up in Italy and England. For the rest, I had an impression of a swamped desktop, stacks of briefs against the wall and that sort of thing.

Umberman was going on, nodding slowly, heavily, with solemn appreciation. 'The Harlem clinic thing. These incidents get around. Many men were bought off. Many others would have been. There's a drumbeat in this city, Harry. I keep my ears to the wind.'

I'd fought the mayor's office to keep the clinic open as he'd promised he would during his campaign. I lost, but Umberman was right, it made some noise. And of the three lawyers on the case, I was the only one who didn't wind up with a choice job working for the opposition. I earned a lot of credit for this in some circles, distrust in others.

'This is the future. You. I know that. The future belongs to reform. That's the way it should be, Harry, believe me. The machine is gone. The machine has lived out its usefulness.' Already, as I settled in, he was lecturing, making grand sweeps with both slabby hands, letting them fall to his stomach with a slap. 'The old days – oh, the old days, you know, you did a favor, you helped a friend. A Christmas turkey for a poor family, a home for someone who was burned out, a job for a young man trying to make his way in the world. It had a point then, a purpose. You didn't ask – Republican, Democrat. You knew where they would be on election day.'

For this I had my Youthful Smile of Credulous Admiration, but we Myerists were proof against sentimentalizing the old days, Tammany. That unfinished courthouse behind City Hall? That sucker cost the grateful poor thirteen million of their tax dollars in 1868 and most of that went straight to the bosses in kickbacks. We Myerists knew our history, see, our facts. In spite of our cynicism, we knew corruption never worked. Never.

'FDR, La Guardia, the New Deal – now, the government does the ˙favors for people. That's the way it should be. I mean that. The Civil Service gives the jobs. There's no real patronage in this city anymore,' said Umberman, his big chin dropping with a thud to his chest. 'In Manhattan – pfft – forget it. The Mayor hates the party Chairman, the Chairman won't make peace with the Mayor. You think there's patronage out of City Hall here? Forget about it. There's nothing to give. And now: TV. Commercials. You don't even need the party to run for office anymore. You go right on TV, you go right to the people. Sometimes I ask myself: what am I doing here? The party is nothing now. The people are what matter.' He spread his hands again and laughed, his jowls rippling. 'And the people, Harry. The people, you know, they want issues. Each one has his issue. It's all division, there's no unity. Each one, you've got to tell him what he wants to hear. See? The people – they like words. You gotta give ˏthem nice words all the time. If it's a *shvartze*, you gotta call him black. Then he wants to be called an African-whosits or whatsis, whatever. If it's a cripple in a wheelchair, he wants to be handicapped, and then that's no good, he wants to be physically challenged. The girls can't be girls, they gotta be women, then something else – uy, they have very high hopes for the English language, these people. But that's what you gotta do. Because it's all TV now, it's all talking to people. And every year, you gotta learn a whole new vocabulary. Why? Because every year people find out – surprise! – a new name doesn't make you

white. It doesn't make you walk, it doesn't give you respect
from men. It doesn't give you a fucking turkey at Christmas
time either. People feel the same goddamned way about you
they always did except now they lie to you about it. You're
an African-whosits, you're a woman – they lie. TV, Harry.
The party's gone, the party's over. A guy like me – what?
I'm an old man. An old hack. I have no power anymore. My
day is past. And this is as it should be.'

All this by way of hello – we hadn't even gotten to Plunkitt
Towers yet. And as I sat there, waiting for my chance, raincoat
over my arm, sympathetic smile plastered to my face, I was
beginning to indulge, all unwillingly, in some slightly more
complex reactions. I responded to his ontology; it spoke to
my not-very-secret secret heart. Well, sure, I too had begun
to notice the language of public life being drained of pain
and human feeling – and therefore of truth. I even suspected
that the Inner Man was feasting on this phenomenon. That
he was thriving on the new, politicized vocabulary the way
the gangsters used to thrive on Prohibition: peddling the
forbidden thoughts I could no longer say aloud. And I
confess: I admired Umberman for speaking out about it
when even Myers simply shrugged and went along. Oh,
Umberman still disgusted me, right enough. Just looking at
him. He was reclining with his hands on his belly now, and
his eyes were narrowed, almost closed, and his breathing made
a damp rumble – it was as if he'd sunk, between diatribes,
into a lizardly snooze. And there was a stream of spittle, too,
descending slowly, slowly from the corner of his mouth. He
was horrible. But all the same, I, wrestling with the prissy
angels, saw a certain courage in his awfulness, I guess; an
honesty – or at least an honest mockery beneath his lies. He
was mocking me – I was pretty certain of that – mocking
and watching me through those lowered lids.

'So?' he said, barely moving now. 'Nu? This is what I
contend with. My kind. No power anymore. Our day is
over, Harrykins. Still – hey – I'm glad you felt you could
come to me, a good man like yourself, a man who cares, an
honest man, not to be had, not be bribed. It does me good,
at the end of my life, to see this, the way of the future, a man
I can admire . . .'

'Well,' I said, weighing in with an earnest expression of respect, 'Ralph Myers felt that in the matter of Plunkitt Towers, a certain number of units might be set aside . . .'

'Ach – that!' He waved it away lazily. He sneered into his shirt collar. 'Consider it done. For a young man like you, that's done already. Poor folks gotta live somewhere too. It's done.'

I gaped, I admit it. My mouth, open on a word, just stayed that way, open, as I stared at the semi-napping fat man. That was done? That was it? We were talking about Seidenfeld, remember, who meant billions in realty deals to the city. And Cohen – they called him The Fixer, he was that tough, that connected. That's who I was up against. And it was done? Oh, I felt this, all right, the unbridled power of this, for only a moment maybe but from my gonads to my soul I felt it go through me with a certain brisk hilarity. On the instant, I ceased to doubt that there were women who would hike their skirts for this creature. The Buckaroo scenario even returned to me for an instant, and I felt the excitement of that go through me too.

For an instant, as I say, only for an instant. Then, settling back, I managed an uncertain laugh. 'Uh – okay,' I said.

And without opening his eyes, Buckaroo Umberman smiled pinkly, damply. 'Harry, I'm glad you could come by,' he said. 'I've been wanting to have a look at you.'

~ 8 ~

About three months after this, a surprising thing happened. It was dreary and cold and December then. Marianne was at the West Side Y teaching her meditation class. Yes, she had taken on the Janet Hastings mantle and was doing Transcendence Seminars of her own now. Janet herself had moved to Santa Fe to paint and it was her parting wish that, as she had continued the seminars of her guru, whose name I forget, others would continue *her* seminars and so on until it was just one big Janet Hastings kind of a world. So this was what my wife was up to in the final month of her pregnancy.

The Y provided a small classroom for this, and Marianne and her pupils had pushed the tablet chairs to the wall and set their blue gym mats down in the center of the floor. Marianne had herself all lotused up at the head of a semi-circle. The midsection of her purple leotard ballooned painfully over her swollen thighs and her breasts sagged so wearily it weighed all the other women down as well. But she, her face, her manner, as always, were radiant, were by Raphael. Her eyes sparkled like the surface of fresh snow as they gazed into the middle distance with inspirational joy. 'When Jesus . . .' she said, and she got just that Janet Hastings swelling of ecstasy in the throat when she spoke the name, 'When Jesus said, "If your eye offends you pluck it out," he was talking, I think, about your rage, about how useless it is to take offense at what we think are the evils of the world. Before you tell your neighbor he has a speck in his eye, remove the mote from your own: don't direct your energies toward the object of your anger, direct them toward the anger itself. Whatever is happening is just . . . happening! You're the cause of your own reactions.'

She only had six students of this philosophy, thank Heavens: six women, six tense faces seared with lines. Each was concentrating intently on how awkward she felt in her own leotard: like a collection of gangling stalks sprouting from lumpy putty. In truth, they'd all given up hope on this stuff lessons ago, and were beginning to drop their false enthusiasm for it as well. Recently, during the breaks, they'd abandoned the pretense of philosophical converse altogether, and had begun gossiping about my wife instead. They'd discuss whether her bliss was merely a palliative for her neuroses, which palliative, by the way, they secretly envied her in any case, feeling nothing themselves at this point between the dentist drill of life and their own exposed nerves. They envied her her baby too and her marriage too – or at least her delusions about them, because they knew, as she did not, what the former would tear out of her and wear down in her and how the latter would scorch the girlhood from her soul as it plummeted in flames, or poison it as it lingered in the blood like gall. Ultimately, they assured each other, she would learn, and then she would be like them – just like them despite her protests to the contrary, which would be just like their protests – with even her day's work robbed of its fulfillments by unseen conspirators as she began to realize that her epiphanies had become a farce wearily played out for those, like themselves, stupid enough to shell out eighty-five dollars on one more straw to grasp at as, notwithstanding the strident battle cries of their generation, they sank into their mothers' dissatisfaction and ultimately death.

'So! Let's try a meditation exercise,' said Marianne, sprightly. 'Think about the person who makes you angriest . . . Oh.' At this point, narrowing her brows, she stopped. Puzzled, she bent over herself, trying to peer down into her own lap. 'I – I must've spilled something . . .'

Whereupon, the once-wealthy matron who had been robbed of both dignity and security in a relentless divorce gasped, 'Oh Christ, Marianne, your waters broke.'

My ditzy wife, still transcendent, blinked at her. 'What?'

And the divorcee, and the single mother, and the out-of-work executive, and the former cocaine addict and the stay-at-home feminist and the terrified spinster who didn't need a goddamned man to feel fulfilled, all cried out together: 'Marianne, you're in labor, you're having your baby!'

Marianne, God love her, was speechless. Simply astounded.

It was a fourteen-hour thing, little Charlie coming. She wouldn't take drugs for it, not any. Natural childbirth was all the rage that year, and of course Marianne swore by it, one of the few women nutty enough to actually stick it through. She wouldn't even let the doctor do that spinal block that became so popular a few years later. She had that with our daughter – there were complications then – but not with Charlie. Charlie she did on her own.

We'd gone to classes about this, the two of us. They gave them at the hospital, at Lennox Hill. A pretty nurse with a model's figure put us through breathing exercises each week or blithely stood at the blackboard with a pointer, telling us what to expect and what to do. When the time came, I was there, phoned in from work by the receptionist at the Y. And I did my bit, sitting at Marianne's bedside, massaging her spine with a tennis ball, feeding her ice chips, coaching her through the contractions and all that. Yeah, and it worked great for the first ninety minutes or so. That, we found out later, was when the other girls in our class started screaming for the demerol. But not my Marianne. Now, as convulsions and agonies and exhaustion racked her, as I hunched fretfully beside her wishing she'd cave in, as the fur on that stupid tennis ball turned to algae in my sweating palm, now she, like a sorceress marshalling her fairy gang, called on all her mysticism, all her techniques, all those mantras and huffings and those stupid eye movements and all that ridiculous shit, and she took it, the pain – or let it pass through her or happened with it or whatever the hell she did – she took it, without a curse, with hardly a complaint, for twelve and a half hours more.

By eight o'clock or so on the next snowy morning, she lay sprawled on the blood-stained and piss-stained and shit-stained sheets with only her blue eyes bright in a face as white as paper. Her limbs lay limp at accidental angles all around her and all the energy seemed drained from her, so that it looked as if she was staring out at me all alive from within a dead thing, a log or a clump of earth. And yet, mercilessly, the contractions went on and on, wringing the dry rag of that poor body, while she murmured and breathed and zenned her way all through it. Even the doctor – an imperturbable Chinese woman – was popping in every few minutes now, begging her to medicate. Not Marianne. She never broke. She held the mystic line. Her mind and her body were one, see, there was no chance of her giving over.

Me, I was demolished by this time. I was the ruins of Harry, a pile of Harry rubble on the hospital floor. Any beliefs I had, any convictions or philosophies, you could basically forget them. I was praying to a God I didn't think existed, I was working out superstitious rituals to ease her pain – trying to appease Baal by pacing between the cracks in the hallway tiles or flipping a coin to prophesy if it would come to an end in the next half hour – generally cowering, as it were, in the reptilian stem of the brain for all I was worth. In fact, when the end finally did come, I was in direct confrontation with Jehovah in a men's room stall. Shaking my fist at the tiled ceiling, snarling, 'Let up, you fuck.' Sweat and tears streaming down my face together.

Well, it wasn't exactly the Lord's Prayer, but it did seem to do the trick. When I stepped out into the hall, there was Marianne rolling toward me, her doctor pushing her, bed and all, to the delivery room with nurses dancing attendance. I grabbed a gown and a hat and went with them. The rest happened very quickly.

And this was the surprising thing:

When I saw my son Charlie born, I was posted close by my wife's tormented belly, clutching her damp, weak hand and looking down between her legs. The only man in the room, I felt worn down by the difficult hours to what seemed an almost edenic humanity, with no feelings but tenderness and protectiveness and dependency for these good laborers of the companion sex. I had a clear overview of Marianne's straining snatch – a part of her, by the by, for which I'd always felt enormous warmth and friendliness: such a raw, living orifice to be set so wittily beneath her delicate blond curlicues, with a bosky odor that was generally female but had a unique taste like sour red wine; I'd always liked it and I was surely rooting for it now. I had a clear view of it and all the proceedings, and was surprised to find I felt no queasiness, but if anything a heightened sense of normalcy. Despite my pulsing excitement and fear, despite the shouts on all sides of 'Push!' and 'It's coming!' and my wife's animal cries and the indifferent antiseptic wall tiles and the bright lights and the brutal metal instruments, it all seemed pretty much to me like the proper business of the day which, again, surprised me.

Anyway, in about ten minutes, Charlie came, and this is the point. It was a messy affair. The doctor said 'Push,' and the nurses were all yelling, and I may have called out something too, and Marianne lifted up on her elbows with a nurse supporting her behind and her whole face balled up like a fist and she bore down. She gave a prolonged, wet fart and a gout of loose shit arced from her exposed anus and splatted dully across the sheets. Then, as she renewed the attempt, there was a great spray of piss from her, angry and yellow and pungent. Charlie's head squeezed out of her into the doctor's hands, not looking like a head at all but white and crusty and nearly featureless and the neck so twisted around that it sent my eyebrows clear up under my hairline. 'One more,' said the doctor, all of us shouting, and the dear girl gave it everything she had. And what a geyser there was from between her legs of blood and water and fetal matter and God knows what else. And out between the lips of her vagina in the very midst of that gush, curled all the while between her bloody thighs as if in peaceful sleep, slipped the baby, our baby, to a chorus of grateful cries.

Now then, the thing, the surprising thing that happened: I had a mystical experience. Nothing else to call it; it was none of your meditative states or exalted periods of understanding but a mental event, a thing that occurred. I felt a rush of love for my wife, and it became a tide – all this, by the way, in an instant – a tide of feeling on which I was washed clean out of my sense of physical presence and into Marianne's – what? – being, essence, whatever. I was washed from my body into her being and then with her into the new baby's – and then, all together, in the final squib of that second, began to mushroom out like a split atom into what I saw to be the Universal Thing.

Imagine: a New York City lawyer. Then right away, back I snapped, the Harry we know and love, crying with joy and generally kvelling as young Charlie Bernard was laid, whimpering, between Marianne's bounteous breasts. I was no different than I was the moment before and knew no more than ever. But as I stood there in my stupid-looking paper hat and medical apron, beaming down on my ecstatic wife and murmuring son, I did have the anxious suspicion that something stinking of destiny had been set free in me, was slowly rising, like the kraken from its watery bounds, and I was half conscious of a painful and childlike yearning which I had repressed for ever so long, and which was attached in my mind to a long-forgotten prospect: the darkening sky above me, and the night's first stars.

In six weeks time, I was pretty well sick of the whole thing: the kid shitting, crying, my wife, all martyred, complaining of too little sleep, me trying to help, not wanting to help, not really caring. Marianne loved the boy so much she could not even begin to imagine my inner shrug at him. Well, he was my son and all that and I supposed I'd come to love him in time, but he didn't do anything and he didn't know me from Adam – why exactly *should* I have liked him, if it came to that? Naturally, at the time, I lied about all this, to Marianne and to myself, but the gibberings of the Inner Man were insistent. Every day, I fantasized that a plane would crash into the house and kill them both so that I'd be free.

I worked as much as I could. Made a great show of it too. Rubbing my eyes wearily, sighing over my workload and my responsibilities, my miserable clients and so on. I had to match Marianne burden for burden, you see, or she'd gain the moral high ground and want more out of me at home. Sometimes, I left for work early and subwayed under the west side down to lower Broadway only to spend the next hour or so alone doing nothing in the Starlight diner, a bagel joint south of Canal. I would sit there at a back table – salt and pepper linoleum littered with sesame seeds. I would sit very still with the *Times* draped over my hands and my bagel half-eaten and my coffee cold. And I would stare into space. Sad. Helplessly aching. Remembering and remembering, after these two decades of forgetfulness, all the details of that spring and summer I was nine years old. And I wanted it back, that season. More than words can say. I wanted to have it turn out right. I wanted it back.

9

My mother, fat as a peasant, had grown into her face somehow. It was as if it had been waiting for her to actually become what she'd looked like all her life: an old, frightened woman in a mind-maze of superstitious terror. Jowls of leather, lips white and tight with fear, eyes overheated with the ceaseless ratiocinative work of fending off any secret betrayals: that was Mom these days. The first time Marianne and I brought the baby out to the Long Island house, Mom could only hover over him and fret. She was afraid even to touch him: the Envious Gods, you know. Marianne, her sweet, whispery self, coaxed her as if she were a child, working Charlie by stages into her arms – whereupon Mom sat rigid with him in an absolute horror of joy, then, quickly, handed him back.

We were in the back room where we'd all gathered in the old days to watch TV. Marianne and Mom were sitting with the baby and his assorted bunny-bedecked paraphernalia on the braid rug. My father was slumped in the cushioned chair. Nearing sixty now, paunchy and bald, he exuded lethargy in long, moaning sighs.

'It's so wonderful what you can do now with them,' Mom said, leaning wistfully over the blessed babe. 'I see the young girls carrying them everywhere in those pouches, those Snuglis. Breastfeeding everywhere, right out in the open. In my day, they wouldn't let you do any of that. The doctors would tell you it was no good, your husband wouldn't encourage you. All the men – they'd get together and talk it over and then tell you what to do.'

'They didn't get together,' my father groaned.

'They got together,' she insisted. 'They got together and talked it over and told you what to do.'

'Where would we get together? What did we know?' he muttered mournfully.

But the women went on talking between themselves.

It was a Sunday afternoon in late February. There was a wet snow falling. I saw it melting on the empty branches of the old cherry tree.

'So,' said my father, cranking around to me. 'How's the job?'

I never meant to get talkative around my parents. I always meant to maintain my privacy, play the cards close to the vest and such like. But so many things came into play, so many impulses. I wanted my father to know what a success I was so he'd be proud of me. I wanted him to know what a success I was and he wasn't so fuck him. I wanted to show off my inside knowledge of political arcana, which I loved. And, maybe more than anything, I wanted my mother to know how honest I remained, how good, how golden with integrity. I didn't know why it mattered so much. I didn't know anything about her father then and the secret reasons behind her childhood poverty. But I felt just the same now as when I was a kid, when we sat at the breakfast table and I rattled off stories about my own heroism. I felt the same urgency to let her know this thing.

So I said, 'It's incredible, Dad,' leaning over the sofa arm into his glazed hostility. 'The things I'm seeing. There's never been a western city as layered with corruption as New York, not since maybe Rome. The *baksheesh*, the levels of bribery and influence. The intricate systems of legal graft – 'cause it's all legal, the way they work it out: legal fees instead of payoffs, hiring the councilman's illiterate brother to do your PR. The stuff you read in the newspapers is nothing – the newspapers are in on it . . .' blah, blah, blah, on and on, flaunting what passed for my expertise.

My father sighed, creaking like a hinge. 'You gotta make compromises in this life,' he sighed. 'You gotta make compromises.'

Naturally, this only fired me up more. That was his life – compromises, moral failure – which in his paternal largesse he wanted to be sure to hand down to me. But not this guy – not Harry – and I wanted Mom to know it. I said: 'You know, the one possible bright spot is this woman Manero in the U.S. Attorney's office. Their anti-corruption unit. She's Republican, for one thing, which means she wants these guys but good. She also wants to be Governor, I think. And she's supposed to be honest on top of it all. Anyway, there's rumors she's dropped some baited hooks into the swamp. I hear there could be some big-time busts coming down soon. I've been seriously thinking of sending a resume over there.'

This was a lie, or at least an exaggeration. I hadn't, not seriously – and I felt like an idiot for saying it, for puffing myself up. And God knows, if I'd been trying to impress my mother . . . Well, I couldn't have been more surprised by her reaction.

'Oh, these people!' she said suddenly, sniffing, working herself to her feet. She stood over Marianne and the baby – not looking at me, looking down at them still. 'These humorless people. Like the Seaburys and the Deweys. With their agendas, with their ambitions. Never trust these humorless people.'

For a second, I wasn't even sure she was talking to me. I said, 'You mean Hortense Manero?'

'Yes. Yes!' Mom said fiercely to Marianne. 'What's *her* racket? That's what I'd like to know? Who appointed her the guardian of public morality?'

'Uh . . . the President, I think.'

'Pah!' she said, or something like it; it took care of the President anyway. But she continued to look down at Marianne. And Marianne, her skirt fanned out around her, sat on the floor, cradling our son in her arms, and looked up at Mom blankly, bewildered. 'They all put themselves forward like little angels,' Mom said. 'Butter wouldn't melt in their mouths. You think they're not into somebody? You think they're not on the take? Seabury – he used to sit in that big Park Avenue office of his and the newsies on bicycles used to bring him his envelope wrapped in the *Tribune*.'

'Seabury?' I said. 'No!' I was shocked. He was one of my civic heroes – all the books described him as dead honest. I'd have thought she'd have loved the guy. This was a puzzlement, a disappointment. Even Marianne, who'd never heard of Seabury, blinked, and Charlie squirmed in her arms and he wasn't even two months old. 'Not Seabury, Ma,' I said.

'Yes,' she announced triumphantly. 'Seabury! You don't know about these people. Oh, they're all . . .' But in her passion, she left the sentence unfinished. She gave another dismissive sniff and marched out of the room into the kitchen.

Of course, my father's whining self-justifications and his subterranean rage, my mother's conspiracy theories and her fearful watching for signs of treachery – these things drove me crazy, but I couldn't get enough of them. I sat there on the sofa for a moment after Mom walked out, shaking my head at her paranoid nonsense, and yet wishing she'd stayed, wanting to hear more. I heard her turn the water on in the kitchen sink – that's what she did when she wanted to get away: drowned us all out with the hiss of the water. And I thought: Seabury? *Seabury?* He really was one of my role models. I mean, I knew it was La Guardia who'd actually cleaned the city up in the Thirties, and I loved the guy, sure, but he was a sweaty Wop-slash-Jew, all energy and uncouth doings: my mother hated that type. Seabury – Seabury was like the marble statue of Anglican Virtue standing behind him, bestowing the blessing of the western pieties on the brash new boy. It was he who gave his name to the hearings that busted the corrupt worker bees of the Tammany machine. I'd have thought Mom would have adored him, really. But newsies? Newsies hiding bribes in the *Trib*? She couldn't have made that up, I thought. Because I didn't know then what had been going on in that mind of hers. The mental stretches she'd had to make, the elaborate 'deductions' and workings-out – the fantasies, basically – she'd had to concoct in defense of her dead father. I didn't know anything about her life really. I thought she must just have gotten her facts confused.

I stood up and went into the kitchen to straighten her out – and also to bait her into some more of the familial craziness that was meat and drink to my lorn soul. She was vigorously working the brunch dishes under the faucet, her head bowed into the gray winter light that came through the casement window. The kitchen lights themselves were off, that was probably why she seemed so pale there and marbly. On the other hand, maybe she was shocked herself at having spoken her imagination like that, having slandered the good old judge with the secret glyphs and scenarios of this obsession I knew nothing of. In any case, the second I stepped onto the mock brickwork of the floor tiles, she raised that Litvak life mask to me and I spied such a hunted fear and so much sadness there that I clammed up and said nothing.

She went back to her dishes. 'Your friend,' she said, above the gurgle and hiss. 'What was her name, that little girl, that Agnes something?'

My lips parted stupidly. I was stunned. Here, I'd been snorkeling in sentiment about her for weeks and I was completely unprepared for the surge of feeling, the loss of equilibrium. First Seabury, now this; what a day. I could only murmur: 'Agnes Sole?'

'Agnes Sole,' she said into the sink, 'that's right.'

'You mean the one whose mother Dad was fucking?' No, I didn't say that, but the urge to tear the veil away was sudden, unexpected and powerful. Yet, again, Mom lifted her face to me – that face that had been imposed upon her and had then molded her into itself – and I hadn't the heart.

'She called me up the other day.'

'What?' More flutterings and pulsings, bewildering how strong. 'Agnes called you? How is she? What did she say?'

Mom shrugged, sniffed, rubbed her nose with a soapy knuckle – all to play it down, as she always did with momentous things. And the suspense, meanwhile, riveted me.

'Well, what did she . . . ?'

'We hardly talked at all,' Mom said. 'She just called to get your address. She said she wanted to write to you. She said she's been wanting to write to you for years.'

The letter didn't come for weeks. It was a period of intense excitement for me. Before Christmas, the Plunkitt Towers affair had been settled and now, in the New Year, Buckaroo Umberman had begun to invite me places. First, I got a printed card inviting me to a fundraiser. Given his favor to me, I could hardly refuse. Then came phone calls and I went to lunches and to club meetings and was introduced around. I had a very serious conversation with Donald Leamer, the president of Queens, about the outlook for development there, and Stu Freeman, Cohen's law partner and the party leader in the Brónx, regaled me one evening with rough stories about his cabby father. Buckaroo even introduced me to the Mayor once at a charity function in the Sheraton ballroom. 'Oh yes, Harry Bernard,' the Mayor enunciated in his precise way. 'I have heard many, many things about you. All of them good,' and then he laughed and all the people around him laughed loudly.

Such occurrences struck me as glamorous and valuable. They were inside experiences in places most people didn't get to go. I had a great drive to see such things, to *see* things in general. I felt very competitive about it. Movies, plays, art shows that my friends might have missed – these were coin of the realm to me. And other things, chance realities, these were even more important. I would walk along Fifth Avenue or Columbus or anywhere, hoping to spot a movie star or a former President or a car jumping the sidewalk to smash into a store window or, if I was very lucky, a gunfight or someone falling dead. It was New York, I was a New Yorker, and you could make these events into exciting anecdotes and put yourself forward and other New Yorkers could only try to outdo them with what they'd seen in the past. Out-of-town friends and suburbanites had never seen anything like it except on TV or in the army, and you could hold center stage with them for half an hour at a time. But, again, these sights were right in the open and momentary. The places Buckaroo took me to: many of them were closed rooms where even reporters were not invited, where men I recognized from the papers and the evening news chatted amiably together and used obscenities and laughed with smoke and whiskey fumes coming out of their mouths. These experiences were very valuable indeed.

Still I knew, unless you stumbled upon such scenes, that you had to somehow get involved in order to see them and that that meant paying a price in time and sinfulness. I knew that people who were envious of my experiences – my father, for instance – would be quick to say I was being corrupted. My intention was to be very careful, to walk and witness and deal, yes, but with radiant probity. Like Myers did. This was no easy thing; the game was afoot. Because I knew too that Buckaroo Umberman was trying to corrupt me in fact.

He did it laughingly, as if for sport. He told me he was doing it, as if that somehow made it all right. But I wasn't fooled, I knew he was out for blood. He was, I felt, fascinated by my honesty. It challenged him, it challenged his view of life, his sense of self. And he had, what's more, an instinct for the Inner Man. It made him laugh to see what a jerry-rigged job this outer Harry was. I, on the other hand, was completely deluded. I felt very strong. I felt I understood my Buckaroo, I recognized my id when I saw him and had been proof against him for years and years. Buckaroo would say, 'You sure you wanna be seen with me, Bernard? I'm drawing you into a life of corruption, ya know.' And I would wink at him arrogantly. I'd tell him, 'The angels will protect me, Buckaroo.'

He made his play finally in March over supper. That Immortal Supper, that will forever shine upon the 'inward eye which is the bliss of solitude.' We went to an Italian place on Mulberry Street. I do believe Umberman picked it because of its mob associations and its mob feeling – gaudily elegant blond wood walls; too many empty tables with white cloths marred by candle wax; abrupt waiters with meaningful glances who didn't depend on you for their jobs; quiet meetings, in the corners, of fat slobs in expensive suits: Buck was taunting me, see, with his sumptuous dishonesty. It was supposed to be dinner with Leamer, which already made it very important. But then, as we began dessert, Freeman dropped in too, and, seeing him, I took a strong gulp of my heavy wine. These three men – Leamer, Freeman, Umberman – they had enormous power here in the solar system's capital. Maybe most of the power, behind the scenes. I felt the great glamor of sitting with them in there, leaning into the candlelight to hear their lowered voices, with all the rest of the world excluded.

Leamer was a jovial, overweight man. He liked to refer to himself as the King of Queens. He kept saying, 'No, I shouldn't, I can't do this, stop me,' as he hovered over his tiramisu, hoisting forkfuls with one hand, holding his tie out of the whipped cream with the other. Freeman was cool and devilish: he cultivated the look with a mephisthophelean goatee. I'd heard he had a sign in his office that said 'Crime doesn't pay – not like politics.' He sat back against the wall and eyed me shrewdly over a glass of red wine.

Fat as he was, Buckaroo had hardly touched his dinner and ordered no dessert. He reclined on his groaning chair with his hands folded on his huge belly, his chins on his chest, all the heavy pouches of his face folding into that sleepy serpent look he got.

'Marsha Zimmerman. Very sick,' he said to no one. She was the city Tax Commission President.

'Cancer. Dying. A shame,' Leamer said, attacking his sponge cake again.

Frowning, drawing a long breath into his big frame, Buckaroo let it out with, 'Todd Winger: not up to the occasion.'

'Who's Winger?' I asked.

'Commission council,' said Freeman quietly. His witty gaze never left me.

Buckaroo again: 'Need a council in there who can run the Commission. For – what?'

'Year. Six months. How long can she last?' said Leamer.

'Then they can move him up to President,' Umberman said.

'Hizzoner can't sack Marsha when she's dying,' Freeman observed. 'It looks bad. "Sorry you're dying, kid – you're fired."'

Leamer laughed around a mouthful of cake.

'He needs a new council,' said Umberman, lifting one thick shoulder. 'He can run the Commission till Marsha goes, then they make him Commission President.'

'Todd they can fire,' Leamer laughed. 'Todd is screwed.'

Freeman shrugged, narrowing his eyes. 'I'll give him something in General Services. He'll be okay.'

All this they said as if gossiping, as if in casual conversation among themselves. That was the technique, and I was so slow, it took several moments of silence before I realized

what they were really offering. I looked up startled from my
crème brûlée. I looked from one to the other of them.

'Well, don't look at me, guys,' I said, smiling. 'I'm an
honest man.'

That got a big laugh. I was very proud of it. They all
ha-ha'd loudly and exchanged glances and leaned back in
their chairs with their teeth flashing bright. Umberman, his
body quivering, reached over and gave my arm a paternal
squeeze.

Freeman raised his wine glass to me as if in a toast. 'That,'
he said softly, 'is exactly what we want.'

That was a Tuesday night, the Immortal Supper, March 13th.
Two years exactly from the day, Leamer killed himself as his
father had before him. After the scandals did finally break
that winter and spring, he snatched a knife from the kitchen
cutlery drawer and drove it into his chest, puncturing his
heart. He was on the phone extension at the time, talking
to his therapist. A year after that, Freeman was sentenced to
twelve years in prison and led away in handcuffs. Umberman
only got six months because his heart was failing, but a good
chunk of his millions was eaten up in fines and legal fees. As
I say, these were important men.

At the office, Steve Weiss was mad with envy at my adven-
tures, which added to their value. I could hardly come down
the hall anymore without he would waylay and question me.
He wanted to make sure there were no new developments,
nothing he hadn't advised me on.

'It's a set-up,' he said excitedly when I told him about
the Immortal Supper. 'What, they're gonna take a guy,
a non-party regular, they're gonna make him President –
President? – of the Tax Commission, it's not gonna be a
set-up? It's Manero, they're scared shitless of her. Umberman
must have some little *meshigas* going on at the Commission,
he wants you to front the thing so the Feds'll stay away.'

I condescended to him, pretending to take him seriously,
which made him all the madder.

Myers' reaction to what was happening was harder to
judge. He must have known already that his little do-good

firm was too small to hold me. Was he envious too or genuinely concerned? As he was my father figure – and as my father was my father – I couldn't imagine he wasn't jealous, as my father was. Yet, if anything, there seemed a weight of sadness to his recitations now. They took on, at least in light of the guilt and arrogance I brought to them, the nature of talmudic instruction.

'The Tax Commission, the Tax Commission,' he said after the Immortal S. He deflated in his chair with a tired moan. His sparkling eyes dimmed as he sank again into his Encyclopedic Reverie. 'It's a small Commission, the President, six part-time commissioners, I don't know that much about it.'

I waited impatiently, silently listing my superior qualities. But when he began again, I listened with all due care.

'The story go-oes,' he chanted cantorly, tilting his head to one side, 'that the guys who assess the buil–dings . . . are all in the MacBride Democratic Club . . . and the hearing officers who hear the assessment appeals . . . and the lawyers who plead the cases . . . they're also all in the MacBride Democratic Club. Personally, I don't know this. But what they say is: the assessor guy goes out and bumps the client's building up to fifty thousand dollars in taxes. Then the client is steered to the lawyer guy who goes to the hearing guy at the Commission. Then the hearing guy drops the assessment to twenty thousand. So the lawyer guy gets a third of the client's savings for his fee which then he pumps back into the MacBride Democratic Club where it's divided among Umberman and the other parties involved. But this,' he repeated, swiveling until his moist, gentle smile was upon me, 'this, personally, I do not know.'

I, meanwhile, was full of hope and energy. I was happier at home, affectionate toward my wife, helpful with the baby and patient with him. I was sharp and quick and tough on the job. Things were good, things were happening in my life, opportunities were percolating. And every day, I looked for Agnes's letter.

She was, Agnes, in my mind at this point, a woman of pre–Raphaelite beauty. I was very unreasonable about it.

Sable cascades of hair I gave her, voluptuous lips, pillowy, maternal breasts against which she'd hold my weary head with a delicate and slender hand. I pictured a big shade tree of some sort up above us. I pictured her eyes as wells of wisdom and placidity. We were going to have an affair, the two of us, when her letter came, when we got back together. I wouldn't have said it outright, but I was virtually certain of it in my heart. Maybe a plane would crash into Marianne and the boy and maybe not, but it would all work out somehow with major, even salvific, ramifications. It had to: I was sure that this secret moral emptiness I felt was not my true destiny.

Finally, on the last day of March, the letter came. Marianne had left it on the hall table with the junk and the bills. It was in a cream envelope and addressed in purple ink in a fine feminine hand which seemed then and there to confirm my heart in its aspirations. There was no return address on it, but who else could it be from? I gathered it up inconspicuously in a handful with the rest. Maybe Marianne hadn't noticed it, I thought hopefully.

Now, our apartment was small, though elegant in its way with high ceilings and ornate molding and wainscot – a pre-war West Side place off Columbus. There was a cramped living room, the furniture huddled together under Marianne's potted plants, the odd rattle and teddy bear strewn on the dark rug. Our bedroom on one side was practically filled by our bed, and the nursery on the other was little more than a closet and packed tight with Charlie's crib. There was no getting away from anybody, that's my point. Charlie, with only a single good inhalation, could send his baby screams vibrating through every inch, even through the heavy doors. And he was screaming now. Shrieking from our bedroom, where Marianne had him. And when Marianne heard the front door close behind me, she was out like a shot, after me like a heat-seeking missile, just as I slipped the mail under my arm. 'Can you take him for a while?' she asked. With the kid over her shoulder wailing at full volume, and her hair in lank strands on her brow, and that look that you see only on new mothers and Save The Children ads.

'Sure,' I said, 'let me just go to the bathroom.'

'There's a letter for you,' she shouted over the clamor as I hurried away.

'Oh yeah?'

'From a woman, it looks like.'

'Oh boy. Hope she's childless.'

'Oh, shut up,' she said, but it got a smile out of her. She thought I was kidding.

Moments later, I had Charlie's screaming muted at least by the closed bathroom door. With my pants around my ankles for realism and my buttocks wedged in the chilly toilet ring, I sliced the envelope open with my thumb and drew out four sheets covered on both sides with the words of a woman I hadn't seen since our childhood, twenty years before.

Hi, Harry.

Remember me? I hope I have the right address — your mother gave me this one. So you're in New York now. God, the last time I thought about New York was after that terrible murder last summer in Queens. A man came into a house and said he was with the FBI, and then took out a gun and made everyone kneel in a line. Seven people altogether, three children, one of them a little four-year-old boy. The man just walked down the line behind them. He told each one in turn to hold still, and they did, and he shot them in the back of the head. Only one teenaged boy survived as a witness because he'd hidden under his bed in the next room. I remember thinking to myself: Why did they just kneel there and hold still like that? Why didn't they try to run or fight — or anything? I had a lot of fantasies about it, about how I would have run or wrestled the gun away from the guy and rescued everyone. And then I realized: Shit, that's just the way people think about the Holocaust, isn't it? I would have fought, I would have done something. I guess it's a way of denying that it could've happened to you. Even the way the story was reported kind of acted that process out. (Unfortunately, you can get the *Times* up here at the General Store so I started buying it again to follow the story.) The first day, it was big front page news, just the basic details. Then on the second day, it came out that the victims were Hispanic, illegal immigrants, so the story got smaller and was only in the second section – because so many white, middle-class editors and readers were saying: 'Oh, they were Hispanic, illegal, they weren't like me.' Then it developed that it was all some sort of Colombian drug thing or other and the story just shrank and shrank smaller and smaller, deeper and deeper inside the paper. You could almost hear this fading whisper of law-abiding *Times* readers everywhere saying, 'Not me, not me, they weren't like me, it couldn't have happened to me.' So the story finally just disappeared, poof. I don't even know if the police solved it, but then I stopped buying the paper after a while. I hate the fucking *Times*. Their shallow cultural sections make me crazy. I used to use them for kindling until Roland made me stop buying it – he said it made me too angry. But that story was interesting. It was just like when I was in Paris at the Rodin Museum about five years ago. This was my Grand Tour. I was still living in New York myself then, although out in Long Island City. Being an Ah-tist, you know. I even had a torn-up leather flight jacket I used to wear. My artist friends and I used to sit in this cafe between the warehouses under the 59th Street bridge talking Theory with a big T and making our eyes look sleepy and our underlips protrude. The trucks from the bread factory used to rumble by and we had to shout things like 'hermeneutics!' and 'anti-aesthetic!' over the noise. Of course, our work was more or less shit. Mine was all metal poles and guy wires, and I used to have to explain it by talking about reinventing positive space and neo-negativism and all that. Mostly, I think I spent my time gossiping about all those dirty bastards who got into the galleries with shit that was no better than my shit. Of course, I didn't care about the fame or the money, you understand – it was just the fame and the money I cared about. Anyway, I don't know if you remember my father at all, but he died about that time and left me some dough – a lot more than I'd expected – so I went to Europe: Italy and France. It was a pretty depressing trip. I was all by myself, first of all. I'd had this really ugly nympho phase about a year before and I'd only been off the tranquilizers for about six months, so I was being strictly celibate. Frankly, I'd have sewn myself up like a de Sade victim but I was afraid I'd have my period and explode. So there I was alone, and the idea was to hit the galleries and see the new Euro stuff and meet some in people, you know. But I figured I ought to at least go to the Vatican and the Uffizzi and so on first. So I wound up spending the entire trip standing in front of things like the Laocoon and Aphrodite of the Cnidians, the Michelangelos in Florence, the Nike in Paris — the Venus fucking de Milo, for God's sake. I'd wear my flight jacket and sort of slouch in front of the statues with this post-modern ironical smile on my face, but all the while I felt this despair seeping into me. My work was shit. Everyone's work after nineteen hundred was shit. The whole age was mediocre shit! Your typical artistic crisis. Very depressing. Anyway, by the time I got to the Rodin Museum, I was on cigarettes again and wondering where I could score some barbs. The museum is this beautiful eighteeth-century mansion on the Rue de Varenne, all grand stone but made featherweight by riddling it with huge French windows and fanlights. Inside, there are these big empty sunlit rooms with towering mirrors over sculpted mantelpieces and filigreed walls and glittering chandeliers and curving stairways with wrought iron railings — and Rodin's sculpture everywhere. In every room, you're surrounded by these tortuous bronze nudes with wracked planes and melting curves, and these really breathless exposures coming together in tidal couplings — and in my chaste condition too! My heart was in my shoes, my knickers were clinging. I wanted to fly home on the next plane and throw away every scrap of work I'd ever done. And outside, there was more: this gorgeous maze of hedges under this enormous aqua Paris sky with sculpture in the groves and on the pathways. And then the really great stuff was around in front: the *Thinker* — with the Dome of des Invalides in the background

– and the Balzac and the Burghers among these rose
bushes – and finally, the *Gates of Hell*. The *Gates of Hell*
is just unbelievable. I'd seen it before in Philadelphia but
it was nothing like seeing it here. Back in Phili, all I could
think of was the art school stuff I'd been swallowing.
You know: no base, the ambiguity of the sculptural
space, the overturning of narrative and so on. The
Gates are a very big deal when you're in art school.
One of my teachers called it the gateway to modernism,
but I think that's crap. People are always saying this or
that is where modernity began. Ever since Constantine
converted – that was the first use of the word in that
sense: it was *modernus* to be Christian and old-fashioned
to be pagan. So then you could just as easily say that
Titus's destruction of Jerusalem was what loosed the
Jewish cult of Christ from its ancient territorial moorings
and sent it into the wider world. See what I mean?
Then you could say, well, the misguided notion that
a revolt against Rome could succeed had its roots in
Modin with Matthias at the altar. Which could take
you back to Moses or Abraham. You might just as well
say the gates of modernity were between Eve's legs.
Did you know that Rodin spent hours and hours just
sketching pictures of pussy? No symbolism, no romance,
just dozens and dozens of pure pussy sketches: spread,
hairy, damp, blood-flecked, sperm-flecked, the genuine
article. Which, anyway, brings us back from Eve's legs
through the Arch of Titus to the *Gates of Hell*. So I
was standing in front of the *Gates of Hell* just exhausted
and horny and miserable. And it's this just unimaginably
great work: these two enormous bronze doors with
the three grim shades on top, imperious, mournful,
gesturing down into the pit, and the *Thinker* is brooding
over it all from the lintel and then all these tormented
figures are being shoveled by demons off the toprail into
Hell. The illusion of depth in the *Gates* is incredible and
there are at least a hundred bodies in there tangled up in
this kind of chaos of inner torture with the empty space
around them swirling like hellfire. And standing next to
me, looking at this, were this reedy British father and his

two kids, a girl of five, say, and a boy of maybe six. And they were very prim and proper, all dressed up, the man in a suit and the boy in this cute blue uniform with this adorable cap and the girl in a pleated navy dress. And the boy, very English, said, 'What is it, Deddy?' And the father, very precisely, launched into an explanation of how, you know, well, children, this is Hell where bad people go when they die – although they don't really, it's just a legend; we don't really know where people go when they die but this is one idea. So, of course, the kids are absolutely terrified. None of this reasonable explanation stuff for them. They're staring right into this nightmare and they're starting to feel pretty sure that this is exactly where people *do* go when they die. And their eyes are getting bigger and bigger. And the father, who knows he's blown it, is gnawing the perspiration off his stiff upper lip. And finally the boy asks hopefully: 'Do . . . children have to go there?' And the father wants to be honest so he says, well, yes, of course, they would, if they were bad, if it were real, which it isn't – you see? But this just gets him in deeper. The kids' eyes get even bigger, they're even more scared. And after a moment, the little girl figures, well, my brother's screwed but maybe I can save myself. And she blurts out: 'Ladies too?' And the father coughs and clears his throat and says, well, yes, there would be, uh, ladies too, yes. Well, the kids move a little closer to each other, still staring. And they lick their lips and swallow hard. And then, all at once, the boy has an inspiration. He studies the tortured figures for another second, and he brightens with hope. And he looks up at his father and he asks: 'But only the French, right?'

I remember I laughed out loud. I thought the father should've grabbed the kid by the lapels and screamed in his face, 'It's you, pal! It's all you! It's not the fucking French! It's not the fucking Jews! You're going to Hell! Bye!' That would've put hair on his chest. Back in my hotel, I sat up all night writing this insane diatribe which I called 'Yes, You!' all about how the post-modern search for positive artistic values was doomed to collapse as modernism had into its own inherent negativity because of its basic attempt to deny — what Rodin and Michelangelo and Praxiteles knew — that even otherness is experienced solely through the repetitive doomed realism of the decaying flesh. More theoretical bullshit. Thank Heavens I couldn't get it published. But while I was writing it: that's when I started to think about wood and the relationship between wood and flesh and so on, the way they both live and decay and betray imposed patterns. So I guess you could say that that — that moment at the *Gates of Hell* — was when I first started on the work I'm doing now. Or maybe it was when Titus sacked Jerusalem, I forget.

As you can tell from reading this, I'm alone too much up here. This winter especially. I had literally no one to talk to: that's why I run on and on. All I really meant this letter to say was: Hi, Harry. How are you? Hope your life's going okay, and so on. My life, by the way, is absolute shit . . .

Well, thank God, she didn't send her return address, I thought. At least I don't have to write back. Oh, well, yes, and I was disappointed too. She wasn't exactly the Eternal Feminine, was she, come to lead me on to salvation. More, I'd say, like a foul-mouthed drug-crazed nympho artist manque with enough problems to drag a man under the earth. I did wonder if she looked pretty, though, in that torn leather flight jacket of hers.

The baby had settled into steady, rhythmic shrieking in the battle zone beyond the bathroom door. I could hear Marianne's increasingly desperate and exasperated comfort murmurs. On top of that, my legs were beginning to fall asleep from the pressure of the toilet seat against my thighs. But scanning the rest of the letter I had spotted some passages that fired my interest — that is, they concerned me. Or they concerned my mother really. But in any case, along with the deadness creeping up my legs, I could feel that other deadness — that emotional deadness which I now knew was my reaction to a mental blow — seeping down from my brain to meet it. At the same time, that old devil Inner Man was saying something to the effect of: well, since you're sitting here anyway, perhaps a nice, satisfying bowel movement would relieve some of the intestinal pressure before dinner, no? That's what he was like.

So, to make a long story short, I bore down and read on:

. . . although I don't know why I should burden you with it. I don't know why I'm writing to you at all actually, it's just you've been in my thoughts a lot lately. But it must be important to me, because it sure as hell wasn't easy calling your mother to get your address. The last time I saw your mother was when she came to my house right after you went to camp that summer. Christ, you might not even know about that. It's true, though: She did. I never, never saw such a look of terror in my mother's eyes as when my father opened the door and found short, fat, steaming mad Mrs Bernard standing on the front step. Mom sent me upstairs to my room right away, and I just sat on the bed up there, staring at my David McCallum poster. And then the screaming started downstairs. Your mother did the screaming. My mother just let out these wild, tearful cries: 'Stop! Please!' And my father didn't say anything. It was an awful-sounding brawl. I finally got down on the floor and crawled under the bed (just like the boy who survived the murder, come to think of it). I lay there, softly singing 'Puff, The Magic Dragon', and holding my fingers in my ears. Even after I heard the door slam, I just lay there. I thought my mother would come up to fetch me or something. Put me to bed and sit on the edge of the bed and explain everything, you know. But she didn't come for the longest time, not until half an hour after my bedtime. And then she just tucked me in with this distracted air and floated off downstairs again. I could see she'd been crying. What on earth did your parents tell you when you got back? Did you wonder where I'd gone to so suddenly like that? Scarsdale, just in case it still matters to you. I really did want to write to you at the time, but you know how it is when you're a kid: you don't. And it was all so fast and traumatic. A

therapist once told me that that incident was the key to
my obsession with roots and the past, and my need for
bourgeois security, and my dependence on men, and my
recurring urinary infections, and a verruca I had to have
removed from the big toe on my right foot. Then she
sent me a bill for fifteen hundred dollars. But what I can't
figure out to his very day is how my father managed to
move us out of town in something less than ten days. For
a while, I remember, we had to live in an apartment, but
still it was incredible: ten days after your mother's visit,
we were gone. I remember the look on his face – even
though I didn't really know what was going on at the
time, I watched him in the days after your mother came,
and his cheeks were all sallow and sunken, his forehead
all moist and sickly. His eyes were the size of tennis balls;
they were practically bugging out with fear. It was like
he was running away from the Nazis, which I guess was
the general idea as far as he was concerned. And it took
months after we'd moved for that look to go away. Then
it became something else, something worse, harder to
define. Before we moved, he used to talk to my mother
with this sort of formal, wistful sweetness, the way an
old man talks to a pretty young girl before he pats her
on the head and sends her off to play with her friends.
But after that, he was just scrupulously polite to her
and I guess what you would call faintly sardonic. He
would look at her with this almost imperceptible smirk
at the corner of his mouth, this terrible knowing look. I
think for my father humanity was divided between the
Pitiful and the Unforgiveable. I was always the former
to him: he was always gentle with me – and I adored
him anyway, which I think he needed from people. But
after we moved, my mother, she was in the latter camp
definitely. Not that he ever said anything, not that I
heard. There was never any shouting or growling or
even sniping remarks that I heard. It was just that
look, that awful knowing. And it was unshakeable,
unchangeable. My mother did everything she could. I
mean, before we moved, she'd had a life. She was always
a very dedicated housewife – she knew my father was old

world and demanded that of her – but she also had some kind of woman's club she belonged to and she went into the city to see shows and did volunteer work at this special teaching program and so on. But after we moved: nothing. Just the house. Cleaning the house. Fanatically. She cleaned and cleaned that place until it was practically transparent. Scrubbed the walls, the floors, down on her knees with a sponge on the floors half the time. And she made these elaborate meals and set them out on these beautiful table settings with linen edged with tatting she'd made herself. She also knitted bedspreads, made needlework pillows, lace antimacassars, and did her own upholstery. I have nothing against any of that, mind you, but there was a sort of fever to it. She worked at it so desperately. It ate lines into her face. It made her old. And the house – it was like living in some Eastern European cottage somewhere, that's what she turned it into. And my father never changed anyway. He just kept looking at her: she was one of the Unforgiveable Ones; 'Now I know,' – that was the look. When my mother finally took me and moved out, he still hadn't said anything, but he might just as well have stood in the doorway pointing us sternly into the Beyond like in one of those Victorian illustrations: 'A Daughter's Disgrace.' My therapist – a different therapist – once told me that I'd never rebelled when I was a teenager because I thought my parents had already suffered too much. That's why I was such a mouse when I finally went off to art school, and a virgin besides. Maybe that's true (it better be, it fucking cost enough!). But after we moved, things were actually better, I thought. We moved to Mahopac up in Putnam, a nice little exurban-type town with a big lake and a little mall to hang out in. And my mother did some temp work and finally got a job in a real estate office and my father always sent us money, and always let me visit him when I wanted to. It wasn't all that terrible really. Still, all my therapists, they always light up like lightbulbs when I tell them about you and this whole story. Roland, also: he's always saying it's the cause of all my obsessions and craziness. The beginning of the modern Agnes. You're my *Gates of Hell*, Harry.

Roland is my husband, by the way. Or he was. I guess he still is technically, but he left me this winter, just after New Year's. It was exactly right of him too: I'd gotten myself on the tranks again and it was getting dangerous for the baby. But anyway, just so you know: I'm Agnes Mallory now.

10

Five months later, I was in my office at the Tax Commission when my old pal Buckaroo Umberman waddled in.

'Hey!' I said, looking up from my files. 'The Buckster!'

He made a comical gesture: stopped short just within the doorway with both of his arms upraised. Indicating my office, or, that is, the ailing president's: the vast oaken presidential desk, the homey sofa, the broad band of glass behind me which showed both the famous skyline to the north and the western view across the river into Jersey. His effect was pseudo-biblical: Moses looking over Jordan; 'There is the land.' Except Buckaroo was so fat and had features like a wax eagle that had melted, and was huffing after his walk from the elevator, his skin filmy with excretions.

'Life,' he said gruffly, 'has meaning!' I grinned. He let his hands collapse to his belly with a slap and held them there as if to contain himself. Wheezing and snuffling with the effort, he crossed the tan carpet to the western window, presenting me with his visionary profile as he gazed out dramatically. 'You have no money, no success, no recognition – what? Life is fraught, am I right? Death looms large, philosophical questions make us ponder. Morality – it's impossible, this one against that one, who can figure it out? Suddenly: poof! A man is somebody. He has some money, some respect. Suddenly – he understands all.' He glanced over at me where I swiveled and chuckled in my high leather throne. He nodded with mock solemnity. 'There is wisdom throughout the land, correct? Life works? God exists – or not, who cares? My point is: the facts can be dealt with. We take our old friends out to dinner. We explain to them in their confusion. "It's just a matter of taking life by the cohones," we say. "It's just a matter of hard work and decision-making and inner strength." You, Harry Bernard, are a happy man.'

'Ecstatic, Buck. I got thirty-two letters demanding a review of phase-in mechanisms and no council to pass them to. I'm thrilled.'

He hoisted his shoulders. 'Give 'em to clerical. The important thing is: you talk to the Mayor, he puts his hand on your shoulder, you meet with commissioners, men kiss your ass, girls want to suck your dick. Creation wasn't such a bad idea after all.'

'Let's not get carried away. It's a small Commission. Practically a backwater.'

'Oh, this, that. You're thirty years old.' He reached down and patted my cheek with a damp palm. 'It's a big suck of the tit.'

He elephant-walked over to the sofa and I watched his vast stern, smiling, shaking my head. He was still taunting me, you see, for my past heroics and my earnestness even now. But he was communicating too, and I understood the truth of what he said. Even Marianne – lifter-of-the-veils-of-Maya by avocation – had recently snuggled naked against me in our bed, her pupils dilated, her nipples hard, her loins in action, and whispered with appealing hoarseness and unnerving honesty: 'It turns me on, you know, that you have power.' This is a very grand thing to hear from your wife, despite the pressures. It was almost enough to make the point. But the *Times* had also picked me out in an editorial as an 'adornment to the administration.' They'd recommended that the Mayor move me 'closer to the centers of power with all deliberate speed.' Anyone can imagine my daydreams at this point and my sense of possibility as well; my overall sense of well-being.

But these other revelations – these insights into the mutability of the moral universe, its relativity as per the discourse of the Buckaroo – these were secrets, secrets of success. They were not for the frustrated or for the judgemental. They were not for the wife either. In fact, with remnants of my old fastidiousness, I had hardly acknowledged them to myself. So it was a relief to hear it from the Buck on these occasional visits of his, all as easy and acceptable as that. It did endear him to me. When he sank down onto my sofa – looking something like a cement truck with a couple of flats – I confess I felt a genuine warmth of affection for him.

'So?' he said, stretching his arms along the sofa back, circling one hand. 'You're still an honest man?'

I nodded. 'Yeah, I'm still an honest man.'

Both his thick forearms lifted and fell. 'So the Buckaroo's not so bad, after all,' he said.

Now Myers, on the other hand, told me a story. Took me to lunch for it – a rare enough event to carry some weight in itself. We went to a Chinese place he favored. It was hidden away in a Pearl Street basement and the government types avoided it, so this too was portentous.

Fired up as I was, though, I had to wait for his purposes to be made manifest. Toying with my plastic chopsticks, smiling shrewdly as best I could. There was no use expecting Myers to talk while he was eating: Suprisingly, the man was one of the most disgusting and voracious eaters I've ever seen. It was the outlet in his gentle Jewish soul for all the demonic powers. He shoveled it in. Tie tucked in his shirt front, napkin over that and tucked into his collar. He worked the sticks like a crank and made sucking noises like a straw at the bottom of a milkshake while noodles and shrimp tails and broccoli spears shot and slithered over his face into the hole. Like a film of a man vomiting shown in reverse. Then, his plate shiny and clean, he sat back as from a job well done and sipped from his water glass – his kidneys couldn't deal with Chinese tea. And he said mildly: 'Hortense Manero. You know Hortense Manero?'

'Sure,' I said. 'Federal prosecutor. Sure.' I picked at my chicken bits with the chopsticks; I always ate very delicately around him, hoping he'd catch on.

'Funny story,' said Myers. 'Remember – oh, about a year ago – the Barco killings in Queens? Guy came in said he was an FBI agent . . .'

'Made the people kneel down . . .' I said softly.

He yanked his napkin free and daubed his chin with it. 'Drug killing, right, terrible, seven people shot dead.'

I whispered: 'Yes.'

Well, this sort of thing happens, of course. You hear a word for the first time and the next day it turns up in a crossword puzzle and so on. Synchronicity; no call for panic. It had been months since Agnes's letter, and it was a fairly spectacular case, still unsolved, anyone might have mentioned it. But for all that, I met this introduction of Myers' with your basic thrill of superstitious terror. I was given to superstition about the letter anyway because its effects on me were both unexamined and profound. My father's relationship with Evelyn Sole – I'd fretted plenty over that now and then through the decades. But my suspicions about my mother's actions lo those twenty years ago, these were unacknowledged, so their confirmation in the letter – and the jolt of that confirmation – were also subterranean events. When Myers mentioned the killings – shot that bridge from the silent imagination to our rollicking, urgent and political world – it was as if I'd dreamed about a specter who handed me a golden key, and then woke to find the key clutched in my hand. I shuddered. I got goose flesh on my arms.

'The FBI part, though, was apparently on the bothersome side,' Myers said. 'To the investigators. They thought it might have accounted for why the Barcos let the killer in. Because they were already afraid, the Barcos, they were taking precautions. So, you know, the investigators were worried the killers might have had actual credentials of some kind. It might also,' he went on in a speculative tone, 'have accounted for why they were so obedient. You know, the killer ordered them to kneel down . . .'

'Yes. Yes, I know.'

'Anyway, Joey Turpentine. He's this guy, this informant. Probably a killer, should be in prison two, three times already, consecutive life terms. Bu-ut – the FBI – he tells the FBI he can get them this, get them that, go undercover: they let him out and he works for them. The question is: who else does he work for? Because recently, he's been making some important connections with the Colombians. In all events, Miss Prosecutor Manero, she should live and be well, invites him in for a chat because she's working with him on some *fakakta* drug corruption thing. "Joey, what can

you tell me about the Barco killings?" she says. Joey smiles –
this is what I heard – he gets out of his chair. He walks to
her desk and there are newspapers all over it: *Times, Newsday,
Post, News*. He picks the newspapers up one after another.
Drops them down. He says, "You see the Barco killings?
Does anyone care about the Barco killings? You solve the
Barco killings, you get, what? One headline, two headlines."
He opens the papers. He starts pointing to stories, like, here,
here and here. "Leamer," he says to her. "Freeman," he says.
"Umberman. The Mayor. You're anti-corruption, Hortense,"
he says. "Stick with corruption. Me – I can get you Buckeroo
Umberman. Umberman – he can get you everybody else."
And Hortense, God love her, Hortense says,' – and here he
suppressed a laugh to signal the punchline – "'All right. That
makes sense. So get me Umberman.'" Myers sipped his water.
He shook his head. 'That makes sense,' he repeated, relishing
the humor of it.

After I'd managed to wrestle my eyeballs back into their
sockets, I found myself babbling, 'Well, I don't know what
Umberman's up to. The assessors are over at the Board of
Assessment. The hearing officers were all in place before I
got there. I hear some cases, I see some files, but half the
time I'm in meetings. I'm swamped under piddling review
requests. I mean, until the president dies, I don't even have
any real power.'

'A funny story,' said Myers, ignoring me. He tilted
his head sleepily to one side. Closed his eyes, lifted his
shoulders, smiled his moist, rabbinical smile. 'I thought you'd
enjoy it.'

It was like a bout of hypochondria for the next week or so,
that sort of waffling panic. Is it cancer or just a mole? Was I
in jeopardy from the Feds or was I not? Did I know anything?
Well, what? That some assessments were ridiculously low?
That some were unnecessarily high and then knocked down
instantly while the lawyers from the MacBride Club took
their fees? What was an assessment but a matter of informed
opinion anyway? And besides, I might not have even noticed
these things. I was scrupulously honest myself, and I had lots
of plans for reforms once I actually took the reins. I was really

in the clear – or was I? Cold sweats in dead of night were
followed by unearned, illogical waves of relief. Yet relief won
out in the end. The panic was just worn away by inaction,
which I suppose is how hypochondriacs finally die.

Nonetheless, when Agnes's second letter arrived a few
weeks later at the start of my August vacation, I was prepared
to read it almost as oracular. What new stage of my life would
begin with this, pray tell?

Dear Harry,
I waited till I was feeling a little better before writing
you again. I didn't want to leave you with the impression
I was in despair or anything. I'm not in despair – or if
I am, I don't want to leave you with that impression.
The winter is just hard up here, that's all. Everyone shut
up in their houses, no one visiting, no one to talk to.
This summer has been better. I can get out and swim
in the river in the morning before going to work and
in the afternoons I can walk in the woods looking for
logs to haul back to my studio. I am back waitressing
part-time at *Fitzgerald's* at night too, so I get to see the
old restaurant gang again, or what's left of them. And
I'm pretty much off the tranquilizers, so the whole
situation is a lot healthier. If I can stay clean for six
months, Roland will let me have the baby as much as
I want. Frankly, I'm not sure how I feel about that after
what happened. That is, I'm desperate to see her, but
also scared. Fucking terrified is more like it. And then
there's my work, which pretty much obsesses me. I guess
I don't know how I feel exactly. I keep thinking about
how simple and great everything seemed in the old days.
When I first met Roland, the *Fitzgerald's* gang used to
come over all the time in the mornings and afternoons.
Everyone would bring some vegetables or something
and I'd make a huge tureen of soup and some loaves of
fresh bread and just leave everything out on the wood
stove for them. They used to call me Ma Sole for a
joke, as in Oh Ma Sole, Rock Ma Sole and so on.
I'd go into my studio and chisel away, but keep the
door open so I could hear them in the living room,

talking and laughing, eating soup, Roland noodling the guitar, Jack on the saxophone or whatever. Roland played at *Fitzgerald's*, that's how I met him. He sang there every Friday and Saturday night, these sensitive folk-rock songs, very early-Seventies. There's a lot of that up here — I think this is where the Sixties came to die. Anyway, here was this lanky six-foot-four guy in jeans and cowboy boots with blond hair down to his shoulders and this cute Mr WASP face. I used to hang around the restaurant late pretending to clean up just so we could have a beer together at the bar and talk when everyone else was gone. Finally, one night, he set his empty glass down on the counter, looked across the bar at me, cleared his hair off his forehead, smiled his Pepsodent, *goyische* smile and said, 'So — are we gonna do this or what?' That was it. It was love.

I think those were actually the best days of my life: after he moved in and when his friends would come by and I would work and they would play and compose. I even had work showing in a gallery then — not a gallery, just a crafts shop off Route 12, but Lily, the woman who ran it, put a few of my pieces in with the handmade potholders and coat pegs and mailbox windmills etc. And she did sell a piece of mine from time to time. And people were always coming up from New York to ski or fish and what-not so at least I had the illusion of gaining a wider audience. Of course, when my really big chance came, I fucked it up completely in typical self-destructive fashion. This was about two years ago — almost exactly two years ago now. This woman, this New York gallery owner, had been spending the summers here and she'd seen some of my pieces and mentioned to Lily that she wanted to see more. So I got very excited. I started working away like a madwoman trying to make enough good new stuff to show. And, at the same time, around May, I got pregnant. Well, I was sick as a dog. And crazy: there were so many hormones coursing through me I looked like Cruella De Vil in that red-eyed close-up just before she drives off the cliff. My schedule was: work, puke my guts out, scream at Roland, cry, then puke my guts out again, then go back to work. I don't usually use maquettes but I was making them then just so I could twist their fucking heads off, that's how I felt. And after this long period when I'd really been feeling good about my work, everything I did started to look like shit to me again. And summer was coming and the Gallery Woman was coming and . . . yaaagh! So just about the middle of June, I got this idea, this inspiration. I had this gorgeous piece of spalted pine I'd found in the forest. It had these wonderful black lines running through it, and it was just at the edge of decay, so soft you could almost gouge it with your hands. I saw this gesture in it, this striving gesture, like a monkey reaching itself into existence out of the core of a tree, and I saw a face, a woman's face, where the monkey's face would be. The wood had only had a couple of years to dry, I knew it wasn't ready, but (with just a brief pause to puke my guts out), I locked myself in my studio and set to work on it. No chainsaw, no compressor – the wood was too fragile. It was just me and the gouge and the mallet whacking away. And a week went by and the thing came free of the wood – perfectly. And another week went by and it was beautiful. Roland and his friends were wandering in from the living room to watch me go. I was almost finished, I was down to the three milimeter chisel, doing detail work. And, all of a sudden . . . I hit worms. I shaved a strip away and found this inch-wide medallion of rot right at the base of the monkey's left breast, and these thick, white hideous grubs came squiggling out of it spilling onto the floor. Instantly, I puked my guts out. I mean, I'd known the wood was spalted, I'd known it was too wet – the whole thing was totally my own fault – but fuck that shit: what was I going to do now? So I thought: All right, I've still got some room to maneuver. I'll dig out the rot, plug it, shape the thing down a little, maybe the bad stuff doesn't go so deep. So I did that – a few hours' work. And I was very lucky – it wasn't deep at all. I didn't even need a plug. I worked the contours down past it. Even I could hardly tell the difference. When I was finally finished, I relaxed on the sofa weeping and retching, and Roland sprayed the piece for me to kill any grubs that were left inside. Then, for the next two days I rubbed varnish on it, layer after layer. Then I painted it. Then I varnished it again. I figured: Any of the little shits that are left are sealed in there for good. Die, you bastards! And that was it. A month went by. As promised, Gallery Woman came to Lily's crafts place. Thin as a spindle, wearing three hundred dollars worth of khaki from Banana Republic. Dropping her g's and pretending to be a human bein' because she was out in the country with us folks. But, for all that, as Lily pointed out, she was at least original enough to be sniffing around outside the city – and looking at wood too, which was still very *outre* – so we had some hope. Her husband saw the monkey first – I'm told; I wasn't there. Hey, look at this, hon, he says. She looks up and stops in her tracks. Lily said she could see the thoughts running through her mind: Whoa! Shit! Talent! Art! Yes, but is it . . . *in*? Can I put words to it that give it a cachet? Fresh . . . no, no . . . radical innocence – maybe . . . a radical retro look at feminist evolution . . . yes, that might fly . . . and the fact that it's heartbreakingly gorgeous that could be a . . . a . . . an ironic post-modern parody of the concept of Beauty . . . Yes! And all the while, she had started moving closer and closer to the work. Circling it, dodging her head this way and that, eyeing it from this angle, that angle, until finally, she was right up close to it, her nose almost touching it – because the wood does that, that soft wood is so beautiful it's like flesh, you want to taste it and stroke it and practically fuck it, it looks so good. So she was right there, right in front of it. And just under the left breast, she slowly became aware of a movement. What's that? Her eyes shifted. A fleck of dust seemed to stir on the surface of the wood. And then there was another fleck. Sawdust – there was a little circle of sawdust gathering there as if by magic. It got thicker. A pinch of it sprinkled to the floor. Gallery Woman followed it down, open-mouthed – then she looked up again . . .

just in time to see the fattest, ugliest, whitest, slimiest grub of a worm writhing and struggling out from inside the sculpture. Her high-pitched scream — her screams, because she screamed again and again, her body rigid, her hands spasming in front of her — could be heard, I'm told, at the campground about five miles up the river. Even I had to laugh when Lily told me. Of course, then I wept. Then I screamed at Roland and puked my guts out . . .

This letter came on the Saturday before we left for the Berkshires. The cream envelope again, no return address. That annoyed me a little. That and all the references to people I didn't know, events I hadn't heard of. The point was: she didn't need me to understand. She didn't want me to write back to her. She wasn't even writing to me really. She was writing to the Idea of Me. She was writing to herself. I was sure of this because I'd been planning to have an affair with the Idea of Her before her first letter came; I knew how she felt. But it annoyed me anyway.

The letter arrived while I was at home, and I was glad of that: Marianne never had to see it. She'd been her usual airy-fairy self, all sensitive and accepting, when I'd declined to show her the last one. 'You don't have to explain yourself,' she said firmly. 'There are some relationships that are just private, that's all.' Yeah, but I'm no idiot, I knew I couldn't push it too far. Still, and to my own surprise, I found I did want to keep Agnes private. I'd never told anyone about her really. My first lover, Kate, I told her, but no one after that. I just felt somehow it wasn't anybody's business but mine.

So, also, I had to control my curiosity. I didn't want to read the letter this time until I could get off somewhere by myself, and this was tough to do on the weekends. There was Charlie, first of all. I had to play around with him all morning. He was crawling now and smiling with his round, rosy cherub's face and just that little token of humanity had changed everything for me with him. I'd discovered suddenly that I adored him. I thought about him all the time, took time off to buy him presents, blocks, busy boxes, fuzzy blue outfits with bears and bunnies on them. I couldn't hug the guy tight enough,

I loved him so much. Of course, he was a bore to actually be with for any extended period of time, but I could overlook even that for love and I spent most Saturday mornings with him when I could. Then, when he went down for his nap, I seized the opportunity to ravish the mystic Missus, toward whom I'd also been feeling very affectionate of late – especially this last anxious week when terror of Manero's corruption investigation had made me sentimental and she and Charlie seemed like the only really good, clean things about my life.

So it was around three in the afternoon of that hot, thick, gray, sooty day before I finally went out on the pretext of buying a novel for the trip. Instead, I stopped into the Greek diner on Amsterdam and plonked myself down at the far end of the counter and started to read the letter there.

Before I was this far, about halfway through, I had noticed several points, at least three points. One: the postmark on the letter was Gaysville, Vermont. I hadn't noticed that the first time. I hadn't cared the first time where she was. But now I saw it and I knew I could find her if I wanted to. How big could Gaysville be? Two: I was beginning to remember her. That is, when I read the first letter, it was so at odds with my fantasy that I was repulsed by it. But now it came to me: she'd never been the sort of girl I'd been attracted to particularly. She'd always been weird. Troubled, deep, crazy. If I kept that in mind, I found I recognized something – I really did recognize something I remembered, something I'd been connected to – in this letter, in her voice. Three: She was falling apart. Mentally, I mean. I could see it coming a mile away. People who are really in trouble are always telling you that a new day has dawned. Spring has sprung, they've had a revelation, they're much better now. It's a bad sign, hope. Healthy, normal people complain constantly.

So she was writing to me because she was slowly falling into desperate trouble. And the strange thing is, this made me feel afraid – for myself, for what I sensed, what I already *knew*, was happening to me. I'm not sure how much of that was the superstitious nonsense again, the stupid oracle business and so on. But I could not somehow entirely separate myself from the poor unhappy woman who wrote these letters. And that made me wonder also, seeing that I could probably find her, seeing that I felt connected to her, and seeing that she was coming apart at the seams, what, if anything, I was supposed to do about it.

What, if anything, did she want from me?

That was the beginning of what I sometimes ever-so-wittily call the Pregnant Pause. A really bad period I had most of the time I was pregnant. I hardly did any work at all, none at all really. I'd decided the worm incident was a metaphor, some kind of sign: there was rot at the heart of my work, you know, the whole concept was misguided. This drove Roland absolutely up the wall. He used to come home sometimes – he was getting more gigs now, and he was doing some studio work for a friend down in Boston – and he used to come home and find me sitting in a chair by the window, smoking a cigarette, drinking a beer. And he'd just go ker-azy. He even got down on his knees once: grabbed my arms, gave me his sincere WASP gaze. Please, Agnes, stop smoking, stop drinking, you're going to hurt the baby. Lucky I didn't tell him I was taking pills again or he'd probably have left me right then and there. Taken the fetus away and brought it to term himself. Why don't you just try to work, Agnes? he'd say. The things you make are so beautiful. We had our first real screaming fight that winter. I told him: that's exactly what's rotten, the beauty of my work. I said, the whole idea of beauty has been the central perceptual ideal of a civilization that has tortured and oppressed and slaughtered my people from its inception. You can't separate those things. The project of creating beauty was inseparable from the project of destroying what they saw as ugliness. Which, more often than not, was represented by the Jews. The Renaissance *was* the Holocaust, I said; they were ultimately the same thing, one inherent in the other. Praxiteles is the same fucking guy who marched my sister to the river side. My father's daughter, Lena. Six years old, clutching her dolly. Shivering in her nightgown. Rodin put the pistol to her head and pulled the trigger and shattered her face and splattered her childish brains. And six million others like her. Six million! A third of all my tribe. If I'm silent it's my father's silence – thus I railed at poor Roland. Because my father *knew*, he was *there*. He knew what the beauty and the ideals and the fantasies of western civilization had been trying all those centuries to suppress. So Roland sort of shrugged and said: So don't make beautiful things. No one cares about that anymore. Isn't that what all the artists are saying now? (I had told him about Joseph Beuys making 'ugly' art as a reaction to Auschwitz.) And that set me really going at him: They're wrong! They've got it all wrong! Beauty *is* beautiful, beauty *is* truth, it's the only thing that matters – that's the whole problem – there wouldn't be a problem if that weren't true! Anyway, what's the fucking difference? Whatever you make, whatever you say – ugly, beautiful, philosophical, political – you suppress the other thing, the silent, invisible thing that you didn't say, that you didn't make. That's the first principle of the Jewish religion: Thou shalt make no graven images. Thou shalt make no graven images, Roland, because the minute you do, you destroy the part of the truth that's unmade, that's suppressed! (You have to picture this pregnant woman in an *I LoVermont* sweatshirt pacing up and down with a cigarette in one hand and a beer in the other, reciting these things to a wondering six-foot-four son-of-a-horse-breeder who's sitting in a beanbag chair with a guitar in his lap, staring at her, open-mouthed, shaking his head.) No graven images, he said finally. Doesn't that make it kind of tough to be a sculptor? Which was when I started screaming. Screaming, crying. I stood in the middle of the floor jerking my hands up and down so hard the beer foamed up out of the bottle and flew all over the place. That's the problem with you people! I screamed. Whenever you're confronted with the great Jewish truths, you have to negate them to preserve your wretched world view. Our insights drive you mad, you go mad in huge masses. How else can you explain Jung and the atom bomb! And Christianity! And western fucking civilization! I think

every brilliant Jewish guy must be followed around
by this humpbacked gentile Igor. And the Jewish guy
says, 'Love Thy Neighbor.' And the goy says, 'Yeah,
and let's build huge churches and not let anyone have
sex!' And the Jewish guy says, '$E=MC^2$!' And Igor says:
'KABOOOM!' I want to carve my father's silence into
the tree of life, Roland. And you just *sit* there? With that
face? With those boots? Look at those boots! (A piece
of advice, Harry: Never get pregnant. It makes you
absolutely insane.) Even Roland, the sweetest, calmest
human being on earth, started to yell at me. You want
to carve your father's silence into the tree of life, go on
ahead and do it, he said; I mean, just do something, all
right? cause you're driving me up the wall. And I drew
myself up to my full five foot six and said, 'I can't do
it. I haven't suffered enough.' Well, you're working on
it, he said, and stomped out, boots, face and all.

  Shit. Here I meant to write you such an upbeat letter
and show you how much happier I am, and all I'm doing
is picking over the bones of my poor, dead marriage
again. Again and again and again. Over and over and
over. And it's not even so bad now really. I really am
happier now than I was before, last winter. I really do
think I'm pulling out of the gloom anyway. I'm certainly
working hard. Anyway, I'm glad that summer's here.
Take care of yourself, Harry.

  Love,
  Agnes.

11

'Come,' said Buckaroo Umberman one evening that September. 'Come fuck with me.'

This was in a little Thai place, right at the point where Chinatown had begun to infiltrate and Little Italy begun to decay. It was an isolated joint on an island at the tip of an asphalt playground; you could see the black guys playing B-ball in the night through the front window. We'd been there for hours – hours and hours – drinking Thai beer first and then wine with the spicy food, and now bourbon. Buck and me, an ambitious mayoral aide named Alvin, and an Influential Chicago Guy named Frank Stain. Younger men on the make, the two others and I, letting Umberman hold court and philosophize. This of course he did at length and we'd been treated throughout the evening to a choice selection of sociological Umbermanisms.

On African-Americans: 'What are they complaining about? Slavery, slavery, you made us slaves, this, that. Christ, if it weren't for slavery, they'd still be in Ethiopia saying, "Thank you for the grain of rice, Mr Relief-man."'

On Germans: 'The bacteria of the western world. Why d'you think they call 'em germ-men? Lookit: who ate the body of Rome? Who caused the cancer of Europe? Every time. Read your history. The Berlin Wall should have a quarantine sign on it.'

On immigrants in general and Slavic taxi drivers in particular. 'They come here. Why do they come here? To be free, to be Americans, only they don't want America to be like America, they want it to be like their country, which is what they're trying to get away from. I'm in a cab, the guy, the hack, is from Russia, he can't get through Times Square 'cause there's a demonstration. He shakes his head, "Too many demonstrations in dees country," he says. "Too much freedom." I mean, fuck you, go home.'

There were also Hispanics, who didn't want us to teach them English so we wouldn't 'oppress them out of being ignorant.' And Those Who Expressed Empathy for the Muslim World, when it was 'An entire culture founded on the principle of slaughtering everyone who doesn't agree with you.'

These little tirades, which we mocked, which we disputed, which we waved off, bound us to him because they liberated the mutterings of our own hearts – notions we didn't really believe but which had been so long imprisoned by the tyranny of liberal decency that they had begun to seem like secret truths. He was our id, like I said; or maybe he was our Miltonic Satan, or the B-side of Plato's *Republic*, or maybe just a fat, sweaty, more or less canny New York pol who, from mere boredom or for sheer glee, had offered us a peek up the hot nookie of the city system and now drew us in for the rest of the show. What I thought about him depended on my alcohol intake, and I'd had a lot that night. And now, when we were all feeling warm and at one and in-the-know, he lifted up his hands in beatification, and said, 'Come. Come fuck with me.'

This was to me in particular. Alvin and Frank Stain were laughing in their sleeves and seemed already to know the drill.

'Hey,' I said, 'you're a cute guy, Buckster-man, but pussy is my beat.'

There was much hilarity at this and Alvin shook his head at the noodle-stained tablecloth, repeating it, 'Pussy is my beat. Pussy is my beat.'

'I love him,' Buckaroo told the others. 'I love him.'

I looked from one to the next to the next, smiling stupidly. 'What,' I said. 'What?'

We piled into the Tax Commission President's Cadillac. Alvin drove, we all smoked cigars, we all laughed very loudly and kept our windows nearly shut. It seemed to

us – to me, I know, anyway – that there was something
wonderful, something terrific and exciting and exclusive –
elect – about the fact that the government car was crowded
with our sprawled limbs and rollicking with hardy-hars, that
it was hot and thick with stinky smoke and the smell of
whiskey. The rest of the city – the country – outside that
car, just couldn't get the half of it.

Out we piled then onto a ritzy block which I saw for only
a moment. An east Fifties cul-de-sac between First and the
river, brick towers with entrances back from the road. Into
one of these we walked, Buck with his chest thrust out and
his cigar nestled in the moist circle of his mouth, the rest
of us following after him like ducklings, chomping our own
cigars or jerking them up from our sides for quick puffs like
movie criminals. Right past the doorman, who only glanced
up and then glanced away; pooling together in the elevator
which was dark with the doors closed, and soft and velvety
with the paisleyed mirrors on the ceiling above.

'So?' I said.

The others faced the door and watched the light moving
behind the numbers and stood like Buck: erect; tin soldiers.

There were four girls but only two bedrooms. Alvin and I
sat out in the living room while Buck and Frank Stain took a
woman each behind closed doors. The two other girls poured
us champagne from a rolling bar and we paired off and sat at
opposite ends of the long room. Alvin nestled with his girl in
the loveseat over by the door, and I could see them, almost
silhouettes, breathing over their glasses into one another's
faces. Juliet and I sat more chastely on the sofa by the garden
windows, I backed up against one arm, she leaning casually
against the other.

She was pretty, Juliet, and young. A little fleshy maybe
at the thighs and cheeks but it was like baby fat and made
her seem even younger. So did her makeup: too much
makeup, like a kid would put on, so that her eyes seemed
to turn up at the corners and the whites glistened painfully.
She was wearing a very short skirt and a halter-top, her
middle bare. Her skin was very white; the word 'creamy'
came to mind. To protect myself, I concentrated mostly

on her face, which was pert and innocent under bobbed black hair.

'Well,' I said ironically – more ironical than I felt – waving my drink around drunkenly – more drunken than I was – 'nice place you have here. Or something.'

She laughed. 'Yeah, it is really nice. I just love it.'

We both looked across the room, for lack of anything better to do, and, yep, it was nice all right. Half moons of low-watt light playing on French poster art and the framed covers of Weimar sheet music. Colorless modern furniture draped with knitted afghans and tasseled shawls for style. A wooden floor with ovals of rich-looking white shag rug here and there. Homey, hip, youthful; nice. Only now, at the far wall, Alvin and his girl were leaning toward each other, for a tentative kiss first and then a longer one. I looked back at Juliet and we both shrugged and laughed.

'Listen, uh . . .' I said, and I went into a sort of bashful, ear-tugging, averted-eye routine which I thought I was pretty good at. 'I don't want to throw a wrench in the works or anything, but I'm not going to do this, okay?'

'Sure. Okay,' she said. She watched me as she touched her lips to the surface of her champagne.

'It's really nothing personal. If I were going to do this, you're the first person I would do it with, really. But I'm married, I've got a kid; my sainthood is pending and I don't want to screw it up.'

I thought that was worth a smile at least, but apparently she didn't get it. After a confused moment, she said, 'No, really, it's okay. It's nice. A lot of guys, you know, aren't like that.'

'Well . . .' Still shyly. 'What can I say? There you are.'

'What does your wife do?'

'Oh, well, you know, our son's only nine months old so he's a lot of work still. She teaches meditation sometimes.'

'Oh, no kidding? That's really great. I'm into meditation. I'm really into Tai Chi.'

'Oh, sure, Tai Chi is great. She does that sometimes.'

'Oh really? Wow, that's interesting. Yeah, I think it's really great. It's so, you know, like: non-violent or anything. But it's really good for your concentration and muscle tone!' She pulled up straight and touched her naked midriff with a long painted fingernail to indicate her muscle tone.

'Right,' I said, watching her fingers. 'Right.'

Frank Stain finished with his bedroom first so we went in there. When Juliet took her clothes off, I was breathless and felt I was truly in luck, maybe even blessed. Her body was white all over. She was short and had round breasts and looked very cuddly indeed.

Frank's girl must have made the bed fresh. It had new sheets – they were printed thick with violets – and was neatly turned down. When Juliet and I were under the covers – the instant I folded myself around her – I went into a state of near-swooning delight. She was so white to look at, so hot and pliant in my arms, she smelled so of youthful talc and fresh perfume – she was so new all of her, and I had not dared to believe, no matter how often I'd dreamed it, that I would ever touch a naked woman but my wife again. She was very wet inside and expansive – I could feel it even with the condom on – and it put me off for a moment because it made me think of other men coming in her; but only for a moment and then it was a luxury. When I kissed her, the lipstick tasted thick on her lips, a fact which seemed to me very womanly and thrilling. I fucked her with enormous happiness and many tender caresses. Every moment of it was mindless joy.

Now, there are some I know who believe an experience – a kiss, a dawn, a work of art – needs no words to complete it, and others nowadays who say the blathering afterward is all, an experience in itself. They can get quite wrought up arguing about it; I know, I know. But had champions of each side been contending on the sidewalk before me as I strolled home alone that blissful evening, contending no matter how ferociously, I think I would've slapped them on their shoulders together and, grinning, said, 'Each thing in its time, me boy, my dearie, each and every thing in its own blessed time.' Because with Juliet – I explained to myself, as I strolled and hummed and considered – I had been just drunk enough to achieve the wordless buzz required for full enjoyment, but not too drunk to perform the required actions, and that was the perfection of the thing. Ah, but now – now, along Central Park South, with the air cool and unusually clean; and the deep shadowy parkland of trees to my right that were not yet dying but luxuriating still in the wind with all their leaves; and the traffic lights and headlights on the boulevard to my left sparkling red and green and yellow and brightly white in the crisp air; and the great stone hotels rising straight up above them like unleashed genies; and my sense that all Manhattan, the city of my successes, was swelling on every side of me like a crescendo – well, there was a good deal of gentle pleasure to be had in contemplation.

That walk home, it wasn't the old walks, the Agnes walks, because it was full of thoughts, but it was awfully fine. The others, Frank and Alvin, had tried to coax me into more carousing – careless, I thought – with their girls out in local bars. But Buckaroo was understanding and clapped me on both shoulders as a father would and, solemnly assuming responsibility for the car, sent me on my way.

I decided to walk – I needed to think – and there was a dark period first. This was as I wandered in a zigzag pattern past the unlit brownstones of the east Fifties and up the sparsely trafficked avenues there, the after-midnight avenues. General principles of conscience concerned me then: it seemed so much illicit pleasure simply could not go unpunished. I reeked of perfume, for instance, I could smell it even in the open air, and who knew what other clues there were to my transgression? As I lost myself in an increasingly complex labyrinth of excuses and stratagems, concealment began to seem impossible to me and detection certain. Then, as I was approaching Grand Army Plaza where the sky first grew broad and the city great, and Fifth Avenue unrolled like a black velvet ribbon from the feet of the magnificent hotel, the specific truth occurred to me. It was nearly one a.m., Charlie would have run Marianne ragged all day, she was sure to be sound asleep by now. When I came in, she might stir, she might murmur that she was glad to have me back, that she felt safer with me in the house and so on, but she wouldn't wake up, she never did. I'd simply put the perfumed clothes in my gym bag and send them to the dry cleaners from work the next morning. I'd shower Juliet's smell off me before I climbed into bed. And it would be fine, everything would be fine.

With this, my mind started to clear and the stroll along Central Park West began. I became blithe as I went, and warm with well-being even in the brisk weather. Precious, heart-held memories of Juliet formed and evanesced within me, making my viscera toasty and my psyche companionable. And my love for Marianne and Charlie, in their sleeping innocence, had risen up refreshed as well, I realized, as did my lost affection for myself, who had turned out to be such a bold and regular fellow. So much of life, I thought, was such a waste of worry when so much turned out so well so often. There was too much strain, too much contention in the world in general, not only in philosophical matters, but in politics, and personal relations too. The whole world, it seemed to me, ought to have a single shoulder so I could slap it genially, and say: Be at peace, my darlings everywhere. Each thing in its time, each little thing trots along in its God-made time.

Again, the sky, the city, yawned sumptuously as Central Park West opened into Columbus Circle. And I admired Columbus up there on his column as I strolled by him, hands in my pockets, on the sidewalks of the roundabout below. I'd read in the papers recently that some liberal scholars were pecking at his reputation now, castigating him for the natives he had dispossessed, the cultures erased, even the Redskins who'd been obliterated after he was gone. But where would they have found the room to think such thoughts if he had not uncorked the crimped nations from their histories and let them light out here over the open land? You see, this was just the sort of thing I had in mind tonight. They had no peace, these critics, these mantis-like intellects who had never been to sea; they had no peace within themselves, as I had, because they could not accept that disasters too will happen, must happen, that all things must happen in their time and – and this was my culminating revelation for the evening – there is never any justice to them, to anything, ever. That may not seem like much of a revelation, but these things depend a good deal on how they hit you, and this hit me there with all the clarity of that cool September. There is no justice. The word refers to nothing. My wife might sometime discover that I'd cheated on her, which would certainly be unpleasant for everyone, but then she might not, which would simply be terrif. It was all a matter of chance and circumstance and maybe the vagaries of the tell-tale heart. Surely others got away with this sort of thing. And worse than this: Take the Buckaroo. And if the Buckaroo was caught out in his indiscretions then what about Joey Turpentine, the FBI informer who'd been sent to get him – he was probably the Barcos killer, for crying out loud, and he was working with the police! And surely, the world over, there were other murderers thriving, drinking champagne through their Decembers, doing the cha-cha and such. Why, Dr Mengele butchered children who climbed onto his table still sucking their thumbs and he drowned in old age, which is a sweet sort of dying, or so I hear. And then other innocent children simply got leukemia and shriveled to death with wide eyes, clutching their teddy bears, and who was going to put a stop to that? You see? I told the wide world, you see? All this fret about the way things simply are. A million courthouses, pharisaical at best, corrupt more likely, each as useful as Boss Tweed's in the end; and stultifying gods to exact imaginary vengeance; and new rituals to keep weaklings safe and new principles to murder for; and blame, blame, blame – we make such villains of each other – all rather than accept this founding nubbin of reality: there's no help for it, there's no changing it over the long run, these are the jokes, folks. There is no justice.

And so, with that little misunderstanding cleared up, I sauntered north on Columbus Avenue whistling a happy tune, content that a wise man might yet live his life in any way he chose and be as glad as health and luck would let him, and every inch as free.

*

Dear Harry,

I must be the only person here who hates to see autumn come. It's so beautiful – the leaf smell in the forest, the watercolors in the hills of trees, and all that shit. But I can't enjoy it. I don't feel like I can enjoy anything right now. Which is utter bullshit really. It's

something that really pisses me off about myself: all this
self-indulgent, bourgeois languishing. It used to make
Roland nuts. He used to say I was just torturing myself
so I could feel like I was suffering because I thought
it would make my work better or reconnect me with
my father or something. Well, he was right. It's bullshit.
I'll never experience real suffering like that, like he did.
Do you know what happened the first time my mother
met him? I love this story. My mother lived in Forest
Hills at the time, that's where she grew up. Her parents
had come over from Poland a long time before, and
her father owned a candy store on Queens Boulevard.
When she was a kid, my mother used to work there
sometimes or play in the stock room. They sold the
usual stuff like magazines and toys and so forth. And
one day, Mom found a little watercolor set in the
stockroom and her father let her have it. She started
painting what she called her 'little pictures', and she was
apparently pretty good at it, although I never saw her do
it, she never did it while I was alive. So one day, when
she was sixteen or so, this handsome young guy came
into the store and he saw my mother working behind
the counter, and she was doing a watercolor because
the place was empty. The guy turned out to be an
art teacher at Queens College which, of course, my
mother's parents thought was very impressive. And he
started going into raptures over my mother's paintings
and saying how much talent she had and so on. So her
parents agreed to let my mother go over to his studio
for lessons after school sometimes. And she would paint
there and he would lean over her shoulder, instructing
her, breathing on her neck, touching her hand – and
pretty soon, sure enough, he seduced her, and she was
in love with him. She once told me she used to lie
on this little Hollywood bed he had and look up at
the passing clouds through his skylight and think how
beautiful the world was. While he was fucking her, I
assume. I remember this shocked me at the time she
told me: my mother having unmarried sex! The whole
story, actually, shocked me pretty much even though

she didn't tell it to me until I was seventeen or so.
Anyway, her affair with the teacher went on for about
three months and — surprise, surprise — she got pregnant.
So she went to him and told him and, to her absolute
shock, he went all thunderous on her and pointed her
at the door saying he refused to have anything further
to do with such a tramp! My mother was absolutely
frantic. What was to become of her? But finally, a
friend told her about a doctor in the city who would
help her out. So in she went, clutching her handbag,
trembling, tearful. And in this dingy little office — a
third-floor walk-up on the lower east side — there was
My Father, The Abortionist. Not that he was really: he
just had a practice of mostly poor Jews, a lot of refugees,
and he believed, as my mother put it, that 'a girl's life
shouldn't be destroyed because of one mistake.' He was
apparently very kind and gentle to her and only took a
few dollars from her for form's sake. I guess he scraped
her — my mother didn't go into the details, thank God
— but she said it was very painful, even though he gave
her a drug that made her woozy during it. Then, after
it was over, she said she lifted up on her elbows on the
table and she saw him standing over the toilet. She said
he must have just flushed the fetus down there. And he
was *davening*, up and down, you know, and chanting
to himself: he was saying Kaddish! I mean, Jews don't
even do that, say the prayer for the dead over fetuses.
And here was this guy who must have seen so many
bodies just a few years before — fields of bodies that
you couldn't walk on without stepping on a friend's
ribcage or a mother's throat or a child's hand — and he
was praying over an embryo the size of his thumbnail.
Which he'd just cut out himself and flushed down the
crapper besides. And I'm not even sure he believed in
God! It's weird. I never knew what he thought or what
he was thinking really. He never told me anything. I'm
not even sure how much he told my mother. She used
to tell me: We couldn't ask, we couldn't upset him, he'd
been through so much already. His daughter, his darling
daughter, my sister, had died, you see — and I was alive.

I had to make him happy enough for two children, my
mother said, both for myself and for the child who was
dead. It never occurred to me, of course, that I had to
do the same for her as well. So I kept quiet, I didn't ask,
I never asked to know more. And when I was a little
girl, I used to watch him, trying to figure it all out.
When he was reading the newspaper or watching TV,
I used to sneak in the living room doorway and stare at
him, trying to get into his head, trying to imagine what
he'd seen and done and what he thought about things.
I remember specifically he had this Bible on the shelf, a
Hebrew Bible, and he used to take it down sometimes
and sit in his chair holding it open and just meditate on
it, just look down at the open book with this intense,
tragic stare, without ever even turning the page. And
I would watch him from the doorway, wondering,
you know: what is he thinking, what's in his head?
When I was about fourteen, just after my mother and
I moved out, moved to Mahopac, I started reading the
Bible myself — just trying to sort of get the feel of
what had been going on in his mind, just wanting
the same words to be in my mind that had been in
his so I would get some feeling of connection with
him. It took me almost a year, but I read the entire
book cover to cover. And I would even try to think
about it the way I figured he would think about it. I
would try to meditate on each page the way he had,
thinking the same kind of intense, profound, tragic
thoughts I thought he would. I took notes on it, I
wrote down my thoughts in my diary and, over the year,
I developed this big theory, being all of fifteen, that the
whole Bible was all just one story about how suffering
and injustice slowly informed a person's understanding
of God. You start with the child's paradise and then
come to a consciousness of good and evil and are
expelled into the world of suffering; then you create
a God who punishes evil and rewards good; then,
when that fails in face of the facts, you get a historical
God who works through nations over the long run; and
finally, when even that doesn't play out, you get the

acquiescence to suffering and unknowability that you get in Job and Ecclesiastes. (For the grownups, that is; for the kiddies, they tack on the Hollywood ending where Jesus saves the day.) I won't bore you with the whole thing, but it was a very detailed theory with all sorts of complex exegeses about brother supplantation and the crisis of Noah and the movement from personal triumph in Genesis to national slavery in Exodus, the inevitability of kingship and empire and so on; I wrote pages and pages. The point is: I imagined I was really getting into my father's mind. I imagined that, when he read that great old Bible of his, he was trying to travel back through all the terrible things that had happened to him, and back through all the terrible things that had happened to our race, and trying to recreate in himself the acquiescence, the acceptance, of the preacher in Ecclesiastes, or of Job — and I thought, well, now I was traveling back with him, so that now I understood him, so that now we were together in this endeavor. The punchline, if you can call it that, is that one day, after I'd finished reading the book and had had all these thoughts, I came home to visit him. And we were talking about school and movies — about nothing, like we always did. And my father went out of the room for a few moments, maybe to the bathroom. And for the first time, I felt worthy to reach up to the high shelf and take down his sacred Bible. Because I knew too now, see, I understood too. And I pulled the book down slowly, reverently — but secretly, because I didn't want him to know. And I held it lightly in my hands — and it opened! It fell open naturally to a page in Deuteronomy. And there, pressed between the pages, was a lock of hair. Blonde hair, silken like a child's. Lena's probably. In fact, I'm sure of it. He probably got it from his uncle, who escaped before the war and lived in Israel. And that's what he'd been meditating on all that time.

He never talked about her either. My half-sister. She was four years old. I never knew exactly what had happened to her. When I was seven or eight — not too long before I met you, in fact — my mother told

me that Lena had been killed with the other Jews in her
town – that they were shot and their bodies thrown into
a ravine. I didn't know what a ravine was and imagined
this big river with my sister floating away in it. That
was the image that stayed with me: that the Nazis had
drowned her in a big river. Mom didn't know much
more than that herself. From my reading, I've figured
Lena was murdered in the summer of '41, when the
Einsatzkommando went into Eastern Galicia. They were
the rifle squads who rounded up whatever Jews the
locals left alive, lined them up naked at the sides of
ditches or ravines – or graves the Jews were forced
to dig themselves – and gunned them down. At that
point, they were murdering the leaders first – Jewish
professionals and rabbis and so on – so I don't know
how or why my father managed to survive. Maybe
he was too young to be a leader. I just really have
no idea. Roland said he was amazed that I never just
out and asked him – when I was older, I mean. But
even then, how could I have? If he was silent, it was
because it would have killed him to speak, wasn't it?
Anyway, I couldn't, I never could. I didn't even begin
to read about it – the Holocaust – until after I was
out of school, after I came to New York. That was
when my father first contracted cancer, so I guess it
was another attempt to connect with him before it was
too late, but I didn't know that at the time. I just became
fascinated with the subject suddenly, reading anything I
could find about it. I mean, I'd read about it before, and
I'd thought about it, but I'd avoided it too, emotionally,
somehow. But now it got me. It started out, I was just
walking by the Strand one day – walking up from Soho
where I was waitressing sometimes – and I saw a book
about it in the bins outside. Maybe *The War Against
The Jews* or Terence des Pres, which had come out
recently. I don't remember. And I thought, hm, that
looks interesting, and bought it and took it home. At
first, I read books like that: overviews and theories.
Getting sort of the historical movement, you know.
That's how I thought about the whole thing anyway:

Jews' rights were curtailed, then their locations were
centralized in ghettoes; smaller, local killing actions
went on and that led step by step to the invention
of the gas vans and the death factories and finally there
came the systematic emptying of the ghettoes into the
camps and the gas chambers. I mean, it was almost an
abstract thing, like following a battle on a map. But
still, it gave me nightmares enough and stomachaches
too. The inevitability of it, you know, the inevitability
of the past, the done-ness. It drives you crazy after a
while. You keep having these fantasies of stopping it,
of changing it, and they're like moths battering against
a window because they see a fire inside but it's a
fire that's already happened, that's over, and the glass,
anyway, is unbreakable. They kept me from sleeping
– the fantasies more than the nightmares – so I would
stay in Manhattan at night and drink in the bars around
St Mark's Place. And I'd meet guys – artists, craftsmen,
hangers-around – and I started going home with them.
I was just glad to be able to sleep away from my own
bed and my books. Glad not to be alone. Before that, I'd
had only two boyfriends, both in school. I'd been very
slow about that sort of thing. Then I'd gone through
this arch-feminist phase for a year or so, because I felt
I'd been hurt, you know, by men. Anyway, I didn't
have much experience. But now, suddenly, it was every
couple of nights. No condoms – we didn't know about
AIDS yet – sometimes not even my diaphragm. I didn't
kid myself about the emotional part – or I did because
I thought there wasn't any. It was all very modern and
ironical and sort of deadpan, humorless. We'd do it
and smoke cigarettes and shrug a lot without smiling,
and then I'd be able to sleep. After a while, I started
reading more personal books – Elie Wiesel and Primo
Levi and so on – books by survivors. And I'd go over
each incident and I'd keep asking myself – did this
happen to my father, did this, did this? Did he survive
like Levi because he had some scientific knowledge and
they put him to work in a lab? Or was he one of the
Sonderkommandoes who unloaded the bodies from the

gas chambers and burned them, or even a capo, who policed his own people in order to stay alive. I used to look for his name in the indices. And of course, the sleeplessness got worse, the fantasies, of rescuing them – him – Lena – everybody. I stayed in Manhattan more and more, slept with more and more guys. Sometimes, I'd hook up with a guy for a week, a while, but then it would be no good, the insomnia would come back. Meanwhile, my father had had an operation and he was very sick, very weak. I would visit him and he was so thin and slow. I used to look at the pictures in the books, the photographs of the death camp inmates, skeletons painted with a coat of flesh – and the comparison was unbearable. As if it had somehow come back for him, as if he hadn't gotten away at all. He would just sit in his chair all day now and watch TV. Nature shows. He loved those documentaries they do on Channel Thirteen, those incredible close-up shots of voles and ibexes eating each other or whatever. He bought a machine and taped them and I used to bring him videos from the store. I used to sit next to him, watching with him, holding his hand, feeling the loose flesh and the thin bones, and just forcing the words down into my throat: What happened, Daddy? What was it like? What did they do to you? Because how could I ask him, how could I make him talk about it? It wasn't as if he'd changed any, being sick. My mother came to visit him once or twice and he turned that same old stare on her – his eyes were very big now but still intense – and she stopped coming after a while. He wouldn't even let me stay with him for more than a day or two. He had a nurse, and he said he preferred to be alone. So anyway, now, when I went home to LIC, I was reading descriptions, any descriptions I could find, of actual, individual atrocities. Reading them over and over. Even hunting out unpublished testimony in the libraries once or twice to find new material. I wanted graphic stuff, see, emotional stuff. A baby being torn out of a mother's hands and bashed dead against the ground near the unloading ramp at Auschwitz. Naked women shitting in terror as they waited their turn outside the gas chambers while the men were killed inside. A husband forced to unload his wife from the chamber, her legs streaked with shit and menstrual blood. A child being given candy and led by the hand to a place where he was autopsied alive. I wanted to stay nauseous, I wanted to have nightmares, I wanted to see it and feel it for myself. And at night, more nights than not, there I'd be, some guy I'd never met before covering me and sliding into me, sucking my breast – or me putting my mouth around his cock and drinking his scum, some guy I hardly knew. I don't mean to make it sound hellish or anything. There was the usual collection of miserable experiences, but no one ever really hurt me or messed me up. Some of the guys were creeps, I guess, but a lot of them were just regular guys who figured, hey, they'd gotten lucky that night. I tried not to think too much about them. In fact, stupidly enough, the only one I really remember very well was this one kid, this total blithering asshole, because he was the one who finally put an end to it all. His name was Norman. He had to be all of seventeen years old. Very tall, very thin, ugly, stringy black hair down to his ass. Wore lots of leather with metal studs and death's heads on them. And he had a particularly small dick which he made lots of unfunny, insecure jokes about. He was into heavy metal, which at the time was kind of underground stuff. I hadn't paid much attention to it so I let him show me all these magazines he had. Pictures of bare-chested guys in leather pants playing guitars and thrusting their hips and scream-ing. Everyone's seen them now – bands with names like 'Satan's Hour of Devastation' or 'Armageddon From Hell' – but at the time I was pretty amazed. Norman explained to me how great they were because they sang these incredible songs, you know, like, about, like, serving Satan by becoming a sniper on Broadway and at the same time, you know, they make these, like, fucking motions with their hips and stick their tongues out like they're eating pussy. And I nodded as best I could and said something like Wow, Norman, that's great. I mean, the guy was a moron, what can I tell you? So then he fucked me which was, as you can imagine, a near-run thing, very desperate and incredibly quick. But he seemed very pleased with himself about it and he was kind of be-bopping naked around his studio afterwards, all energized, pretending to play an electric guitar and chewing gum and cupping his testicles in his hand and so on. And he noticed the book sticking out of the pocket of my flight jacket, which was hanging on his chair. I remember it was testimony from the Eichmann trial I'd found somewhere. And he kind of casually drew it out to see what it was. And he said, 'Ooh, Nazi shit, wow, I love this shit, it's really a turn-on.' Then I guess he must have glanced over at me, because he said, 'What. Hey, don't look at me like that, man. It turns everybody on. How do you think they sell fucking newspapers? I mean, it's not like it's real people dying or anything. It's just words on a page, you know. It's just going on in your head, like a fantasy or something. It's SM, man, everybody digs it.' I'd like to say that I stormed out or threw up or something. But I just waved him off and rolled over and tried to sleep. Which, I'm sorry to say, made him giggle and get on top of me again. And he had at me from behind, more sure of himself this time, thwacking my ass with his hand, singing under his breath. I did manage to bury my face in the pillow so the little bastard wouldn't hear me come.

Anyway, that's how my Holocaust reading ended. Norman spoiled it. It just tapered off to nothing after that night with him. And my nympho period ended too. I still couldn't sleep, but I started going to doctors for it, collecting prescriptions for tranquilizers. That's how that got started. I guess I was pretty much tranked up most of the time until after Daddy finally died. Then I kicked the habit and went to Europe, like I said.

So now, old Harry – whoever you are – I hope my tale of woe hasn't managed to alienate you completely. I do have that effect on people, I suspect. I did on my husband anyway, although I'm sure that had more to do with what I did to our baby. I never told him this stuff, not all of it. In fact, I'm probably going to burn this letter as soon as I finish it. Except maybe I won't, you know. In which case, my nine-year-old hero:

All My Love,
Agnes.

I did a funny thing when I got this letter — an odd thing. I didn't read it right away. I could guess the tenor of it and I didn't want to ruin my good mood. So I carried the cream envelope around in my pocket for a day or two, shrugging it off when Marianne archly asked me what my 'old girlfriend had to say.' Then, one slow day at work, I drove out to Long Island with it and read it there. It was October, and the leaves were changing here now too and the hometown kids were back in school. The side streets were quiet, nearly empty. I parked the department's Cadillac at the top of Piccadilly and walked down the road, past the ghost house, which was still there, to the Sole house, the muse of my old melancholies. It was painted an ugly tan these days with black shutters. The Finkelsteins were gone, and there were tricycles and a stroller on the grass out front. A lot of the houses on the block had been repainted or rebuilt, and whole new ones — big, gauche monsters — had replaced the humbler antiques in some places. The place was all changed, in other words, and yet it still managed to accomplish what I wanted. It made me nostalgic, brought up some gilded traces of the old emotions, gave me a context in which to bear her dissolution. It still had that power. That stupid, bourgeois little town. It has no meaning in the scheme of things, I know that. But I do believe that if you wiped the world clean, I could still walk the places where its streets had been. Maybe even if you wiped the world away, I could call it forth whole out of the interior terrain and walk it. Maybe, if it comes to that, I'm always walking it, every day. Maybe I've never walked anywhere else.

— 12 —

I did not hear from Agnes again for nine months, the worst nine months of my life, when I was invulnerable and full of joy. The Tax Commissioner finally died in that time, and I officially replaced her. My salary rose and Marianne began hunting for a new apartment with a feminine pleasure that made me feel manly and proud. She took pleasure, too, when the papers wrote about me, which they did once or twice, predicting good things. Her crystal blue eyes glistened, and she clipped the articles and saved them in one of those ring binders with the plasticine holders inside. Charlie, to our delight, was growing chunky and handsome and good-natured. He would walk beside me of a Saturday, holding my hand and looking up at me, or ride on my shoulders, beating a fond tattoo on my head. Marianne loved to see this, and would watch us from the window as we headed for the park together.

On the nights when I stayed out late – when I told Marianne I was working – she would leave a snack for me on the dining table and a little love note signed with a heart. The time I went to Florida, she packed my bags for me and made jokes about what an important man I was: I had told her I was going to a conference of some kind. All of this I enjoyed immensely and was grateful for. And, in the early spring, Marianne became pregnant again, which made us both very happy.

Then, one jolly morning, a Saturday morning just after summer came, I went out to get the newspaper. It was nine a.m. The weather was pleasant. Blue skies, warm air, not too humid. I went to the Iraqui's shop on Amsterdam and got the *Times* and scanned the headlines on the front page as I walked back to the corner.

Feds Used Killer To Crack Drug Ring. I guess, subconsciously, it was the thought of Joey Turpentine that made me pause on that one, but I don't think I was actually thinking about him. Still, I glanced over the article and, sure enough, there he was: '. . . convicted murderer Joey Turpentine . . .' It was a Chicago story, broken originally by the *Tribune*. I had no premonition of danger as I read it. I was even pleased to have some small personal connection with an exciting yarn. I stopped at the top of my block and read on. Then, at the very bottom of the page, I saw: 'Turpentine, who frequently goes by the alias Frank . . .' at which point the story broke off, to be continued inside.

Now I did feel a tremor. In my heart, in fact, I was already certain of disaster, but I tried to chalk this up to superstition as I quickly pulled the paper open. There it was, though, bottom right-hand corner of page thirty-five: '. . . Stain.' Frank Stain. Joey Turpentine, the federal informant whom Myers had warned me was coming after Umberman, was our frequent drinking and whoring companion, Frank Stain.

I don't remember ever feeling quite that way before: the earth was an elevator and the cable had snapped. My stomach rose and a cold sweat broke out on my forehead and palms. Dazed, swallowing, I lowered the newspaper.

And I saw two men, waiting for me.

They were leaning against a brownstone stoop right across from my place. Young guys in suits with short-cropped hair. They were grinning at me in this horrible, over-friendly way that made me more nauseous still. The moment I spotted them, they pushed off the stoop and started walking toward me. Smiling, casual.

I folded the paper and moved forward. They have nothing to do with me, I told myself. I'll walk right past them, just as casual as they. Only I'd forgotten how one does walk, exactly. I had to guide my body stiffly through the motions. I met up with the two men in the middle of the block.

'Hiya, Harry,' one of them said. He was the older one, dark-haired, flint-eyed, self-assured. His grotesque familiarity puddled my spine. The younger guy backed him up with his awful G-man grin.

'What?' I said. It was all I could get out.

'Been reading the paper?' he asked me. Deftly, he pulled the paper out from under my arm. He held it up to me without glancing at it. 'Why, look here, Mark. Joey Turpentine is in the news again. That's Frank Stain to you, Harry. You know Frank, doncha?'

'I don't know what you want. Who are you?' I said – my one crummy attempt to say the innocent thing.

The dreadful man didn't flinch. 'You know who we are, Harry.'

'Look,' I said. 'If you have business with me you can call me at my office Monday.' But I mumbled this, staring at the pavement; a miserable performance, nothing like my fantasies.

'Oh, but Harry,' said the horrible man, smiling horribly. 'Today is the most important day of your life.'

I looked up, my throat closing. I knew that phrase. Buckaroo joked about it sometimes. It's what they say when they've got your balls in their hand, he said, and they want you to start talking or else they'll make a fist.

'You see, Har,' the man went on, 'we're not here to hurt you. We want to help you. We know what you did wasn't so bad. Anyone might have done it. What was it? A few trips to the whorehouse on Buckaroo's dime?'

'Twelve trips,' the younger man said quietly.

'A few days in Florida at his expense.'

'Seven thousand a hundred and fifty-four dollars it cost old Buck,' said the other, 'counting the girls.'

'So what?' said the older one. 'So in return you let him jigger the tax assessments, skim the profits – it's a favor for a favor. He buys you some fun, you turn a blind eye to what's going on in your department now and then.' He snorted, shrugged it off. 'We don't want to put a guy in prison for that.' I tried to snort back at him, nobody's fool; I tried to gird my percolating loins. Christ, I had been planning to *join* you guys at one point, I thought desperately. I used to work with *Myers*! But I saw in his eyes what I was to him, his hard eyes. 'It's Buckaroo,' he said quietly. 'He's the one we want.'

Of course, he might just as well have smeared shit on my head as that patronizing routine. As if I were some punk criminal willing to seize on their secondhand delusions about myself. My eyes stung with tears of humiliation and terror. My throat felt like a crushed straw. I opened my mouth to tell them both to go to hell.

'Please,' I said, 'I have a wife and child.' And my heart was breaking, but those wretched men, those horrible men, they didn't care, what did they care?

'You probably should've thought of that before, Harry,' said the younger man with oozing sympathy.

My lips were trembling now, but I managed to say, 'I want a lawyer. All right? I want to call my lawyer.'

'You do that, Harry.' And the monster slapped my shoulder with one hand as he gave back my paper with the other. 'In fact, you bring your lawyer with you down to Police Plaza Monday morning at ten a.m., okay?' He wagged his finger in my face. 'Ten a.m., Harry. Because at Ten-fifteen, there'll be a warrant out for your arrest.'

When I came into the apartment, I heard Charlie whisper gleefully to himself, 'Daddy here!' He left off his puzzles and rollicked to me full speed in his clumsy way. 'Zoo, Daddy! We going zoo – to zoo – and see Grandma and Grandpa!' I knelt down and caught him in my arms and held his little body against me. I forced out a whisper, 'That's right, pal.'

After a second or two, he struggled out of my grasp. 'I have new puzzoo, Daddy!' he told me, pointing to the mess of toys at the kitchen threshold. I'd given him the puzzle the week before. 'I do new puzzoo for mysef!' he said.

'Wow,' I said hoarsely, 'Let's see.'

'We should – we should *see*!' he echoed, running on before me.

I followed him weakly. Marianne smiled sunnily at us from the sink where she was washing dishes. She was beginning to show the bulge of the new baby, and her smile and her eyes and her cheeks all seemed to give off light.

'What's it like outside?' she asked me.

I shrugged, glancing at the window. I couldn't remember. I stood there a moment, gazing at her: my wife. She knew nothing. Nothing. And I wished it had all been a dream.

Slowly, I sat down next to Charlie. Concentrating hard, he was fitting the puzzle pieces into their slots. First the farmer, then the farmer's wife, then the little animals. I reached out to touch his fine blond hair.

'I doing it mysef, Daddy,' he said.

'There you go,' I whispered.

Meanwhile, my Inner Man, in a paroxysm of regret, was flinging himself about from wall to wall, clutching his face with both hands, tearing at his temples. 'Oh!' he was shrieking, weeping, grinding his fists into his eyes. 'Oh, that I ever cheated on my darling wife! That I ever strayed from my beloved family that I adore so much! Oh, I want to hold them forever! I want to eat them up, num, num, num, num. Oh, that I ever wanted to do anything at all but be with them and love them and protect them! Oh! Oh! Oh! Oh!'

The shit. The miserable piece of shit.

The Central Park Zoo was crowded that morning. Lots of children, lots of children's voices rising to the open sky, lots of balloons, plump and colorful beneath the cloudless summer blue. The sea lions were barking and splashing in their fountain behind us. And before us were the little brown macaques, which Charlie loved, swinging from the dead branches on their stony island, grooming each other tenderly in niches in the sheer rock, showing each other their pink rectums, coupling in the tangle of low pines.

Charlie clomped back and forth along the fence, ducking his head so he could see through the plexiglas divider. Shouting to me, 'Monkeys, Daddy! Monkeys swinging!'

'Monkeys, Charlie,' I called back. I stood behind him, beneath the pergola, my hands in my pockets. A pillar of ashes. My father stood beside me.

'Oh, your mother,' he moaned. 'Her crazy sister.'

I had asked him why Mom hadn't come into the city with him, but I wasn't listening to his answer. I was watching my excited little boy as he peered through the monkeys' fence. I was turning into lead.

'Her crazy sister, she sits in her health spas and her,

whatever they are, her beauty farms. She goes from one of these places to another, she has nothing better to do. She sits there going crazy from eating celery and wearing mud packs. Then she calls your mother with her craziness. "Daddy did this, Daddy did that." Like they were still ten years old, the two of them. And who's paying for all this so she can call your mother and make her all upset?'

'Monkeys, Daddy!' cried Charlie with wide eyes. 'They swinging in – in twees!'

'She's upset?' I said vaguely.

'It was a million years ago!' said my father. 'Who knows now what he did? In those days, you wanted to make a living, you chased ambulances. Today it wouldn't even be a crime. Today you can advertise on TV.' He made a dismissive noise, pushing the air through his teeth. 'Some hotshot reformer – big Mr Seabury – wants to make a name for himself, be a Governor: indicting this one, indicting that one. Over what? Over nothing. Regular people have to suffer so he can be a famous judge.'

For a moment, I turned to him, startled and afraid, but then I realized he must be talking about someone else, not me. I watched Charlie again. He was poking his head through the fence, pressing his nose flat against the plexiglas. I heard him chuckling to himself. 'I'm watching the monkeys through the glass,' he said.

I bundled Charlie home early, ringing the door buzzer, waking Marianne from her exhausted nap. I did not cross the threshold, but only handed the boy into her arms.

'I saw monkeys, Mommy,' he said, clumsily patting her blonde hair. And then he climbed down and ran off to play with his puzzles.

'I have to go out,' I said.

'Ralph Umberman called,' she told me. 'He says he has to talk to you. It's urgent.'

'I know.'

'Is everything all right?'

'Yes, yes, fine,' I said. I was irritated with her just then. For her innocence. And for her ditzy point of view too. I knew what she believed: The mysterious Spirit of a man knows right from wrong in quietude. She had actually said that to me once, she had written it for one of her classes. She had said that Modern Man was angry with God as with a father because He hadn't protected us from ourselves. But like a Good Father, see, He had given us this Mystic Conscience of ours, and if we strayed from that it was our fault, so that was all right, wasn't it. Who could believe such shit at this end of the millennium I don't know. Anyway, it was easy for her to say, with all her mystic bills paid up by evil me. I didn't want to talk to her.

Then, when I had brought the Volvo up from the garage, when I was alone inside and on clear road over the Triborough, I wept and sobbed for her, for what I'd done to her and in pity over what was going to happen to her now. The newspaper and TV stories, the court dates, the truth that Charlie would one day know, the looks from friends. That sort of thing. I thought it would destroy her in her fragility and I wangled with God to spare her and choked on my tears as the road blurred beyond the windshield.

As I entered Westchester, I calmed down, snuffling. I felt hollow now but steady enough. I suppose I had started out with some whimpery hope that Buckaroo might still deliver me from my fate, but that was beginning to pass away into a colder feeling. As I tormented myself with images of Charlie at the monkey island that morning, I recalled what I had once seen on a television documentary about macaques. When a chief monkey wants to show his supremacy over a lesser one, I remembered, the lesser bends over and the chief mounts him for a moment in imitation of sodomy. By the time I pulled into Umberman's driveway, I hated the bastard with an icy hatred. I began to consider strangling him. I imagined it. That mean man, I thought. That bad Buckaroo.

He lived in a long ranch house surrounded by sloping Japanese gardens, about fifteen minutes from where I live today. His wife, a coarse, leathery creature with a voice like a crow, led me fretfully to his study in the back. He sat there enthroned behind a glass desk in a modern leather swivel chair with a high back. There was a wall of glass behind him that looked out on a rock garden and a sunken pool.

Amidst this snazzy modern magnificence, he looked sunken and small and jowly; sickly, withered and white.

'O-o-o-oh, they . . . o-o-o-oh, o-o-o-h,' was all he could say at first, moving his hands vaguely over the papers on his desk.

'Christ,' I said. He too had thought he was invulnerable. I shook my head over him. I did not sit down.

'They'll come, they'll come, Harry,' he groaned. His whole fat body had started trembling. 'They'll want, they'll want you to talk. They'll want you to tell them.' He leaned toward me with cancerous intensity. 'Guatemala. You have to go to Guatemala. I'll call you. I'll be in touch.'

'Guatemala.' I laughed.

'Money. I'll give you money so you can go. I . . .' He searched the surface of his desk with bulging eyes as if he expected to find the cash right there. Then he looked up in terror at me. 'They want me, Harry. Me. The Buckaroo. They want me.'

To my dismay, I had to fight back tears again. 'If you wanted an honest front man, why the fuck did you corrupt me, you son of a bitch? Why couldn't you control yourself?'

Buck grabbed a fistful of the loose flesh of his own cheek to indicate exactly whom we were talking about. 'Mmmmeeeeeeeee,' he said desperately, shivering the jowl in his hand.

I turned and walked out.

'Guatemala, Harry!' he called after me.

So that was the day Agnes's last letter came. It was waiting for me when I got home. I clung to the Jungian timing of it as if there might be some sort of rescue in that. I patted it in my pocket with superstitious hope. I did not read it until that evening because I spent all day sadly hovering around Marianne and Charlie; her lucency, his sweetness, clinging to the aura of them like a blanket in the night. It was just the way I had hovered round my mother that day before I went to camp. Then, when my son was in bed – and my wife lay weary on the sofa reading Boehme – I sat in the stuffed chair with the leaves of her umbrella plant tickling the back

of my neck and opened the envelope. The letter inside was
not long. It had been scrawled quickly by a troubled hand.

Dear Harry,
Don't worry. I won't write to you anymore after this. I
won't even send this, I will burn it this time, I promise.
It's not that I expect you to save me or anything. That is,
I do, but I don't really. I just have no one else to talk to –
even in the summer now no one comes. And I don't go
anywhere. I just work and work. And the work sucks.
Everything sucks. (Always a pleasure to hear from me,
isn't it?) Roland says I should take my daughter back
now, at least some of the time, because I've been off
the barbs again since April. He says it would be good
for both of us. I've been stalling him, but I know it
won't work. Christ, why does he think I let him go in
the first place? In his fat-cheeked decency. Why does he
think there were no lawyers and lawsuits and hysterical
scenes? I mean, he knows how much I love my baby.
My baby. She's almost two and a half now. But I still
wander around the empty cabin nights mewling 'my
baby, my baby' over and over like in a mad scene
in a play. I don't even know if the sentiment is real
anymore. I was never sure which was the real stuff
and which was for form, for show. I remember, when
I was about six months pregnant, we all sat around in
the cabin together, Roland and I and all our friends.
We sat in a semi-circle of chairs in our living room,
and Roland made a little speech: 'We want you guys
to be part of naming the baby because we want the
baby to be part of all of us.' And I sat at the head of
the semi-circle. Leaning back with my hand on my
belly, smiling serenely, feeling her stir. Everyone was
grinning at me. And I was watching them all through
my secret valium haze, and thinking, Oh, my friends,
my friends, they're so wonderful, I love them so much, I
can get by with my friends, and so on. And after Roland
spoke, there were a few nervous jokes and then this
solemn silence. And after a long pause, somebody –
Margaret from the restaurant, I think – spoke up and

said: 'Lena. We have to name her Lena. That has to be her name.' And everyone nodded. Solemnly, solemnly approving. Solemnly raising their bottles of beer. And I nodded too, approving. And thinking: Yes, yes, it's all so perfect, they're all so decent, we're a new generation mending the scars of the past. And believing it! As if you could replace someone, as if you could undo something, as if you could put anything right ever anywhere. Well, I was tranked out of my mind at the time, what did I know? But it was real for them, or they thought it was. All my decent, clean-living, back-to-nature friends. And nobody suspected their anti-Holocaust madonna was floating cross-eyed through the borough of loons. It was how I occupied myself, now that I couldn't make art anymore. Finding the doctors to prescribe by phone, finding the different pharmacies, driving to Rutland to pick up my stash. Oh, that would've made them solemn if they'd found that out, my friends, migh-ty solemn indeed, indeed. But no, they were too busy being righteous. And 'healing'. Naming her Lena! I mean, that's exactly what I was afraid of, wasn't it? Even with the drugs, I was lying awake half the night thinking about it. Imagining all the atrocities that could happen to *this* baby, the new Lena. She could be born with half a skull. She could be a staring, dribbling mongoloid. She could be strangled on the umbilical cord and born hanged. *These things do happen!* I tried once to tell my friend Julie. Because she was an artist too and she had two children. I thought she might understand. And she said, 'Oh, Agnes, every mother-to-be thinks things like that sometimes.' Which may be true – but it doesn't mean those things don't *happen*! And then she went on to tell me how I ought to have natural childbirth – no doctors, no drugs – how wonderful, how natural it would be. She had a midwife she knew who was just so wonderful. We could do it right in my house. Oh, sure, I thought. So wonderful, so natural. I mean, when exactly did Nature become our friend? When she was inventing stillbirths? Or germs? Or pain? Or tornadoes? My pal

Nature. Not for me, boy. I'd had amnio once already and would've gladly done it every goddamned day till my delivery. Christ, I was ready to check into the hospital now. I wanted a team of doctors choppered in from fucking Manhattan. I wanted to be drugged until the baby just wafted out of me. Leave it to fucking Nature and I was sure there would be nothing but racking, violent pain until my baby was spewed out of me in this bloody mess of organs and twisted limbs. And then I would have to survive. That's what really frightened me. I would survive to live with that. And I loved her so much already.

Well, it was the hospital for me, old friend. Lena was born in about an hour and I was practically comatose the whole time, thank God. I don't remember any of it. I just woke up and there she was suddenly. In my arms in her little blanket. With her little face and fingers. Little tiny Lena. Oh, people who don't have children don't know. They talk and talk and I don't know why they're talking because they don't know anything. They don't know about love or terror or bliss or remorse, and not even grief, which they think they know. Maybe they can know math or how to play chess or something. I'm not sure. But for the rest of it, I think they're looking at a closed door. It's like a closed door with a *trompe l'oeil* on it, a painting of the room beyond. And, oh yes, they think, we know the room, we do know. But it's really just a door, a closed door, and they don't know. Anything. I loved that little baby, Harry. The fact that I'd thought I loved her before – the fact that I thought I understood the word love before – were just tokens of the hugeness of what I didn't fucking know. That was real, definitely. No one ever can say I didn't love her, because my atoms had turned to love, there was love in the interstices.

But, hey, Har, you know me: What's love for this gal if not an opportunity for unthinkable suffering? Oh, I had it all worked out. Sitting at home with her in my arms, at my breast, looking down into that tiny scrunched face, loving her impossibly, I had thought it all through: Crib death. Undetected congenital heart disease. Choking. A sudden fever in the night. And how impossible it would be to live after you came into her room and looked down and found her glassily staring out of her crib. I pumped a lot of drugged milk into that kid, I know. But taking drugs was better than the alternative, than just sitting there, thinking those things with nothing to protect me from the fact that they happen, they *do happen*. Drugged, at least, was plausible, was bearable. So that was me and my baby. Mother and child.

Roland, of course, got wise eventually. It was pretty hard to hide from him after a while. He pleaded with me to give the drugs up, reasoned with me, screamed at me finally. I promised him I'd try. I tried to stop. I failed. Then, when I just couldn't do it, he got this look in his eyes, on his face. This wary look. Watching me all the time when I was with the baby. Following me around, pretending he wasn't. I guess he thought that any moment I was going to do some terrible, druggie thing, like drop her or cut off her finger instead of her nail or God knows what else.

Well, my personal choice, finally, was the river. Lena was almost six months old by the time the water was warm enough. But then, in the afternoons, when the sun had been on it, I could take her down there through the woods for a bath. We have a private place on my land where the water gets deep, a swimming hole. Roland and I used to skinny dip there sometimes. I still swim there every morning. There's a little backwash upstream a few yards with gentle eddies over a bed of smooth stones. It's about two feet deep, if that, in mid-summer. Lena just loved it. I'd sit on the stones and hold her around the middle. Lower her in and let her legs swirl in the current and dandle her up and down to make a splash. She used to positively scream with glee and slap her hands around on the surface. And I remember she would stare these big serious stares at the frogs and the fishes going by. We had a wonderful time the two of us. Or the three of us. Because Roland came down with me whenever he was home. He would pretend he wanted to watch or help out or have a swim or whatever. Then he would sit on the bank and stare at us playing. With this frozen smile on his face. I knew he was thinking that his wife was such a drughead that she might let the baby go any minute, lose hold of her and let her drown. Or possibly it was just me thinking it. Because I did think it, all the time, every minute. I'd be sitting in the water, splashing her around, laughing with her, and my heart just swelling up with all that love. And I was terrified. What if I did let go? What if she drowned? What if a water moccasin swam up and bit her? While she was shrieking and splashing, I could see it all happening in my mind. I could see her slipping away from me. Pulled out of reach by the current. Pulled down into the deep water, her white body still visible under the surface, her suffocating face. I thought of her giving one last uncertain little baby cry before going under. I saw her hands waving helplessly. I thought of it again and again. I saw the whole thing happening over and over.

So when I actually did let her go, I just sat there helplessly. I mean, for a second, I couldn't make the transition from my imagination to the real thing. The baby just slipped away. She went straight under. She was gone in an instant. And the current did pull her away from me over the stones toward the deep water. If Roland hadn't been there, watching me, distrusting me, I really don't know what would have happened. I came awake and he was already splashing into the river. He grabbed Lena not two feet away from me. Hauled her up while I was still struggling to my feet with my mouth hanging open, trying to call out. Lena was coughing and gasping and fighting to breathe, smushing her face with her tiny hands, then flailing around with them, reaching for me. Then – a tad too late, I'd say – I was all over her, sobbing, hugging her, kissing her. I put my arms around her as best I could, considering the fact that Roland wouldn't let her go.

Well, you can bet your boots we had a solemn

discussion about that little event, by golly. Roland explaining in a quiet, measured voice why he thought separation might be best for all of us for a while. And how I would be able to see the baby anytime I wanted and so on. And me just sitting there numbly, dumbly, staring, nodding. Thinking: Yes, yes, for Christ's sake, save her, get her away from me, shut up and go. I was still sitting there when his face crumpled and he walked out of the room to do his crying in private. I was sitting on the sofa, staring, thinking: Ah well, what the hell, it's high time I get back to my work anyway. I'd been blocked by then for almost a year. But I knew it would come back now. The flow, the ideas, the sureness in my hands. I was thinking: yes, yes, I've suffered now finally. Now finally, I've suffered enough.

It broke off there, no signature. I folded it quietly and put it in my shirt pocket. I felt a certain lightness with the burden of hope taken away. I don't even know what I'd been hoping until then, but I wasn't hoping it anymore. I stood up, sighing, at loose ends. Marianne glanced at me from the sofa and smiled placidly. I started wandering among the crowd of potted plants and creepers. I wandered past her head into Charlie's room. I stood by his crib in the dark a few moments. I watched him sleeping with his baby intensity, his whole face set on it. Fucked up your life for you, Chuckster, I thought. Sorry, little guy. Then I had to pull out before I broke down and woke him.

I checked my watch. It was ten pm.

'I'm going to go see if the Sunday paper's out yet,' I said.

Marianne nodded, giving a sleepy snuffle, rubbing her pregnant belly with her hand. 'I may just haul the old anvil off to bed.'

'Yeah, don't wait up. I may take a walk.'

I bent over the sofa and kissed her gently, which made her smile up at me again. I pulled my windbreaker from the hall closet and headed out the door.

The streets were bopping. It was a summer Saturday night and warm and easy. Everyone seemed young and walked with long, loping strides. I headed down to the bank on

72nd. I went into the foyer where the cash machines were. We had three different accounts and every day you were allowed to take up to five hundred dollars out of each. I took out fifteen hundred dollars, which left plenty behind. Then I stepped outside and hailed a cab and rode down to the Port Authority. The place was hell at that hour. Carpeted with sleeping beggars, reeking of urine. Hustlers shimmering dangerously along the walls. Black faces slowly turning to follow me with sallow eyes. But a bus to Vermont was parked outside one of the gates, its engine already thudding. As easy as sleepwalking, I was in it, and we were pulling away. And what was strange − what I hadn't expected − was how free, how fine, I felt suddenly; when we had crossed the George Washington Bridge, I mean, when we were rolling past the black Hudson and the looming palisades. As if you could really get away like this, lighting out for the territory, as if the idea were still there, anyway, dyed in the wool, even with the territory gone. After a while, I pressed my face against the window almost eagerly, shading my eyes from the reading lights with my hand. I thought I could make out Pegasus rising over Rockland County. And I remembered a poem I'd read once, something about Chaldean constellations over crowded roofs. Christ, it seemed like forever I'd been stuck in that light-blinded city. It seemed like just forever since I could look up and see the stars.

'Agnes Mallory,' I said now to the girl. Her on the couch, nursing her coffee, bathing her nose in the steam. Me by the mantelpiece, elbow on the mantelpiece, scotch in hand. Trying to keep the emotion out of my face. And the wind falling and rising outside, the rain hissing and pattering. And the fire crackling. 'Agnes Mallory,' I said. 'The name's familiar. Why do you want to know about her?'

The girl did her impression of a thoughtful gaze across the surface of her coffee mug. 'Well . . . because . . . Like I said — or like you said — I want to be an artist. A sculptor. And as a woman sculptor, she's, like, this important influence for me. I feel.' And she tucked her legs up under her and swiveled that ingenue kisser on me, all blinky with youthful candor.

I could barely stand to look at her — I could barely stop — now that I recognized the face. 'So read her biography,' I said.

'Oh, great.'

'There are several. Three, I think.'

'Great. Are you gonna, like, toy with me?'

I, like, might, I thought. 'Dweller In A Secret Place. That was one, wasn't it?'

'You know, obviously.'

'Yeah. Arthur Levine. That was the best one, I thought. The heroine artist. From the psalm: "Thou shalt not be afraid for the terror by night . . ." and so on. Then there was Shaping the Night, the critical one. Sheila Solotoff. Which wasn't bad either as far as it went. Agnes chisels the horrors of the twentieth century into art. Simple, but not stupid anyway. Which brings us to the feminist one, what was it . . .?'

She sucked her cheeks in to hide a smile. 'In the Valley of the Dead Elms.'

'*Right, right. Those sterile, phallic elms standing envious guard over the fruitful valley. Those bad, bad elms.*'

She pressed cute lips together hard; raised pert chin defiantly. '*You were there, weren't you? In the actual valley?*'

I snorted and swigged scotch, to show I couldn't be tricked out of my eternal silence that easily. Then I treated her to a nice, hard study, swirling my drink, feeling the heat of the fire on my calves. Feeling her face, the memory of her face, the memory of the mornings in Vermont. '*So who are you?*'

'*What do you mean?*'

'*Well, what's your name to start with?*'

A suspicious pause. '*Uh . . . Anne Truitt.*'

'*Honk. A lie.*'

'*Anne Truitt! That's my . . .*'

'*Sorry. She's a famous sculptress.*'

'*Well . . . I was named after her.*'

'*Both names?*'

'*Well . . .*' She burst out laughing. '*God. You're being such an asshole.*'

I laughed too, mighty pleased with myself. I shook my head. '*Mystery and romance,*' I said into my drink. '*Mystery and romance.*'

She forced herself to stop laughing — and then went right on with the melodrama, solemn and watery-eyed, as if her laughter had just been erased, edited out like a blown take in a movie. Kids. '*Look, it's just important to me, okay? It's something I need to know about. You were, like, right there. Right in the valley of the dead elms and everything.*' She actually said that. In the valley of the dead elms. Like something out of H. Rider Haggard or Conan Doyle. The romance was suffocating, the past like a hand on my throat.

'*Christ,*' I said.

'*You knew her. You were with her. You were there when she died.*' And she really wound up for the next pitch, setting her coffee mug down on my cobbler's bench, lifting her eyes — where did this cherub get such a range of gazes? '*And you have her letters too, don't you?*'

Nothing from me. I watched it go by.

'*Arthur Levine wrote about it in the* New York Times. *He said you had no right to keep history from people.*'

'*Oh yeah. History.*'

'*He said you admitted you had them by refusing to give them to him.*'

My scotch was gone but I grinned at the ice cubes. 'I told him if he didn't get off my lawn I'd stuff them so far up his ass he'd be eating her words.'

'*Then you do have them.*'

With nothing to say, I rattled the cubes against my teeth. This was no good, I thought. You could get to enjoy this. The fencing with her. Even the fencing with myself, knowing who she was, not quite letting myself know. Like one of those relationships where you spar about sex so much it becomes impossible, the sparring becomes everything. What was I going to do about her? that was the question. I thunked the empty glass onto the mantelpiece.

'*It's like I said,*' *I told her. '*I don't need my life interpreted for me. It bugs me. I've resigned from the zeitgeist. Okay?*' *I wanted to leave it at that but, ah, bitter, bitter, bitter boy; on I went. 'I was there — you're right. And somehow, call me shallow, but I missed seeing the heroic artist unafraid of the terror by night or the sculptor shaping the chaos of the twentieth century and — hey, maybe I just don't get it, but I didn't even see any phallic elm trees, silly me.*' *I managed to shut it off. 'Ach! Have you got a car somewhere? I'll give you a lift.*'

'*But I'm not a biographer.*'

'*That's right. You're Annie Truitt. Not that Annie Truitt, this one. Only not. Have I got it now?*'

She was having a problem hiding that smile of hers. I guess she was enjoying it too, all this sparkling dialogue. But she soldiered on. 'Listen, Mr Bernard,' she said. Leaning forward earnestly now with a Listen-Mr-Bernard sort of expression worked onto her tilted face. She rested her crossed arms on her knees in a manner meant to be engaging. 'I understand it must, like, hurt you to talk about these things. And I don't mean to be mysterious. It's just . . . Well, I'm not supposed to be here. Okay?'

Her father again, I thought — and then wondered if I'd muttered it aloud.

'*And I need to know, that's all,*' *she went on anyway. 'It's not, like, so ridiculous or anything. She's an inspiration. A lot of people say so. I mean, when someone dies, a famous artist — especially, for me, a woman artist, you know — and they die and no one knows who they are and then their art, you know, becomes recognized, becomes famous . . .'* I was nodding now: yeah, yeah, yeah. *'Well, it's, like, inspiring. You know? It is. I mean, it's like . . . she didn't die. Like . . . her art lives on. Or something. And so, like, if you're going through a hard time, you can think to yourself, well, this happened to this other person too, you know, so it's not so bad. You can think: well, look at Agnes Mallory.'* A noise aloud from me: exasperation, disbelief: gah! *'Well, you can,'* she said. *'It can teach you, you know, how to live. And I happen to be having kind of a hard time with that right now. How to live. So, like, I need to know.'* She gave a simple, ingenuous shrug. Was there no bottom to the girl's performance?

'Christ,' I said. 'The Easter story of art.'

'What? I don't . . .'

'An artist dies obscure, or kills herself or whatever? And then her work is resurrected and she ascends into the heaven of our admiration and the faithful learn how to live? Horseshit. She just be dead, kiddo. All of them. John Keats. Jesus Christ. A million and a half murdered children. Dead, dead, dead. That's the only thing you need to know. That oughta be the headline every fucking morning.'

Anne Truitt (the younger) closed her eyes tight and opened them as if she were having an hallucination and wanted it to go away. 'Uh – what murdered children?' she said. 'Like, what are we talking about?'

I laughed. I put my hand to my forehead, dragged it down over my nose, over my mouth, wiping my lips dry. Trapped in the cinema of her soul. One of those chubby-but-hardboiled character actors was going to play me, I could tell. With a gravelly voice and narrowed, twinkling eyes. How could I tell her this story, if she wasn't wise enough to despair?

'Tell the truth and shame the devil,' I said. 'You're Lena, aren't you?'

Caught out, her reaction was less than subtle. She looked like the heroine in some B-movie thriller. Backed to the wall by the claws of an oncoming shadow: panicky, trapped.

I pulled up the other Windsor – the one she hadn't put her dripping things on. I drew it nearer the sofa and sat down on the edge of it, leaning toward her over the cobbler's bench, elbows on my knees. I did this because my legs were getting tired from standing, but perhaps it was suggestive to her of greater kindness, more earnest

*intimacy. At any rate, she settled down. Her face went still, blank.
She waited.*

'Evelyn,' I said quietly. 'That's who you look like really. You
look like Evelyn.'

*She pressed her lips together, casting her eyes down in sensitive
distress. Yes, this was better. This was the kind of melodrama she'd
had in mind all along.*

'How is she?' I asked. 'Is she still alive?'

She nodded slowly. 'She's pretty much all right right now, I
guess,' *she said.* 'But she's been sick a lot lately. She had a blood
clot in her leg or something. And she has arthritis, which bothers
her because she likes to work in her garden. She has a house in
San Mateo. My father got it for her. It has this, like, really nice
border of flowers around it — these impatiens — and then a trellis of
roses on one wall. They were really, really nice when she could still
keep them up. Sometimes I go up and help her with it, with the
gardening. She likes to see me. And I like her too but, you know,
I don't get to go up there too much. Uh — what else can I tell you?'
She shrugged. 'She's, like, getting old, you know. She must be, like,
almost seventy or something.'

'No. I don't think so. She's not that old.'

She shrugged again. 'Sixty-five.'

'And so she lives all alone there?' *I asked her.*

'Well, my Dad has a woman look in on her every day. He's
offered to bring her down to Los Angeles, but she says she doesn't
want to be a bother. I don't think she gets along with my Mom
very well.'

*I nodded. I was moved. Moved simply by having news of her.
And by her old age. And by the girl's father — Lena's father — and
his kindness. He was always like that. A good straight guy, didn't
question the verities, did what had to be done. I sometimes thought —
and it was a thought I could really torture myself with late at night,
a thought that could close my throat with tears on a moment's notice
— I sometimes thought that he was the man I had wanted to be
when I was nine years old. The kind of steady-shooting hero-type
I pretended to be back then. Which, with my Marianne theory,
would pretty much bring the Agnes-Harry circle to its miserable
close: she had married what she thought I was and I had married
what I thought I loved in her.*

'I went and saw her just before I left,' *the girl offered now.* 'I told her I was coming here. She's the only one who knows. She said to say hello.'

'Did she?' The feeling welled in me and that was all I could trust myself to say.

'Yeah.' She hesitated. 'We wrote down some questions. I mean, I wrote them down, but I talked them over with her: the things we thought you could help with. Some of them − the questions − were hers.' She made a diffident gesture at the wet clothes on my other chair. 'They're in my vest.'

With an expression of long suffering, I indicated my permission. She lifted off the sofa and reached across me for the soggy down vest. She hung there across me, futzing with the vest's inner zipper, so that her armpit was in front of my nose and I could smell her sweet deodorant and the rain in her hair and steal a look down over the curve of her backside as she lifted her leg up to make the stretch. I toyed briefly with the idea of reaching inside my chest and squeezing my heart to cinders to stop its agony of longing, but I figured another thirty years or so and I'd be dead anyway. And then, anyway, she sat down again.

She sat down again, and she had a notebook in her hands. One of those small, thin ones reporters use. It must have been part of her original disguise. She flipped it open quite professionally too; maybe she'd spent nights practising in her garage. Goofily − attractively − she made nervous circles in the air with one white, glossy-nailed hand − she went into a ditzy preamble that went like this: 'So these are . . . It got a little wet in the rain. These are just, like, some things I just sort of, you know, wrote down.' I chewed my cud and watched her, damned if I'd help her along. 'So, like, one thing I wanted to know was, like: Were you, like, in love with her?'

I laughed. 'Is that what you wrote? Were you comma like comma in love with her?'

She deflated; made a face: I was being a paternalistic asshole.

'Here. Here,' I said. I extended my hand. 'Don't sit there reading them to me. Let me see.'

She had another face for this: reluctant, but what the hell. She handed the notebook over. It was damp, thickened with the rain. The pages were gray at the edges. Some of the writing near the edges was blurred. But it was all legible. She'd made her list of questions neatly in a round, schoolgirl script. Each one numbered,

*with a few lines under it left blank — space for the answer, I guess.
This was the first page:*

1. Were you in love with her?
2. Did you recognize her genius?
3. Do you know how she died (accident? suicide?)?
4. Do you have any of her letters?

*It went on. Four or five more pages, four or five questions each. I
riffled through them. When did you first see V. of D. Elms? was
one I picked out.*

I leaned back in my chair, back against the fanned spindles
supporting the headboard till the whole apparatus creaked and
crackled. I fixed a sardonic smile on my kisser and opposed it to
her bobbing, eager, teenaged anticipation. All the same, I knew I
was weakening. The habit of silence was wearing thin. Somehow, I
had to re-immerse myself in the ethic of it. I had to think of Perseus,
of those poor waifs playing Perseus and Andromeda in the vacant lot,
all that stuff, its reality, the privacy that kept it real. Confession, I
thought: Confession is the enemy. Confession is the secret weapon
of a society crazed with envy and suspicion of our private lives, of an
empty, jealous society trying to root out individual reality before it
strikes. Confess, says the priest; confession is good for your soul. So
you confess, and he prays as they burn you at the stake to cleanse
you of your sins. Confess, says Officer Bill, get it off your chest,
son. So you confess, and he shakes his head sadly when they hang
you from the highest tree. Confess, says Reporter Shitferbranes, the
people have a right to hear your side of the story. So you confess, and
the public and the press and the professors and the true believers —
they swarm over you like red ants with their judgements and theories
and interpretations and opinions until your moral compass and the
general imbecility of the age become inextricably intertwined.

I gritted my teeth triumphantly. I was on a roll now. I had some
big thoughts and stupid generalizations on my side too.

And now she comes to me, I continued, working myself up. This
Lena-ghost, of all people, this white-washed American specter of the
thoroughly Jewish dead, this sungrown pipsqueak who thinks history
is a factory churning out guiding lights for her improvement, she comes
here and she says: Confess — because this country is all highways and
no signposts and I'm lost as hell; confess — for me — because I'm so

cute, and Daddy wants me to go to college and gee I don't know what to do and maybe hearing about how Agnes died in agony and terror would help me figure out what I want to major in; or confess — yes, even better — confess for yourself: free yourself from your own history and join the national pastime of regeneration, the great American nulling of the tragic sense. Liz Kicks Drugs! Jill Kicks Cancer! Rock Kicks Bucket! I mean, for God's sake, man, tell your story, triumph over your suffering, inspire us, teach us that life can be mastered — Christ, what do you want to be, obscure? *The magazine cover is there for the taking.* Inside This Issue: Scandal Attorney Harry Bernard Learns to Live Again, and Gets Multi-Mil Contract to Write The Agnes Story. Plus, Learn How to Make the Best Holiday Truffles Ever! *Just open your mouth, my son. Surrender your memories to our understanding, and we'll make you a star. Confess.*

I breathed deeply, squaring my shoulders. Nothing like some bitter railing to restore your resistance, refresh your failing strength. Thus fortified, I resolved once again to defy her. To continue to defy them all — I alone. I alone am survived to not tell thee. I insist on Agnes's life to myself, not because I'm worthy of it but because I was there. I insist on her real life, unredeeming; on the details unstained by theory; on the uninterpretable sensations; on the utter incomprehensibility of her blind, head-clutching stagger from the vagina to the grave.

And so I sat there, leaning back in my chair, with Lena leaning in waiting to be saved, with the storm at the window setting the scene, and the snickering fire lighting the stage. I sat with her water-rippled notebook flipped open in my hand, and the questions in her round schoolgirl script staring up at me. Were you in love with her? Did you recognize her genius? Do you know how she died (accident? suicide?)? Do you have any of her letters?

And I thought: Yes. Yes, yes, yes.

Then I slapped the girl's notebook down on the cobbler's bench between us. 'It's no good,' I told her. 'I want you to go.'

That seemed to spark some actual emotion in her finally. Frustration, more than likely. How deep do you go in your teens? She pulled back on the sofa, pulled straight, out of the firelight, with a noise of exasperation. The wind rose and the hail spattered on the windows. Her hands went up and down, up and down, and her bottom seemed to hop and bounce on the cushion.

'How can you say that? How can you say that if you know who I am? How can you refuse to tell me anything?'

I shrugged. 'I just don't want to, kid.'

Suddenly, she bounded off the sofa, striding away from me across the room. I expected that, though: the next scene. I had the rhythm of her dramatics pretty well down now.

'It's not fair!' *she said, and there were tears in her voice stretching it to a thin whine. She went pacing back and forth before me in the energy of her tantrum, her arms still going, her hands palm-upward, flopping around as if she were trying to shake some water off.* 'You can't just sit there, you can't just go, like, "Oh. You must be Lena," and then go, like, "Oh, sorry, you've got to go now." You just can't, like, do that.'

'I guess someone forgot to fax me the new rules,' *I answered with what I hoped was infuriating calm.* 'I thought I could go, like, any damn way I chose. That's why I love America, darling. If you can pay for your own groceries and cut a deal with the prosecutors and ignore the women and the children and the press, you can still say just about anything you want. I'm saying nothing, Lena. I really do want you to go.'

Well, I thought that was a pretty good speech right off the top of my head like that. She obviously thought so too because she started crying then, when I thought she might have stretched the tantrum out a little more.

She did the crying well, though. She didn't push it too far; underplayed it rather. Swiping her eyes angrily before the tears even fell, swiveling with real petulance away from me.

'There's a box of Kleenex on the windowsill behind you,' *I said cooly. But I must admit: I wished she'd stop. She had that instinct for my weak spots, this girl, she made her mark. With these memories of mine alive and electric and with the traitorous clamoring for confession loud, she had Marianne's tears to reverberate off of, a real woman's tears of betrayal and pity: you can't just pocket those, they made embers of the nerve ends yet. Annoyed, I sat stonily and watched the girl. The fireglow was lambent in the shadows around her as she trumpeted her nose into a tissue. The space between us, firelit — the rumpled sofa, the smeared notebook on the cobbler's bench beside her coffee mug — seemed very empty and depressing with her gone. I suspected it was going to be rough again for a while, when I finally kicked her out of here. Lonely until I hardened over again. That was the whole trouble, of course. That was my incentive to keep this argument going between us as long as I could. Silence is no business for the weak, I tell you.*

'I need her, Harry,' *she said now* — *and didn't snuffle much; was annoyed at herself, in fact, and erect and struggling for dignity. Or at least she played it that way.*

I cleared my throat. 'Mr Bernard,' *I said.*

That set her off again. I knew the sort of liberal parenting crap she was used to. 'Mr Bernard. Mr Bernard. It's not fair!' *She daubed at her eyes with the crumpled Kleenex.* 'I'm not some historian or reporter or something. I don't want some, like . . . idea of her. Or theory or whatever it is you're afraid of. I want . . .' *She raised her hands, clutching the tissue. She searched the rafters for her thought.* 'You know? To touch the things she touched, to read the things she wrote. I want to talk to you* — *or listen to you* — *because you knew her. Because . . . like, you were there, where she was. When she left* — *when she died, I mean.' She leveled her glistening eyes and begged.* 'And I'm here, see. I'm still here, and I need to know why she did that. I just need to hear. I'm not going to judge you or anything. I promise!'*

Well, even I had to smile. Lowering my chin to my chest, clasping my hands between my knees where I sat. It really was cute. Just the sort of promise a kid would make, like I'll walk the dog or feed the goldfish. To not judge me. To go into the thing, open and quiet like that; to hear my story. To let the juice of it into her marrow, no babbling, no theories, no questions asked. I mean, hadn't she read the newspapers? Didn't she keep up with politics? The Tao of No-opinion — *that Negative Capability* — *it was like mummification or piety or something: a lost art. Some people didn't even believe it had ever existed. Christ, with any luck, I would've been one of them. But again, she had that girlish talent for my underbelly. I'd worked with Myers, after all, the mellow Hebe; Christ, I'd married Marianne, the ditz: I knew that transcendental quietude was still around, could still be done, even now. It was just* — *like silence* — *no business for weaklings.*

I heaved a sigh, genuinely tired of this. 'Look, kiddo,' *I said, almost kindly,* 'your mother made two, three dozen works of art, genius some of them, lots of them. And I led your father to them.*

I did my bit for mankind. Go to the museum and touch those, and glom those with your no-judgements.'

She stepped forward urgently. 'I have! I do!'

'Well, then you've got the best of her.'

'I don't want the best of her!' Another step brought her over me, back into the range of the fire, between the white bricks of the hearth and the sofa's edge. My sensation when it happened was of a desperate warm relief: I mean, I was glad the room was full of her again. Dangerous stuff that. I really had to close this up. She looked down at me. 'I mean, you know, it isn't like I'm trying to, I don't know, get a grant or something or write an article or a book about her or something. I mean, like, I see your point about that. Then you could go, like, "Okay, you have the best of her, don't be an idiot, buzz off." Okay?' Her hands fell, she went limp and plaintive. 'But I'm different. I have a right to all of her. It's part of who I am.'

'Oy,' I said, pinching the bridge of my nose. The kid was killing me. It really would be tough to take when I finally gave her the boot. But then again, the suspense was trying too. And this weariness was a downright peril. And I had to toss her out sometime anyway if I was to keep on. Raising my head, still forced to smile, clasping my hands again in a fatherly way between my knees, I went, like, 'Lena. You're a nice girl, and I wish you well. But I really do want you to go. I'll drive you to your car, if you have one . . .'

'Forget it!' she said angrily.

'I'm sorry about the storm. I didn't ask you to come.'

This to her as she streaked past. She was already marching to the other chair. Snatching her sopping vest from it, pulling it back on, shrugging it into place over the stained patches on her workshirt. The earmuffs she snapped on too in her huff. And while I sat, still looking mildly upon the space where she had been, she tromped away behind me to the door.

I took a breath and braced myself there on my Windsor. This was not, I knew, the end of Lena yet, not quite. Once she had her hand on the knob, the urge to dart a savage glance over her shoulder at me, the pressure to pose like that and make a final, dramatic, even devastating speech before her triumphant exit was sure to be overwhelming. I dreaded it, but at least I knew it was coming. It was, I hoped, my one big advantage over her in the way of self-defense: She'd never heard of the Parthians, but I had been to the movies.

I had every gesture she was going to make down pat.

~ 13 ~

I stood above the White River on a ledge of rock. Below me was a swimming hole, empty in the early morning. To my right was a high metal bridge; it led across the water to a dirt road that snaked up into the wooded hills. Beyond the bridge was a campground, yellow tents on the river bank, the smoke of breakfast fires rising. To my left, upstream, the river wound around a bend and out of sight. There would have been heavy rapids up there a month or two before. Even now, it was white water, sluicing into view around jutting gray boulders, slapping into the sides of the ledge upon which I stood before smoothing out over the deep water below me. As I looked in that direction, there came a high, delighted, feminine cry. A girl rounded the bend of the river, riding a yellow inner tube over the swift waves.

She had a tangled blonde mane. She was suntanned and sleek. She wore a small bikini that left the sweet upper globes of her breasts bare. She dangled her hands in the water and threw back her head as she rode and screamed and laughed. She was in her teens – in her twenties maybe – and how she made me ache, my soul in my groin. I watched her sail under me, heard her cry out wonderfully to her boyfriend, who now came around the bend after her in a tube of his own. I could have died of the longing. Oh, oh, oh, I thought. Oh, youth irretrievable. Oh schmuck, schmuck, schmuck.

Then Agnes called me from the bridge. 'Harry!'

I looked up and saw her striding across, waving to me over the rail as she came. I picked up the overnight bag I'd bought in Rutland and scrambled down the rock with it and up a scrubby path to the road. I walked onto the bridge to meet her. She strode on toward me, grinning. I couldn't take her in, not all of her, not as fast as she came and with all my expectations blown away. I don't know how I'd pictured her. Wan and nervy and overquick, I guess. Not like this. Small, lean, muscular, so brown her smile flashed white; all the leopardy vibrance in her visible sinews, all the powerful vibrance in her eyes. Her face had thinned — I remembered the grim, round, monkey-featured face of yore — and now the features were very sharp and strong and framed in a downpour of long, straight, black, black hair.

'Welcome to disaster,' she said, and I tossed my bag to the pavement and we threw our arms around each other.

And so I was a blank, and held her hard, pouring myself over her, closing my eyes. I smelled the sun in her skin and felt the strength in her arms and the pressure of her breasts against me. She was wearing just cut-off jeans and a black halter top and I pressed my fingers gratefully into the hot skin of her bare back and her bare shoulders.

We broke. She held me at arms length, looking me over. With that white smile and those eyes, their overpowering liveliness.

'So?' she said. 'Are you an asshole?'

'Pretty much,' I managed to get out. 'Yeah.'

'My luck — and here I've been praying you'd come.'

She had a deep laugh that rung in me. I picked up my bag, and she took my arm, wrapped her arms cozily around mine as we started walking back across the bridge.

'So what's the plan?' she said up at me. 'We fuck each other and the Dionysian and Appolonian merge in a great white flash and all nature's set aright?'

'Uh . . . well, yeah, that was my general outline.'

'I'll bet.' We strolled to the dirt road. 'God,' she said with a comical sigh. 'If we could really just be what we meant to each other! Instead of what we are.'

I laughed too, looking down into her sable hair.

I had had no idea it would be so good to see her.

The road climbed steeply and more steeply still. Past an inn on an acre of cleared land, and a pinewood vacation cabin back in the trees. Past a few more driveways and then into thicker forest, becoming a rutted switchback as it climbed.

Agnes waved at the windshields of a jeep or two that came bumping down past us to the bridge below. But after that, we were alone together, the forest dwarfing us and pressing in on the roadsides with spills of mulch and beer cans, and drawing back into superstitious depths strafed by the morning sun. It was a tough climb for me and I was breathing hard. And I was beginning to feel nervous, with this sense that I was climbing away from everyone everywhere. And Agnes said:

'So I shouldn't have written you all that shit, huh? I really was praying you'd come.'

'No, no,' I puffed. 'I wanted to hear from you.'

'Well. Since you are here, would you mind making everything in my past have been all right?'

'Sure, no problem.'

'And there's kind of a clunking noise in my refrigerator too. God, it's nice to have a man around the house.'

I smiled, but she was way ahead of me. I couldn't think of anything clever to say and, in fact, began to feel almost a panic of solitude and misgiving. She spoke as if we both knew why I was here, and I didn't. And she cursed so much, which made me uncomfortable in a woman. And she didn't shave under her arms, I noticed too, which made my heart sink and even repelled me. I didn't know her, I didn't really know her. I gazed off into the forest to avoid her now, huffing hard with the steep climb, and huffing harder to fill the silence. No houses anywhere, no view but trees. The tortuous forest interior murmurous and chilling as a monk's chant. Low bursts of birdsong coming from its invisible reaches, call and response, intimate and strange like conversations on the streets of other countries. I mean, where the hell was I? What the hell was I doing here? Where was my family? Where was everybody? I had a shock as I noticed some crouched thing peering back at me from in there: a car, it turned out; the rusted skeleton of an abandoned Pontiac, staring like a giant toad from its decaying headlight sockets. That did it. My fragile sense of escape broke open, and I got a full blast of the insanity of what I'd done. My poor wife! The police! And to be here alone, with this stranger, this neurotic woman who could barely hold her own life together . . .

I turned to her, meaning to pull away, and then I saw her

and it was all right again. She had her face confidently lifted
to the mountain breeze, and strands of black hair playing on
her browned skin — and I did know her; that hadn't changed.
And I did understand what was going on, sort of, though
I wasn't as precise and glib about it all as she. Well, it had
always been like that between us, hadn't it. She was one of
these artist types, after all.

'I didn't just come here, you know, for you, because of
your letters,' I said, without thinking. She didn't get me at
first — and then she did, before I finished: 'I'm in trouble of
my own.'

Her reaction wasn't everything I might've wished: her
energy did falter, her chin jerked a little to one side as if
she'd taken a blow. But she showed me that bright white
grin again. 'Sure, right,' she said. 'We'll talk all about it.' And
I had my first glimpse of how strong the force still was in her
— joy, I would say now, the force of joy — and how battered
it was, how she staggered inwardly, and reeled.

'Look.' She pointed proudly up a final, steep ascent.
'There's my house.'

It stood behind red pines on the top of a hill. A long,
one-story log cabin with a low, shingled hip roof. There
was a round tin chimney gleaming up from the roof's center.
Black smoke chugged from it steadily, blowing off to the side
as it cleared the trees and dissipating beneath the clear sky.

'It's great,' I gasped, working hard up the slope. 'But I hope
you know CPR.'

'You're an old New York City fart,' she said, tugging on
my arm.

'Thanks. I needed you to tell me that. Christ!' I pulled
up, halfway there, trying to catch my breath, looking around
me. There was a view from here, over the forest top. Your
basic green hills in misty distance, with swathing strokes of
light and shadow. 'Great spot,' I said, like any New Yorker
admiring a country house. 'How much land do you have?'

'Oh, acres and acres. Woods and The Swimhole and The
Meadow of Wildflowers and the Path Through The Pines
and the Valley of Dead Elms and after that there's a nature
preserve that goes on forever. We used . . .'

She barely said this last, but I got the picture immediately. We used to wander through it together, she was about to say. And I imagined Roland and her to the sound of violins, tripping sweetly hand in hand, discovering and christening the mysterious regions of their domain. Sad stuff now that it had all gone sour. 'Wow,' I said, still leaning on my New Yorkisms. 'How the hell could you afford it?'

'My Dad's money, when he died. We built the house ourselves, my friends and I. One of the good things about being an artist is you know all these craftsmen who are out of work. Come on.' She had let go of my arm and was continuing up the hill easily, the big muscles showing on her thighs. 'You can explore while I work.'

'Work? I just got here. And it's Sunday. And I haven't seen you for twenty years.'

'I know, but the light. I gotta use the light. Come on.'

She waved me up as I labored after her. Seeing her above me, framed against the red shafts of pines, vital and at home and with her butt moving in her short jeans, I had a momentary impulse to catch up with her and take her by the arm, to swing her round to some violins of my own and pull her to me. I had the momentary sense that if I kissed her like that, like in a movie, this would work out, whatever this was, like a movie, and I would get clear of everything somehow. Of course, I was a little long in the tooth already to believe that and probably didn't have the courage anyway. And I was just glad, finally, to pull alongside her again and be next to her again as we continued on to the top.

The cabin stood on a circle of dark red earth. An old gray pickup was parked out by the perimeter. The site was set back from the edge of the hill and the high pines screened and shaded it making it feel tenebrous and secluded. She led me inside through a flimsy screen door which slammed loudly behind us.

'It's not big or anything,' she said, as I blinked at it after the sunlight.

This central room was most of the house, it seemed, too small to be sprawling, but broad enough under the cathedral beams. Dark but airy, with small windows all thrown open.

Rustic and spare: just a sloppy purple sofa and some exhausted log chairs pulled haphazardly around a wood stove in the middle of the floor. The night cold lingered indoors and the stove was lit. The fire outlined the iron door in orange, and I could hear it breathing harshly, one long exhalation.

At the first sight of the place, I felt another small surge of loneliness, of misgiving. I couldn't have said just why.

'The kitchen's over there,' said Agnes, pointing to a railed alcove on the room's far side. 'There should be some food or other if you're hungry.'

'Yeah, I am.'

'That's my bedroom and the bathroom, and that's my studio. And that's it.'

Dutifully I ambled over to the bathroom door, holding my bag before me in both hands. Then I moved to the bedroom and peeked in. It was darker in there with the pine trunks outside pressing close to the windows, but it was light enough to see the bed unmade and toiletries scattered, and her clothes for days, maybe weeks, tossed down on chairs and the floor and anywhere. I glanced over at the studio too, but that door was shut.

'The place is a mess, I know,' she said.

I nodded at it all, the way one does, ambling back toward her. 'It's great. Really.'

She nodded too, looking the place over herself. I came to stand in front of her.

'It's not the light,' she said up at me. 'Obviously. I mean, about working, my having to work. I *need* to work. I just . . .' She shrugged.

'Oh, no, yeah, sure, right,' I said. And I nodded some more. 'So what are we, like, in love with each other? Or we would've been, or . . .'

'Just what in tarnation's going on around here?'

'Yeah.'

'Beats me,' she lied blithely – good thing I hadn't mentioned my sudden agony of terror and yearning. She went up on tiptoe to kiss my cheek: mwah. 'Why don't you explore the place till I'm done. There's paths all over.'

My frustrated urge to connect with her was nearly desperate as she walked away. And now here was something really

strange, something practically gothic, to make it worse. As she
went to the studio, she drew a single key from the pocket of
her cut-offs. I mean, the house was wide open, but this one
door had a deadbolt. She unlocked it. She opened the door
only slightly too, and slipped secretively through the gap.

'Don't get lost,' she said, smiling brightly one more time.

I tossed my bag down by the sofa. It's a little late for that,
I thought.

She closed the door behind her and damn me if I didn't
hear her bolt it again from within.

I'd planned a moment then for a gander at the details. The
framed pictures on the wall, the flower vase on a rough-hewn
dining table, the mugs and crockery I'd spotted hanging from
hooks on the kitchen wall – to search for a clue, I mean.
Because something really was off about the place: that aura
of a dangerous despair wasn't all coming from me. It was
something simple, basic, and it bugged me: a forgotten song
sort of thing. But it was no good trying to figure it out now.
Now, it was body time in flesh city, the functions had had it
with mystery and romance. I was starving, I needed to take
a piss – and tired, God, I was exhausted, nearly sick with it,
nearly swaying.

Agnes began to work. I heard her going at it. Whack,
whack, whack, chuck, chuck, chuck behind the bolted door.
Mallet and chisel on wood. I stumbled roughly into the
bathroom. Even the bathroom door had no lock, but I was
just too tired to think about it anymore. I pissed with my
chin on my chest, my eyes closing. Then I forced myself
to the kitchen and scarfed handfuls of fresh-baked bread
and Swiss cheese at the open refrigerator door. Woozily,
I resolved that this was what I would do from now on:
eat only healthy, simple foods like this; and I would move
to the country when my troubles were over, and learn the
names of all the trees and birds.

I tottered to the sofa and dropped down on it. To the inter-
mittent rhythms of her chisel, and the steady warm breathing
of the woodstove beside me, I fell into a black sleep.

When I woke up it was well into the afternoon. The fire was

out, and I was chilly, though the air through the window was warm. For a few seconds, it was quiet, and I lay on the sofa, hoping Agnes had finished. But then the mallet started in again behind the studio door. No wonder she had such muscular arms.

I sat up, got up quickly, washed up quickly, putting some vigor into it. I'd decided to take Agnes's advice and go out for a while — before the ominous atmosphere of Castle Mallory began to oppress me again. On a shelf braced up beside the kitchen railing, I found a row of books, solemn women's novels and a few paperbacks on art and a few on nature. One of these last was a handbook on wildflowers. I picked it out, ready to make a start on this new, organic life of mine.

But the first thing I did, I admit, when I got outside, was wander round the house to the studio side. Just curious — I wanted to see if I could look in through the windows and see what all the secrecy was about. I passed by with a great show of innocence, hands in pockets, glancing all around. The windows were all hung over, though, with stained canvases. Stepping back, I saw, on the slope of the roof, two plexiglas bubbles through which she got this precious light of hers. So that was that. I set off on my own to explore.

The day was fine. There was a fresh, poignant undercurrent in the breezes. A path of spongy duff angled down westerly through the woods, and I took that, marching briskly. Hut, hut, good exercise, good for the mind. A little sweat to ease the wracking woe-is-me routine.

After a few minutes, I became aware of the steady hiss of the river off to my left. I could see it then through the trees, foamy and rippling over its rocky bed. I figured I must be approaching the Swimhole; my flower handbook wouldn't be much good there, so I turned off at a dog's leg I saw and headed deeper into the forest.

The biographies of Agnes go on forever about these acres, her property, and its importance to her, the place-names she gave. Roland gives poetical interviews from his Hollywood home, and art school girls make pilgrimages, and every other year or so some jerk waxes half-smart on its effect on her work or even its symbolism in her mind, God help us. But for all that, it was a magical place, I felt it right away. Maybe it was her, the way she loved it, the way she moved in it, as I'd already seen, as its creature, in such off-handed communion. Also, though, there were patches of it that simply resonated in the mind somehow. They were beautiful, but they were so weirdly familiar and effortless too, like just one more grand view on a picture postcard. You couldn't admire them, you could hardly really *see* them at all. They just drew you in, fairy-tale fashion, to some zone of natural imagination, as you moved along.

I felt the effect even then, as I headed down this narrowing trail. Low hornbeams and half-sprouted elms closed over me to form a descending tunnel. It thickened and gloomed as it curled around, and I could see ahead where it opened again into a sedate medallion of mote-hung gold. Anyone can imagine the metaphors, the symbols – this shadowy passage into radiant light – it's all been done; it's a small industry these days. But they botch up the fact of it, the feeling of it. Because it was somehow all so *known* already; it was defiantly unremarkable.

I collided with the fabulous web of a tiny spider and, dragging the sticky silk from my lips, bowed out of the tunnel and into what she had called The Meadow of Wildflowers. It was a great, stout crescent of grass bordered by forest on three sides and by low hills along the northwest fringe. It was very green, and wonderful with sprays of purple, and yellow and white – loosestrife and goldenrod and Queen Anne's lace, that is, with white moths and monarchs bobbing around over it, and gnats dancing in the beams from the sun, which had sunk now to the crest of a hill.

I walked out into it, bugs springing from the grass before my feet and chittering and rattling all around me. Redwinged blackbirds ditching their blinds and making for the trees as I came on farther. And I reached the center of it, where the colorful meadow was all around me, the hills and the trees and so on. And again, it was all so placidly present, so *there*, it felt, within as well as without, that it really beggared thought; so beggared thought, in fact, that I found it a bit hard to bear.

So I got me out my book, I did, and started naming off the flowers. Kneeling over clover with a scientific frown, chucking the bellflowers with my finger. Sticking my shnoz in the milkweed and watching the grubs shimmy up its boles. That reminded me of Agnes and her monkey statue with the worms in it. And looking up, I noticed that the whole place brought Agnes back to me in the way she hadn't herself. The old times were with me now: the stream in back of her house, the walks home – the ache of regret, too, which I guess was part of what I'd come for.

Well, after enough of this, I could stand the place a little better. And I got to my feet, and the sun was just down, and the sky was royal blue with an undulent line of tangerine above the hills, and what do you know? I was one serene Harry suddenly. Or at least a more solid Harry, a more actual Harry, who had a real, calmer sense of his situation, who knew the score. I did know it, to my surprise. There really wasn't much mystery to it, after all. I had a pretty good sense of what would happen next – with the Feds, I mean, and the newspapers, and my wife. I realized I had to call my wife too. She'd be terrified I'd killed myself or something. The doofus. I could've kicked my own ass, just panicking, just running out on her like that.

So I sighed. I gave the meadow a last once-over. A magical spot it was, absolutely.

And then the sky went a shade darker and the big empty place began to seem kind of creepy, so I hied it the hell out of there.

Incredibly enough, our heroine was still locked up and malleting away when I got back, lamplight now seeping under the studio door. But then, just moments after I came in, she seemed to give over. I heard other noises briefly as I replaced her wildflower book on the shelf – sweeping maybe, and some heavy piece of furniture scraping the floor. And then the bolt thunked back, the door opened a little. She slipped out, and with her back to me, shot the bolt home once again.

Christ, what was she building in there, a vampire? Whatever it was, it had sure drained her. All that morning's vim was history. She looked limp and weak, her tan a thin layer over sunken cheeks and deep pallor. And she seemed irritated to see me waiting for her, as if I were one more problem than she could tolerate today. *This is the woman who wrote those letters to me,* I thought.

'You okay?' I said.

'Tired.' She tried to smile, brushing her hair off her forehead. 'Why don't you pour yourself a drink while I make dinner?'

'No, that's all right.' I was a purified, natural man now, see; no more booze. 'Well, on second thought, what have you got?'

I had a beer, leaning on the kitchen rail with the bottle. Watching as she shuffled wearily from refrigerator to stove. She made Spanish omelettes, pretty expertly it looked like. I'm attracted to domestic women, and the sight of her cooking fueled my warmth for her and my vague fantasies of escape.

I told her how I'd gone to the meadow, which seemed to brighten her up a little. A few times as I described the experience, she lifted a smile to me and said, 'Yes. Yes.' But then she'd sink away again, and go on about her work without speaking; blinking with exhaustion sometimes, or coming to a stop for a moment, forgetting what she had meant to do.

She was silent for a long time too as we ate together at either end of the rude wooden table. I was pretty much out of conversation myself and there were longer and longer lapses: the sounds of metal forks on clay plates, the miserable concentration on grains of rice and scraps of egg, the steady traffic of frogs outside and the crickets between the floorboards. All depressing as hell, because I wanted so much to be with her, to feel close to her, not to be alone.

Finally, and with an effort I think, she raised her face. But she regarded me none-too-pleasantly and her voice was hollow and wry. 'So?' she said. 'Are the police after you?'

I nodded. 'I would think so, by now.'

'You're not a murderer or anything, I hope.'

'No.' I leaned back heavily in my chair with a second bottle of beer. 'Just a scumbag basically. Overlooked some minor political bullshit, took some illegal gifts, cheated on my wife. You know the routine. The screws want me to rat on Bugsy and Big Al.'

'Uh huh. And will you?'

'No.' This is what I had decided in the meadow. 'I actually hope they nail the bastards. But I'm not turning them in to buy out of my mistakes. Ricco squeals on no one.'

She kept up the sardonic tone, but I could see she was suffering in those live-wire eyes. I hated this. 'Will you have to go to jail?'

'I don't think so. To be honest. They haven't really got that much on me. I didn't do that much. They'll just lean on me, make sure it all gets in the papers. And I'll be disbarred, probably.'

'What about your wife? What'll she do?'

I shrugged. 'Forgive me, I would think. I couldn't bear that. I'll have to leave her.'

'Do you love her?' I didn't answer. 'Ah, you do,' she said. 'She was made for you. You adore her.'

She was studying me with unnerving directness, so I studied her back. High cheeks, deep eyes, thick lips and a beakish sort of nose, all intense and overpowering. Not beautiful. It was her energy that made her so desirable, I figured. Or maybe the beer. I sure wanted those cut-offs gone just now; I wanted in between those muscular legs of hers.

'I do have to call her,' I said.

She gave a tired snort, sitting back from her empty plate. 'You'll have to take the truck into town. My phone's been cut off.'

'You're joking.'

'This morning. About ten minutes after you called me.'

'Because of money?'

I think she considered lying about this. She turned in her chair and glanced at me sidewise. It made me feel my position: this nostalgic fugitive intruding on her years of solitude. But she gave in. She said: 'Oh, it was on purpose, more or less. Roland's been badgering me. He's getting annoyed. You know, he has some big offer to go to Hollywood and score a movie. He doesn't know what to do with the kid.'

I suppose I wanted to get back at her for the crack about Marianne – before I could stop myself, I said: 'Maybe you ought to take her, Agnes. Obviously, this shit is just killing you.'

She laughed once, a sound like something falling to the ground. 'Maybe you should just stay out of it, Harry.'

Tilted back in my chair, I raised my bottle to her. 'Right,' I said, 'that's what I meant.'

The night had gone colder fast, the way it does in the mountains. Agnes closed the windows while I cleaned up the dishes. She brought in logs from outdoors somewhere and built the fire again in the woodstove.

When I was finished, she was sitting on the couch with a glass of wine, staring blankly at the blaze through the stove's open door. I sat down next to her. She put her head on my shoulder.

'Sorry, Mr Har.'

'No, no.' I put my arm around her. I kissed the white part in her black hair. I breathed in wood and work-sweat and some feminine shampoo.

'Evil Agnes mustn't hold you to her imagination,' she said. 'I can't be much of a thrill for you either.' She sighed. 'It's all just who you are in the end.'

'God, I hope not. I haven't the faintest fucking notion of who I am. That's how I got the shaft.'

She gave a low, appealing giggle into my shirtfront — by which time, of course, my hardon was caught painfully against the crux of my thigh. An intrusion on this gentle moment, but there you are. I looked away from her to cool myself down, concentrating on the melancholy reaches of the room.

And then, as they say, it hit me: what was so wrong with the place. What was so oddly morose and somehow suspenseful, even frightening about it, as if some ceaseless minor chord echoed in its atmosphere.

'Where's all your work?' I asked her.

'Hm?'

'It can't all be in the studio? I mean, you've been at it for, like, what? Five years? Seven years? Vere's da art, Chahlie?'

She raised her face to me sleepily. 'Oh,' she murmured. 'Don't, Harry.' She let me kiss her, and kissed me so softly on the lips that I wanted to rend my garments with the unfairness of life and with my desire.

'I'm finished,' she whispered up at me. 'I love you, you know. I've always loved you. But I'm finished. I'm already dead.'

It was a little tough to sleep with my hair standing on end like that, my eyes jacked wide open and the tip of my dick somewhere up around my chest. Still, I did manage to doze off around three in the morning, clutching my blanket around my chin on the sofa as the last of the fire died.

It was the clang of the woodstove door that woke me in the morning. Some time near six, with the sky just barely light. I pulled my nose out of the dusty upholstery and rolled over, squinting. Agnes was retreating from the stove to the front door as the fire snorted to life again. She was wearing a thin, ratty bathrobe of green tartan and I could tell, by the flow of her body, that she was naked underneath.

'Ssh,' she whispered at me. 'I'm going for my swim. Go back to sleep.'

I pulled my blanket close around me, glad for the warmth of the fire, and watched through narrowed eyes as she worked the wooden door open and pushed out through the screen. I listened to her light footsteps fading on the path into the forest, and then lay watching the orange outline around the woodstove door while the pall of fear and sadness settled over me.

Agnes, though . . . I was dressed and showered when she came back, and she was full of bright smiles and energy again. Rubbing her wet hair with a towel she carried, her breasts and buttocks printed in water on her robe and she all wifely unconcern. Electrifying it was, though I clung to my self-pity.

She dressed in her bedroom with the door open, while I wandered into the kitchen. I pondered the old-fashioned coffee pot helplessly and listened to the sounds of her tossing her wardrobe around, searching for an outfit.

'Go on, old Harry, I'll do it,' she said, rushing in – in shorts now and an *I Lo Vermont* sweatshirt – chasing me away. I managed to put some butter and knives on the table, all dolefully. And she made corn bread – fresh corn bread from scratch – chattering the while about the pleasures of the

Swimhole. 'Go down in the afternoon, when the water's warmer. About three o'clock, it's perfect. You have to wear a suit then, though, cause all these fucking, you know, tubers and canoers go by,' and on and on like that. She was very enthusiastic about it.

Breakfast took a long time, more than an hour, first juice, then coffee, then the hot bread when it was ready, and coffee again with our feet up on the extra chairs. She talked about the property and the places I should go and explore while she was working, and it was enviable and charming how much she loved the place. Thinking back on it, I realize she didn't mention the Valley of Dead Elms again, but I didn't notice that at the time. She directed me to the Path Through The Pines and Cathedral Ridge and something called the Elf Hollow, and described them excitedly with her black eyebrows hiked up and her hands held open in the space in front of her. I suppose there was a touch of mystic back-to-nature stuff in the way she talked, but I felt I understood it, having been to the Meadow of Wildflowers, and anyway, she was very appealing as she talked, throwing herself back in her chair sometimes as if startled and laughing a lot at her own raptures. I confess, I would have liked to steer her back to this fascinating business about loving me, and even to have shared a comforting groan or two over the impossible situation we were clearly heading for. But her mood would not allow it, and the force of her interests – the force of her in general – was far greater than mine, which I also understood and acknowledged even then in my manly pride.

As we refreshed our second mugs of coffee – and I picked more chunks of corn bread from the pan – she moved from exalting Vermont to dishing New York and its corrupt world of art galleries and theorists. I guess every failed artist sings this tune – that's what I chalked it up to then – but it did sound awful, especially this business about galleries taking fifty per cent of the sale; I was aghast at that. Mainly, in any event, this was her springboard into her own concept of the enterprise at hand. And talking about this – about art, I mean – made her eyes downright hypnotic with excitement. I couldn't keep up with everything she said, but the way she said it – it sure did make me want to lunge across the table and kiss her mad and fuck her silly. All right, that may not have been the response she was going for, but it was mine own, and I'll hold it up to any of the claptrappers who dissect her nowadays and who'd have to run back under their toadstools clutching their various genitals, I swear, if ever she strode back onto the scene. They've never come near understanding her, never guessed the half of it, never touched it, committed as they are to their own notions and careers. She was all over the place, all over history, with huge, sweeping, inflexible ideas – the kind you get when you argue mostly with yourself – and a vision that covered mankind from the creation to the night before last. The Holocaust was a big part of it – the chamber doors of Auschwitz being a sort of modern *Gates of Hell* – and the *Gates of Hell* played their part and the Industrial Revolution and Newton and Darwin and guys like that – Freud; and the Death of Faith, which had to do, so help me, with her Bible theories, and a general picture of humanity as a single organism, going through childhood, maturity and death eventually, and all the while deluded into feeling that the inevitable cycles and developments of each stage were its own creations and within its power. Artists just needed craft and inborn genius – *Craft! Craft!* she said, *Genius! Talent!* – simply to capture nature, and it was nature, not art, that would change in the evolving human mind. That's the Harry version of it anyway. 'Abstraction,' I remember she said, 'is the panicky reaction to the materialistic revelation of the human form; the discovery of the real body, without magic, without any bullshit about the soul is what sent us into a panic of abstraction. That's why every new abstract trend is always being described as 'bold' or 'daring' or 'shocking'. To hide the fact that it's all just cowardice and horror really. And the fucking theorists who hold the structure up are just like the Catholic monks except with God taken out of it. The inner systems of speculation outlive their purposes. They just can't stop stuffing their angels onto the heads of pins. That's why I fucking hate New York. It's the new Vatican. It is!'

Well, we all have our lives, I guess, and our ideas, smart and stupid, are just our emotions made to sound like objective truths. That's how I see it now, at least, though at the time

I had no thought, no clue, that there was anything desperate in what she said, any last plea to the gods or powers for exactly that sort of courage and realism which she demanded from the unable age but in no way possessed. Oh man! was what I thought as I lifted my coffee to my lips once more, as I watched her across the rim where she gestured and railed, her aspect turned to neon: Oh man, would I like to ball her! God! What she is! What she could have been! Christ, what *I* could have been if I just could've loved her long enough to discover . . . something, myself, anything.

She tapered off in the end and became watchful. Still pleasant and full of beans, but careful of the light, see, expertly gauging the spread of daylight at the cabin windows. My loneliness seeped back into me as I realized what she was waiting for and that she was going to get up soon and go lock herself into the studio again. I tried to keep her talking, questioned her, diddled her vanity, but eventually she set her mug down with a definitive clump and stood from her chair, stretching.

'The keys to the truck are hanging up in the kitchen,' she said.

Which was bad enough – because, of course, this call I had to make to Marianne was weighing a ton on me. But when she had unlocked the studio again, and slipped so cautiously inside, and shot the bolt; when the whack and chunk of the mallet and chisel started – to go on, I knew, until the daylight failed – it was worse still. I found that the oppressive sadness of the cabin had been thrice magnified by the sudden absence of her vitality. All that talk, I mean, all that sexy, jazzed-up yammering about art and man's destiny and so forth – and now there I sat alone at the breakfast table with the birds cheeping indifferently in the pines outside and, around me, the big dark wooden room gloating and cavernous. And empty. Empty.

Where was her sculpture, for Christ's sake? All that yammering. All those years of work. Where the hell was her art?

I bumped down the dirt hill in the pickup. Over the metal bridge with the campers waking on the banks far below, and a few kids diving off the boulders to the right. I drove the curling mountain two-lane down into Gaysville. Not much of a town. A few gas stations at the edge of the road, a restaurant, which was closed, a few general stores. I bought myself a *Times* at one of these last and sat in the truck's cab reading it over. Parked on the slope, I was, of the little asphalt strip outside, in the far slot, next to the old-style glassed-in phone booth. The sun shone through the booth, the phone waited expressionless inside, and the blood, in my throat, in my heart, in my whole body, was as heavy as molten stone.

I was there, in the paper, all right. Front page, a one column lead. *Commissioner Vanishes As Inquiry Nears*. A good story. The Feds had slipped them everything. The assessments, the Florida trip, the hookers. Even the connection to Umberman, who was quoted saying he was 'deeply hurt' that a young man he'd trusted and supported should have shown himself to be blah blah blah. Well, at least Marianne knew the story now. That ought to have made it easier on me. But it took a long time before I kicked my way out of the truck, and walked heavily to the phone.

It was not at all how I'd imagined – and I'd thought I'd imagined it every way it could be. She didn't go noble on me, or hysterical or cold. After the first long trembling silence of relief when she heard my voice, she was the same Marianne whom I knew and lived with: we talked it over as husband and wife would, as if discussing a child's sickness, say, or the loss of a job. Her voice was quiet and measured. She'd been terribly worried about me, she said. Was I all right? Did I have a place to stay? Stuff like that. Charlie was at the park with a sitter, which was a blessing: I didn't have to hear him babbling in the background. Yes, I thought, this can be borne, I can get through this. It was only later, when I was driving back to the cabin, that I saw the big picture of it, that I had to pull over to the roadside for a moment to pound wildly on the steering wheel and spit curses at my own stupidity and ignorance. It was then, finally, that I understood how much she'd looked up to me and respected me, the way women do when they love you, and how I hadn't begun to realize that – wouldn't have believed it if I had – until I'd blown it all. For something. For what? I couldn't remember.

But on the phone, I just concentrated on getting through. I explained to her what I thought would happen. I tried to make it sound as endurable as I could.

'Where are you now?' she asked me softly.

'I shouldn't say that,' I told her, fumbling for a reason. 'The Feds, you know, they might ask you. I don't want you to have to lie. I just need a few more days.'

And then she said: 'Are you with that girl? The one in Vermont, the one who writes to you?'

'No, no, of course not,' I said. 'I just need to be alone and think, that's all.'

So then, when she did start to cry, I figured it was because I was still lying to her, even now, which meant the marriage was pretty well over, which only I had already known.

It was a few seconds before she got her voice again. 'I'm sorry,' she said.

'Christ,' I said, clutching my breast in my fist. 'Christ, don't apologize to me, Marianne.'

'Well,' she said, after another silence. 'Come back soon, all right? And don't hurt yourself anymore. We love you.'

I tried to tell her I loved her too, but the stone wouldn't clear my throat.

My hike that morning was not so successful as the first. I was too miserable, for one thing, and I got lost in a particularly scrubby patch of woods for another. I managed to learn the names of a few trees from another of Agnes's handbooks, and then gave it up and worked my way back to the cabin around one o'clock. I ate a couple of cold chicken legs while Agnes hammered away behind her door. And then I drank a beer, which knocked me out on the sofa after last night's sleepless hours.

I was awake before the day started dying in earnest. I lay where I was, listening to the mallet go, my soul like an anvil. When I got up, it was to push back the grinning emptiness of the place a little. The room was beginning to gather shadows in the corners and basically get on my nerves.

I paced the room a while and read the books on the shelf and paced the room again to the chisel's rhythm. I found myself eyeing the bolted studio door every so often and I felt its draw on my curiosity and my yearning. I stepped outside only once – to break that attraction, and to breathe the cooling air beneath the pines and watch the sun setting into the green hills. Then, going back inside, I eventually wandered over to the clapboard wall that separated the main room from her bedroom. I studied the pictures hanging there; I hadn't taken much notice of them before.

It was a little gallery, five pictures in a straight row. Just photographs torn out of books or magazines and sloppily placed behind the glass of cheap snapshot frames. All were of sculpture from different times. I suppose I could identify them now, but I couldn't then. There was some typical Egyptian king or other sitting stiffly on a throne; an absolute gas of a Greek soldier with a neat-o helmet and a face as noble as a god's; a Roman emperor – Vespasian probably – pointing grandly over his dominions; a sexy Michelangelo nude seeming to rouse himself languorously out of the rough marble; and some sort of unpleasant mish-mash of slates or stones arranged out in the desert somewhere. I went over them carefully, to pass the time, feeling there must be some point to the arrangement. Great moments in sculpture, great sculpture on parade – something like that. Which shows you how much I knew about it.

I was surprised by the sound of the bolt thunking home and turned to find Agnes already there. Leaning back against the studio door with both hands behind her. Still and stiff as a statue herself, as if petrified by exhaustion. Her cheeks were heavy again and her complexion sallow. She glared at me – sneered at me almost, I thought, as if to say: who let this idiot into my house?

It didn't matter: I was delighted to see her, and my mood warmed and rose.

'Hi!' I said.

She snorted. She asked thickly: 'Like my gallery?'

'Uh . . . Yeah, sure.'

She pushed off the door as if to come toward me, but instead she stopped where she was and rubbed her face with both hands, wearily. When she looked up, wincing, she headed past me for the kitchen. She waved the pictures away, going on as if it bored her.

'Jew killers I've known and loved,' she said.

Puzzled, I examined the pictures again, even scratching the side of my head with a finger. 'I guess I missed that.'

She was in the kitchen now, out of sight. I heard her uncapping a couple of beers.

'The Egyptians enslaved us,' she called out. 'The Greeks laid the groundwork for anti-Semitic theories.'

'Did they? Man, they were clever.'

'Their ideal of perfection inspired the Nazis. And the Romans fucking flattened Jerusalem, the Vatican set us on fire for laughs . . .'

'And the modern guys bore us to death?' I called back.

She carried in the beers with a tired strut. Handed me a bottle. 'That's our answer. That inhuman, meaningless crap. Who would look at that shit if you could look at Michelangelo?'

As she knocked back the brew, she fixed such a gaze of intimate rancor on the photographs that I gave up trying to kid her out of it. It was another of her humongous theories and typical that way, but more connected, I suspected from her letters, to these after-work depletions of hers.

'I don't get it,' I said. 'You mean, if we want to make good art, we have to be anti-Semitic again?'

Her laugh was ugly. 'What do you mean "we", Jew-boy?'

I managed to let this ride. 'I guess I'm just not up on all the Jewish stuff, to be honest. I wasn't raised that way. Hell, everybody hates everybody else most of the time. I figure you can't get obsessed about it.'

That's what I said, all right. And why that – which sounded reasonable enough – should've seemed insipid to me at the moment, while what she said – which was kind of nuts – seemed profound, I don't know. But Agnes gave me another what-an-idiot look, and I somehow felt I deserved it. Then she threw the whole thing over, half-smiling, letting out her breath with a whiffle.

'Okay,' she said, still not altogether pleasantly. 'D'you call your wife?'

She asked this, and then drifted away, yawning, to the front door. It was still standing open, despite the chillier dusk, and she leaned against the frame with her beer, looking out through the screen at the pines.

'Yeah,' I said softly, and hoped she'd leave it at that.

And she did. She leaned in the doorway without speaking again. I swigged my beer, alone where I was. I was annoyed – disappointed, I guess, having been so eager to see her. In fact, I was beginning to feel a sort a grim ire against her depression, and against mine, and against the whole cabin's blackening atmosphere; a sort of sturdy defiance, like those brave Englishmen feel in ghost stories when they go crouching with lanterns down the hallways of their haunted homes.

Then bang went the woodstove door and up I woke – up after about two hours of sleep, having spent most of my time getting wretched over Marianne and Charlie and the Feds and how withdrawn Agnes had been over dinner last night and how much it all made me feel alone, poor boy. But now, as the throaty sussuration of the fire deepened, I rolled over on the sofa slowly, and there Agnes was, crouching right by me, her face close to mine, our noses nearly touching. And her smile was what you would have to call sunny. And she said, 'Hiya, cutes. Wanna swim naked?'

'Yeah!' I said, and I sat up, throwing the cover aside.

The Swimhole, as she'd named it, was where I'd figured it would be: down lower on the western path, past the dog's leg which led to the meadow. Another turn off, on the left side this time, took us fairly tumbling down a steep forest slope until we spilled out onto a little sandspit at the river's edge. Here, the White, though narrow, deepened into a strongly flowing pool, decorated with grey rocks by the banks and screened in by thick trees on either shore. It was a lovely place: the river winding out of view to left and right, the mountain's morning mist hanging low over us, black birds shooting out of the trees and across the water to the far trees, and the air loud with the water's confidential swash: it was a place of reminiscent mysteries. Indeed, a city boy like me had to wonder if some primordial Harry hadn't summered in some such place and loved it well enough to work the memory into his generations: like the tunnel to the meadow, like the meadow too, the pool seemed to greet in me some inner impression of itself so that I had that sense again of an overriding stillness.

'It reminds me . . .' I said, then hesitated, but she rewarded me with such a lively grin, that I finished: 'Doesn't it? Of the place behind your house?'

'A little, I guess,' she said.

'Sort of anyway. I don't know.'

Agnes dropped our towels on the sand and stepped away from me. She moved out onto a flat boulder that cantilevered over the pool in a perfect diving surface. As she moved to the edge, she slipped the tatty green robe off and let it fall to her heels. Naked, from the back, she looked scrawny and brown and muscular, with a full valentine of a bottom only slightly paler than the rest. Along with your basic aching joy at seeing a woman nude, a powerful romantic sadness welled up in me, so that I wasn't sure whether I wanted to dance a wild pan-dance to a frenzied bacchanal or just rip my own head off at the intolerable sweetness of mortality.

I opted for getting out of my clothes: I peeled my shirt off. Agnes dove in. I stopped and watched her, grunting softly when I caught the fruity flash between her legs. Then, talking my dick down to a respectable angle, I worked my jeans off too. I was glad I'd been going to the gym, I'll tell you, but a little ashamed at the pallid pinkness of my skin. As Agnes surfaced, whooping at the cold, I jogged quickly out onto the rock and hurled myself into the river.

Well, it was cold all right, and we screamed and shivered our cheeks. And the current was stronger than it looked and swept me steadily downstream so that I had to splash and fight to pull up level with her.

'Watch,' she called – she had to shout over the White's great murmur. 'Like this.' She did the sidestroke, facing me, strong graceful sweeps of her two hands. 'You can swim and swim like this without moving.' Because she was headed into the current, see, and it kept her right where she was.

I followed suit, and there we lay together, motionless in the water save for our strokes, breathing hard into each other's faces. Her nakedness was soft and ripply – and riveting – just beneath the surface.

'Was I a total bitch last night?' she called to me.

'Not total,' I gasped. 'I think I'm falling in love with you too.'

'Agh!' she said. 'We should be seventeen! This should be happening when we're seventeen!'

'I know. That's what I keep thinking. Is there anything worse than not being seventeen?'

'Being seventeen?'

'Right,' I said. 'Right.'

Soon, I was exhausted, out of breath. Vanity-exercising in a gym, I was finding out, means just about nothing when you start hiking in woods and swimming in rivers. I had to head in. And that was hard work too. Making it back to the rock against the current, trying to climb but finding no good purchase for my fingers as my legs were pulled downstream. Eventually, I shuffled my way around, gripping the boulder, until my feet touched the pebbles on the river bed. Then I hopped and danced my way over the sharp stones to the strand.

I toweled myself off while Agnes rolled over discretely on her other side and kept on stroking. Even after I'd dressed again, she went at it for a long time. I sat out at the end of the diving rock and watched her, and listened to the water and the sudden calls of birds, saw the mist burn off and the sky come out pale blue, watched the sun angle in through the downriver trees, felt my heart breaking. That sort of thing.

Often, remembering, prick in hand, I have asked myself why I didn't clasp her as she came out of the water and try my luck at drawing her wet body to the sand. The answer is unacceptable to me as I've become, and even taunts me, but at the time there simply seemed a mysterious rhythm to the thing. Having seen or sensed that it was this – this natural metabolism of desire – that had been shattered on our first go round, I was superstitious and careful of it. And in the mornings, when she was so charming and vital and all, I indulged my sadness and my panicked terror with the fantasy that, tended lovingly, the rhythm could be restored. I had it all backwards, of course: it was her morning cheer that was the most horrible thing about her. But how – as I always end up asking next in my scummy anguish – how was I to know?

That morning especially, of our handful of mornings, we seemed a possibility. We climbed back to the cabin through the dawn woods hand in hand. She taught me – pretty comically – to make muffin batter while she zipped through the arcana of the coffee gizmo just as if by the way. We sat at the table with our feet up on the chairs, and for the first time, we talked about being children together. I recited my idylls about our little stream and our evenings, and she imitated her own witchy voice and rituals so that I had to smile a lot to hide how much they affected me still. Then we stopped for a while. We sat silently. For myself, I was afraid to go on any farther. I was afraid our old friendship would begin to seem strange or even sick in some way, if we talked about it too much. It's the details, you know, that get you. I was afraid to murder the romance.

But Agnes said: 'So? Don't you want to hear about your father?'

I shrugged. 'We never really had a chance to talk about it.'

'Yeah, well. What would I have said? "Having a wonderful time with your Dad. Wish you were here?"'

I kept my smile plastered on, gazing at the floor.

'I mean, most of the time when he was there, with my mother, I was at school or something. I mean, obviously. But sometimes, I'd come home and he'd be there. I'd have my milk and cookies and he'd ask me what I was learning in school and that sort of thing.'

'And he'd tell you those stories. The ones you used to tell me,' I said, not looking up. 'About astronomy and stuff.'

'Yeah, that's right. It sure seems like they were taking a hell of chance, though, doesn't it? I mean, I could've just babbled to my Dad about the whole thing. They never told me not to.'

I answered heavily: 'Maybe you knew you'd lose him if you did.'

'My father?'

'Mine.'

Now we were both making a careful study of the floor. I was beginning to feel a little ill.

And Agnes said: 'Look, it was probably a lot easier for him, you know. We were like this make-believe family he had on the side. He didn't have to deal with our problems – he just got all the good stuff. He could just come by and fuck my mother, charm the kid, then do all his farting and stuff at home.'

'You don't have to talk about it that way,' I said. I washed the taste of it down with coffee. 'I'm sure it was nice for you.'

She rolled her eyes. 'It *was* nice. Sue me.' I snorted. 'Forgive me,' she said.

'Oh Christ.' I laughed. I pinched my eyes shut. 'Oh hell, hell, hell. The man was just such a *shlub* at home. Whining, you know. Mourning all his lost chances. "I wanted to be an astronomer," he used to say, "but . . . I had a family to support." Like his life was my fault.' Agnes leaned forward, listening sympathetically. It annoyed the shit out of me, her sympathy, but I went on. 'What can I say? I wish I was there too. It's just so weird to think there was this whole other Dad . . . or not maybe, I don't know; maybe I just couldn't see it or something. It's like I used to wish sometimes I could've been there that time he was pitching woo at Aunt May. Before I was born. They oughta let you do that. Just watch some scenes before you're born, just to fill you in. Then later you can say, "All right, the guy's a beaten asshole now, but he did have this moment of romance or integrity or something." I mean, it's kind of like being half an orphan otherwise.'

Agnes grinned and put her elbow on the table, her chin in her hand. She said wickedly, 'Gee, Harry, and I thought you loved me for myself.'

I made a face. I almost echoed that back at her but thought better of it – finally, finally, beginning to get the idea that it was I who was by far the stronger of the two of us. 'Oh, shut up,' I said.

Staring at the floor, I heard her chuckle, and then sigh – and then drink and set her mug down with that definitive thud. She pushed her chair back. I looked up and saw her stand.

'So when are you leaving?' She always said the hardest things just as she was moving out of reach.

'It better be goddamned soon,' I said bluntly – and I was still surprised to see it hurt her, to get that glimpse of punch-drunkenness in her eyes. More gently I said: 'I make it worse by staying. You know. I mean, Jesus, they could bring me back in handcuffs if they find me. I mean, not to put too fine a point on it, but I happen to be scared out of my wits.' And I still thought this was because of the police and the scandal and so on.

Maybe Agnes knew better because she offered this as if to relieve me: 'Well – anyway – I'm going to work now.'

I sat where I was as she moved past. Sat and listened to the sounds of the studio door – unlocked, opened, shut, locked again. After a moment of suspense, I flinched: the mallet had started for the day.

I hiked out and found the Path Through The Pines, which was kind of the property's tourist attraction: not magical, like the other places, I mean, but just fun to see. The trees here had been cleared, I guess, at some point and replanted in tidy rows – half an acre, say, of white pines and then another half of red. When you walked from the first section to the second, the effect was of moving through a stark gray landscape – past empty silver shafts with their first branches high above eye level – and then into a field of rich shade and colors where the orange trunks rose from the red earth and bloomed in low boughs everywhere, bearing green needles and brown cones. You could even stand between the two halves, looking right then left, heightening the sense that you were on the border of two countries, two worlds. I found myself searching for some meaning to this illusion. I tried to read some hopeful omen into it, a pep-talk from the gods about my future. But that annoyed me soon enough. I couldn't work up the superstition. I mean, how much pull was some dead lumberjack likely to have with the Feds?

So I turned back – which provides only this small irony: that I must have been less than fifty yards from the southern ridge of the Valley of Dead Elms. Not that finding it those few hours earlier would have made much difference to my slow, unconscious ratiocinations. Laying aside any regret-filled daydreams I might have, I sincerely doubt I would've gone galloping back to the cabin to rescue Agnes from her personal krakens. I didn't even know I was in that story. I thought I was in the Harry and Agnes Have A Bittersweet Romance story. Oh, and anyway, I didn't find it, so what the fuck's the dif?

So it was home to another merry afternoon of staring at the locked studio door, listening to the mallet hit the chisel, the chisel bite the wood. This though it was a fine summer's day again and I might well have lunched and napped and hiked back out for hours. I did make myself some lunch and I caught up on some of the sleep I'd lost last night, though I think I was beginning to have nightmares, because I woke up sweating. But then, despite my resolution to return at least to the meadow and drink in some of that wisdom and serenity stuff I'd had the first day, I stayed where I was. Lying on the sofa with an unread book. Staring at the studio door. Feeling oppressed and irritable, curious, and drawn to that locked room as by an hypnotic command. Listening to the mallet within, which seemed to me more swift and furious today than ever before.

Once, toward evening, she stopped, the mallet stopped. And I, who had been pacing aimlessly, stopped where I was and watched the door intently. I heard a sound from in there, which might have been a cough, which might have been a suppressed sneeze. But which might also have been a strangled sob, as of someone weeping violently but trying to hold down the noise.

I began to creep quietly toward the door. The idea was to listen, though I'm not sure I'd have had the courage to knock. But a floorboard creaked under me, and there was some swift shuffling in the studio, and then the hammering started up again — so I retired in defeat.

All this put me in a dark and heroic mood. That feeling of defiance rose in me again. It was beginning to seem as if my capacity for self-pity might not be bottomless after all, nor my willingness to submit to the cabin's grim and esoteric atmosphere. On top of which, I wanted her — though she cursed a blue streak and she wasn't blonde and didn't shave beneath her arms — I was crazy for her, had been cheated, so I felt, of some natural, formative intimacy with her, and did not want to waste another evening tiptoeing round her miseries while the law threatened to separate us again.

So a couple more hours went by. The sunset shift of birds came on outside, singing mostly low notes and sadly. The light beneath the pines around us thickened to a reddish loam. Agnes's hammering tapered off — a little earlier than usual, I thought. And I heard a thud and a rattling clank, as if she'd dropped both mallet and chisel to the floor in sheer exhaustion. So I imagined it, anyway. And I stood prepared for her in noble pose in the center of the floor. Waited while the usual sweepings and shufflings went on in the studio unseen.

Then back went the bolt. The door opened — just that exasperating crack. She slipped out so carefully, turned to shut the door so quickly, that she didn't even see me there, but was re-locking the door before our eyes had met.

But she knew I was waiting, must've known. And she stood with her back to me a long time, resting her forehead against the door, as if she barely had the strength to stand unaided. Still defiant, I stayed as I was, planning to outlast her, to hold my ground until she finally came around.

But my resolve broke. The silence in the cabin went on — in the cabin and its shadows — and I was suddenly afraid — I didn't know of what. I had some idea that when she did turn, she would fix me with a skeletal stare and whisper again, *I'm dead, Harry. I'm already dead.* I'm not sure I could have stomached that.

'Agnes,' I broke out. 'Come on, Agnes. Where's your work? Show me what you've been doing. Where the hell is all your work?'

Slowly, slowly, she pushed off the door, as if lifting a great weight that held her against it. She showed me the side of her face, and gave one of those belittling snorts that cut right into me.

'I need a drink,' she said. 'I need a beer.'

She looked, when she turned, too forbidding to mess with. I let her walk past me to the kitchen.

'Shit,' I muttered.

Nonetheless, I did go after her. I stood at the kitchen entryway. And when she swaggered into it, bottle in fist, I confronted her, my hands in my pockets, my face set.

She sighed, as if I were just a bother to her. She swigged her beer arrogantly. She shrugged.

'All right,' she said finally. 'I don't know what good it'll do. But come on, if you want. I'll show you.'

She led me down that first path I'd taken, her beer bottle tapping her thigh as she walked. The sky, which was clear, wasn't quite twilit yet, but was just beginning to lose its substance in a richer depth of blue. This changed – the light, I mean, changed as we headed down, and as the trees closed in around us. There was real gloaming beneath the leaves and when it brightened in open patches it was never as bright as it had been in the patch just before. We heard the river as we went down, a thin hiss and gurgle at that distance. Then she turned off, as I had, onto the dog's leg, and I followed her, bending over, into the tunnel of low-hung boughs. The shade beneath them hurt the eyes, being not like night but just as deep; grainy and strange to peer through. And it wasn't much better when we came out into the meadow, where now the first dusk was spreading downward from the sky and staining all the wildflower glories a uniform grayish blue. With the grass high around her bare legs, Agnes crossed the meadow quickly, hewing to the eastern border of forest. I lagged behind, and panting at that. And my broken attempts to make conversation – to liven things up a little – did the proverbial lead balloon.

It was a long meadow, longer than it looked. I remembered that – how far you had to go to reach the center. By the time we came to the hollow of its crescent, where the woodline bulged out into the grass, the day was ending truly, the twilight becoming smoother and more dense. We came upon a white rag tied to a bowed sapling. It marked another trail, and Agnes turned onto it.

The forest was now diffusing into forms and shadows – fingery extensions, and jutting, grinning boles, tortuous vines and startled stones upstanding. As a New Yorker, I confess I began to grow a bit concerned about coming upon the stray werewolf in here or confronting a rampaging troll, say, in the dark. I told this to Agnes – it was a good excuse to pull up closer to her – and she surprised me with loud, delighted laughter, her white teeth flashing. I suppose I was consoled a bit that she, at least, had come into her element.

The trail went on, but she turned off it. 'Hey,' I said, because she seemed to have stepped into an impossible thicket of scratchy brush. But when, in a hurry to be with her, I forced my shoulder through the first mass of briars, I found there was a way through where the foliage had been well trodden down. All the same, it was a narrow passage, and the whip-like branches lashed my face as I went after her, and thorns caught at my clothes.

So on we went, and the brush grew thinner after a while, and slowly, we emerged onto a scrubby plain where the trees were sparse and low. The pall of dusk was full upon us now, but the light was better here than in the forest. And I could see, there before me, with Agnes a small featureless shape moving beneath them, a staggered row of huge dead trees, their leafless branches reaching far into the dissolving sky. They were creepy all right. They looked like witches' brooms: going straight up then spreading raggedly from the vertical. They towered above us and loomed over us darkly.

'Agnes!' I called out, spooked. She stopped for me. I kicked quickly through the high grass to her side. She raised her white eyes up to them and I raised mine.

'What are they?' I said. 'Why are they all dead?'

'Elm trees,' she told me, and sipped at her beer. 'Dutch elm disease. It came over in the Thirties with the European logs they used for furniture. The bark beetles take it from tree to tree. Almost all the old elms are dead up here now.'

'Yiminey cricket!' I said. But she didn't laugh. In fact, when I glanced down, she was gone – she was moving off under these giants and past them. I hurried the hell after her.

It was unnerving to pass under those louring figures, to shuttle so close by their stout, knotted, staring trunks. I was glad to catch up with Agnes where she now stood, on a rim

on the far side of them. She swigged more beer – swigged
fiercely – and gestured before her. I looked out. Beneath our
feet here, a gentle slope led down into a small, marshy valley.
Just a sort of unkempt bowl in the earth, loud as a swamp
with trilling insects and guttural frogs. Above it, all along
the valley's rim, the dead elms stood, spraying up against
the violet sky, their gnarled features sinking into silhouette
slowly, as if reluctantly, as the night came on. Impressive,
they were – they looked like the solemn guardians of the
place. They were so impressive, in fact, that all my first
attention was on the eerie effect of them, and it was several
moments before I understood what I was actually seeing in
the valley below.

'Oh, for God's sake, Agnes,' I said then. 'I mean, for
God's sake.'

Now, it's a famous sight, of course. The pictures that
little shnook from the local weekly snapped have been in
newspapers and museums around the world. I even heard
some crazy dame on TV once explaining that it was really
Agnes's post-modern feminist masterpiece, and that poor
old Roland destroyed it in the interests of some phallacious
commercial conspiracy or something. Well, okay, that's her
planet. But I was there, there with Agnes. I came on it in
that gloam as if it were some jungle ziggurat in an impossible
clearing, and there was no theorizing about it, I tell you, I
knew right away: I was looking down at an epic work of
pure self-destruction.

They were everywhere in the bottom of the valley. Their
hands clawed up from the swampy earth, their faces gaped
at the dying heavens, their bodies contorted with agonized
grace into the heartbreaking blur of mulch and decay below.
Some were lying on their sides, some stood like columns,
most jutted at angles, half-sunk in the mud. The shrill,
unceasing burr of the insects vibrated up from all around
them, and it made me think at once both of the slugs and
beetles ravening in their wood and of their own brainless cries
– because they seemed to me to be rotting alive down there,
all of them. And when that image came to me, I turned my
face away.

Agnes took another pop at her bottle. She sat down

on the slope, leaned back on her elbows, observing this masterpiece of hers with an insolent smirk as aggravating as any adolescent's. I felt it as a challenge to me, and got fired up again. Well, all right: I turned back and started edging my way down the slope.

The mud squelched up over my shoes as the land flattened under me. I had to pull up hard as I worked my way farther out toward the middle of the valley. The dead elms strung along the ridge stared down as I moved in among the discarded statues, and I felt chilled by that and unanchored, afloat, with all the empty space going dark all around me.

I came first upon an angel, fallen back on its Renaissance wings, and with a body carved in the final bloated stages of starvation. Its passive, beaten eyes looked into mine and I actually shivered at the sight of it. Part of one wing had liquefied and I could see the crawlies moving on the mulch. And I heard them busily chirping, which was horrible. And I staggered on through the mud. I came to a muscle man with the body of a snake, and then a small centaur raping a woman twice his size; further on, I found some sort of hunkering creature with a countenance like Apollo's – and they were all half-rotten, their color changing from the brown of sodden wood to a crumbling black which was indistinguishable from the earth. I splashed and stumbled from station to station, bracing myself on the thrashing tail of a lamia or the friable arm of a centurion gone mad. And, after a while, I paused, my figure at the center of those wooden figures everywhere, all those sculpted limbs and faces half-upreaching, half-submerged, surrounding me – and I looked up at her where she lay watching on the slope beneath the towering elms. And I thought: *What the hell is wrong with her?* And my blood ran sour as if, really, down deep, I knew.

By then, too, for all my inexpertise, I think I had begun to realize – what everyone says now, what I couldn't have exactly put into words – that even though the sculptures were melting away, they had remained artworks, somehow, still. The various forms and passages of their ruination had become part of them, even lent them a mysterious depth of time, like the lost arms of Venus de Milo, say, or the missing

head of Victory. And just as I had when I was a kid – when
she made that Play-Doh skull for me and I carried it home?
– I had started thinking: Gee, you know, if she put her mind
to it, she could really do something with some of this stuff.
So that's the thought I held onto, the thought I resolved to
carry up to her. And I pushed the other knowledge away.

It got darker – it was almost night. The hundred struggling
shadows of Agnes's work were being dragged almost violently
into the blackness as the surrounding elms frowned somberly
down. Mosquitoes had already made a meal of my ankles
and were now biting my arms and making that disgusting
zeet noise in my ears. Swatting at them with both hands, I
hauled my way back through the mud to the edge of the
valley. I climbed up the slope again to Agnes. She still lay
where she was, sneering triumphantly, insouciantly tipping
her bottle up, though it was almost empty now.

I stood over her. I scratched my nose. I tried to think of
the most encouraging response.

'Gosh, honey,' I said finally, 'some of that stuff looks
pretty good.'

Agnes blew out a quick laugh. I wanted to slug her.

'Well, come on,' I said. 'What the hell do you want?'

She gave a frown – as if she were considering the question.
She raised her bottle up before her and cocked her head like a
painter viewing his canvas past his thumb. 'If I could make a
child,' she said. 'All right? A real child of glory, so that every
one who looked at her, or heard about her, or just sort of
knew from the cultural buzz that she was there would feel
. . . not just love . . . but that unbearable tenderness you feel
when you see your own child and it's like your – body
almost – your own body except exposed to life, stripped
of that sense we all have of our own invulnerability, you
know, and stripped of our crusts of caution . . . if it would
make people feel that kind of desperate love, parental love
. . .' She lowered the bottle, brought her hand to her mouth
and wiped her lips with the back of it, but all the while staring
out over the valley. 'And then,' she went on cooly, 'And then
. . . if I could destroy her. See what I mean? Just smash her,
pulverize her, reduce her to something that hardly had even
existed because . . . well, for no reason, just because I wanted

to, because she was what she was, because she filled some role in some play going on in my mind. Because she was a Jew. And then, and then, if everyone would feel her, see, *being* ruined, just feel it almost in the air, and every . . . caring or even uncaring heart would just . . . break open . . . just burst open and out would spill this – hot poison, this black grief all down the middle of their souls so that there would never be an end in all their lives to the grief, to the grief and the poison . . .' She flashed her hollowed eyes up at me, her mouth contorting. '*That* would be a work of art.'

'What are you, nuts?' I said. 'Ya dumb broad! That would be an atrocity!' She glowered at me so angrily that I felt possibly I'd misspoken. 'Well, I don't know much about art,' I added, 'but I mean I know what I like.'

At that – and at my idiotic smile – she groaned, loudly. She fell back on the grass, throwing one arm across her face, shaking her head. I stood there stupidly, but that didn't seem to help much. So finally, I gave a shrug and sat down on the slope next to her.

After a moment or two, her lying there like that, I began to get the sense that maybe she was crying. Not that she shuddered or gasped or anything, but just from the way she opened her mouth to breathe and wouldn't take her arm away from her eyes. I tried to think of what to do, surveying the weird scene meanwhile: the tortured shapes in the valley striving up from the muck – or sinking down into it really – and the black forms of the elms standing grim watch over them on the ridge. I spoke over the racket of insects.

'So am I being, like, a gormless mooncalf here or what?'

She laughed – and I thought I was right: she was crying. She dragged her arm across her eyes – to dry them, I guessed – and maybe they would've glistened when she looked up at me, but it was too dark now to tell.

'Oh, shit, Harry,' she said. 'Don't go.'

'Oh, come on, sweetheart, look . . .' I said. Sure, but what was the rest of the sentence? We'll work it out? We'll think of something? Nothing's as bad as it seems? Wait till the sun shines, Nellie? 'Oy, shit,' was my choice finally. I collapsed onto my back and lay beside her.

We lay still. We didn't talk. I felt her shoulder brushing

mine. I felt her fanning hair blow soft against my temple. The sky, I noticed, had taken on a strange appearance. A sort of iron solidity, low and suffocating, as if the valley had a lid on it. Just clouds, I thought, moving in fast the way they do in the mountains, but I couldn't be sure in that darkness and I began to feel trapped there and claustrophobic. I peered up to see if I could make out any stars to gauge the clouds by, but there were none at first. Then one, right in the center of the sky, winked and faded, then winked again, and shone. Vega, by God, I thought hopefully. Vega in the lyre.

'Hey, look,' I said. 'Make a wish.'

And Agnes answered at once: 'I wish everything had been fucking different.'

I laughed – well, it really was dreadful. And the clouds – because they were clouds – proceeded to make their cheery contribution to the night by sweeping over that awful valley in great thundery gobs, catching a-hold of that cute little star, and just smothering the shit right out of it.

It started to rain as we hiked back and, right after we got inside, it started to pour. Loud, heavy fists of water drumming on the roof, in the pine branches, in the puddling dirt. Agnes made us sandwiches and we ate without speaking as if overwhelmed by the pervasive noise. I even found myself eyeing the ceiling as we sat there, half expecting the torrents to pound their way in – it was that heavy, that loud. I made a few comments on it, but got no answer. And finally Agnes stood up and wearily carried her plate in to the kitchen. She paused at my chair when she came back. I took hold of her arm and she bent to kiss the top of my head, almost pityingly. Then she shuffled away into the bathroom and began to get ready for bed.

I lay on the sofa that night listening to the downpour. I thought about the rain falling on the Valley of Dead Elms, of the soaked wood and the insects breeding in the water. For the first time, I think, I began to get a sense of what Agnes had wanted from me, how much she had wanted and hoped for. I even started to fantasize more supernatural expectations as well, wondering if maybe, in my cowardly escape from Manhattan, I had been Brought Here For A Purpose after all. Well, better to consider such bullshit, I guess, than to meditate on how ill-equipped I was to serve this imaginary purpose, to serve any purpose whatsoever; or to consider how disappointed the poor girl must be, how desperate it must've made her feel to see her last chance of a white knight come riding up the hill and have it turn out to be Sir Schmuck himself – of all creatures most corrupt, dear Lord, a New York City politician!

The unrelenting rain put me to sleep at last, but powerful blasts of thunder woke me in the night, startled me from nightmares in which the elms stared down as the decaying carcasses in the valley bottom began to move, began to pull themselves slowly from the rising muck and claw their way up the grassy slope with bright eyes to come crawling home to their creator . . . Yuck. I didn't sleep again till nigh on morning, and was slow to rouse myself at the sound of the woodstove clanging shut. I came to consciousness by small degrees: of the cold first – and it was plenty cold in the cabin by then – and the comforting breath of the fire next, and then the rain. The rain hadn't slackened, was still hammering down, splashing raucously outside in what must be great pools of mud and water by now.

Then I heard the screen door slam, and spun around, throwing off my cover.

'You can't go out in that,' I croaked – but she was already passing by the window in her green robe, already drenched and her black hair matted. 'Agnes!' I shouted. But she didn't hear, or pretended not to, and continued on down the path to the river.

Blear-eyed – blear-all-over – I padded into the bathroom to piss and shower and shave. I made myself as fresh as I could, with great helpings of deodorant and the cleanest clothes I had – even some underwear I'd washed in the sink the morning before. Some lingerings of last night's sense of mission were still moving in me, some vague idea of trying to live up to her romantic imagination of me. Whatever: I'd managed to make myself look as lawyerly and competent as I knew how by the time she came gallumphing back to the cabin through the mud and rain.

It was a waste of time. She was too miserable to notice.

For all I knew, she was past hope as far as Sir Harry was concerned. She came in clutching the soaked rag of her robe around her, shivering, breathless, her eyes dull, her lips blue. She made small, unhappy noises through her chattering teeth, and hurried straight past me into the kitchen. She tried to make coffee, her robe falling open as she fumbled the pieces of the percolator in her trembling hands. I moved beside her and helped her put the gadget together, disconcerted by her grey nakedness and by my yearning for her – and by her wide-eyed, shuddery countenance, which put the kibosh on any ill-formed fantasies I might have had of earnestly urging her to success and salvation.

She went in to the bathroom while the coffee perked. I waited on the sofa through her long shower. I watched the steam coming out beneath the bathroom door and heard her gasping with relief at the heat. She rushed out without a word, mummified in towels, scurried to her bedroom, and dressed. I watched through the open door as towels and clothes went flying across the room. I eyed the ceiling some more as the rain kept battering away.

When she came out, she was wearing full-length jeans and a baggy plaid shirt. She smiled at me briefly, and returned to the kitchen without a word. This was pretty subdued stuff for the morning, when she usually seemed most alive. So I trailed in after her with dark misgivings, prompted by her glumness to a tremulous urgency and zeal.

She was slapping some bread in the toaster, her back to me.

'Listen, Agnes . . .' I said.

She raised her hand and made a rapid movement with it, signaling me to stop. 'No, no, no, don't. Okay? Let's not talk about it. I shouldn't have taken you out there. I just get bitchy when I'm tired. I did it to bother you. It's not your problem, all right? You've got enough fucking problems of your own, really.'

'It took me by surprise, that's all. I didn't know what to say. But listen, we should talk about it. There's some really good work . . . It could still be treated, preserved and . . .'

'*Stop!* Please. Okay?'

She said this loud enough to shut me up, half turning to

me with a stern frown. Then, briskly decisive, she grabbed a mug and splashed some coffee in it.

'Listen,' she said. 'There's toast; butter's in the fridge. I'm not hungry. I'm going in to work.'

'Oh, come on, Agnes,' I said, in a reasonable voice – but in truth, I was starting to panic. I was losing her – I could feel it. I'd lost her already – lost her again. I'd failed some test of response out there in that god-awful trashcan of a valley of hers. Well, all right, I knew I'd failed. Hell, what did I know about artists and their sensitive souls and what you were supposed to say to them and when? I needed a chance to figure it out, that's all. I *was* figuring it out, sort of. And now, before I could, this iron veil was between us suddenly – and in the morning, too, when there was most to hope for. What she would be like by nightfall if she was this way now, heaven knew. I couldn't stand the thought of so much loneliness. The urgency went up me like fire and, before she could pick up her coffee and leave, I stepped forward. I took her arm.

She yanked the arm up, but I held on.

'Harry!' she said. I yanked her to me. I took her by the elbows. 'Don't,' she said.

'Let me.'

I kissed her – a botched job – she turned her face aside. I pulled her, wrestled, like a bloody teenager, to work my body against hers. Well, I had a hardon hot as fever: I wanted her to feel how much I desired her, as if then she must surrender herself unto our redemption. Like a teenager – what choice had I given her? – she cried out: 'Stop, stop, *stop!* Jesus!' And she twisted away so sharply that I'd have hurt her if I'd held on. I released her, and her own impetus sent her stumbling back a step.

'For Christ's sake, Harry,' she said – said sadly, rubbing her arms where I'd gripped them.

I blinked – and came to a sense of myself. Too appalled for words, I leaned against the counter and slugged myself in the forehead with the heel of my palm. She made a noise at that – amusement? Disdain? Disgust?

'I'm going to work,' she repeated.

She snatched up her mug and walked away. Sir Hardon the Stupid stayed slumped where he was.

That was my last full day in the cabin – her last full day alive – and the worst, with the rain and all, the never-ending rain. It was so loud sometimes even her mallet blows were lost in it – or became part of it because they seemed not so much inaudible as ubiquitous, and all the more nerve-wracking for that, if that's possible, if that can be believed. If I could have gone out, taken a hike, worked off some of the energy of my embarrassment – my shame, that is, my failure – it might have made the hours almost tolerable, or so I thought. I even considered driving into town, but I knew I'd see the papers there and couldn't stand to rub my face in yet more of my own inadequacies. So I just sat, or paced, or stared at the blurring pages of books, or stared out the window at the gray curtain of water which showed no sign of letting up, or swung my beetled brow back over my shoulder to cast foul glances at the studio door as if it were my enemy. By midday, I'd exhausted myself with such occupations and yet got myself too wrought up to sleep. After an hour or so of tossing on the sofa, I was up again and at it, my fingers in my hair. I couldn't think by then, was too confused to think, and could only submerge the revving faculties in a sort of sludge of memories and daydreams occasionally broken by blazing jets of raw, dumb wanting and rage; anger at myself, at her; like fires burning in a bog.

It was out of this mess that I fashioned my decision; in the late afternoon – plucked it like Jack Horner, like revelation, proudly, surely – and with a little smile of vengeance at the locked door. I was getting out of here – that was it. I was leaving. Going home this very evening, as soon as I had a chance to say thank you, ma'am, and goodbye. I wasn't going to just hang around, making trouble for myself. Nursing some crazy would-be artist out of her aesthetic doldrums. I had my own life – I had a wife and family to destroy. Scandals to be buried under. Jail time to serve. I was a busy man, for Christ's sake.

With the heavy rain keeping jig time, I gathered up my belongings – my toiletries, my clothes. Stuffed them in my overnight bag. Set my overnight bag decisively by the front door. That done, I went in the kitchen and got me a brew, yessir. Carried it out into that dreadfully empty room, and swigged it manfully, using the bottle as an adolescent prop the way she'd done with hers the night before. It was almost time now. I waited for her. The sound of the mallet rose out of the sound of the rain and spread back through it again, and was everywhere.

What happened in that studio, behind that locked door, what happened to change everything for us — if it did change everything, if it changed anything — I can only conjecture. Some people make a living of such theories; me, I just pass the awful time. But I do have a guess. Based on what I heard and saw and what happened. I do have an image of it — the nights of self-laceration wouldn't be complete without one.

Agnes — to set the facts down first — Agnes made a sound. I heard it when the mallet suddenly stopped that evening. I heard it even above the noise of the rain. But it wasn't loud — she didn't cry out or sob or shriek or anything. It was just a low, throaty, shuddering expulsion of air. A sort of drawn-out 'Uh!' sound. And in my opinion — and I'm the only one alive who heard it — it was a genuine exclamation of horror.

That *is* just a guess, though. I'd never heard one before. I've never heard one since. It's not really something that comes up that often. Even in a situation where the horrors follow thick and fast — a war or a hospital or something — I imagine you get inured to it and such noises swiftly cease. So whatever her revelation was — if it was a revelation — it had to have been the grand premiere of it and a hell of a shock to boot. And my guess is . . . not that she saw herself, not that she realized what she was doing — she saw fine, she knew already; 'I'm finished. I'm dead,' she'd told me, and that pretty much covered it. She already understood — a lot better than I — how her powerful instinct for joy had been hollowed out, eaten away from the center until it was really only the armor of an old habit, mostly rotten, holding her up, loving, lamenting, creating and destroying by rote according to the pure, loveless logic of psychosis. It was only a matter of time before the whole thing went finally down; she already knew all of that. No, I think what she saw was the rest of us, everybody else. Me, for instance, for inspiration – because I think it was my half-comprehending dismay at the sight of the valley, my ridiculous attempt at salvation-through-ravishment that gave her the clue. That made her realize, as the day wore on, that I really did love her. Blundering lowlife that I was. And maybe, when that notion worked its way into the impeccable reasoning of her insanity, maybe she saw at the same moment that Roland loved her too, better yet, in his decent, shallow way, and her baby – her baby was doomed to adore her, the way kids are. And maybe also – still guessing, just guessing remember – maybe also it occurred to her, by corollary, that there was this whole gang of people, fractious, tedious, snooty, high-living bourgeois snobs, who were also ready to love her – her audience, waiting to love her – because the things she made were beautiful, had a beauty that hadn't been achieved I think for almost a century, and because that beauty would give them pleasure for a moment and a moment's peace. I imagine that all that – the love, the beauty – if she had thought about it at all before – had seemed pretty small potatoes next to her visionary mission, the Great Truth she was trying to convey; had seemed an irrelevant point of culture or chemistry to her, and explicable to the point of nothingness beside the sweep of human history she had in mind. So the image I form finally is that her mallet hand and her chisel hand fell dramatically to her side, and her lips parted as her perception shifted just that little. And it suddenly seemed to her that to fuck with love and beauty in the interest of a mere Great Truth was a terrible folly and an unpardonable sin. And she was horrified at what she had done.

Well, we all have our lives, and our ideas, smart and stupid, are just our emotions made to sound like objective truths. And that's my idea about what happened in the studio.

A moment later, anyway – without the usual noises of sweeping up and rearranging – the bolt shot back. She slipped out into the room with her usual stealth, but quickly now, as if escaping, as if she couldn't get out of there fast enough. She took the time to lock the door again, the key clacking on the rim of metal before it would go in, but then she swung around with her eyes jacked wide, searching the room desperately until she saw me right there in front of her. She saw me – and stood still, and hugged herself hard, trembling, and tucked her chin down, pulling into herself, pulling herself small. 'Harry,' she said, her voice shivering. 'Harry.'

I set the beer bottle on the floor and went to her. 'What's wrong? What the hell's the matter? Agnes.' I put my arms around her. She burrowed against my chest, trembling all over. 'Jesus, Agnes,' I said. I put my hand on the back of her head and held her against me. After a moment, she freed her arms. She braced her hands on my chest and lifted her face as if she wanted me to kiss her. So I did. She kissed me back hungrily, our tongues coming together, my hands going over her with passion and relief.

When she broke off, she took my hand – clutched it in both of hers, and hers still shaking. She went toward the bedroom, my hand captured like that. And I followed eagerly, trying not to think, letting my thoughts get washed away by the overriding rhythm of the rain.

Well, it was pretty good sex. Not bad at all, really, considering: first time together, too impatient for much expertise. A bit of anxiety in the opening moments, what with all the frenzy and expectations. And we banged our teeth in the heated kissing, which sent a shoot of dull pain up into that little hollow spot just behind my right eye. When I managed to wrest my hair out of her fingers, I nuzzled my way over her hard belly to bury my face between her thighs – and that was good, she seemed to really like that. But she had a bitter, sweaty smell and taste that took some getting used to, and then when I did, and when I looked up along her and saw her arching and red-faced and got the image set in my head of how this pussy I was licking, this tangy purple heat was part of her, was part of Agnes, well, I got so excited that I couldn't carry on at it maybe as long as I should have. So I reared up, wiping my lips with my hand, and went into her, which was dynamite, just great for all concerned. We got a rhythm going between us for a while, and that was pure pleasure too, even a joy, her face beneath me wonderfully mottled and lovable and her breasts thrilling to see in motion and sharp and urgent between my lips. I even dug my nose into the dank black hair beneath her arm, God love it, and it wowed me, truly, and made her laugh and cry out. Naturally, you know, with all that inning and outing, the mind wanders sometimes, and there were murky patches of fantasy – My Highness commanding obeisance from some model I'd seen in one of Marianne's magazines, to be precise. That brought me too close to climax too soon so that I had to pull back and then I got doused with thoughts of federal prosecutors and my wronged wife and child, which in turn nearly did me in. Still, still, there were whole expanses of really spectacular clarity, moments like lakewater, when I was pumping into her with great sweetness and assurance, quiet-hearted with awareness and feeling the world and all its creatures were right well-made. She was very precious to me then; I wanted to pour my soul all over her like honey. And when, at last, she came – and she really came; I had my finger in her ass and could feel the contractions – it was so poignant and exciting that it carried me along, and we slammed together in a last spasm that spread through whole seconds of mindless unity.

Of course, after that, right after that, in the calm of mind that followed, when I rolled onto my back and lay sprawled beneath the white wash of the thudding rainfall – with my brain clear of boiling semen, I mean – I saw at once how impossible this whole thing was. We could never have made a go of it, we two. She all geniusy and impassioned and crazy, and me – leaving my troubles and entanglements aside – basically conservative and solidly middle class. I couldn't see it with my stones on fire, but it was instantly clear to me the minute I came. Well, I thought, gazing up at the ceiling, what do you know? You live and learn.

And Agnes rolled away from me onto her side and started weeping.

It was very violent – it was frightening. She was curled up with her knees to her chest and her hands clenched at her mouth and the knobs of her spine stuck out at me looking fragile. And the sobs, as the saying goes, racked her. Really made her quake and shudder as if some animal in its death throes were trapped inside her.

I propped myself up on an elbow over her, raising my

eyebrows as another bout of sobbing was swept under a rising gust outside that made the rain splatter noisily. I laid a hand on her shoulder, but she didn't react, and it was scary to feel the seizure come up through her flesh into my palm.

'Gee,' I said faintly, 'was it good for you too?'

She laughed and moaned and sobbed all at once, moving her hands up to cover her face. I started to speak again, anything just to bring her down to earth, but she pulled away from me, unfolded her legs and, climbing off the bed as I called to her, hurried, naked, weeping, out of the room.

Unsure what to do, I stayed on the bed at first. I tried to listen, over the racket of the downpour, to hear where she was, what she was up to. I figured she'd get herself a beer or something, maybe cry it out alone on the sofa. Maybe go back into the studio and work her feelings off on the wood – that's what I thought she'd done when I heard the door shutting. But then I heard another noise through the wall – a noise from the bathroom: she was opening the medicine chest in there.

I threw myself off the bed and got out of the bedroom fast. I grabbed the bathroom doorknob, yanked the door open just as she was screwing the cap off the bottle.

'Don't do that, Agnes. You don't need that,' I said.

Crying, trembling, she shook about seven tablets into her palm. I stepped forward and grabbed her wrist.

'*Let go!*' she said – she practically shrieked it. She tried to pull away, dropping some of the tablets to the floor.

'It's too many,' I said. 'You'll kill yourself.'

'Let me go.' But with another sob, she went limp in my grip. She hung her head and cried miserably as the rest of the tablets dropped noiselessly from her hand.

'I mean, that's crazy,' I said, feeling awful for her. I tugged the bottle gently from her fingers and set it on the sink. She tilted against me, and I held her, held her up, feeling her tears running into the hair on my chest. 'What did you expect?' I said, just to say something. 'We're just people here. I mean, what did you expect?'

After a while, she let me lead her back to bed. She was much calmer, and even lay with her head on my chest, watching her own hand toying with my shoulder. I kissed her hair and petted her and murmured to her, my stomach only slowly untying its knots. I felt good that I'd kept her from taking the pills: I hated the thought of her trashed on that shit, with all her energy gone. And as I lay there, thinking about it now, realizing that our future as a couple was what you might call limited, I began to think that maybe my best bet here – maybe my Purpose, if you will – was to try to talk her into meeting with Roland, and she'd have to be off the pills for that. Maybe if she made some peace with him, I thought, logged some time with her daughter, you know; maybe it would get her out of this depressing eyrie of hers and back into some semblance of a normal, healthy life.

But thick-skulled as I may have been, other suspicions were beginning to condense as well. It was pretty obvious I'd touched on something more – worse – than till now I'd understood. Working my way so close to her – by virtue of my claims on her past and imagination, by virtue of my love and my lust and my panic and despair – I'd clearly set one toe into the Sea of Bad she held inside. And there was more Bad than I could account for by what I knew of her. More at least than I'd figured on anyway, knowing what I knew.

I really did want to help her – and I was curious to get the whole story. So, lying there, holding her, warmed by her body against the cold sound of the rain, I conceived my nocturnal project while Agnes sunk away, finally, exhausted, into sleep.

I didn't wait there long – less than half an hour. I was afraid the constant rain rhythm would lull me and make me doze. Besides, I'd read somewhere that the earliest part of sleep is the deepest – and I was also afraid she would wake up hungry, because I didn't think she had eaten all day. So, soon as she started to snore fairly steadily, I slipped out from under her. Tensely, I watched her roll over. I watched her resettle on her other side till she began to snore again. Then, kicking through the clothing that lay strewn around the floor, I moved to the spot where I had thrown her jeans, picked them up, and began going through the pockets.

The studio keys were there in the right front. I gripped

them in my fist as I removed them so they wouldn't jangle.
I went from the room on tiptoe – flinching, bracing, looking
back every time the boards creaked underneath me, though
I doubt the creaks could have been audible to her over the
noise of the rain. At any rate, she still lay quiet when I reached
the door. So, steeling myself as best I could, I moved into the
other room.

I'm not, I suspect, particularly courageous – I knew she
would find this a terrible betrayal, and the suspense as I
reached the studio door was murderous; I nearly gave it up.
But I managed to work the key in the lock, and made a great,
elaborate, slow business of turning back the bolt. I pushed the
door open, slipped in – my plan, at this point, being to take a
quick look and then run like anything back to bed.

I found the light switch on the wall. I flipped it up. I was
thinking, God, God, what if she comes in now, what could I
say? But the next moment, my thoughts were obliterated by
a jolt of surprise – because the room, at first glance, seemed
to be empty.

It was a big rustic room of rough log walls and unfinished
floorboards. Sheets lay crumpled here and there along the
edges, and there were pencil sketches on newsprint tacked
up at eye level all around. There was a jumble of various-sized
logs and branches just to the right of me too, with a wicked-
looking chain-saw tossed in among them. But nothing else,
I thought – until I looked left, and discovered all the rest.
Under a rain-splashed skylight in the corner, stood her small
worktable. Her chisel pack was unfolded on it and the chisels
lay skewed, some in, some out of their pockets. Her mallet
had been dropped beside the table's leg – so much smaller,
the mallet, than I'd pictured it. And there was her high stool
for sitting at; and a plywood stand with a covering sheet
fallen into the woodchips at its base. And atop the stand,
alone atop the stand – there stood the one statue; that's all;
just the one.

Well, that was strange – wasn't it? – I thought that was
strange right away – that there was just the one work in
progress. No models, no maquettes, no other works at other
stages. Just this one – and it looked so small too, no more
than three feet high – less – and so little completed. She was

in here chiseling away so much, so many hours. Was she throwing everything into the valley? As I crept closer to it, the screeking boards crying up to the pattering ceiling, I saw that only the face had been finished really. The rest had just the vague shape of a human figure chopped into the surface by a few rude strokes. And then, and finally, these thoughts also were blown away as I came right up to it, as I got my first good look.

Agnes was right about at least one thing, I've noticed: artists, critics – they are always describing their creations in very melodramatic terms: shattering, breathtaking, shocking, revolutionary. Personally, I think it's just because they lead such boring, solitary lives and need to put some fireworks into them. I mean, everyone dreams of heroics and having a hand in world events and so on, and they spend their lives in their rooms making useless little things. Once I even heard a writer say he wished he lived under a more repressive regime so he could endure the torture and censorship which make art important. I thought he ought to just stick his penis in an electrical outlet to get the feel of it – because none of that really is ever to the point in the end.

See, I saw that child, her statue, Agnes's Child of Glory, and it wasn't a dramatic or shattering thing at all. It was apparent, even at that stage, even to me, that she was getting it right, getting exactly what she wanted, and the effect was one of – I don't know – a depth of recognition more than anything. It was an impression that met the impression within, like the meadow full of wildflowers or the swimming hole: almost a cliche but revivified by its insistent presence and individuality. Man, I wish I could see it again now, stand before it again – now, I mean, that I know a little, have studied a little, albeit studied in my half-crazed, alchemic efforts to bring the dead woman back to life. But even in my ignorance then, it did finally dawn on me that this exasperating gal o' mine had been up to something incredible here on her mountain top, was accomplishing something historic even, if out of so repetitive a thing one can make a history of sensation. All fearful of discovery, all keyed for interruption and the incriminating cry as I was, I still looked at her Child, at the barely sculpted face of it, and felt that still, sad hallelujah of release that comes when the substance of great things feared and hoped for is revealed to have been obvious all along.

It was Lena, I guess — her half-sister Lena — I'm almost sure of it — I mean, wasn't that what she'd been trying for even as a kid? Lena at the edge of the ravine, at the very end of her life. So young, little more than a toddler, still trailing clouds of glory as it were, but also, somehow, staring with knowledge if without comprehension into her own meaningless destruction. Now too — now that I've seen the model for it — I guess it was the other Lena as well, Agnes's daughter. I didn't know that at the time, I didn't even think about it but, sure, I guess that was also part of the point of what she had been doing here.

Anyway, my reaction to this discovery was almost comically stupid. Well, it was pure resistance at this stage. I had all the facts, I knew everything; it was pure denial that kept me from putting it together. Instead, I went positively radiant with hope and determination. Ho, ho, thought I, a small, rapt smile creasing my idiot features; ho, ho, if I could bring *this* down! If I could help bring her down with *this* from the mountaintop, guide her through our love to a happier life creating such things as *this*, well then, young Harry, my son, my pal, well then, even your scandal, even your selfishness, your unkindness, your very corruption would become mere footnotes in the Book of Art, mere quibbles beside your magnificent contribution — nay lad, next to your salvation, after all!

This called for a sandwich. Back I tread to the formerly hated door with a last fond glance at the Child — and a quick check to make sure I hadn't left footprints in any stray sawdust — and touching the lightswitch, I gently shut up the studio, and gently locked it.

I went to the kitchen and slapped some goat cheese on wheat, and stood at the window chomping away and chuckling in what must have been an hysteria of impossible aspirations. I watched the rainwater streaking the pane, and listened to it spanking the slates of the roof and, hey, it was letting up a little, I fancied. Yes, it was. Oh, how symbolical, I thought, and how right it would be — how perfect, I thought, popping the last of my sandwich in the old gob – how perfect if tomorrow should dawn bright and clear.

The day dawned bright and clear, all right, the storm finally abating in the last dark hours, the big clouds just blowing over and away as the clang of the woodstove door in the next room woke me. I lay there gathering my thoughts a moment, memories surfacing. I had awakened at one point in the dead of night, I recalled, and found Agnes lying also awake beside me. She'd been staring quietly up at the ceiling, a small, unpleasant smile on her lips; a sneer almost. And I had shuffled close to her and nuzzled against her neck and murmured I loved her as I fell back to sleep. Some hours after, as dawn was coming, I woke again – or became aware, at least, that the rain was stopping. The raucous thwacking at the roof had become a scattered drip-dripping from the eaves and from the trees . . . What else did I remember? Oh yes: nightmares – I had had nightmares – those came back to me last. Ominous, importunate dreams, full of eager faces staring through inky murk. I suppose my subconscious had been working things out, assembling what I knew. The valley, the routine, the disconnected phone, *I have to work*, the one statue. They had come back to me in my dreams as whispers, messages, urgent, distant, muffled as if through fog. I closed my eyes, straining to hear them again. *If I could make a child* . . . The little clay figures in the stream back home, the baby she had almost drowned, *a child of glory* . . . I guess, in my sleep, defences down, I had finally let the whole picture come together because now, as I lay there, casting for my dreams, the facts began to arrange themselves. Agnes's evening depressions – it occurred to me, as if out of nowhere, that these were glimmers of her better self – her happier, saner self, I mean. Signs that the weight of the love she still could feel, the beauty she still could make had been resurrected, were threatening to overwhelm her grand ambitions and intentions. I ran my two hands up into my hair. Yes. That was right. I understood. And in the morning, she was cheerful – cheerful because she had triumphed again, her intentions, her artistic mission had triumphed again, was marching on. I mean: nuts. What if she was nuts, in other words! Caught in one of those ritual treadmills of insanity like some guy on a street corner arranging buttons in a gutter. Christ! It could have been going on for months. Long before I came: days, weeks, months literally, before I showed up to disturb her. Doing the same thing day after day after day, again and again going into her locked room, chiseling out the same face, the same child, over and over and over until her heart sickened with love, at what she saw as this trial of mere love against her revelation, and then every morning, every fucking morning . . .

'Jesus Christ!' I said aloud.

The clang of the woodstove door.

I got tangled in the covers as I hurled myself from the bed. Cursing, I ripped them off me, and hurtled, naked, over the bedroom threshold. The peaceful susurration of the stove was deep and chesty. The orange glow around the door sent out blinding spokes of glare. I grabbed the door handle, searing my fingers. Threw the door open and stuck my hand into the blaze.

'Damn it!' I shouted. 'God damn it!'

For a single instant, I had hold of it, even drew it to the edge of the fire. Saw, as through a dancing red glass, the face already shrinking into flaking char. And then I fell back, hissing in pain, gripping my hand to my chest and gritting my teeth as the red flesh blistered. And the thick log shifted back into its bed of ashes and was hidden completely by the unbroken shroud of fire.

'Oh . . . bah!' I said. Furious, I stalked back into the bedroom. I yanked my pants off the bed's footboard, yanked them on, up over my nakedness, barely remembering to push my penis down clear as I yanked the zipper up with another curse.

I stomped back through the central room with a convulsive sneer at the jolly stove. I kicked the screen door open and stepped out, barefoot, into a muddy puddle up to my cuffs.

I sloshed to the edge of the Swimhole trail. There was no sign of her.

'Agnes!' I shouted, clenching both my fists. 'Agnes!'

And then, with another harsh expulsion of breath, I threw my hands to my sides in disgust. I shook my head.

And then — standing quiet like that — I heard the river.

Well, I was a city boy. It hadn't occurred to me — what happens to a river, I mean, after two nights and a day of torrential rains. I suppose I knew in the back of my mind; I suppose I could have answered if someone had asked. But I was a city boy. I just hadn't thought about it. Not until I stood there, not until I heard that sound.

I started running. Down the trail — all mud now, mud and puddles and swift rivulets of brown water. I had, I guess, some crazy hope that it was just some sort of aural glitch — that steady bellow rising through the forest to my left — that it was magnified between the banks or something, that it sounded worse than it was. But there was no mistaking the fact of it as I splashed, mudspattered, nearer to its source. The thing was roaring — roaring — like a giant trapped in a pit, that sort of echoing, hollow, interminable roar. I rushed past the turn off to the meadow — I was wheezing for breath — and saw the other turn off up ahead, and the steep forested hill to the river's edge, now sliding with mud. I saw the river then too, through the trees. Unrecognizable as the river I knew. Half again as wide and twice as high, whipped by tornadoes of frothing white, and the driving current scored atop its surface in long, moving sinews of implacable force.

I left the trail — before the turn off, I just cut off it and raced into the trees. Immediately, my feet were swept down and out from under me. I dropped hard onto my ass, sliding in the mud, rolling in the mud to find my feet again. Grabbing hold of tree trunks, I got a few more steps — let go and charged and fell again, forward this time, thudding to the wet earth on my shoulder as the filth sprayed up over my mouth and eyes. Again, I rolled. I grabbed at a tree, and dragged myself up. I worked myself, sliding, to the next tree and the next . . .

And already, I was at the edge of the water. It had risen that high, that far into the woods. The sandspit, of course, was gone, was buried under the rushing current. Even the diving rock was wholly covered, and where its extension had been was now a lashing serpent's tail of green-white spume.

Agnes stood naked there, on the far side of the rock, with

the foam thrown up around her. She stood at the very brink of the forest, at the brink of the water, between two trees. Her green robe was lying in the mud behind her. She was poised to dive and I, braced against a tree twenty yards away, had no chance of reaching her. I suppose I could have shouted – assuming she could have heard me over the river's roar – but I knew there was no point to it. This was part of the ritual too – this she did after the burning in remembrance and communion – and for all I know the secret motive of the whole business had always lain in the fact that the river would one day rise. If I'd ever had a chance to break the spell, it was probably when she'd taken me along with her to swim here, when she'd allowed me to come that close to the mystery. Maybe I should have ravished her on the beach that day and just hoped like hell she'd love me. I sort of doubt it would have worked like that. Then, after all, she'd been in her pride – and even last night, when the terror struck her, me and my precious dick and my cut-rate humanity had just been things to mourn over and sneer at in the dark; I had nothing near the power of her compulsion.

So, leaning on the tree, I closed my eyes and said, 'Aw, Agnes.' And when I looked again, she dove.

Maybe she had a moment of comprehension then – because she buckled as she fell, as if to stop herself mid-air, and she plunged into the water sloppily. The current slammed her into the diving rock and the serpentine waves grabbed hold of her and tossed her over. Her body was pulled down beneath the water, her limbs splayed, as if she had no power at all, as if she were a doll or a puppet. But she was still conscious, I think, because she surfaced once in the next second or so, and I saw her chin tilt up and her mouth open as she fought for air. She was facing upriver. The next whirlpool was just behind her. That dragged her under finally, and she was drowned.

This I remembered, but hadn't told. Still hadn't told, though the fire was snickering down now, and the wind and the hail were rising. And the girl was at the cottage door — the model, the beneficiary. Lena. She stood soggy and forlorn in her wet earmuffs, still hesitating with her hand upon the knob, composing some savage or penetrating or triumphant exit speech to clobber me with because she thought she wanted to hear about how her crazy mother fashioned her likeness every day and then used it every morning to cut down on her heating bills. What ode of inspirational joy would she make of that, I wondered. What would she console herself with — it would be kind of interesting to know. Well, Agnes probably did save her life back then by refusing to let Roland bring her home to the cabin. And the great sculptress did get a little glum of an evening because she still felt enough mother-love to intrude on her madness — almost. For myself, I know — because none of us lives without consolation — for myself, when I get tired of rehearsing it in my lonesome bed, and the stars have revolved toward sunrise in the unseen sky — not by way of mitigation for my crimes, incidentally, but just to get some sleep, dear God, to get a little sleep — I remember that I did jump into the river after her, I did try to pull her from the water in the end. As I say, I'm no hero; I was plenty scared and almost certain I'd get myself killed. And it was ridiculous, of course: she was a much better swimmer than I was. I even knew it was ridiculous at the time, which is part of what helps me sleep. Because I certainly wasn't suicidal or anything. I just loved her and was pissed off and had to do something, even if it was useless, even if it killed me. So I jumped in.

Hilarious how the river dragged me off and sucked me under. Hilarious, I mean, because I'd had some idea of swimming after her on the current. I don't think a person's imagination contains any

image of his own helplessness. Complete helplessness like that. Even
in retrospect, you always wonder if you could have fought harder or
thought smarter or done something to gain the upper hand. Even
when it was happening, come to think of it, I struggled and thrashed
as if it made any difference – which it didn't; I could've floated limp
and the river would have carried me off the same way, wherever it
went. I can still feel the inanimate fact of it, the insentient, irresistible
strength big with its guiding laws. I might have been one of the broken
branches spinning and shooting past me. I might have been a twig off
one of those branches, just part of the river now.

And the fact that I was stronger at heart than Agnes, that I was
saner, that I had a better grasp of the minimum daily requirements
of life; these things, like whether she was smarter or kinder or better
or more creative than I, had nothing to do with the fact that I survived
and she didn't. There just happened to be this rock, this boulder,
out in the middle of the river around the bend, submerged but still
visible in the rising shelf of waves that curled above it where the river
struck. The current at that point carried you out smack toward it,
and the water seemed to flow in equal measure around either side.
If I'd hit that thing – and there was no chance of missing it – and
spun around it to the right – and there were good odds of that, being
positioned as I was – I would have died for certain because there was
nothing beyond it on that side but a thrashing stretch of white rapids
to the brink of a thunderous falls. But, tumbling helplessly about as
I was, I was tossed up to the surface with my legs in front of me. My
thigh smashed against the rock, sending my whole leg numb, but my
upper body, most of my weight, was on the left side of it, so I was
carried off, by this chance, to the left, where a tree had been brought
down on the bank by the storm. The tree – a maple, I think – was
still anchored firmly to the earth by its roots and its branches reached
out several yards into the water, much of it above the current. I went
crashing into the branches backward – else probably I'd have lost an
eye – and, half-conscious, I held onto them, and the tree bore the
pressure, and so I dragged myself to shore.

'You're just afraid – really,' said Lena at the door. This was her
valedictory now. Spoken to my back because I was still sitting in the
Windsor, facing away from her. Hands between my legs, shoulders
slumped a little. Ready for the speech to wash over me with whatever
force it had. 'You're just afraid that no one'll, like, give a damn about

you anymore. I mean, it's like: you think the only thing that matters about you now are your secrets. All these people, these reporters, my mother's biographers, me — we all come around here, like, begging you to tell us what you know. And then, like, what if you tell us, right? What if you tell everybody what happened? I mean, it's not like it'd make you famous or anything. It's not like Agnes was a movie star or anything. She just made art. So no one would care, right? No one would come here. They'd just write about what you said and they'd pretend they knew more about it than you did, and what you thought wouldn't even matter. And you wouldn't matter. And that's what you're afraid of, right? They'll go away and I'll go away, and then you'll just be here with yourself and no one'll care. You're just a coward, that's all. You're just afraid to be alone.'

That was it. That was her speech. I lifted one shoulder. Not bad, I thought. I mean, nothing an adolescent ever says is true, of course. It can't be. They can't possibly have lived long enough to discover how the most grave, urgent and human decencies are only to be achieved through self-deception and hypocrisy and lies. But because of that — precisely because of it — some of the stuff they come up with has the ring of truth to it, the aura of something hidden away, half known, and then uncovered, the way truth often is. And I confess, when she spoke, I felt the old inner shudder, and I quailed at the bleak prospect of what would follow if I gave in. I could envision the rosy glow of triumph in her cheeks, the misty gleam in the youthful eye, as she crammed this miserable series of circumstances into some salvific mold or other. Oh yeah, I could see her marching off, into whatever personal destiny, with whatever fresh lesson of life she thought she'd learned, leaving me here alone with the unredeemed history of it, empty of solace, having been there, standing at the window, my hands in pockets bulging with events and sensations and whatever few meaningless patterns I could discern. I would watch her, through my own reflection, as she strode off forever into the dead, the winter woods. And she had a point: I didn't think it would be tolerable.

Sensing — as ever, unerringly — her advantage, she let go the knob and came toward me: I heard the floorboards squeaking at my back.

'I had this dream before I came here, Har . . . Mr Bernard,' she said.

Uh oh, I thought, a dream; this wasn't going to be good.

'I mean, I know it was just, like, a dream and everything but I *had this dream where she came to me. Okay? I was walking in the woods, just wandering, you know, the way you do in dreams. And then I came out into this really scary place. And she was standing there. It was really dark, it was night, but I could see her. Just like this shadow sort of in the distance, waiting for me. And I walked toward her, and suddenly I realized: we were in the Valley of Dead Elms. Just like in the photographs, you know. All the statues lying in the mud everywhere, and the big dead trees hanging over us all around like they were watching us. And she was standing in the middle of it and I walked up to her. And I could see her face. And she was, like, smiling. This really happy smile. And she said I could come with her. I could come and live with her forever. And I was really frightened because it was such a horrible place. You know? I looked around at all the statues and everything and it was . . . it was horrible. But then she said, no — see? She said she didn't really live here, in the valley. This was just the place she had to come to so she could meet me. Where she really lived was in the meadow, she said. In that meadow, you know, that was full of wildflowers. And she said it was really beautiful there, all the time, and if I came with her, she would take me. But I didn't know what to do. I was afraid. I was too afraid I would have to stay where we were, stay in that valley.' I heard the child swallow. I heard her breathing. 'Like, forever,' she said.*

She stopped. And I do believe — I do believe I moaned aloud. What mystic chord she hit with that one I couldn't say offhand, but it rose up through me full of sadness, full of phrases, full of images and redolent, I have to say it, with the very spring air of my youth and of the little stream where Agnes and I first met.

I heard her take another step toward the chair — and she was right behind me now — gazing down at me with what last hopes, what silent prayers I didn't dare imagine.

'Tell me about my mother, Harry,' she whispered.

I leaned forward and buried my face in my hands.

Abacus now offers an exciting range of quality titles by both established and new authors. All of the books in this series are available from:

Little, Brown and Company (UK),
P.O. Box 11,
Falmouth,
Cornwall TR10 9EN.

Fax No: 01326 317444.
Telephone No: 01326 372400
E-mail: books@barni.avel.co.uk

Payments can be made as follows: cheque, postal order (payable to Little, Brown and Company) or by credit cards, Visa/Access. Do not send cash or currency. UK customers and B.F.P.O. please allow £1.00 for postage and packing for the first book, plus 50p for the second book, plus 30p for each additional book up to a maximum charge of £3.00 (7 books plus).

Overseas customers including Ireland, please allow £2.00 for the first book plus £1.00 for the second book, plus 50p for each additional book.

NAME (Block Letters) ....

....

ADDRESS ....

....

....

☐ I enclose my remittance for ....

☐ I wish to pay by Access/Visa Card

Number ☐☐☐☐☐☐☐☐☐☐☐☐☐☐☐☐

Card Expiry Date ☐☐☐☐